The Girl a

Be

A Lamentation of Fates

By

James D. Stone

The Girl and the Goddess

Copyright © 2018 by James D. Stone

First edition published 2018 by James D. Stone

Cover artwork by Edoardo Taloni

Email James at
jamestoneauthor@gmail.com

Follow James on Instagram at
@jamesdstoneauthor

Follow James on Facebook at
www.facebook.com/jamesdstoneauthor

Follow Edoardo on Instagram at
@stevoleblanc

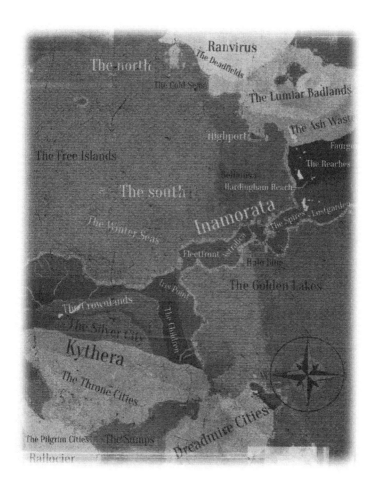

The Known East

~*Part One*~

JAMES D. STONE·2

One

Praying was easy. Hearing the answer was always harder. And each time the girl prayed, she would feel a warm hand brush across her scalp, though when she looked up, there would never be anyone there but the snow. And that was seeming like the only response she'd ever get.

A myriad of thorny trees stood tall around her and blotted out the clouds above, all while fresh snow fell to the grass and snapped beneath her feet. But the tree she knelt before was different from the others. It had been a place of worship as its trunk split in half, stretching up to the sky like a mother's legs as she gave birth. But the girl had always just thought it looked pretty.

'*Let's go back,*' her friend Jayce had once said under that same tree, a lifetime ago when there was something still of a willowy blonde left in her. '*I don't like it here. It's damn cold.*'

It had been summer then and in truth, it had been damn cold. But the girl hadn't wanted to hear that.

'*Leave then*,' she had said, wishing her away.

It turned out that had been the only wish of hers to come true. She'd only kept Jayce around because she'd laughed at her jokes, but her father had run away to the Free-Peoples, taking his daughter with him.

'*You'll catch a chill!*'

'*Don't be such a bitch*,' she had called back with something of glee (bitch had been a new word at the time, and she'd liked the way it tasted when she said it) and stomped briskly about the muddy grass.

'*I'm not—*' Jayce stuttered in that shiny red dress of hers. '*You don't know the meaning of afraid! You've never even seen a cold siren*,' she huffed.

'*And you have?*' she'd spat back, dropped to her knees and prayed that pretty face of hers would disappear.

In hindsight, that wish had come true too.

And it was under that same tree she prayed still. She'd never prayed for good things then, but they were all she prayed for now. She thought to her little brother, Rache, and found herself praying for him too. 'Gods give me the cure,' she said as she had every day before, but each time she returned to the palace, her brother was still a cripple.

She felt her mind wandering to her father, to Kharon Vorr, and prayed for him as well, but in a different sort of way, she supposed. He was the chancellor of her home, the city of Orianne, and very much a cock, so she prayed he'd have the decency to fall ill.

She even prayed for her bastard brother, Albany Moore.

She'd only been five years old when he was born, but she could still remember his mother—she'd seemed so warm and kind, not at all like the woman who came to besmirch her family. Perhaps that was why she and her false brother had never got along; she loved Rache to the end of the earths, but ever since she'd become a woman-grown, she'd always thought Albany was vulgar. Perhaps the gods could've had a hand at fixing that too.

She picked herself up and looked out to the starless skies, wondering if anyone would answer.

Oh; she'd forgotten—there was one more to make.

She considered praying that she wouldn't have to be sent off to fight in whatever Kharon's next war would be, but she found herself quickly changing her mind. He'd often said the nameless gods favoured the warriors and frowned upon the cowards, and she was tempted to believe him. *Best not,* she decided, even if they weren't real.

Besides, like with Rache, she'd prayed a thousand times before, and the world was yet to do her a favour. When she'd been a child, she'd attended communion every second week, and there she had prayed and prayed and prayed, and when that hadn't worked, she had spent every second she had alone praying too. *Not anymore,* she told herself, but not a moment later, she clasped her hands together again.

'Take me south,' was the last thing she said before she forced herself to stand. *It's a pathetic dream,* she told herself, *the only ones in the north who still have any ships are the Tyla, and gods know they can't care less for the south.*

Albany's mother had been a southerner, though— and everyone in the north wanted to fuck a woman from the south, her uncle had said. And when they had arrived in that galleon all those years ago, her uncle had been proved right.

The girl collected herself and cavorted through the frost, the mountain air prickling her chin.

She studied the roses as she passed them, fragile things like untreated wounds—the bloody symbol of her city. She followed the trees as they crept up the hills until they met the brass spires and great glass towers which spanned the skies above. It wouldn't be long before she reached the pond where nobody could find her, lost in an orchard left to rot.

Magmaya Vorr smiled the same way a caged bird took flight.

It was here when the hail grew tired, and the geese wandered, she could at last just breathe in the thin air while the jagged moss and twisted roots eclipsed her from the clockwork city above. And when she was finished, she'd return home before a soul realised she'd gone amiss.

It was in the forest she would get the closest to hearing the maidens sing their sweet, sweet music she'd so longed to hear and watch the multi-coloured lights overhead which she had so longed to watch. But she had lost herself here.

Now each time she visited, the waters in the pond appeared to shrink while her reflection grew larger. And in it, the pale moonlight stripped her eyes that insisted on ageing faster than she did; after all, her youth had come with all the delicacy of the old, chipped paintings that stared down from Kharon's boardroom.

The ice startled her as it glistened and rumbled, small bubbles creeping to its surface and fish, too, dead from a mid-winter spawning. From the pond, a valley cut between the trees, beyond the Silver Mountainside and into the night her people called the enemy. She was inclined to believe them—there were places farther north no one had ever dared to travel, save for barbarian tribes and electric-worshipping sorcerers who had all but disappeared.

Magmaya had only crossed out of the city's grounds twice; once as a child riddled with intrigue and summer dare, and the next as stern, cold retaliation for being scolded for that first time. To Kharon's dismay, she still dreamt of stealing a small boat and rowing herself across the Cold Seas and then perhaps even farther south to meet all the 'fuckable' ladies in their Silver Cities and then to whoever lay even farther south of them. She needn't worry about not getting home either—they said if you travelled far enough south, you'd end up back where you started.

Besides, she didn't want pennies, power or promiscuity—how hard was it for people to leave her alone? *The nameless gods probably thought the same,* she reminded herself, *but people were always bothering them.*

Magmaya skimmed the surface of the water again, following the incisions and imperfections where the barbs weaved through small cracks, gasping for a taste of the winter sun. She skirted around the edge of the frost and knelt beside them, her throat aching from the cold—she would've killed for some warm wine, but Kharon had taken all of that for himself.

She found herself reaching forward and snatching up a thorn. The spines tried to bite at her, latching themselves into her skin, but it was too fragile just to drop. It was the stem of a rose, but where the head should've been, grizzly entrails hung lank between her fingers, before a cusp of winter breeze tossed the limp thing away.

It joined the dead among a garden of roses, sewn into the snow and defying the winter.

No, they aren't roses, she quickly realised.

Just a trail of petals remained, barely a day old as they still glowed like red summer wine. They rested on the freckles of frost, so precisely and intricately placed— nature could've never been so delicate.

As Magmaya followed them, her heart began to sink. She reached a small clearing where nothing grew, yet the petals sprouted like severed veins. There was even a mound in the clearing's centre where they clustered, creeping out like encroaching tendrils.

But she wasn't alone. There was a man with her. Some silvery man, laying cold in the frost. He was armoured with a floral tunic and a mess of golden hair, but his mouth had been forced open, rivers of frozen blood spilling down his cheeks and filling the reservoirs of his dimples. Where his eyes should have been, black crevices gaped, and bloodied rose petals blossomed.

The world around her grew loud, and snow began to pound the ground with a vengeance. She reached about to find a weapon that wasn't there, gasping and stammering and shouting, but the cold of the night was suffocating.

What's this I'm feeling? It hurt like new fire. It clouded her head like thick smoke.

And all around her, there was Jayce, screaming at her still, *'Let's go back,'* she said, again and again. *'You don't know the meaning of afraid,'* she'd told her. Now she damn well did.

The air seemed to disappear beneath her as she ran, the white branches above thirsting for her skin. The mountainside shivered while the humming city above her rose and fell, and Magmaya called and called and called before a brass bannister appeared up ahead, marking the edge of the forest.

And then there was a grey warmth against her chest as she forced herself forward. Yet the warmth's grip proved sturdy, even as she kicked and screamed and spat.

Magmaya's eyes stung, and her throat was dry; she must have looked like an unkempt crow.

Siedous Harluss was a fair and kind-looking man, though, not yet sixty, and yet, a certain cold persisted within him; he was one of Kharon's advisors, a retired swordsman and the closest thing Magmaya had ever had to a friend. But he knew better than to hold her against him.

'Magmaya?' His voice was a bulwark against the snow. 'What are you doing...?'

'Siedous!' Magmaya's voice was rough and brittle. It hurt to speak. 'Albany—he's...! ...Kharon's bastard is dead.'

~ ~ ~

Brazen spires and onyx arches stood tall about the palace like the gods had placed them to perch on their tips and watch the world burn. The chandeliers above swayed under the pounding hail, while scowls of long-dead angels danced in the shimmering marble floors around him.

The same angels the southerners warned us about, the old knight remembered. *Though we carved them into our ceilings before even they came.*

There was tranquillity in admiring the artefacts about the hall that made Siedous wonder what exactly his purpose was. One moment he had been inspecting a defiled corpse, and the next, he appeared to have ascended through the gates into the heavens.

Some heaven, though, he thought as he looked at the grey skull on the podium; its fangs stood in rows like columns of soldiers, and its eye sockets buckled and warped under its jaw like a devilish thing. He wondered if such a beast had ever thought it would be a museum piece. Perhaps one day he would be too.

'Beautiful? Don't you agree?'

Siedous looked to the voice in surprise, almost having forgotten Nurcia was standing beside him. She looked at him plainly; she had the face of a woman who lived by a rule of discontent. Her hair ran long over her blue-grey dress, lined with draping furs which curled like dead hands around her neck. It was a rare sight to see her in the palace; she'd spent much of her recent time scouring the haunted Deadfields for some old relic buried beneath the ice. Whatever she found out there was a mystery, though; she was hesitant to tell anyone.

'It's lovely,' he stuttered, scratching at his beard. 'Yes, Kharon will be pleased. He made the right decision to have you decorate the halls.'

'I'm most delighted.' Nurcia smiled. She looked around, her elegance surpassing the saints above. 'I do think it will help the chancellor recover from this week's happenings, no?'

It had been a monstrous week in truth, only made worse by the investigation into Albany's death. Seven men had been put on trial, and all seven of them had been forced to confess. But Kharon didn't believe a single one, which only meant more board meetings for Siedous.

Not only that—the city had been crowded by shamans summoned from the Free-Peoples. They'd claimed they would get to the truth and through their rituals, give rest to Albany's soul, but with each bloodied prayer, and with each silver turned to gold, Orianne just suffered more.

He raised an eyebrow. 'He was a false-child, but Kharon loved him like a true son. I should've been there to find him.'

'It was a tragedy.' She nodded. 'That forest has bewitched us—I say we burn it to the ground before any other conspiracies can start there. We must honour Albany's death—he was our vessel to the south.'

'If only I'd been there an hour earlier,' he replied. 'Or two hours, dammit! That southern woman—she—I would board the first ship to Kythera if I could—if ours could sail so far. I would drag her back here, so maybe I could make some sense of this all, I—'

'My lord, I feel as though you're speaking out of place.'

'Perhaps you're right.' He nodded. 'It's a lovely skull, but I can't bear to think of dead things anymore—Albany—I—Now, if you would excuse me.'

He tried to shuffle away, though he couldn't help but think of Magmaya. What if it had been her? What if she'd been there at the wrong time? He could hardly live with himself as it was.

'Siedous!' Nurcia called louder than she should've, averting the eyes of quiet preachers around the hall. 'Before you leave, I pray you speak to me.'

'About what?' he grumbled.

'About whatever you're hiding from me.'

Siedous sighed. Then he said, 'Come this way.' His shoulders drooped.

The pair began stalking the empty halls riddled with candlelight. A harrowing silence seemed to wisp through the air, and despite his thick furs, Siedous felt the breeze. When he was certain no one else was in sight, he turned to her and explained, 'This is bigger than you might think.' His voice was brittle. 'I've heard Kharon say he knows who killed Albany.'

'My lord…' Nurcia placed her hand on her breast. 'Who…?'

'The Mansel.' Siedous heaved a sigh. 'That's what the chancellor told me, anyway. But he was drunk and threatened me not to speak of it—I do hope I have your confidence?'

'Of course,' she replied. 'But how would he know?'

'He said he found a letter containing the Vorr family tree with his children's faces scratched off by Mansel runes. And, of course, the next morning Albany was found dead by Magmaya, eyes stolen and filled with rose petals. I think if anything, that confirms it.'

'I—!' Nurcia looked around for some kind of comfort which didn't present itself. 'Did you see the letter?'

'He said in a fit of rage he threw it in the fire.' Siedous sighed.

Nurcia nodded. 'And you've told no one else?'

'Only you.' Siedous bit his tongue. 'If anyone finds out, Kharon will have our heads swinging bloody from the ramparts.'

'I know.' Nurcia frowned.

'There's more,' he continued on. 'The chancellor is planning a military display outside one of Mansel's strongholds.'

'I don't understand,' Nurcia said. 'Is war not what *they* want?'

'The chancellor plans to send a convoy of two-hundred men,' Siedous said. 'His broth—Lord Shalleous, is going to lead them, he says—along with—' His heart ached. 'Along with Magmaya.'

'Two-hundred?' Nurcia's nose twitched. 'Mansel strongholds are fortresses of iron barbs. Vargul Tul is at their feet! Perhaps the old masters could've faced them down, but Magmaya? She's scarcely a girl who played swords with you. She's never fought.'

'If this escalates, we will lose the heirs to Orianne,' he said. 'We risk even the city itself. The Mansel are savages, they won't stop for a minute to consider backing down. It was your home they took, you know better than any—'

'I know, I know,' she cut in. 'Are you sure he's sending Magmaya?'

'Yes,' he said, flustered. 'She's only a few years past womanhood! She has scarcely left the city before, dammit.'

'We must have faith in our chancellor, still.' Nurcia swallowed. 'Perhaps through all of this, he wants to strengthen our city.'

'I fear he has no intention of strengthening the city—he wants to break it,' Siedous groaned. 'If what he says is true about the Mansel, then something must be done. But not like this. Not with Magmaya. If they see it as an invasion, she'll die.'

He'd considered over the last few days volunteering himself, but he was too old and not even that would allow Magmaya to be freed from duty. He was a low-born, truly—Kharon wouldn't want him as the city's representative.

'My lord.' Nurcia frowned. 'What would you see me do?'

'The chancellor will soon ask you make ready his men. This march to Mansel will likely begin in a couple of days.' Siedous paused. 'I'll prepare Magmaya ahead of time, but you must delay his orders for as long as possible, understood? He trusts you the most out of anyone on his council, but I will do what I can.'

'Of course, my lord,' Nurcia said. 'I'll be on my way.'

'I'm grateful, Nurcia.' He nodded, and she scampered down the corridor, her dress seemingly floating above the floor below.

Magmaya, he thought, *dammit!* He should've taught her to run away.

~ ~ ~

The bitter swelling of honey carried through the sculleries and tickled her nose like an insect landing on a petal. There was a wantonness in the wine she poured down her throat, but she let it bubble there and poison her all the same. Magmaya knew soon it would reach her head, and she wouldn't be herself for a little while; she didn't even like the taste, but it was sweeter than any silk tea the maids tried to make her. Besides, from time to time it would let her recreate that happiness she had felt a thousand winters ago and the warmth that had come with it—but it was never the same. Her body felt so damn old. Moments became memories before they even passed.

Magmaya laughed as the wine trickled down her chin and stained her shirt, sullying her blouse with the colours of the forest she'd ran from. She laughed harder and harder—and choked. It was even more so droller now—the corpse, the blood—the empty eyes.

It had all happened in a moment's notice, and Siedous was there too, somewhere. She remembered the warmth of his chest against hers as she'd ran to him. When she'd been younger, she might have dreamt of kissing him—but he was over double her age and his breath smelt like salt.

She took another mouthful of wine and choked again as she laughed, spitting it across the floor. Magmaya heard someone enter the room and raised the nigh-empty bottle into the air, wailing, 'Tonight we drink!' She sniggered, 'Tomorrow, we go to war!'

'Mistress?' The voice was shocked to see her, but Magmaya wasn't confused. *It's only me.* 'Let me return you to the chancellor, my lady.'

The voice tried to pry the bottle from her hands, but Magmaya held it to her chest like a mother did a babe and began to nuzzle the rim. Pearly white lights began shining down, and for a moment, the world made a little less sense. Why wouldn't she want to catch those moonbeams in her sinful hands?

But before Magmaya knew it, the scullery had disappeared from beneath her, and there was a crash. The bottle was trailing behind her; glassy shards scattered about in a spring of scarlet. She wanted to cry for it and scrape for the remains, but her lungs felt like they were about to collapse, and her nails could've never jeered deep enough to dig her back.

The lights are roaring multi-coloured now! She tried to grab them, but they just trickled between her fingers, and she felt herself be dragged away. Her stomach was groaning, and her mouth had gone dry—if only she could get back to the cellar...

Doors and nameless faces stared in wonder as she passed, and Magmaya couldn't help but smile. *Thank you,* she tried to say and bow but tasted bile instead. Corridors turned and twisted and before long, hands became cold and brittle until, at last, she recognised their owner.

The same hands tore away from her and left red cuts up her arm. And then a limb twisted up above. Before hammering across her face.

Magmaya cried and stumbled; her cheek began to burn as it always did when she was around Kharon. The boardroom seemed to appear around them at last, but what she saw at his hip was much more interesting— Moonbeam—the sword of Orianne and symbol of their home. They *were* readying themselves for war then.

'You stupid wench!' the chancellor stuttered. 'Pathetic girl. Had I found you myself, I would have struck you harder!'

Magmaya watched Kharon's eyes glimmer as they glowed in the candles overhead. She stayed quiet, but she was afraid that whatever she did, he would lash out at her again—when he spoke, he was like a tempest thrashing a feeble village off the shore.

'You're pathetic,' he spat. 'What do you expect me to say when I'm told my heir is caught drinking in the common kitchens?'

'I don't know,' she stuttered. *But you could tell them I'm more than a reminder of you not knowing where to stick your cock,* Magmaya thought. 'If I knew you were sending me out there—I, I would have never told you I found my half-brother's corpse! This isn't just *your* kingdom.'

'I have no kingdom,' Kharon groaned.

Magmaya reeled, holding her cheek. *Leave the palace and tell me that again*, she thought and felt a wave of tantalising nothingness reach her head.

There was a deep and unbroken silence as the wind screamed, and one of the candles flickered out.

'I've a request for you,' he said at last. 'If it's not too much of a burden.'

'And what could that possibly be?'

'Shalleous is leading the troops tomorrow.' Kharon's breath was heavy, and it reeked of wine and onions. 'I don't want you to be among the ranks. Instead, you will be his banner girl.'

'I beg your fucking pardon.' Magmaya cocked her head, and suddenly, the layers of numbness she'd built up in the morning fell away. She was feeling again, and the heat from where he'd struck her was burning red.

'If, damn me, you're to represent my city, then I won't have you lost in a crowd of guardsmen.' His words were cold, like the man he had perhaps once been. 'One day you may be the last of my legacy, now start acting like it.'

Something of a melancholy tackled Magmaya, and she stumbled to the centre of the room. The fine, wooden table trailed through her fingers, and she almost tripped over the leg. From afar, the wind curved around the spires, calling and howling.

After some quiet deliberation, she turned back to the chancellor and mumbled, 'There are easier ways to kill me.'

With a shudder, Magmaya left the room and let the poison take her. It wasn't long until she reached the stairs and then the door and finally found herself in the forest again. At least there, she could watch the snow fall and bless her with the knowledge the trees would never sing if she wasn't to arrive home.

Two

She woke from a dream about a temple. It was a temple of blood and stone, ivory and brass. It was like she'd lived there in a past life—a realer life than this one. And all around her, there had been fire, clouding her thought, though it was the kind of place she forgot about once she came around.

And when she did, it was to the snapping of greased iron sweeping over the hillside as if it never had before. The air reeked of sweat and rain where the winter had lashed the muddied ground apart like the whipping of an outlaw's back. And across it, the guardsmen stood about in wolf-skin and metal plate, wilting roses carved in their chests; each of them insisted on sporting thorny antlers that pricked the clouds and wearing extravagant feathers like some aloof birds.

But all Magmaya could fathom was that it was freezing. Speckles of sunlight were beginning to beat the snow away from the palace grounds, but the ice seemed incessant on eating at her. She had started longing for the warm morning before in the armoury where she'd clipped the cuirass onto her chest, all while her servant had scurried around, tending to her every need. She longed to be there again, to be rolling her shoulders back and feeling the cool metal burn through her clothes.

Even then she'd longed to be elsewhere, though; she'd longed for the evening before in towers when she'd slipped into the warmth of the baths, the water burning her skin. Then the hours had done nothing but embrace her.

But now, she just stood quietly in the corner of the grounds, though even that didn't stop the women occasionally looking to her in scorn, while the men tried to make out the curves of her breasts beneath the shimmer of her armour. She'd learnt to close her eyes each time and let the steel encase her. If they thought she was a dazzling white swan, then she would do her very best to muddy herself in the rain.

The tides of guardsmen began to shift as someone trudged through the snow clumps, taller than the rest. His armour shimmered brighter, and his long brown locks were slicked back above the dark stubble that crowded those wrinkles she'd known so well. Shalleous Vorr locked eyes with his niece and allowed himself a swift grin.

'Magmaya Vorr.' He looked down at her fake sword. 'Perhaps your father doesn't underestimate you after all.'

'I don't think he wants me to actually hit anything with it,' she murmured. 'I'm only here to look pretty or die trying.' She laughed feebly. She had a habit of doing that when she was nervous, but it often did her more harm than good.

'Why not both?' Shalleous let out a roar of laughter, and the murmurings about the grounds fell silent. Her uncle's mere presence seemed to uplift them, though; he exuded raw enthusiasm, even in the face of the cold. 'Are you afraid, dear girl?'

'No,' she lied, keeping her teeth clenched. 'Kharon says fear is for men.'

'The chancellor has many such sentiments,' he remarked. 'Once on a drunk summer's evening, when seventeen were slaughtered in the square, he looked to me with a smile and said, Drink until it is over.'

'And he hasn't stopped since.' Magmaya grinned.

'Even so, that is not my favourite of his,' Shalleous began, laughing. 'When my son was born, the chancellor told me how he'd dreamt that the moon became the sun at day. And then, the next morning, a star had fallen from the sky. Except it was no star, no; it was something of clockwork. He described the thing in wonder as if he had seen it himself, but whe—'

There was a stammer of sodden footsteps, and the chattering was cut off as Kharon strode towards them, a trailing gown of white following his every step. The harsh light didn't feed his features well; he looked an age older with every passing second. But he nodded to his troops as if he were a king, and so they hid away to let him pass.

'My lord.' Her uncle bowed.

He looked to the pair with a venomous smile (only made more so by his crooked beard) and shouted through the downpour, 'If I hear you turn tails, they'll be no place for you at Orianne.'

How inspiring, Magmaya grumbled.

The chancellor turned away to the guardsmen and cleared his throat, basking in their adoration like he was a saint among disciples. And when he spoke, he chose his words precisely and vindictively so that when he was done, perhaps in the eyes of a few, a saint he would become.

And Magmaya could only watch, blinking steadily as spit caught her cheek. She drowned out the words in her mind—they were all the same: pleas from a man who wouldn't dare leave his wooden seat. She just wished Siedous was around, but he was far too old and weary to come. The lines in her uncle's face were beginning to show too, though—he wasn't much younger. Maybe the rain would see to that.

After a few minutes more of droning on and rites and prayers from a number of priests, the battalion erupted into wails of adoration; all around her, there were fists held out to the chancellor's cloak. The applause illuminated the blackness of the morning long enough for Magmaya to sink into the shadows.

There was a heavy muttering as Kharon waded back through the crowd, ignoring his daughter and almost throwing himself at Shalleous. His brother embraced him, and the pair stood high with something almost primal about them.

'Before we go, my lord—' Shalleous began.

'You were my first choice,' Kharon cut him off, voice muffled as rain caught his lip. 'I wouldn't be without my brother.'

'Of course, my chancellor.' Shalleous nodded, and Magmaya watched on. Her father was facing away, but she knew he was watching her, even as guardsmen flooded between them. 'Though I must let you know I've decided to head for the Sultide first,' her uncle said. 'We'll be able to better afford strength if we camp out there for the night.'

'I care not how this is done, only that it is.' Kharon smiled, patting his brother's shoulder. He looked around, and his smile dropped. Magmaya ducked. 'Look at you all in your furs. A pack of wolves,' Kharon remarked. 'Some things never change. That's what mother used to call you, wasn't it? A wolf?' There was a hint of warmth in his voice for what seemed the first time in a hundred years.

'And you were the Bear.' Shalleous blushed. 'Though I'd hoped my little name had been forgotten...'

'There's nothing disrespectful in a title,' Kharon remarked and began ambling about the puddles, watching the streaks of rain cut across the valley.

'I do hope your daughter gets one after this fiasco is finished,' Shalleous said. 'She's grown strong.'

'It's an exhibition,' Magmaya heard her father say and shrunk down again.

'No, it is not,' he asserted. 'Kharon, today is the day we challenge a fortress! Scarcely any of us have seen Mansel territory with our own eyes but if it's anything like in the stories—'

'Nonsense,' Kharon barked. 'Magmaya Vorr is the heir to Orianne. She must advocate for the city. You and I did all those years ago. She's no different. Besides, the Mansel have suffered a harsh winter; they're in no place to retaliate. Her sword isn't southern steel, either. She couldn't stick herself if she tried. She will grow bored if anything.'

Gods, I hope so, she thought. *I'd rather be bored than flayed.*

'She better be—for your sake.' Shalleous raised an eyebrow. 'I'll be going.'

Her uncle disappeared down the hillside, and she watched as the chancellor turned away, confronted the shadows and called for her curtly.

'I'm here.' She crawled out from between a pair of guardsmen and wiped hair from her eyes.

'It almost slipped my mind, but Rache wanted to see you again before you left,' Kharon muttered. 'See to it.'

'This armour's bloody heavy.' Magmaya gestured to herself. 'It'll take me a week to get back to the palace.'

'Make it a short week,' he said, and so she did.

Miniature infernos flickered off Magmaya's cheeks when she arrived, but she couldn't help feeling like an intruder. They were mere façades of the children they had once known themselves to be, chasing one another around the courtyards. To Rache, she might have been some wise woman—the valiant defender of Orianne and its name. But now that she was dressed for the part, she wasn't valiant at all.

Magmaya ambled over to him, ran her palm across a pile of leaves he had made a habit of collecting, and perched on the end of his bed. 'Rache,' she called for him, and the room came to life; the crackling of the fires above began warming her skin with a pearly caress.

The boy stirred, wiped his forehead of sweat and looked to her with a glance that she might have once mistaken for disregard.

'We already said goodbye.' She smiled. 'What's the matter?'

'I want you to read me a new story.'

She pursed her lips together, half-annoyed, half-joyous. 'I thought you preferred uncle's? Or did his just scare you off? Oh gods, he hasn't been telling you about the moth again, has he?'

'No, no,' he whispered. Rache thought for a moment, before he heaved her a book from the many resting on his bedside. 'Look at this one.'

Magmaya leaned over and took it in her arms. She ran her fingers over the brown-leather cover and flicked it open. The heavy scent of raw musk rose up like a rich perfume.

'What's it called?' Magmaya asked.

'The Emperor's Bride,' Rache stifled the words. 'Did father send you?'

'Yes. Did you ask him to?'

Rache nodded. 'I didn't want you to leave.'

'Are you worried for me?'

'How can't I be?' Rache said, and Magmaya couldn't help but grin, prying the pages apart.

'*The mountains crossed my path like daggers from the earth,*' she began, '*but I walked to the harbour instead. I was full enough from my luncheon, and I didn't need any royal feast. Besides, the boats were warmer than the inns at that time of year.*' Magmaya turned the page. '*My day changed the moment I met a fair lady on the road to the shore. She was eight and ten and covered in green perfumes and wore a dress sewn like honey—*'

'Oh, that reminds me,' Rache cut in. 'I heard some man about the halls earlier. He said he would rather you be sewing than doing all of this.'

As would I, Magmaya realised and finished the page before forcing herself to stand. She pressed the book back into his arms and bent over to kiss him on the forehead.

'How long will you be gone?'

'Long enough,' she said.

Rache looked up at her and his eyes filled with a pining that seemed every bit as unbearable as going out into the cold again. She'd been visiting less and less after she'd found Albany dead—it was hard to talk about things anymore. The conversation always led back to their false brother.

'Don't leave,' he said at last.

'Rache—'

'Don't leave!'

'I have to go,' she crooned. *Would he always make things so hard?*

'Don't—!' he persisted, but before long, she was out the door and listening to him shout at the walls.

'Mistress...' a shrill voice called as she left, and she turned to find Nurcia, standing in the dim light of the hall.

'My lady,' Magmaya replied quietly. She'd never been so comfortable around the chancellor's advisor after she'd once thought it had been her who'd mothered Albany. Then again, finding out it was some southern woman wasn't much better. She did spend an awful lot of her time in private, though.

'I was hoping to catch you here,' she said. 'You and your uncle are leaving now, yes? I didn't want to intrude...'

'It's quite alright. Can I help you?'

'I only wanted to wish you luck,' Nurcia remarked.

'Thank you.' Magmaya curtsied awkwardly. 'Is something of the matter?'

Nurcia shrugged. 'It's a long way to Mansel territory,' she said, 'and Shalleous is a hardy man.'

'How do you mean?'

'How long has it been since his lady died?'

'Four... five years?' Magmaya recalled. 'I still don't understand—'

'From one woman to another... be careful around him,' she replied.

'Nurcia...?'

'In truth, my lady, it's that last night, he...'

'He...?'

'I woke to find your uncle in my chambers,' she said at last. 'He had his breeches down, I had to shoo him away. He said, um.' She paused. 'He said he wanted to fuck me.'

'What?' Magmaya exclaimed.

'It is only the nature of men,' Nurcia answered. 'I just want you to be careful, my lady.'

'I...' She was struggling for words, looking to her feet. *Shalleous tried for her bedchambers?* That wasn't at all the uncle she knew. 'Nurcia—' she began again, but when Magmaya looked up, the chancellor's advisor was gone.

The battalion stormed through the night, fastened to the hides of shaggy silver deer which were said to be able to take a man around the world and back. But each step sent a jolt up Magmaya's legs and through her spine, only furthering her desire to get off the bloody thing. *Around the world and back?* she asked herself. *I'll barely last a mile.*

There were hundreds of them too, jutting and wailing and reeking like something feral. Sometimes, a convoy would wander off, hauling their foodstuffs with them. And each time, the entire host would have to stop for half an age to rally them out of a ditch.

They hadn't been delayed in over an hour, but (as if to compensate) the storm was getting worse; the guardsmen ahead were fading into the white of the clouds, and the snow was biting at her lips. It was cold, yes, but it filled a pit in her chest that nothing inside the city gates could have ever done. When she'd snuck out of the city as a child, she'd felt nothing but excitement. It was the same now, but it felt like fear this time.

Shalleous was riding a few men from her left, edging farther forward. Magmaya had never ridden for more than an hour, and so as the night grew closer and as the snow cast ghastly shadows across the mountains, her inexperience began to take its toll. It wouldn't be long until they arrived at the Sultide, but that watery plain stretched out for miles, and by then her back would have surely broken in two.

They would find refuge in the caverns at its shore, though; there, the heavy thermals would warm them better than any fur would, and perhaps then Magmaya might get some sleep. They would set off again at midnight and reach the Mansel stronghold before sunrise, but she was already feeling herself grow limp under her own weight (she had almost slipped from the reigns twice already). Her dream of leaving the north wasn't so sweet anymore—if she couldn't even brave a few hours out in the Deadfields, she hadn't a chance at surviving the journey south.

She looked over to her banner boy as he rode shortly on ahead; he was no older than sixteen, and the brass sigil he jabbed at the heavens seemed likely to crush him at any moment. His name was Gilbus, but Magmaya had only remembered that because of how reluctant he had been to tell her. He rarely spoke, and when he did, it was more of a giggle. Still, even he appeared more comfortable in the snow than she.

'Steady.' Shalleous veered over and gripped hold of her deer, steering it straight. 'You won't want to find yourself separated.'

He had his breeches down, I had to shoo him away. He said he wanted to fuck me.

'Sorry.' She recovered timidly, and the two began to ride alongside. 'How long until we reach the Sultide?'

'An hour, perhaps,' Shalleous replied. 'We're ahead of schedule—we'll arrive before nightfall.'

'We'll barricade the caves, yes?' Magmaya asked. 'Kharon told me wolves lurk out here when the sun's down.'

'You know little of the cold,' Shalleous remarked. 'After the Transmutany, the first northern travellers killed all the wolves. If anyone tells you otherwise, it's a faery story Magmaya.' He looked to his feet and back to her, wise eyes sunken deep in his head. 'You would always dance about the sculleries as a wee child. Your father said, *Aye, she will make good for her prince*, but I insisted your dancing was good practice for swinging a sword and apparently, you did too.' He was pleased. 'Siedous taught you good,' he said. 'Are you happy with where the stars have taken you?'

'The stars?' she asked.

'You may think me a rugged old man, but I have something still to pray for.'

'My bastard brother's birth caused the greatest scandal the city had ever known,' she remarked, 'until his death caused a greater one. What good have the *stars* ever done me?' She remembered praying at the foot of her tree, praying there wouldn't be war. *Look at me now,* she thought. 'If they cared for me really, I'd be praying for a little warmth.'

'If a girl says so, then certainly it must be true,' Shalleous remarked, a flash of guilt about his lips.

Magmaya tried to say something, but the wind cut her off. Even her furs weren't keeping her warm any longer, and it was beginning to grow dark.

'We near the Sultide, my lord,' a guardsman called through the snow. 'Better us ride on ahead to scout the caverns?'

'You and four others,' Shalleous agreed. 'May the stars carry you to safety.' He winked at her.

Magmaya found the nerve to laugh at that.

There was a clattering of hooves and an incessant screeching of deer before the scouts carried on ahead. They rode in silence as glimmers of sunlight caught the edges of the world, silhouetting the peaks as they scowled down like the gods which Magmaya sought so hard to turn away.

I would *pray for some silk tea, though,* she thought. *Gods know what they put in it, but at least that would warm me before going to my head.*

Before long, the riders returned, deer wailing and snorting. The Sultide was clear, and so they rode on; the haze of the day began slowly dissolving until the clouds retreated to the mountaintops. As the sun struck them, they began shimmering like they'd been carved from iron and silverwater and not from the dull black rocks she'd found scattered about the palace grounds. But with the dying of the light, the day drew to a close, and with dusk, the valley grew sparse.

Magmaya looked back through the dark, finding nothing but endless plateaus and mountaintops; there was no sign of the brazen spires or glass domes she had called her home for so long—the sight made her wonder if it even had existed. There was a terrible fear that came with being alone and lost on a mountainside; it was a fear ingrained in her bones. It almost made her calm.

For a moment, she found herself remembering the silver vessel from the south, looming like a moon on the sea; she remembered the way the smaller boats had flocked out, disgorging those silvery faces from so far away. There had been boys with dark skin and girls with brown eyes, and they spoke of pearly angels and delicious fruits and stars and—

Magmaya watched the horizon, half expecting the ship to return, but instead, she was met with a face-full of snow. Sometimes, she felt as if her heart had sunk so far, it would beat as cold as brass.

'We're nearing the caverns,' she heard Shalleous call, and she turned back to the cold. 'Keep your wits about you.'

It was true; she had missed the opening to the Sultide through the valley. She was getting distracted.

'Scout ahead and find a place to camp.' Her uncle turned to the riders. 'Thermals reach deep, so don't dare leave unless you find them.'

The thermals reached so deep in fact, they spread out beneath the whole of Ranvirus like a sprawling spider's web. The ones beneath Orianne had for centuries been used as priest holes or sewers, but the pilgrims who'd first travelled north wouldn't have survived to build the city hadn't it been for the heat that rose from them. And neither would she if they didn't find one to camp on for the night.

A couple minutes passed in silence, and Magmaya couldn't help but feel anxious; she doubted she'd get rest anytime soon either—the temperature had only dropped since they had arrived at the Sultide. Was it not for the coat that kissed at her neck, she seldom would've had the strength to carry on.

She longed for even a feast with Kharon now, sat in silence and pushing meat around her bowl while she sipped from a goblet not made for women. She had often watched the Deadfields and wondered what the cold would make of her. Now she knew.

'Something's moving on the horizon,' one of the guardsmen's voices broke the silence, and Magmaya couldn't help but be relieved. 'A black shadow. It gets larger every second, my lord.'

'Nothing moves on the horizon.' Shalleous remained stern. 'The glow of the water does something to the faint of heart. Look away if it scares you.'

'Could it be a torgulus?' another shouted through the heavy wind.

'The torgulus are dead,' Shalleous called. 'The wolves are dead, the bears are all but dead—the oracles, for the sake of the gods, are dead!'

'My—'

'Don't scare yourselves with the fantasies of long-dead men,' her uncle interrupted. 'You'll catch a chill like no other. I can assure you of that.'

Magmaya pursed her lips together and waited. She too had noticed a grey shadow growing beneath the mountains, forged in the moonlight. She was more worried about the riders, though—they hadn't returned yet. But there was something else too…

'Shalleous…' she said after a moment.

'My lady, I swear to the chancellor himself, if this is more speculation about that bloody shadow…'

'No, it's not the shadow.' She looked forward with dismay. 'I can hear something. Some heavy stammer.'

'It's a small tremor. That or our riders have returned with eight legs apiece.'

Silence fell again. The shadow *had* grown larger, distinguishable without squinting; it was splitting across the horizon.

The stammer was getting heavier. Magmaya's heart was sinking.

'Shalleous,' Magmaya began, 'issue a rider to a taller viewpoint.'

'No, the others are taking time enough,' Shalleous barked, and Magmaya looked to him, but couldn't make out the same man from the morning before. This man had lost his beauty; his skin was grey and cold. 'We'll ride on and inspect more caverns. You can get a better look at your cursed shadow from there.'

'Then we do so now,' Magmaya ordered, and to her surprise, the men began to pick up pace.

The Sultide was farther away than it had looked, though, and there was still no sign of the riders returning. The thin waves lapped feebly onto the icy rocks below, and the deer slowed as they approached, yapping and snorting wildly as they stamped at the thin streaks of light.

'If the moon's behind the clouds, then what's casting the shadow?' she asked him.

Shalleous didn't reply. Instead, she found her uncle gazing into the distance; a look of horror was spreading across his face. He raised his left hand high, ordering the men to stop.

And so, the battalion stood still, cramming the gorge's opening. The wind was near silent, but in time, the deer grew restless, and Magmaya heard every last heartbeat.

'Fall back,' Shalleous muttered quietly, and then louder, 'Fall back!'

The deer began to call, the snow fell heavier, and water sprung up around them. Magmaya looked to the black shadow in earnest.

'I've made a terrible mistake,' Shalleous hissed. 'That's not a shadow, girl. Those are a hundred Mansel warhorses.'

'But—but—we outnumber them, yes?' Her eyes watered, and her expression turned to panic.

Shalleous smiled. 'You and your brother were both summer children. You're so young. You've only heard fables of these men, Magmaya. They're merciless, cunning, cruel. They would have you skinned and hanged—eaten by their hunting hounds.'

'So, what do you propose?' Magmaya asked, flustered.

'Vargul Tul is their castellan—he leads their cavalry,' Shalleous said. 'I'll ride forward and take his charge. It may leave time enough to turn tails and spread news to Orianne.'

'Shalleous, you know you can't,' Magmaya insisted. 'We can't outrun them.'

'What other choice do we have?' her uncle roared, and before she could hazard a reply, he tugged at his deer's reigns and rode off.

She found herself looking to the horizon. The shadow had faded, but in its place stood the silhouettes of charging men, inching closer with every passing second. There would be little time to spare. She followed quietly on after the fleeing men, though by the time she pranced a metre, the Mansel were already closing in.

After a couple of minutes, Shalleous raised his blade and called into the night. Several of his men rallied around him and met the Mansel charge at the hilltop. They came together like a drum hammering through the sky, and after a moment of valiant charges, their fervour devolved into something terribly primal. Men went for men's throats; horse hooves became intertwined with deer hooves. It was pathetic, the way they all fell. Like nothing she had heard in the faery stories.

Damn it! she cursed. *I won't live to see tomorrow.*

She could do nothing but watch as his men soiled themselves as they died, and their deer buckled and ran. *You're making a mistake*, she thought and cantered on ahead, the others forming ranks around her. There was no time to think now, only to run.

Cries and curses echoed from behind, and the Mansel lurched forward; black lances met her company's rear. They cut swiftly through the middle ranks before a second battalion emerged from the fog.

A terrible screaming cut through the night and then an echo and then a hailstorm. Once again, the horses reared, and the Mansel held. Her men weren't so fortunate—their mounts betrayed them. In a mess of tangled limbs, they tossed their riders to the icy ground and trampled them as they fled.

Magmaya turned and drew her sword. It was lighter than what she was used to; it was a flimsy thing made for show. She was never meant to fight.

She peered through the field of mangled bodies, and then she passed the corpse of Gilbus, hands still clawed around that banner pole, and found some strength rise within her.

'To your lord!' Magmaya shouted, but she should have shouted louder. Though a loyal few rounded-back, several of her uncle's guardsmen disappeared into the night. She wanted to scream the command again, but Nurcia's voice was nagging away at her still: *He had his breeches down, I had to shoo him away. He said he wanted to fuck me.*

The snow was beginning to fall quicker, and so Magmaya didn't see the next charge. The riders spared no time to cover the ground between them, and in a shower of upturned mud, a spear met the hide of her deer.

It was then Magmaya could almost feel the warm touch of the candlelight from her chambers and see the scorched bricks on the ceiling; the portraits that hung above seemed wiser now and the statuettes of naked maidens that lined the halls even more gracious. The snow began to fall, and the world grew white. A star flickered in the distance. She was home.

But only for a moment. She had been living by her mother's love and dying by her father's. Her deer had erupted into a wailing, thrashing about with its antlers. Its spasming limbs cut the air above, and Magmaya kicked out, but her feet found nothing but the wind. And as it tossed about, she felt something hard meet her chest, a hoof, and for but a second, a ringing burst through her ears and the world turned black.

A shoulder blade met rock, and a hip met ice before Magmaya lay still, cupping her bloody gut as the water lapped at her. Her head was pounding as the men who had come to her side were slain, one by one. And as she finally accepted peace, the water didn't seem so cold anymore. As her body sank beneath the waves, it was warm like milk from a mother's teat. Her counterfeit blade had been lost in the fall, but she had no strength left in her to stand anyway. And as she folded her legs into her stomach and let the nameless gods take her, a fractured smile crept on her blistered lips.

And yet, more of her men came to defend her— why was her life worth so much to them? *More than a banquet. More than gold,* her mother had once told her.

All around her, bodies piled upon bodies in the tides, intertwined with the carcasses of horses and deer seemingly too innocent to live. The wind howled, and the night fell silent again—that was until Magmaya saw someone else emerge from the fray.

He was a head taller than the others, and he had copper skin, buried beneath layers of barbs and fur. The face was too hazy to make out between the falling snow and her failing eyesight, but at his knees, there was someone else: Shalleous, bloodied and alone.

'Magmaya Vorr, my castellan.' One of the Mansel pointed at her, his voice cold and dry.

She raised her hands to cover herself, smearing her eyes with her own streaking blood. But between red fingers she saw the bigger man nod and advance on her, dragging her uncle's knees through the water.

He muttered something, and Magmaya shuddered; his voice was like cracking ice, and his eyes were like black pits. It wasn't what he said that scared her—it was the way the words formed in his mouth—like something unnatural. 'I want you to watch and listen closely.'

'You dare touch her!' Shalleous called, but his voice was a whimper, and his mouth was overflowing with blood. Yet her uncle persisted all the same, shouting, 'She's the heir to Orianne! Without her, you have no leverage.'

Vargul Tul wasn't listening, though. He put a pair of blades to Shalleous' neck, and the Wolf collapsed into the snow.

Three

Magmaya had convinced herself fear was a figment of the wind. And yet, she was falling slowly, but all at once; shards of glass were cascading from the heavens and shimmering like snow in the moonlight.

It was like an ecstasy of colours, and it hurt to watch. Her head pounded, and in the back of her mind an icy voice scratched away at her and burned like fire, *'You must inform them.'*

The words stung her throat.

'Tell them, girl, and you will be free.'

Who? Whose voice was that? Magmaya's mind wandered as she fell, and the sky twisted. The clouds bent, and the red sun turned black in the edges of her vision.

'Inform them,' the voice said, intruding her. Magmaya's mind grew foggy as she tried to free herself from it all, but each time she tried to resist, the voice only got louder.

Needles prickled her skin and ran up her spine, ate at her arms, and bit her neck. There was an empty crying in her ears, and the stars were falling around her— falling fast! Faster than ever before! There were violet ones, blue ones, orange ones and ones of bursting green which no man could've ever even imagined. It hurt her eyes to stare too long.

Magmaya Vorr was floating, yes, but there was no sinking into her mother's arms; there was no feeling the warmth of the sun. Her life did not flash before her eyes, and neither did the pain stop—it became a part of her.

And as she fell, the ground didn't grow closer, but it was over in but a moment all the same. She could feel it: her heart beating out of her chest, rising through her lungs and spiralling into her throat, spreading like a wildfire that couldn't be tamed.

For a moment, there was a dull ring as the fall came to an end, and there the girl lay sprawled on a bed of crimson.

Magmaya could almost smell the dust and entropy. The wind beat at her face, and for a second, her heart felt like it was clapping behind her closed eyes. Ice groped at her neck and seeped down her thighs where she just sat and shivered.

She still felt herself falling, though. Would the nameless gods ever let her rest? Couldn't they just let her die?

'You must inform them,' the voice rasped again. *'Inform Orianne. Tell your father to surrender the city,'* Vargul Tul had said, and she felt herself smile; no doubt would the fleeing troops have reached and warned Orianne by now. But would her people have enough time

to prepare? It was a question she would ponder until the end of time, whenever that may have been.

As Magmaya dreamt again, she found her thoughts turning to the Paradise Lands and to the Silver City. It was said to shimmer above the earth like it was amongst the stars itself; chrome spires pointed to the skies as the people below sung and chanted and smiled. And yet, she was just another girl that lived in an inconvenient place in an inconvenient time. And there had been so many like her, and they had all died, wishes unfulfilled—why should she be any different?

The cold bit sharper, and Magmaya screamed.

'Gods!' she cried, and her face flushed with ruby. 'Gods, I'm alive.'

Her eyes snapped open, light lashed at her, and beads of tears spilt down her skin. The wind and ice beat at her eyes, but she didn't dare shut them and face the dark again.

Magmaya's body ached, and not an inch of her skin wasn't sore, it seemed. As tears pooled in her mouth, she lowered her head, found the mane of a horse, and let out something of a laugh. She watched her spit dribble down her chin and smiled. Snow whipped against her back. Colours melted behind her eyes; they were violent and strong—stronger than the wind.

It was only when she looked up at the winter sky that she felt the holes in her heart and lungs where something warm had been. And as the horse carried her begrudgingly through the ice, at last, she began to appreciate her predicament. *I'm no captive,* she realised. *Captives are only of worth when their home wants them alive.* If she thought for a minute that Kharon cared for her enough to surrender the city, she would have been sorely mistaken. Vargul Tul knew the clockwork politics of her home as well as she did. Eerily well.

Instead of holding her to ransom, the Mansel had sent her back to Orianne. The city would let Magmaya in, and she would tell them to surrender. She had seen what the Mansel had done to her uncle. There couldn't be any more bloodshed—surely?

As she pressed her face into her hands, she noticed her own blood had dried between the crinkles in her skin. *It might have been hours since the clash at the Sultide,* she realised, *and the Mansel would have inevitably outpaced Orianne's men back to the city.* If they were truly sending her as some kind of scout, then they were biding their time.

Magmaya felt her gut tighten, and bile filled her mouth as her fingers found something wet, threatening to spill into her hands. She looked to find a gash in her belly; it was bandaged to a degree, and yet, blood still ran thick through the cuts. But in her, there was no pain; there was only a dull ache.

In a moment of heat, she gripped the reigns, tight, and looked down to the Mansel horse. It was steadfast and strong enough, but not an inch of its coat was spared from a number of bloody lacerations and cuts. Magmaya felt her fingers brush over her bloody navel and looked on feebly. She raised her arm and struck the horse's hide.

With a jolt, she felt herself running. The mountains became fainter and more distorted than they'd ever been, and ice glided past faster than it could fall.

She felt herself fading, yet a mad whirring inside seemed to take over. Something greater and more diabolical than her began to take the reins.

'I shall inform them...' Her voice was brittle and breathless. 'I shall inform them...'

She found herself thinking of Rache and the gardens of Orianne; she thought of the flickering candlelight and the marble halls. She thought to the white sun and the pale moon, the pearly men on the seas and the hoary vessels at night. She thought to the bitter taste in her throat and the blood spewing from her gut. Anywhere but home—surely?

The horse was intent on taking her there, though. It scaled the mountainside as if it had a hundred times before, but occasionally, it would grow quiet and settle by a small frozen stream and force her to drink. It was so terribly cold, and Magmaya feared each sip was going to kill her more than the last.

And with each sip, she looked to the mountains and wondered if she could run that far. Jayce had— perhaps she was just over the hillside with that stricken face. The pair wouldn't look too dissimilar anymore. Besides, the Free-Peoples would take anyone in, but she didn't have a clue about where she even was.

And with each sip, she managed to convince herself still to get back on that damned horse and let it carry her home. She was starving, though, and she would've considered eating the bloody thing had she had any less restraint.

Whenever it stumbled over a rock or tumbled down a nearby slope, Magmaya reached out, half expecting Siedous to be there and catch her as she did, and each time, she found herself a mouthful of snow. If the nameless gods had indeed saved her, then surely it must have been for a cruel joke. If Vargul Tul wasn't going to kill her, the cold certainly would.

It's better to die now anyway, she decided. The falling snow felt so warm. She wanted to dive in and let it take her. But before she could move another inch, a sudden stench of liquor overpowered her. Magmaya's eyes twitched, and she heard herself calling for someone who wasn't there. Before long, she drifted into the clutches of a dream again.

Magmaya found herself dreaming of Allister Julne. All those years ago, he'd alerted his servants in the early hours to feeling unwell, but there hadn't been much remaining to feel unwell by the time they'd arrived. The man had stood by her side for as long as she'd remembered, attending courts while she lazed and speaking on her behalf when she hadn't a clue what was happening. Magmaya remembered, and he was alive again, somewhere in her head.

Allister had seen many rulers come and go, and it had been his legacy that ended hers in the end; he'd been a beloved man throughout the palace, and one day they'd all woken up without him.

By the afternoon, a scribe had arrived to see Magmaya about the ado. They had always been quick, hoisting those endlessly long scrolls through their clockwork machines as he did in those sangria robes that day.

Magmaya had hidden her wine out of sight.

After their curtsies, she'd looked to the man that perched before her and sworn he must've been two-hundred years older than Allister ever was; his garnet-lined eyes and porcelain skin were like mirrors, though she tried better to hide her cracks. He had a kindly smile that gave the warmest embrace, but it was the embrace of a snake.

She'd felt a sickness in her throat, and she'd begun to grow cold. The man looked right through her, but all she could see were shadows dancing about in those glistening brown eyes.

'Allister was an advisor to you, no?'

'Yes,' she had admitted.

The scribe had jotted something on one of his many scrolls, ready for its preparation in some old tome. Ever since the Dark Age of Transmutany, Orianne had made a great habit of recording everything; most of the continent's past had been long forgotten then. According to the southerners, the clockwork ships and the Silver City were the only remnants of the golden ages that were remembered so far north. But they were beginning to forget.

'We all must lose someone close to us, in time,' he said after a while, and she'd looked up, perplexed.

'What a strange thing to say,' Magmaya remarked.

'What is?'

'Whatever you just said.' She'd frowned.

'Perhaps it was,' he'd admitted. *'Or perhaps I would like to know what came of my son.'*

Magmaya sat back, eyes wide, and composed herself. She had felt awfully relaxed.

'Your son was a traitor and tried to break the city,' she replied, recalling the young lad and that cursed smirk of his. She felt herself remembering her sword through his neck, his blood on her skin, the sweat down her legs. *'My father would have you hanged.'*

'My days are few.' The man stifled a laugh. *'If you want that, you should hurry.'*

'*It's lucky I'm not my father, then.*' Magmaya grit her teeth. '*Where did you flee to anyway? The Free-Peoples?*'

'*Where else would a dead man flee?*' He raised an eyebrow. '*I may be old, but I have not lost my wits. The Free-Peoples taught me patience. I'm no convict, my lady, but it's lucky for* your *kind I'm not my son.*'

'*My kind? No. Not just my kind, we all are.*' She had sighed. '*Are we done?*'

'*It seems we finished long ago.*'

The scribe stood abruptly, and Magmaya had sworn the walls had shaken. She wanted the man out of her sight, and if the scribe was to die as his son had done, it hadn't bothered her.

Magmaya had stood before he left and called, '*Guards!*'

Her voice was frail, but it was enough to make him look on in horror. The door was thrown open, and a pair of armed men had charged in, clad in rosy-steel with hands to the hilts of their blades. Magmaya's mind had whirred as she looked to the scribe, deciding his punishment. '*Assure he's exiled to the Deadfields or—I don't care. Just get him out!*'

It was effortless—the way they had taken him and pinned his weak, old hands to his shoulders. He was nothing to them as they stood over him like colossi of old—like the pearly men in her dreams.

'*On what grounds?*' the scribe asked, his eyes wide.

'*He attacked me,*' she'd said. '*Went right for my throat!*'

'*Lies!*' the scribe had screamed, but her men weren't listening.

'*This man should be put on trial, my lady,*' one of the guards suggested.

'*No,*' she'd paused. '*Let him go where he belongs.*' A bead of sweat rolled down Magmaya's cheek. '*The cold. I want this matter forgotten.*'

She remembered watching as the old man fell to his knees, pleading, only to be dragged out across the stony halls. The guards marched mercilessly either side, and Magmaya forced herself to turn away, whipping sweat from her forehead.

Allowing herself the warmth of the wicker chair, she raised the bottle of wine from beside the seat and produced a small ritual knife from beneath her dress; it had been rusted and chipped, sporting an embroiled grip—forged in the south, no doubt. Magmaya had noticed it under the scribe's robes as he had entered, and during their curtsies, had made an effort of snatching it before he'd had a chance to set to work with her.

She'd put the blade to the bottle, weened out the cork, and watched the red mist foam. A life for a life was what he'd proposed, but it was an empty debt. *If only it was so easy,* Magmaya had thought, though she couldn't quite decide whether the gods had been cruel or kind.

And when she awoke again, she could still feel the knife pursed between her fingers. No—she wasn't going to the Free-Peoples. She wasn't going to find Jayce. She was going home.

Four

The screams and shouts of the night had become one with the cool air, but at last, her journey had met its end. And she was glad for it—her thighs were beginning to ache like all hells, and her hair was frozen and knotted. Besides, she wasn't quite sure what was even happening, nor where she was, nor who the people were that carried her back to her city.

'*The way back is always quicker,*' she remembered Siedous saying, but it didn't feel true anymore. As a child, she'd run back and forth across the city all day in pursuit of geese but getting to the hospice seemed to take a month. No, not the hospice—she had pleaded with them to take her to the palace and to Kharon Vorr.

'It'll be all right, girl.' At last, she heard a voice she recognised—Kaladeous, one of Kharon's advisors—as he walked and murmured over and over, 'It'll be all right.' But it wasn't all right, and her lungs were on fire.

There probably wasn't a single man or woman in Orianne who didn't know who she was—heir to the household and champion of its name, the scrawny girl born during a summer heat. But as she limped inside the boardroom, even her own father (no matter how distant) scarcely recognised her.

Hair fell like wet straw over her nose and sullied the threadbare carpets. Her cuirass was broken and chinked, shattered beyond repair. But something else was missing too. All her strength had been drowned from her, and the blue across her skin had become a violent colour. And amongst it all there was Siedous, holding her in those warm, grey arms she'd known so well.

'We found her on a Mansel horse riding from the Deadfields,' Kaladeous said with a flash of urgency about him. 'She might've been poisoned, my lord.'

Despite the spit rolling down her lips, her mouth was dry. She cried and tore a chalice from Kharon's table, downing whatever was in it. It was sour, and it hurt, but it was warm enough still to make her forget.

'We thought it best to take her to the apothecaries, but she insisted on coming here. She wanted to speak with you, my chancellor,' Kaladeous continued as he ripped the drink from her hand. 'She's bleeding heavy enough and— Magmaya, sit down!'

She did as she was told, but her head was throbbing. She gasped for air; the ache was in her heart and in her bones.

'Magmaya, what happened?' the old knight asked, and she couldn't help but laugh.

'A lot of things,' she told Siedous, 'although I doubt I have time to tell you them all.' She spluttered.

'Well, get the shamans up here, damn it,' Kharon replied to Kaladeous at last, but it a gruff whisper. His eyes were empty as if it was not his daughter lying before him but some animal-thing instead.

'They're on their way, my chancellor.'

She scanned the boardroom, and her eyes froze, finding a small, gold vase. *That'll be worth enough coin to take both me and Rache south,* she reasoned. Her mouth crinkled with pleasure at the thought. It was a cursed vase, her father had once told her, bestowed with magic from places even farther north than they. *Good,* she thought with something of mirth, *people love to play with cursed things. It'll fetch an even higher price, and I'll be able to run farther away.*

But before she could grapple for it, something sickly jolted up her back, and she collapsed into the old knight's arms again. She cried, 'They made me drink something.' Tears welled in her eyes. 'I'm going to die.'

Siedous leapt up, and before she knew it, Magmaya's head was between her legs, and she was pale all over. Brittle fingers were forced down her throat. Her head turned heavy. After a short moment, she vomited.

'It's Dew of the Honey,' she heard him say, frantic. 'She's drunk Dew of the Honey.'

'And what's that?'

'A killing potion from the Summerlands,' he croaked. 'But the Mansel use it for torture, my lord.'

'And what's it doing to her?' Kaladeous asked.

'Numbing her.'

'The Mansel are coming,' Magmaya heard herself shout. There was some burning behind her eyes willing her on, but no one appeared to be paying attention.

'And will it leave her?' the chancellor asked.

'Listen!' Magmaya screamed. 'Vargul Tul let me live. He let me live to tell you—'

'Tell me what?'

'Stand down,' she spluttered. 'Surrender the city.'

'Likely!' Kharon scoffed, looking about. 'Where's Shalleous in this madness?'

A thousand footsteps rumbled outside the doors, and her world fell into something an ocean. After a few moments, a legion of physicians charged into the boardroom, and she could only watch as they took her, their robes snapping against the cold until the light of the blade at Kharon's hip sent her into a daze.

'He's dead,' she murmured, and the last thing she saw was a look in her father's eye she might have once described as conceit.

When Magmaya woke again, it was like her feet had been kissed by fire. There was a pit in her chest that had once raged with hellish pain, but now, there was just a dull ache where something should have been, gnawing away. And all around, shamans looked to her with relief. But most of all, there was silence—bar the static that rang out from hour to hour.

She'd watched her uncle die, his head loosened from his shoulders, and no matter how many times she tried to shake it free from her mind, it just kept happening over and over. There was no warmth left inside her—the snow had seen to that.

She tried to call out and scream, but nothing came out save for silence and empty gasps while she raged and flailed against the monsters above. They opened her mouth and forced her to eat, pressed incense up her nose and dragged metal needles through her skin. The sourness of it all had turned her eyes nimble and dim, yet there were dry fires behind them, and she heard herself spluttering, 'I'm Magmaya Vorr—I'm heir—gods! I'm...' *alive.*

But then, all the strength left her like the last breath of a dying man, and the hours passed into silence. She could almost feel the Dew of the Honey coursing through her veins still like a sickness.

Strength returned to her slowly, and then as a landslide.

And with the passing of the hours, the room had emptied, save for the stains, so she forced herself up and pushed her way out of the room, finding a complex of endless freezing corridors leading into oblivion.

In each one, a thousand different mirrors and a thousand different choices stared back with coals for eyes. She must have collapsed a thousand times, but in the end, she found a girl in a white bodice ambling out the snow and into the light.

Damn this cold, she thought. *Did Orianne not know how to even light a fire?*

Magmaya stopped, felt something wet, and watched her drapes turn a deep black. She was holding herself like a new-born, and yet, there was a rush of zeal spiralling through her head, and so she ran, tripping over her own footsteps.

And suddenly, there was a stairwell before her, spiralling up to the palace above. Hours appeared to have passed, and her head was pounding by the time she reached the top, and when she did, it was only to meet the outstretched spears of a dozen brassy guards, the embezzled roses on their armour blinding her.

'Stand down,' one of them called through the snow. 'Do you know where you are?'

'Let me through,' Magmaya hissed. 'The Mansel are coming—I must—you know me, yes? Magmaya Vorr?'

'My lady, my apologies.' One of the sentinels lowered his spear. 'The chancellor sent notice to the people—he wanted to see you...'

'Good,' she jabbered. 'I wanted to see him too.'

She held her gut and followed the beads of blood as they ran down to her hands, filling the crevices in her bony thumbs. Magmaya turned to the sentinel and trailed drunkenly into the palace. She felt naked in the dust and chalk of her home; she might as well have not even worn her drapes.

The guard's plate clanked about the hall and seemed to bend in the light from the braziers above, and Magmaya began to feel a little more unwell. *Keep a hold of yourself,* she scorned, but her head was warm and dizzy. She was surprised she was able to think at all.

They soon arrived at the boardroom and peered in to see Kharon Vorr standing at the balcony, watching the snow float through the wind like it was trapped in an hourglass. 'Kharon.' She started over to him, but her head was dizzy. She almost tripped over that damned table leg again.

'It seems not all Vorr are so easy to kill,' he muttered.

'They're coming for the gates,' she crooned. 'Why did you summon me?'

'You think I don't know that?' He took a seat by the window, waved a hand at the sentinel and watched him leave.

'You can't stand idle when a monster is out there trying to burn our city,' she scorned. 'Take the fight to him.'

'Stupid girl,' he murmured. 'There's no fight. The Mansel are prepared for a raid, not a siege. They'll all starve before a single drop of blood is spilt.'

Magmaya shook her head and took the seat opposite his. Sitting made her feel calm, and besides, the chair was draped with several of Kharon's discarded garbs, and even they were warmer than her bloodied gown.

'You're in a state, girl,' he droned on.

'I know. But you wanted me here all the same.' She began to slip one of his tunics over her head; it was far too big, but it was warm, and that was all she needed now. 'If you can't tell me why you wanted me here, then let me go to the gates,' she said and eyed the shimmer he had left on the table behind; it was the shimmer of Moonbeam, the blade of Orianne.

And then she turned back to the chancellor and found him quiet—she'd never seen him so silent. Or sober.

But then, as if in response, Kharon moved to a chest of drawers and plucked a wine glass up between his fingers. He took a sip, and he was a different man.

'There's fighting at the gates, still.' He cleared his throat. 'Siedous has gone to hold them, but—' he coughed. 'Besides...'

'Besides what?' She put on his trousers.

'Magmaya,' he hushed her. 'Just... just be quiet.'

'Why did you send Shalleous and me to Mansel?' she asked at last. 'You claim it was to showcase the pride of the city—'

'No more!' He turned and, all of a sudden, he seemed to notice she was getting changed, and his eyes glowed red.

Damn him, she thought. If only he'd boarded that damned ship and fled south while he still could've, then none of this would've ever happened. Then she could've been chancellor and—well, it was best not to consider that.

'So be it,' Kharon snapped. 'Nurcia has betrayed us.'

'What?'

'We've reason to believe so.' He sighed. 'She was meant to be tending to the hospice, but we've reports of her going down Low Path to bow to Tul.'

Magmaya got up and dusted herself off, but her hands became slick with blood. The bodice they'd given her had only appeared to encourage her bleeding, and she'd sullied Kharon's garbs too.

'How do you know she will?' she asked at last.

'She stabbed Kaladeous on her way there,' he murmured. 'Seven times.'

'But she was your advisor...'

'Yes, I am quite aware,' he groaned. 'But she made it no secret that she and Tul had history. He sacked her home before she even flowered. Seems likely she turned her tail in fear it would happen again.'

As far as Magmaya had always remembered, Nurcia had been a devout and quiet woman—and she'd betrayed the city? She had been so beautiful...

'She's too scared to see through this,' she cursed. 'What now, then?'

'I said there would be no fight,' he began. 'But if she tells the Mansel where the thermals are…'

'She'll lead them right into the city…' She nodded. 'Send out guardsmen, then. Take her back before she can reach the front.'

'I've sent out a contingent to find her,' he said, 'but if she knows we've discovered her betrayal, she might just run a little faster.'

'None of this makes any sense,' she remarked. 'I knew that woman, she…' Magmaya sighed. 'I'm going after her.'

'What?'

'You said it yourself. When your contingent arrives, she'll flee. If I can go down and approach her…'

'You will die, and she will run.'

'I can talk some sense—'

'No,' he roared, and he was certainly the man she knew again. 'I'm the chancellor. Not you. You will not decide what happens in this city.'

'You sent me to represent Orianne, now let me act like it.'

'You can scarcely fight.'

'I can swing a sword.'

'No, you can't.'

'Siedous taught me all I needed to know. I *can* swing one hard enough, harder than you can,' she spat. 'I'm no use here.'

'What are you going to do?' He laughed. 'Take her in?'

'I'll kill her if I have to.' She gripped her abdomen as a flash of pain blinded her, but she felt some strength course through her still.

She remembered that night at the forest when she'd found Albany lying dead. *The Mansel had sent their message then, and I had run away. That wouldn't happen again.*

Kharon threw his head back. 'You storm in here, and you speak to me like a fool, you steal my clothes—'

'Your *discarded* clothes.'

'Quiet!' he stammered. 'Siedous will go. You, to the hospice.'

'Siedous is at the gate. You said that yourself.'

'You're going to lose us this fight—'

'There is no fight,' she crooned. 'Now, thank you.' Magmaya couldn't quite believe the words she was saying. 'For telling me.'

'Go and kill her, then,' he snapped. 'Take a sword from some dead man and bring her head back here.'

I will. She turned, and there was Moonbeam.

'Time is fragile.' Kharon sat, reaching for a glass that was empty. He was looking away into nothing. 'Almost as fragile as you, you damned piece of shit.'

As Kharon Vorr threw his head back, Magmaya Vorr caught herself smiling. She crept over to the table and took the leather of the sheathed sword between her fingers. It was heavy—heavier than any sword she'd held before, and if she'd held it any closer, she swore it would have blinded her.

The air outside reeked of iron and sweat. The night was breaking in again, and the last of the cold sun's rays were seeping beyond the horizon. And as Magmaya strode away, she couldn't help but want to collapse. She didn't want this! Ranvirus was a small, insignificant realm far away from anywhere that mattered. She was nothing; this was nothing, and no matter which way it all ended, no one would weep for her.

I would weep for them, though, she thought. *If the south fell and I never saw it, I would kick myself until the day I died.*

She'd always told herself there would be a day when all the ice would melt, and she would feel the green grass beneath her feet, but that thought was quickly becoming a fleeting thing. If she were to ever feel a warm sun beating down on her back, she would spare her new self the pleasure of a heart. Perhaps she would rip it out and replace it with something cold.

She turned a corner, and without warning, a hailstorm of crossbow bolts fell from above. Magmaya threw herself to the ground, feeling them spear the earth around her.

Once the metal rain had fallen, she tossed herself aside. The crossbowmen above began to reload, but not before they shouted out to her, 'My lady!'

'We thought you were that traitor...' another called.

Magmaya coughed and pulled herself up from the carnage, scowling. She dusted herself down and turned away. She wanted to vomit again, but by the time the sickness had left her, all her energy had too, and she found herself collapsing into an alleyway.

A large, empty building awaited her, broken windows shimmering in the new-born moonshine. It scattered haloed saints and broken angels into the shadowed snow and for a moment, the night seemed silent.

Magmaya rose and approached the edifice as if something was drawing her in. Somehow, it felt colder inside; mist clung to her skin and ate away at her eyelids. It was sparse and quiet with a bruised checked floor that glistened under invisible braziers above.

And when she looked up, she found humming arches and grey pillars staring down at her. Her strength was leaving her quickly, dying like the setting sun, and she was forced to remind herself, *Not yet.* She told herself, *You can die later.*

She carried on and prepared the words between her lips: *I'm looking for a woman by the name of Nurcia Vyce. She works for the chancellor. I'm afraid she's in terrible danger.*

That ought to get someone concerned. She had the face of any common girl now, too. *No one will mistake me for Magmaya Vorr.*

When she left the building through the other side, the winds returned, and the snow started falling again, filling the streets. She looked around, and there was Low Path—a trail of broken cobblestones and abandoned market stalls sweeping down the rocky crag of the Silver Mountainside. The path had often been where the commoners had bartered, but now, it was empty, save for a quiet chitter-chatter about the streets.

She could make out the street's end about a hundred yards away, but from there, the path would just twist and turn, continuing on until it reached the gate. She just hoped she'd find Nurcia along the way.

One day, this will be all over, she told herself. There was another sun out there, and it shone like gold and yellow and warmed those who stood in its light. When the winter ended, and the clouds cleared, the whole world would know of spring and dance in the flower fields—she could look forward to that, at least.

It was even said there was a whole continent across the seas called the Summerlands where girls worshipped the light. There, people were truly free and bore their own fruit, as priestesses and valiant witches prayed for good harvests under their holy bells that gave them rain and fire. Perhaps across the seas, she might feel warm at last—she just had to make her way to the shore...

And then there was a sound, and her fingers felt for Moonbeam. She was awake again.

But each winding stair she struggled down seemed gnawed away at her chest, and though she couldn't feel the pain, the pressure on her navel felt as if it would snap her in two. She hadn't even realised her palm was wet either—a token from one of those crossbow bolts no doubt—what a pitiful way to die!

Not yet, not yet, she told herself. *Find Nurcia; that's all you have to do. Not a drop more of blood needs to be spilt.*

But the path ahead was choked with fog. Another step forward would plunge her down into a maze of clouds, and then she and Nurcia might be lost forever. There would surely be no chance of her finding the traitor anymore.

She carved her way through the mist anyway, until she was but a sound amongst the dark of the city streets. A number of burning braziers and glowing candles speared through and caught the corners of her eyes, but they were just noise to the hum of the moon above.

'Magmaya,' she heard someone croon and turned to the open air behind her. But as she scanned the streets, she found herself alone again—holding herself and cold—oh so cold.

And then sounded the grizzly snorting of horses and with it, a faint neighing. But Orianne didn't have horses. Only reindeer.

'Surely not...' she whispered to herself and found Moonbeam.

I'm looking for a woman by the name of Nurcia Vyce. She works for the chancellor. I'm afraid she's in terrible danger. The words were nothing now.

Magmaya peered through the fog and continued on. Each alleyway led to another like an impossible puzzle, and at the heart of it, eclipsed in the light of the moon, stood Nurcia, waiting about the streets.

Now what? she asked herself and sank back into the shadows. She could still make out the neighing of horses and Nurcia whispering to herself, muttering something strange about the darkness.

'The old knight still rides,' she heard her say.

But then, another voice said, 'Dead by sundown'—and a chill went up her spine.

The voice was cold and brittle; it was part of the falling snow. And when she peered out again, she found the figures of perhaps a dozen Mansel, hunched in barbs and fur.

Five

Nurcia smiled like she knew when the world would meet its end. Her horse cantered quickly through the desolate streets, wisps of ice beginning to nestle in its fur, coughing and whinnying in a pale effort to free itself from the cold.

She was a skilled rider (that much was clear), and as she rode, her blue drapes beat behind her in the winter winds, and a look of disdain spread wide across her lips. The scarred Mansel strode tall by her side, quite at odds with her snowy white skin. Soon enough, the fog began to spread, and she disappeared into the dark again. There was no longer any sign of her or the Mansel, let alone the tall spires that seeped into the heavens above. Magmaya was alone.

'Once this is done, take your leave, my lady,' one of them echoed through the fog.

'Of course.' She heard Nurcia say, 'But I will triumph still when my lord takes the city. And soon, he shall sail for the south. It has been prophesied in the sea star that moves.'

'Yes, my lady,' a pair of the Mansel answered.

A humming of metal rang out, and one of them grunted, ambling about the stone streets. Another drew his blade and tightened his fist before a couple others followed suit.

'Someone's here,' he said. 'There's someone in the fog.'

'No one's here,' Nurcia scorned. 'Mount. Vargul will be at the palace in time.'

Vargul at the palace? Magmaya wondered. Was it better to fall back and warn Kharon? Or kill Nurcia before she let anyone else in? She feared she'd already made up her mind. Besides, she could hear something too. There was something more barbaric coming.

There was silence for a moment. And then one of the Mansel buckled. His legs tightened, and his chest cracked as he let out a final, breathless moan and toppled into the gutter. Magmaya clasped her hand over her mouth. It was all she could do not to scream.

Nurcia's horse reared up and tore itself away, but she rallied the mare, stared down her foe and drew a dagger. But she wasn't a fighter; she never had been.

'Leave the shadows, whoreson,' the turncoat called into the dark.

But it wasn't *a* whoreson, Magmaya soon learnt. There were twenty.

Kharon's contingent arrived. Nurcia disappeared into the fog. But the Mansel weren't so quick; four were struck down before the chancellor's daughter moved an inch, and another two were slain in the ensuing skirmish. And then began the haunted chiming of locked blades, ringing out through the mist.

Magmaya could do nothing but dart from cloud to cloud until there was a Mansel beside her, already engaged with one of Kharon's men. Without a thought, she ripped Moonbeam from its sheath and drove it through his back.

She'd never struck a man through his back before. His shoulders seized up and locked around the blade, and it took her what seemed a lifetime to drag it out of him. And by then, the contingent had found her.

'My lady?' she heard the guardsman call to her through the night, but she had already taken off, following Nurcia through the streets.

The mist was suffocating, and it was becoming harder by the minute to breathe, but some fire in her willed her on. And then sounded footsteps from around a wall, and so she followed them down an alleyway.

She found Nurcia in a small courtyard where roses grew in the summer, with an arrow in her back and enmity on her lips.

A lone bowman gave a cheer from atop a nearby building and turned back to her, nocking his arrow, but Magmaya protested and gestured to Nurcia.

She wasn't dead yet. She was still useful.

'Kharon sent you here to kill me, didn't he?' the turncoat asked, trying to pull herself up from the mud. But her back had forsaken her, and so Magmaya just watched as she collapsed again.

'No, but I don't have time to consider anything else now.' She was trying to be brave like she'd been brave all those years ago when she had executed that prisoner. *Remember how easily you put that sword through his neck, remember how quickly it was over,* but this wasn't quick, and this wasn't easy, because the girl she was trying to kill was writhing and sad.

'Why, you want to stop the Mansel from getting in?' She spat blood. 'They've been here for years.'

She narrowed her eyes.

'You don't quite understand, I know,' Nurcia said, and Magmaya felt herself lowering Moonbeam to her neck. 'Kharon Vorr truly is a fool if he thinks I turned to Vargul out of fear,' she mumbled. 'We're not all like you, slut. Not everything we do is driven by our need to run away.'

'Enough!' Nurcia lifted her head, and Magmaya drew Moonbeam across her face. It laid her open from eye to chin, but even as she bled, she just smiled, knowingly.

'Bow to him, Magmaya,' she said. 'Your city is lost. Bow to him, and you might finally find a cause you believe in.'

She was infuriated already. She just had to keep telling herself, *remember how easily you put that sword through his neck, remember how quickly it was over.*

Nurcia wasn't making it easier, though. 'Don't you want to know who killed Albany Moore?' she hummed and pressed her finger to her heart.

Magmaya's eyes twitched, and she found herself stepping away, tripping over her feet. Her vision had become hazy, and all she could see was some pathetic thing, a thousand lifetimes away. A pathetic thing that might have one day advised her, befriended her. Now she was bleeding.

'I should have you skinned and buried,' she heard herself say, but her voice had gone shrill.

'No, you wouldn't,' the turncoat spat. 'You wouldn't wish that on yourself. Kill me, and I'll always be a part of you.' She paused. 'I'll always be a part of your brothers.'

Brothers?

'You—? Oh,' Magmaya stuttered. And then she began to cry.

'Does that displease you?' Nurcia turned her head, smearing blood across her furs like an animal at the height of its hunt. 'You would rather Rache be out here instead? I did you a favour with his legs.'

'No more,' Magmaya said, but there was impatience in her eyes. 'Just shut up.'

'I wouldn't threaten me again, girl. You wouldn't bring down Vargul Tul upon you.'

'You really believe he'll take this city?'

'I need not believe in a god I see walk the world.' Nurcia looked up longingly.

'Your god has forsaken you,' she heard herself say and struck her cheek. It was as soft as the snow around it, and the same proved true for the rest of her face. When she was done, Nurcia's eyes were wide and frail, frantic and grey.

Magmaya stood back and watched in a sort of glee as she struggled to stand.

Good, she thought. *She can die slowly at least.*

She let her run and followed on quietly, tracing the trail of bloodied snow through the empty streets. She'd collapsed down an alleyway, so Magmaya dragged her by her furs into a small alcove where surely no one would bother to search and left her there. She would come back for her later, she vowed, but for now, she would let her bleed.

She returned to Kharon's convoy shortly after, finding a myriad of corpses strewn about the streets, Mansel cavalrymen and Orianne guardsmen intertwined.

'My lady,' one of her father's men started, 'the traitor...?'

'She escaped,' Magmaya said. 'Just take me back to the palace.'

They arrived at High Path in good time, collecting the plate of fallen men as they did—but then, a violent, animal scream brought her attention back to the harsh lights of the city, and she looked up across the rows of guardsmen making their way to the front. There she found the old knight, brittle and stricken.

But when she came face to face with him again, Magmaya had quite forgotten what Siedous looked like. Each time she went the palace, memories came to her in broken fragments, telling of how she'd once frolicked in the snow and how only the dead, white trees had known of her little chubby fingers. And with each memory, she recalled seeing a wolf move along the horizon and watching Siedous wield his sword against a thief in a dark alleyway.

It had been from then on, she wondered if there had ever been a child within Siedous; even when he was afraid, he never seemed to turn to a mother's touch but to his chain-mail instead. He'd told Magmaya how a wise man had once said that a knight was nothing in light of love, but as she watched the ages betray him, she had forgotten what the story had even meant.

'My lady,' he said, concerned; there was something haunted festering underneath. 'I thought you were in the hospice!'

Me too, Magmaya thought. 'They expelled me.'

'Are you hurt?' He paused. 'I heard a scream.'

'No, it wasn't me.' She looked away, but when she turned back, she felt different, like her skin had turned to stone.

The old knight looked to her intensely, and she to him; his eyes were red, perhaps more so than they had been that night in the forest when she'd found Albany dead. But she could tell what he thought of her; it had been a long while since Kharon's affair and her own infancy, but it appeared the years had betrayed her even more so than they had him.

'You're armoured...' he said at last, quiet like a little girl.

'There are a lot of dead men around here.'

Siedous ignored that comment. 'The Mansel have already taken the east of the city,' he told her. 'The chancellor has sent his guardsmen there—'

'But he's left the palace exposed...' She nodded.

'Magmaya,' he said, 'I need you to go the stables and take a deer. Go to the Free-Peoples—you'll be safe there.'

'No.' She shook her head. 'I'll never make it in time, besides—Rache!'

'He's safe in the keep—'

'No!'

'Magmaya, listen!'

'Siedous,' she spoke up again, but it seemed no words she summoned would remedy the situation. 'Nurcia.'

'I know, I know—I made my way back to the palace as soon as I heard,' he stuttered, 'but then I heard—'

'I found her.'

'You killed her?'

Magmaya shrugged. She feared Siedous would never look at her again if she told him the truth. 'She was on horseback,' she explained. 'But she ran into an arrow and...' She paused, taking a heavy breath. 'Siedous, she never turned her back on us. She's been with them all along.'

'What?'

'*She* crippled Rache, *she* killed Albany,' Magmaya insisted, remembering. 'She let the Mansel in. She caused all of this.'

Siedous nodded, but she could tell he felt sick to the stomach. Something in those sombre eyes she had known so well had been whisked away to dust.

'Where's Kharon?'

'The boardroom,' he fawned.

'Damn him!' Magmaya spat. 'We can't have him and Rache together.' *This is not how my brother dies,* she cursed, *I prayed. I prayed!*

'My lord,' a breathless voice called out from wide eyes across the hall. 'Vargul's been spotted in the inner city. He's already at the palace!'

'We only just left the gate!' Siedous' eyes were wide. 'There was no sign that he passed here—We assumed...'

His voice was wavering in her ears. Magmaya was already gone.

A distant hum rang about the halls as she ran, and her blood became one with the threaded carpets. Vargul had already made his way in and had surely taken the front, but at least the thermals would allow her to reach the palace without meeting any more of the Mansel than she needed to.

As she ran, the light from the chandeliers and candles above turned cold and dry and made her sick with every metre she left behind. Confronting Tul seemed all but inevitable, but if she was able to hold him off for a little while, perhaps Rache could escape the keep with the others.

She shook her head—it was madness to even consider keeping up with him—had she seen herself? Her chest was slick with blood, and her legs were growing weaker with every passing second.

Yet something drove her onwards still—something hollow in her veins that tasted like a vile liquor on her lips.

And then the wooden doors to the boardroom appeared before her like they'd always been there.

Magmaya froze and closed her eyes, reaching out to touch the scars in the wood, tracing her nimble fingertips across each splinter. When she was a child, she had once carved something into the oak (she couldn't remember what it was now), spending hours etching away. Now she was carrying a bloodied blade—if only she could've just sat for hours and scratched away again, thoughtless and forgotten while Albany cruised the halls, naïve to all he had caused...

She began to lose track of the passing seconds until, at last, she realised time was running out—she couldn't hold herself back any longer; she raised Moonbeam high.

There's nothing to be afraid of, she told herself. *Death will embrace you with all the lips of a lover.*

It's a dream, anyway, another voice told her. *And this dream will soon become another.*

Magmaya stole a breath and wrestled her fingers to Moonbeam's hilt. It was cold, even through the light padding she'd been given. She couldn't remember it being so cold before. It was glittering still, though, and that was all she needed to reassure her.

The doors opened with a jolt and Magmaya stumbled through, haloed in the moonlight and hacking at the air. Wrinkled eyes scanned the room, and a gust of wind blew hair in her eyes. The back of her head was pounding, and her arms were covered in goose prickles.

And then, a face lurched for hers.

Magmaya slashed at it without a thought, but Moonbeam missed its mark and was met with a flash of cold steel. That, and a pair of burning black eyes staring back at her.

He looked taller than he had before, but for the first time, Magmaya gazed upon Vargul Tul with eyes which she could claim were her own.

It was an ugly sight, though; his face was cold and red all at once, stricken with scars and throned with an iron gorget. But there was something else too—a crossbow bolt nested in his spine. No—there were three, she realised.

She was distracted. Something sharp grazed her thigh, and Magmaya collapsed into the embrace of some porcelain tower. An iron claw groped at her leg, tearing thread and silk.

Magmaya screamed and drove Moonbeam at the hand, gouging the fingers apart, but before she could move another inch, a second grizzly talon came for her neck.

Vargul stumbled forward, and Magmaya threw herself aside. She didn't see her blood spill, but she felt it, running down her hands and neck. She swung again, cumbersome, and she heard a crunch as the sword bit hard.

But then, the Mansel's shoulder met her chest, and she collapsed to the floor again. Pottery smashed. Papers fluttered. A golden vase shattered.

And then she found Kharon, weeping and holding his chest in some vain effort to stop the bleeding; it formed a pool around him, sheathing his stomach and flailing robes. He was still breathing, it seemed, as he clung to the air above him with wide eyes. There was a knife trailing from his palm.

Strength rose in her. She turned back and heard herself shout, 'Nurcia is dead!' The words felt warm in her belly, and the heat was flowing through her like a river.

Vargul ignored her, though his face contorted to something terrible.

'I slashed her throat,' she boasted again, feeling an eagerness overcome her, dizzy—the longer she made him talk, the more time Rache had. 'I watched the snow fall as she pleaded. She was weak. Weaker than me.'

By the time he reached her, all her breath had been stolen. She felt for Moonbeam amongst the threaded floors but found her hands warm and lightless.

Go back, she told herself. *Go back to the Sultide and get back on that beaten horse. Ride to Jayce; ride to the Free-Peoples and never be seen again.*

But before she could, there was a crash. The Mansel pinioned her against the floor, and all her wind left her. She opened her mouth to scream, but a knuckle came searing across her lips. His ruptured face had become the world, it was all she could see, but there was something different about him. The crossbow bolts had to have hurt him. Otherwise, he would've killed her by now.

By gods, if that's my dying thought, she cursed herself. Her nails jeered against metal, and her leg met a thigh, but the beast of a man was heavy like a corpse. And as a gauntlet closed around her throat, her face turned blue, and for a moment, there was peace. She still tried to scream, though, but nothing came out. She would've sooner pissed herself.

But then, there was a thump, and the Mansel's back arched. He collapsed off her and pulled a crossbow bolt from the back of his shoulder, and then he was running, and the floor was shaking. He cleared the boardroom, finding the bowman at the doors. The chancellor's daughter didn't have time to catch her breath. She could only watch in horror as the bowman's shaking hands were torn from him, and a shard of cursed gold was put between his eyes.

Magmaya had never moved faster. She cleared the boardroom with a quivering Moonbeam in her hands. Vargul was turning back around, but it was too late—the sword was in his knee and then his back where the bolt had struck him, searing and festering.

Whether he screamed or not, she didn't hear. But as she stumbled away, she caught sight of the Mansel's leg and admired her craftsmanship. And then, at last, he began to buckle.

Vargul Tul kneeled beneath her, and Magmaya couldn't help but smile. He didn't look at her; perhaps out of shame, or perhaps out of spite, but she didn't care.

'In the end,' he wretched, holding his bloody stump of a knee, 'your father wanted you dead more than I.'

'I know,' she said, sighing, and then she killed him.

For a moment, the chancellor's daughter spared a glance at the remains, following the bloody lines in the carpets, the red that began to flood his summer furs and the fountain of black ichor where his head should've been. Whatever was left wasn't quite a man anymore.

An urging came over Magmaya, to lie down and weep or slumber and die. Out the window, the fighting continued on; even without their castellan, the Mansel were taking the city. But a greater ache persisted still, so she stumbled over to it.

A lurid reflection of herself shimmered in his blood, and in it, Magmaya could scarcely recognise her own eyes. Streaks of red garnished her features as if she were a spoiled art form and the purple around her eyes and scarred jaw were only details on the canvas.

The chancellor looked no better, though; his eyes were sagging out of his skull, and each line and incision on his forehead was clearer so. A white fringe settled over his red, venomous eyes like some wretched albino creature with a spotted cloak dyed a dazzling scarlet.

The pair shared a subtle look of innocence, and for a mere moment, the sins of the past seemed to have been forgotten. *Maybe a moment will be enough,* she told herself and said, 'I don't know if this is all over.' Magmaya conceded, 'But it is for us.'

She expected some sort of insult—some sort of cry of defiance. The chancellor had fallen! If she had ever feared a man, if she had ever feared a ruler, it was not anyone who she'd sentenced, nor Vargul Tul himself, but instead, the man that lay limp and bloody before her.

Magmaya ignored the sentiment and found his wounds beneath old, bony hands where she'd nuzzled him as a child, where the flesh was pink and spilling. His blood was a black patch around them, growing wider like the pulsating of a collapsing star.

And in it lay a small knife, rusted and chipped, sewn together with battered embroidery, and inhaling the blood around it like it was alive.

It was a little older but shimmered all the same as the light caught the engraved lettering that a fool might have mistaken for art. But it was scarred now and cut and broken at its point; it was fastened and carved to a sharper edge as if imitating the tips of Vargul's own blades. It had felt like an age ago, but it was it the same—that much was certain. It was a ritual knife from the Free-Peoples—the very knife with which that old scribe had attempted Magmaya's life all those moons ago.

It reeked of betrayal, more so than Nurcia ever had, and Magmaya realised at last how she felt—she was disappointed. Her mind went to Vargul—*'your father wanted you dead more than I,'* he'd said, but now, the very proof of it was glistening right in front of her like something heavenly.

Kharon Vorr had sent her to the Deadfields to die. How else could've a man defended his lineage? If Rache were to ever to succeed his father, she and Shalleous would both have had to be dead, all guised under the

Mansel's onslaught; why else had he fashioned the blade to match Vargul Tul's?

Magmaya plucked it from the floor and let the chancellor's blood lick at her fingers, filling the gaps beneath her nails. 'Kharon Vorr.' She shook him.

He groaned, and she sighed.

'Speak to me,' she said, her voice soft. 'Why's this here?' She showed him the knife.

A couple of seconds passed, and then a scream rang out from beyond the balcony. And then a stampede. Time was running out, but she had done all she could've done. If Rache had ever a chance at escaping, it would've happened.

When she was sure there was going to be no reply, Magmaya slumped against the wall and sighed. 'Damn you,' she cursed softly and looked to the heavens with a smile. 'Damn you,' she whispered again, softer still.

She weighed the blade in her palm, turned back to her father and said, 'We haven't long. At least let me make it quick for you.'

Magmaya held it out and pressed the tip against Kharon's chest. Her lungs raged, and she wanted to collapse, but she didn't even have the strength left for even that anymore.

'Do you want me to end all of this?' she asked, louder this time. But her voice wasn't strong anymore; it was all broken and weary, fractured and distant. So, she shouted instead, 'Do you want me to kill you, father?'

The light of the room faded away, and even the snow turned dull. The blade in her hand turned from silver to grey and the empty chalices from gold to a sickly brown.

Kharon made the slightest of nods, and Magmaya dusted the hair out of her eyes, and then the tears. She heaved his body over and watched his blood shimmer in the candlelight like something holy and brazen, rancid and wet. His chest seemed to concave around his wound as if his entire body was drawn to where his skin was broken: his sagging chin, his flooded robes and crown of lank, white hair.

With a tender touch, Magmaya pressed her hand against her father's breast. She felt the soft wool of his tunic against her skin and then the faint beating of some mechanical heart beyond.

And then, without a thought, she pressed the dagger through.

That's the only way you kill a man, she decided. *With his own bloody blade.*

His eyes were wide but, like the clapping of butterfly wings, they closed, and at last, he slumped against the wall.

Magmaya stood, heedless to the corpses either side of her, and took the bloodied knife from the floor. She made her way to the balcony, out the doors and into the moonlight where the snow and the fighting raged beyond. And without hesitation, she raised the wretched thing and tossed it out into the clouds. She didn't stay to watch it disappear beneath the veil of white.

Six

For what seemed years, she had dreamt of a grey house with empty halls and tumbling columns, steamed with roses and an ocean of muddy rain. She had walked invisibly amid the halls until Vargul Tul had come again, tearing portraits, and crushing oily flowers in his iron grip. His face had been bloody and deformed; black pits had waited where his eyes had once been, but she had just smiled and stood still—frozen.

Occasionally, the paintings changed to Kharon Vorr, Rache and Siedous. And as she fled from them, Moonbeam crumbled to dust, and her armour melted away. At the end of each hall, the corpse of Vargul waited still, pressing his hand to his throat in a wretched effort to speak again. But when he finally stifled a curse, her eyes opened with a fluttering. The grey house disappeared.

She opened them to find a dozen robed figures hustling around her with faces like masks, and with each giddy movement they made, a sickness came over her. Magmaya had to resist the urge to vomit. If the world had granted her life against all odds, then so be it. But it could've at least allowed her to wake up first.

The room blurred again, and she remembered— decapitating Vargul, killing her father, and waiting in the window as Siedous had arrived. She remembered the blood that had stained his lower-lip and the gash above his right eye as she'd fallen into his arms like she'd withered away to ash.

And as she drifted, warm snow pressed against her lips. But when she awoke, there was nothing left but cuts and dead skin. The Silk Tea had seen to that before; Ranvirus was awfully cold, and she'd woken up with broken skin a thousand times before. But this time it was in her very bones—in her very broken heart. Though Siedous had always told her that hearts would mend, she'd come to realise hers never would. It wouldn't mend—it would change, but perhaps that would be enough.

Magmaya stretched, and her scars did too, and the world grew a little quieter. And this time, the pain washed from her before she even drifted to sleep.

It felt like only seconds had passed before she awoke again, but the light had become so scarce that it must have been hours—perhaps half a day even. The pounding in her head had begun to lift, and all that remained was an ache where it had once been.

No longer were there metals embedded beneath her skin, nor around her throat, but instead, there was only a stained ceiling, free of the incessant surgeons that plagued her. At last, she was able to stretch and breathe and live, away from the scent of roses, and away from the stench of blood and dust and sweat. And for all the parricide she had committed, it warmed her to remember it was done.

She turned, glimpsed a reflection of herself in the window and followed the dried blood and purple bruises down her cheeks. She traced a black eye to a torn gum, a broken arm to a crushed chest—and then a voice called, 'My chancellor.'

'Yes,' she replied, looking out for Kharon, but a different figure stepped forward.

He was garbed with flowing tunics, and had a book slung under his arm; his face was still stricken with cuts, but now they were clean and kind and soft. Siedous gave her something pitiful she might have once called a smile and made his way over to her.

'I brought you something to read.' He held out the book. 'Rache asked me to, my chancellor.'

She accepted the leather-bound tome but hardly felt it in her fingertips. 'Just call me Magmaya. I can't take any of these niceties, certainly not from you.'

'Magmaya.' He perched on a chair by her side. 'I—I—how do you feel?'

'Tired,' she said. 'I would die for a drink.'

'You've come too far to do that.' Siedous turned to a small table behind him and produced a large flagon, poured a glass, and passed it to her.

'I didn't mean water,' she remarked, but downed it all the same, and though it was warm, she had never felt so avid for more. It drowned her in relief, and by the time she was done, she was spluttering and coughing and watching her body tremble.

'I suppose you don't remember the last we talked.' Siedous looked to his feet. 'After Vargul...'

'I don't remember speaking,' Magmaya admitted. 'All I can remember is the blood. Gods, that man had a lot of blood.'

Siedous nodded and said, 'Your father, as you probably know, has passed. It seems it was indeed Vargul's work.'

Good, she thought. *Keep thinking that and I'll only have to keep pretending until the day I die.* 'Siedous, I don't want to hear this,' she said, voice raised. 'I know.'

'I apologise.' He nodded. 'Though you must know, we've also captured four of the Mansel. They're in the cells awaiting the confessor. Nurcia Vyce is there, too.'

'She survived?' Magmaya was almost relieved.

'Just about,' he remarked. 'She was petered with arrows and doesn't have much of a face left, but she's alive.'

'And how's she?' Magmaya asked, trying to mask her excitement.

'Being fed. I don't think she can quite understand that Vargul died.' He paused. 'But how she managed to orchestrate this all under our noses? Well, I hope the confessors can get that from her.'

'I hope so too,' she agreed. She knew why, however. And it was the simplest answer Magmaya could've thought of: every girl in the north wanted to go south.

'Kaladeous passed too,' the old knight said gravely. 'He succumbed to his wounds from Nurcia shortly after the Mansel arrived. I don't think much could've saved him.'

'My blood's boiling,' Magmaya said. 'I want to visit her.'

'I was afraid you would want that.'

'She killed Albany,' she protested. 'And she tried for Rache too. If anyone should be afraid, she should.' Magmaya wished she was strong enough to walk there with a basket of salt and sprinkle it over each incision in her face, but her legs betrayed her with each toss and turn.

'Her trial will be in a short number of days,' Siedous said. 'You can decide what to do with her then.'

Days? she asked herself. Was that even time enough to convict her?

'Magmaya,' he began again, 'you were the one, weren't you? To kill Vargul Tul?'

She thought for a moment—she considered making up some elaborate lie. But a moment later, she caught herself saying, 'Perhaps. I'm quite tired, though.' She yawned. 'If you let me come around, I'll be able to give you a clearer picture.'

'I've been awake for hours upon hours, and I still can't give you that,' he said.

'You could try.' She was growing impatient.

'We're all trying to make sense of it, Magmaya. The city was all but lost,' he said. 'But I hazard to say we were saved.'

'Oh?'

'We have new company now,' he said. 'In the form of the Tyla.'

She was surprised. The Tyla? She'd always assumed they had no interest in the rest of the world's affairs. But the last she remembered, the Mansel were still fighting outside—they were at the palace! It was all too late, surely?

'A scout of theirs spotted the Mansel warhorses at the Sultide and sent for cavalry,' Siedous explained.

'Needless to say, we must be thankful. As you are unwell, I shall be attending council with them on your behalf this afternoon.'

'Oh,' Magmaya said again, her face pale. 'I've so many questions now.' She paused for a moment. 'Can we trust them?'

'No.' His voice was gruff. 'Their leaders are candid in their scheming. Likely because they want to hold Ranvirus to themselves. But we have a common enemy. I don't think they're yet a threat.'

'Kharon said they were prideful.'

'Our chancellor was right.' Siedous nodded. 'They will question your authority, your defeat of Vargul—your everything. But now that the wolves are all dead, and the bears are too, you can be a pretty little rose.' He smiled and stood. 'I'll talk later if I can find time. Until then, rest.'

'You tell a blind man to see.' Magmaya sighed.

Siedous smirked and left quickly, light glimmering off his tunic like the armour she'd known so well.

From then on, the minutes passed slowly as if Magmaya was listening to the steady beat of a metronome, but surely enough, frost began to cloud the windows, and she felt herself ache for something more.

The morning after was always the hardest, she had to remind herself. It was when she would sit in a bath of boiling water and wait until it grew as cold as the snow outside. It was when she would recount the night before in her head and chant the words she should have never have spoken: *I don't know if this is all over. But it is for us.* She would have taken Tul's head any day, but her father's...? It hurt when you hated someone who loved you.

She began to feel restless, and her feet ached to touch the floor again, to walk, to run. Before long, nimble footsteps traced the room like beads of rain on a window, and the chancellor was gone.

Magmaya plucked a rose from the crisp, white snow, mesmerised by the fountain of petals that led to its core and the icy prisms that melted on the stem the moment they were born. The last time she'd held the flower was as she'd stumbled across Albany, petals streaming from where his eyes should have been. It had been Nurcia's work; she had entered her secret place and defiled it, but she was their hostage now, and the birds were chirping again as the first signs of spring began to arise.

Nonetheless, she sat, and breathed, and smiled, eying her own pale glimmer in the pond below; its frozen surface was grazed and cracked as white sunbeams beat down from above. It was only when her brother spoke that the world seemed to appear around her.

'There are strange people here, Magmaya,' Rache said, and the sun felt real again, warming her arms like it hadn't in a thousand days.

'Yes,' she found herself admitting. 'They *are* strange. I've never seen a man wear such a bright shade of blue.'

It hurt to speak and even more so to look him in the eye. Nurcia had maimed him, and she had killed his father; a man, despite everything, who loved Rache more than life. Moments came when she wished she could just let it all spill like she had as a child, but she couldn't bring herself to share even how she felt about the purple clouds that hung above.

'They're marching around like this is their home,' he said. 'My own sister is the chancellor. If I were to go somewhere foreign, I would smile a little more.'

'And where would that be?' Magmaya looked to him. For all her life, her brother had only spoken of Orianne; never before had he given any inkling of wanting to leave even the palace grounds.

'There are places I've heard of that I would visit if… if I could. I don't know if they're real or not.'

'Tell me about them.'

'They say the Free-Peoples make ships to travel the cold seas,' he started. 'They find islands and faeries and pretty girls with tails like fish who sing to them.'

Magmaya smiled and paused for a moment. 'You don't think about going south?'

'The men about the palace say that the Mansel wanted to go south after they were done with us,' Rache said. 'Whatever place *they* were to go to must be hideous.'

Oh, but it is not, a voice inside told her. How could he sit idle *here* when he could bask in *warm* seas under *warm* suns? It need not be there, but perhaps anywhere else—anywhere but home.

'One day you'll see those fish-women,' Magmaya said at last. 'Whatever happens, I'll assure you of that.'

'I hope so.' Rache nodded. 'Is that your decision as chancellor?'

She nodded, but the voice inside insisted it would be her only decision. *'Chancellor' they may call me, but Siedous sits in my place,* she realised. *He was a knight and an honest man, and now he's a politician. There is none better than him, but it should be me.* She wasn't made for this.

Magmaya smiled. 'When summer comes, we'll come here again.' She paused. 'No one can hurt us now, Rache. The fight against the Mansel is over.'

She knew in her heart it was far from over, though; she had slain a single warlord—not a city. There would surely be more to come. If one thing was constant, it was turmoil. But maybe when Nurcia was dealt with, all would be better. Rache needn't know about her, though.

The pair set off, and Magmaya carried her brother to back to his room and into his crib where he began his slumber again. She crept back down to the hospice, following her swollen eyes in the windows until she stumbled back through the door.

And when she entered, she found Siedous perched on her bed.

He was dressed in a grey tunic, belted against his waist—and he was armed. He looked furious, and the second they locked eyes, he rose to meet her startled gaze.

'Gods!' he spat. 'Where in the world have you been?'

'I was seeing to Rache,' she pleaded. 'I was with him in his quarters.'

'Don't lie to me,' he said. 'We searched his chambers, and he was gone too. Someone came to feed you, and by the gods, we hear that our chancellor has gone missing—? We've already been betrayed once, Magmaya. Answer me, where were you all these hours?'

'I took Rache to the woods,' she confessed at last. 'I wanted to show him the roses—the uh, the water!'

'Damn it,' Siedous cursed. 'Our allies lie in a fragile balance. Now, they think our chancellor was playing truant and ran away to play. You're no longer a child!'

'You're no longer in a position to insult me, Siedous!' she found the strength to spit back. 'I don't mean to offend these Tyla, but you yourself said we can't trust them. If I want to go to the forest with my brother, then I shall. That is why you've taken on my duties. Kharon Vorr would have done what he wanted.'

'Kharon Vorr is dead, and you killed him,' Siedous roared, and his mane blazed as if he were a terrible beast. But a moment later, he shrunk down to a mewling kitten. 'My chancellor... I,' he stuttered, but he was as speechless as she was becoming.

'Why would you say such a thing?' her voice had broken. 'Siedous?'

'Forgive me, my chancellor.' He lowered his head.

'Why?' Tears began to form behind her eyes. 'What do you mean?'

'Forgive me—'

'Siedous!' Magmaya screamed, and he looked to her, solemn.

No longer did her brave knight stand before her; instead there was a turncoat and a coward. This was some crude man wearing his skin as a cloak.

How long has he known? she asked herself. *How many people has he told of my crimes?* Perhaps there was already a tall price on her head.

'My chancellor,' he started nimbly, 'I served your father for many years as a knight, and not only have I seen every flesh wound, I have received every flesh wound. The puncture in Kharon's heart was splintered and broken, not at all like the blows Vargul struck.'

Not at all? Hadn't Kharon cut his blade to imitate Vargul's? Perhaps that was just something else he had been poor at.

'So you blame me?' she asked.

'I found a knife.' He ignored her, 'fashioned like Vargul's own, but imperfect. And at the angle of the wound, there would've been no way for him to be able to stab himself. Magmaya, you were the only other person in the boardroom, save that dead crossbowman...'

'You lie.' Her lips quivered. 'You're trying to frame me. You're trying to take my place...!'

'No. I want to exalt you,' he said, but his voice had gone cold. 'I wanted none of this, but I'm growing old—far too old—I can't hold my tongue.'

'I didn't *want* to bloody kill him, Siedous.' She frowned.

'It was an act of mercy, I understand.' He nodded. 'But if anyone finds out, they'll twist the truth. They would have you tried, Magmaya—hanged, even.'

'You haven't told anyone else, have you?'

'Not a soul!'

Magmaya nodded and threw herself back onto the mattress. The wind howled, and the night began to draw in like the most sudden of storms; she was pulling her hair out for another way—a way to escape this all and soar far, far away.

'Rest, my chancellor,' Siedous said at last. 'On the morrow, you're to meet with Lord Rallun of the Tyla and apologise for your discourtesy. You must plea it was Dew of the Honey that made you act so impulsively.'

'Yes,' she agreed. 'And when the sun rises, whatever happened in that boardroom shall be forgotten.'

'It already has been.' Siedous nodded and started over to the door. She noticed a limp in his step as he did, and at last, she saw him in the light of the setting sun. *Perhaps the old knight is not so strong,* she realised with a heavy heart. *Perhaps the old knight is fragile after all.*

Seven

Rallun Black was as cold as he was tall. Charcoal hair fell upon his forehead, and blazing nostrils shadowed his wrinkled lip. His eyes were red like a bloody storm, and they wept into his cheekbones and dripped from his pale lips. The way he and his men frequented the boardroom unnerved Magmaya as Vargul had as if they shouldn't have been there; as if they weren't quite welcome.

There were glimmers of Kharon Vorr in him too that she couldn't shake. She found herself scraping her feet against her heels in an effort to free herself from the corpses that had once surrounded her, but all she could see was the blood and the unwatching eyes. She traced their outlines against the floor before a snapping of fingers sounded through the room, and she turned back to Rallun, glowering.

'My chancellor,' he said, and Magmaya found his voice to be deeper than she'd expected from such a spindly man. She turned to Siedous who stood tall by her side, prompting him to nod, before she turned back to the Tyla.

She'd assembled her council out of the survivors of the siege: Siedous, of course, as well as Sir Locheart, Knight of the Deadfields, Castellan Vuan of the Northern Banks and Iglis Purturn, a local lord. She hadn't an inkling of what the new additions would help her with or even say, but Siedous had promised she wouldn't lack counsel; she just hoped none of them would double-cross her.

'My lord.' Magmaya bowed, snapping out of her trance. 'I owe you my thanks for holding Orianne. And I apologise for my improper nature yesterday. I have been feeling quite unwell, you see—'

'It's no matter.' Rallun waved his hand as if to dismiss it, although whether he believed her was something else to be considered. 'I bid your people warmth and friendship. It is forgotten.'

She nodded. 'We're in great debt.'

'If the north fell, there would be no coin left to fight over. There is no debt,' he said. 'Besides, if we hadn't halted the Mansel today, we would've had to tomorrow. But still, I request your aid.'

'Of course.' She perked up. 'Where are my manners? Pray sit, Lord Black. Your men too.'

Servants came forward to pull out the chairs from beneath the table before retreating to their corners. The Tyla sat, followed by Magmaya and then her council.

Her head was low as she watched Rallun's reflection move in the shimmering wood. And then he spoke, and she looked up, dazed. 'Am I correct in understanding you were the one to kill Vargul Tul? At first, I heard it was some crazed swordsman...'

Crazed swordsman? That's a good start.

'Yes, my lord,' she said, but it hurt to speak. She could still smell the blood and sweat, the mud and piss. It hurt to remember. 'In this very room, it was…'

Siedous coughed loudly and tapped Magmaya's heel. She scowled and straightened herself.

The Tyla looked around, curt. 'Well, I'm glad you were able to rid him from this world. He was a terrible man.'

Before she hazarded a reply, Siedous nodded, motioned to a servant and asked, 'May we drink?'

A moment later, the servant returned heaving a bottle dwarfing herself and poured its oily-black contents into a number of clear glasses. Forgetting herself, Magmaya stole for one and pressed her lips to the wine, letting it tickle her gums. But the Tyla weren't far behind her.

'Now,' Rallun started after they were finished, 'whatever is spoken here today shall not be discussed again once we leave.' He gestured to the woman beside him, who in turn, produced a small, bronze container from beneath the table. It was an ornate piece, Magmaya observed; vines constricted its surface, and torn wings beat at its flanks. Although it looked dull, she felt a sudden urge to reach out and touch it.

'What that?' she asked, inquisitive.

'The Promised Papers.' Siedous cleared his throat. 'Excuse me.'

Rallun made poor work of masking his smirk. 'Your knight is correct. And familiar with them?'

'I saw them when I was a boy of few suns,' he explained. 'Orianne was in possession of them before Kharon came to power.'

'They were entrusted with the Tyla shortly before he did,' Black said, embarrassment flashing across his face. 'Anyway, petty grievances.'

The Tyla know my home far better than I, Magmaya realised. *I shouldn't even be here.* Though she'd heard tales of boy kings, not even yet men, who ruled from thrones and broken battlements, it had been their advisors who'd suffered the clockwork of politics while they sat back and toyed with their dominion. Magmaya couldn't misguide the city if she wasn't guiding it at all; she was no impetuous boy king. All the same, she didn't exactly have a heart of gold to guide her either.

Rallun put his hand to the container and span a small brass key in its lock, and Magmaya watched as her advisors practically threw themselves forward for a glimpse. Moments later, she felt herself reaching forward too, peering in to see its contents that were oh so revered.

They were underwhelming, to say the least; just several tattered brown papers piled upon one another. She reached out to touch them, but one of the Tyla whisked the container from beneath her fingers.

'I apologise, my lady,' he said, 'but the Promised Papers are sacred. They're only to be handled by their owner. It's tradition.'

'I see.' Magmaya was taken back. *The old men always seemed to know what was best.*

Rallun fingered the papers out of the box and laid them out across the table. As Magmaya studied them, she noticed a myriad of writings she couldn't quite decipher; teachings of the south, ritual circles and drooling signatures scrawled down the pages. For what felt like an age, she couldn't tear her eyes off the mesmerising patterns that shifted across them: grey sketches of feathery monsters that swallowed fire, and priests that hailed the heavens.

Something in the drawings looked alive, though, whispering secrets of a time everyone collectively agreed to forget. They were moving, shifting about the pages—she was sure of it!

'Star charts.' Siedous pointed to a well of blackness on another paper, speckled with white. Between the stars, there were lines labelled in a language that certainly wasn't the common tongue. The closer Magmaya looked, the more she saw; there were outlines of running deer and dancing fish-women lost in the blackness of the heavens.

What was farther south than south? she asked herself, and suddenly, she knew.

'Some southern cults still use these to perform rituals for their Maiden Gods,' Rallun explained. 'When they first travelled north after the Age of Transmutany, the Promised Papers were forged detailing agreements of its founding. Though that's beside the point.'

'So, what is the point?' There was a tap against her ankle again.

'The Papers order that if a northern power threatens another, then the rest of the north must ally against their oppression,' Rallun continued. 'And so, the Tyla declare themselves for Orianne to starve out the Mansel's strongholds by the year's end.'

'Is that even time enough?' Siedous asked.

Spring's here, she remembered. *That wouldn't give them long.*

'The Promised Papers suggest so.'

'I don't care what some paper dictates,' Magmaya heard herself snap. 'Because of the Mansel, my family suffered. I suffered. It doesn't bother me whether this is all arranged by me or some paper, so long it is.'

The Tyla nodded. 'Are we decided, then?'

A murmuring of agreement came from the boardroom, and Magmaya smiled. No matter how much she thought Rallun was suffocating her words, she let herself fall into his embrace.

'As for the hostages,' he said at last.

Magmaya froze. 'Yes, we have a number,' she stuttered. 'And the traitor.'

'The others are mere Mansel cavalrymen, no?'

She nodded.

'And the traitor? Who is he?'

'*She* turned to Tul long ago,' Magmaya said. 'She was a member of the board, and she let the Mansel into the city.'

'Is she valuable?'

'She was to Vargul Tul.' Magmaya remembered how his face had contorted when she'd told him Nurcia was dead. The pair had an interest in one another—that much was certain.

'Then we ransom her off to the Mansel,' he said and shot Magmaya an unctuous smile. 'After this woman is exchanged, hang the others.'

Magmaya felt a sickness wash over her. She wanted to scream. 'She has yet to be interrogated,' she whimpered. 'We're not to be hasty.'

Rallun nodded. 'Of course not, my chancellor,' he said, though he seemed to do anything but care.

He chattered on long after with terms Magmaya could barely fathom and complex agreements beyond count, while she just sat in a daze, following the lines across the papers in her mind's eye.

Magmaya moved from scroll to scroll, scanning the inky trees that crawled between the blotched script. Circles and triangles led from one to the next by thin trails—oh how she wished she could've held them for herself and plotted her own trek through the stars. She only awoke from her haze once Rallun reached his hand out to hers after what may have been days of conversation for all she cared.

Magmaya looked up and took it with a gracious smile, but only before Siedous ushered her up.

'You're a pleasant woman, Magmaya.' He kissed her hand. 'I do hope we can speak again soon.'

Gods, I hope not. She curtsied, feeling a wetness on her knuckle, and the Tyla and her own council flooded out of the room, the Promised Papers with them.

And finally, when they'd all left, Magmaya was able to breathe.

'You scarcely listened to a word, my chancellor.' Siedous wandered back over, smiling sympathetically.

She looked to the window and watched the Tyla rush out of the halls to their own camps in the city, before she turned back, sighing.

'Some things are not made for girls like me,' she said at last.

Siedous giggled to himself. 'I'll admit, you were engrossed in those papers.'

'I suppose I was,' Magmaya said. 'Rallun is—oh,' she stammered, flustered. 'I had a question for you, Siedous.' She paused. 'Did you ever go to the Cold Seas?'

'Kharon Vorr had me travel there once,' he replied. 'And I have seen no water duller, I'm afraid.'

'Duller?' Magmaya exclaimed. 'I shan't tell my brother that.'

'He talks about the fish-women, I presume?' Siedous smiled. 'Many men I knew spoke of things they would've done if they'd seen such a girl. Vile things, in truth. Your brother doesn't want any of that.'

'I suppose you didn't see them, then?' Magmaya asked.

'Me? No,' he admitted. 'But my comrades did. Then again, they were starved for girls and would've shagged the icebergs, had I not pulled them away.'

Magmaya half laughed. 'Do you remember how to sail there?'

'South.' Siedous smiled. 'And then south. And south again, until the water gets cold. But not too far south, otherwise you'll reach *the* south.'

'It's always cold.' Magmaya shivered. 'Siedous, can I ask a favour of you?'

'Of course, my lady.'

'If there comes a day when Rache can find the strength,' Magmaya started, 'sail him to the Cold Seas and let him see the fish-women. No matter how real you find them to be.'

'If that's what my chancellor requests.' Siedous looked grim. 'And as for you, my chancellor? Would you travel the Seas too?'

'Of course.' Magmaya smiled. 'Why wouldn't I?'

The days passed as quickly as they came, and Magmaya span the wheel of Orianne all while the shadow of Rallun loomed over her; he smiled when they met at the boardroom—that snake's smile that made her cold. And when he spoke of finances, he spoke of blood, and when he talked of reform, he talked of ruin. She found herself passing laws she scarcely understood, all while Siedous turned to her with warm eyes. She sat through hours of folly as lesser men came to the palace, begging for money or some other common matter.

She was alone when she filled the pockets of beggars, but whenever they left empty-handed, Rallun was standing by her side, insisting it was for the best. A man with dark wavy hair and eyes like shadows had come to her once, not pleading or begging but standing stoically as he described the scene of a butchering he had witnessed at the square. The way he spoke of the warmth of the blood made Magmaya near sick. Soon enough, she found herself visiting the forest daily.

In time, the leaves began to change, and at last, spring was truly upon her. And with spring came the clear skies, where she could watch the moon hum overhead with a monolithic dreariness and feel the warmth lash down upon her back. Occasionally, she swore she could spot another (as she always did) nestled amongst the clouds in the pale sunlight. Yet when she looked away, there would only ever be a whimper.

And when the sun beat down, she stripped and swam in the pond, holding her breath tight until she touched the muddy base with her toes, rose petals fluttering around her body. But when she surfaced, no matter how long she was down there for, the world was much the same.

On other days, she scoured the markets in guise, shopping for fruit and lemon-water. She passed stalls with gaunt old things waving talismans, and down darker streets where strange creatures sold their own flesh. Once, she found a queer leather book hidden among some other rusted devices and took it home to Rache. Its pages were battered and broken, and yet, the scripture was unmistakable—it told of the Cold Seas and the terrible women who dwelled there.

Magmaya spent not a second in the boardroom more than she had to, for each time she passed its entrance she feared she'd spot Vargul Tul standing tall in the light of the window. She remembered the times Kharon had sat there, muttering to the heavens and drinking himself to an early grave, and she began to detest the memories that the daylight brought with it. But when night came, the bed felt cold and empty, and as she stretched her hands across the sheets, she felt a thousand roses pressing against her back.

When Magmaya slept, it was an ill affair too. She had the same temple dream from time to time—but the worst dreams were the good ones. She'd be kissing a perfumed lover or travelling far, far away, only to wake up and feel cold again. She began longing for the nights when she didn't dream at all.

Although Magmaya could hardly call it a summer heat, there was at least something reassuring about the haze that enveloped her while she lay alone. Leering faces hung above as she looked to the ceiling for an answer, but by dawn, none had come. Instead, there came a day she had dreaded more and more with each one that had passed.

It wasn't even snowing, so she didn't have an excuse to be late, but she found a way to be anyway. It was a short journey from her quarters down to the dungeons, where she passed all manner of Mansel captives, stripped down and screaming, or sipping on rat piss.

When she arrived at Nurcia's cell, the interrogators were already there, holding their brass balls and chains, wafting incense around the room that they swore would bring out the truth. And between them stood the arch-confessor, reading prayers from his holy book and moving the procedure along. It was the same procedure there always was, and there was almost always a confession, but Magmaya needed to see it; she needed to hear it.

People always talked about how vile the cells looked, and how they'd either starve a man to death or have him eaten by hound-sized rats, but no one ever mentioned the stench. It was as if something terrible had washed over her—a sickness of sweat and faeces. She flared her nostrils and turned back to the confessor.

At a glance, he might have been less human than even the Mansel. But that thought quickly abandoned her when she caught a glimpse of Nurcia behind him.

Despite the abundance of wooden benches, she chose to huddle, nude in the corner save for the brown sheet she clung to. Her face was near unrecognisable. It had become a mutilated mess of scars and red incisions. She had once been stunning—Magmaya had idolised her beauty, but her looks had abandoned her. Her skin was stained with the dirt of the cell, and she was groping her stricken back, writhing about the floor.

'Nurcia Vyce of Orianne,' the arch-confessor began, reciting off his scrolls. 'You stand accused of a number of treasons and murders. Are you to confess?'

'Yes.' Her voice was dry, and her words were broken and weary.

'Nurcia Vyce, you stand accused of the murder of Albany Moore. Do you confess?'

'I confess,' she said.

'Nurcia Vyce, you stand accused of the murder of Kaladeous Garneth. Do you confess?'

'I confess.'

'Nurcia Vyce, you stand accused of collusion with Mansel against the interests of Orianne. Do you confess?'

'I confess,' the traitor croaked again.

'Nurcia Vyce, you stand accused of allowing the thermal tunnels beneath the city to be held open for the Mansel to enter. Do you confess?'

'I confess.'

'Nurcia Vyce, you stand accused of provoking the military display headed for the Mansel stronghold, thus leaving the city vulnerable. Do you confess?'

'I confess,' she said and curled into a ball again.

There was silence for a moment.

'Thank you, Miss Vyce,' the arch-confessor finished. 'Upon your confession, we have found you guilty of treason and—'

'No,' Magmaya heard herself cut in. 'There's one more.'

'Yes, my chancellor?' he asked, and she turned to him, whispering. After a moment, he began again, 'Nurcia Vyce.' He said, 'You stand accused of the mutilation of Rache Vorr. Do you confess?'

She was silent.

'Nurcia Vyce,' he repeated. 'You stand—'

'I heard you,' she spat, and Magmaya's heart sank.

'And are you to confess?' the arch-confessor asked.

Nurcia's ears pricked up. And then she shook her head.

'No,' Magmaya called to the air and then to the interrogators. 'No, she did it—make her!'

The pair took a step forward and began waving their scented batons about the cell, spreading their incense, and driving their barbs into Nurcia's cuts, but all she did was frown.

Magmaya's heart was racing—she *had* done it! Nothing made sense otherwise. All these years she had blamed herself for Rache—she could plead innocent to any other crime, just not that one.

'My chancellor,' the interrogator turned to Magmaya. 'It matters not of this last confession. She has already been found guilty enough to incriminate herself in the eyes of the nameless gods.'

'I don't care,' she spat back. 'Do anything you can, I need to hear it. I need her to say it.' Her mind was racing. *I confess, I confess, I confess*—the words rang through Magmaya's ears, but Nurcia did anything but open her mouth.

Eight

Siedous wasn't much help when she returned to the boardroom. It was darker than usual as the sun set across the Sultide and then the seas beyond, though it bathed the room in a sickly orange glow. But Magmaya couldn't help staring at the red stains on the carpets.

'Apologies, my chancellor,' the old knight said, 'but if I may, you smell of... piss.'

She might have once laughed at that. Now all she could mutter was, 'At least I'm not drinking it.'

The pair were alone again, as it felt they always were. Rallun only appeared when he needed something, and Magmaya was having a hard time to find any suitable advisors after the last few had mysteriously left. After all the deaths of the siege, a thousand opportunities for work had opened across Orianne, but no one seemed to enjoy the business of high lords.

'And?' he asked at last.

'She confessed.'

'It's settled then.'

'She confessed to everything but maiming Rache. So, it's not settled, no.'

'I'm sorry to hear that.' Siedous sighed.

Magmaya stayed quiet. There was nothing much else to say.

'We decided that if she confessed, we were to ransom her off,' he broke the silence, 'in exchange for the prisoners the fleeing Mansel took.'

'We?' Magmaya spat. 'I can hardly believe what I'm hearing.'

'Rallun, I and the committee.'

'Of course. A committee.' She laughed.

'That's not the point.'

'No. The point is she can't get away with this so easily, Siedous.' Her heart burned. 'I forbid it.'

'Four of our men,' he persisted. 'No, four of your men. It is your duty as chancellor to see they come home safely.'

'She killed my brother!' Magmaya shouted. 'She killed Kaladeous. She was behind Kharon's and Shalleous' deaths too! My father would have never let this happen.'

'You're better than he was,' he said. 'And you will do better than he did.'

'Perhaps I shouldn't,' she shot back. 'Perhaps when someone hurts you, you might just have to hurt them back. Perhaps I should do what I know to be best, rather than what a committee tells me.'

'Magmaya, as your friend, I'm telling you that it's your choice to make,' Siedous admitted. 'But as your advisor, executing her or having her tortured, or whatever you have planned, is the wrong one.'

'It's not fair,' Magmaya tugged at her hair. 'She has to die.'

'No, it's not fair,' he stammered. 'But that is the way of the world. We need our people back.'

'Ransom the other prisoners for them,' she sulked. 'You'll see, Siedous, I'll get that damned confession out of her. I'm finished arguing with you.'

'This isn't an argument, my chancellor,' he began. 'You know those other prisoners aren't worth much. I understand how you feel—'

'Do you?' she spat. 'Tell that to Kaladeous. How many times did she stab him?'

He was silent.

'I *will* get that confession,' Magmaya swore. 'I'm going to see her again on the morrow. I'll force it out of her if I have to.'

'Be careful, my chancellor.'

'I don't need to be careful.' She skulked away. 'I need to be dangerous.'

She would see Nurcia again tomorrow, yes, but she had already decided she was having a walk about the village first. She awoke with the rising of the sun, got changed and headed out into the city.

Her footsteps carried her through snowy alleys and bony streets in search of something she didn't want. Ice sparkled lightly under her feet, and by the time she made it to the markets, it had melted to puddles, and the blizzard had turned to rain.

As the crowds begun to muster, Magmaya hid her face behind her leathers. That was until she found the same shadowed-eyed man from a few days before, collecting some bronze piece from a nearby vendor. The chancellor stopped at the stall next to him and peered through the screaming crowds that bartered between them. She tossed a pair of her own coins on the countertop, and a hot drink was thrust into her hand. When she looked up, though, the shadowed-eyed man had gone.

Magmaya downed the drink as she ran through the alleyways that made the morning glow and under crumbling bridges and arches devoid of the streams that once had crashed and raged below. Even though she hadn't been able to study his face for long, something about the man was alluring, like she'd seen him in a dream.

And as she ran, she saw the alley where she had left Nurcia. It felt empty now; the lack of the turncoat's body was a strange sight as if the street had only existed to see her fall. She made note to defile the place, to burn it down after she was dealt with. Would all of Orianne feel like this now? Would each street and every room bring back a memory she couldn't dare face?

Perhaps the shadowy man had disappeared into an aether or perhaps he had never existed at all, for a moment later, he was nowhere to be seen. Magmaya was beginning to doubt herself; it felt like every step she took was washed away like sand on a beach.

She turned a corner to what felt like a hundred-thousand people watching her. 'Magmaya,' they whispered in a foul tongue. 'The chancellor of Orianne.' 'She killed her father.' 'She slew the chancellor.'

'Leave me alone,' Magmaya whispered under her breath, feeling it burn. 'Leave me alone!'

She waded through an endless crowd and trampled a thousand wooden stalls, feeling herself break and squirm as her muscles sprang to life again. She had bled enough from her own womb to feed all of the city, but she feared soon there would be little left to give until her dishevelled wings were all red. She had to leave.

Stares seem to follow her every move like they were tracing her body beneath her robes. Silvery hair ran lank before her eyes and gleamed in the morning light. This dominion was hers to rule over as she saw fit. The people that gazed at her were at her every command, and that included the shadowed-eyed man as well. What she controlled was not to fear, surely?

But when she looked into the eyes of her people, she felt their skin against her skin. She saw in their eyes that they too had suffered the wrath of Vargul Tul; they too had lost loved ones to his onslaught. All of a sudden, the leather that warmed her was constricting around her throat.

She broke away from the crowd and disappeared down an alleyway; there at least no man but the Silver Mountainside could judge her from above.

As she held the wall to steady herself, her fingertips met wet stone, and dampness washed through her. Magmaya brushed her hair out of her eyes and felt herself slip into the embrace of the dark. But instead of the cold, snowy ground to break her fall, there was the hardy grip of a man.

Magmaya squealed as if she were a babe and pulled herself away, ruffling her hair to disguise herself again. Her heart pounded, and the alleyway began to close in on her, tightening around her breasts. She still felt the presence of someone or something behind her, watching over her with scorn—or was it endearing? She couldn't tell which.

'My chancellor,' a voice sounded, and she turned.

The shadowed-eyed man was perhaps a head taller than she'd remembered. He had deep, grey eyes and dark, lank hair that covered his face like pitch. 'Look to the horizons,' he spoke quickly, with a gracefulness about him. 'Watch the stars shine and blink. Watch one move.'

'Why are you following me?' She ignored him.

'You followed me.' The man scowled. 'A star moves. We are dying.'

'What star?' Magmaya spat. 'Who is dying?'

'A pale star, a blue star, a black star. They're all the same.'

'Who are you?'

'Young child.' He smiled deeply. 'Kind child, I have heard your prayers.'

The shadowed-eyed man took off down an alleyway, but Magmaya felt no inclination to follow. She watched him rush along the cobblestone until he bled into the crowd.

A moment after, it was over—like the whole affair had never happened.

He'd clearly been a naysayer or a lunatic. But every naysayer she'd met before had made themselves very clear; she hadn't an inkling of what he wanted.

She found herself back to the palace as if only seconds had passed and yet, as soon as she did, time began to slip through her fingers again. The evenings passed into nights as if they were footsteps behind her. Rallun was at her side as always, dismissing people so she didn't have to and filling the pockets of the rich. But whether she could call it a blessing or a curse, there was no sign of the shadowed-eyed man again.

And when the clocks struck noon one day, Magmaya trembled and made her way back to the dungeons.

She instructed her guards to stay outside the cell before she stepped through into the shrill light. Nurcia was still huddled in the corner as if she hadn't moved an inch. There were two scraps of bread beside her, uneaten, save for when a lone rat scampered out of a far-off hole and retrieved a crumb or two.

Her skin had grown muddier by the day, and the dirt and stained blood had become a black smear beneath her skin; her hair strung down her back, thick with grease and dandruff. She looked up to Magmaya, her eyes stuck together with sweat, only to crawl back into a ball a moment later.

'Can you see me?' Magmaya asked, her voice echoing throughout the cell.

Nurcia shook her head, her cough dry like a witch's laugh, and said, 'I'm afraid not, my chancellor.'

Magmaya nodded to herself, and yet, she felt a twinge of embarrassment. She had once been so radiant; was this truly how she wanted her to suffer?

Still, she needed Nurcia to be able to see her, and be in the right mind to confess—she couldn't be dying of an infection either. That would make things far too easy. She turned to the guards outside and said, 'Get her clean. Shave her and wash her down.'

About an hour passed before Nurcia returned; her skin was still stained with dirt, but she was unmistakably a different girl. Her eyes had been flushed open (save for where the scars ran across her face), and her back no longer twitched and arched where she'd been filled with arrows. Magmaya watched her stumble back into the cell, bound in chains, and settle into her pool of dirt where she hugged herself again.

The chancellor took a seat on one of the benches, feeling the damp crawl up her back, and looked down to her, frowning.

'That's better,' she crooned, but Nurcia was silent, and so she sighed. 'I can't start or even pretend to understand how you did what you did.'

'You don't have to,' Nurcia said. 'I—'

'Though I do think it starts with *he said he wanted to fuck me*,' Magmaya interrupted.

Nurcia shrugged and said, 'I told you what I told you. I never lied about having to shoo your uncle out of my chambers that night. Whatever you made of that was the fruit of your own labour.'

Magmaya scowled. It was that distraction that had caused her to abandon Shalleous in the Sultide; it was that distraction that had killed him.

'Well, I suppose it doesn't matter now,' she said. 'Shalleous is dead. But so is Vargul Tul.'

'No,' Nurcia replied. 'For as long as I am alive, our conquest lives on. You didn't know him. You didn't know what we had planned for this world.'

'I did know him,' Magmaya shot back. 'I killed him.'

She shook her head. 'They keep saying that. They keep taunting me. But you couldn't have. I saw how bloodied you were. You were in no state to kill a god.'

'He was an arrogant god.'

'You took his head off.' She laughed a hysterical laugh. 'That's what they said.'

'Then at least you know the truth of what happened to your love.'

'Oh,' Nurcia remarked. 'That's what this is about. I should have known.'

'Just confess.' Magmaya sighed. The day had drained all her will from her.

'I can't remember everything.' She held her head. 'Perhaps if you fetch me some Silk Tea I might be able to think clearer.'

'Do you want Dew of the Honey in it?' Magmaya spat.

Nurcia stayed quiet.

'I'm glad you can understand one thing, then.'

'My chancellor,' Nurcia said and sprung up. 'What if I sit here? What if I never answer any of your questions? What if I never move a muscle? Would you cry again?'

'I would make your life hell,' she said, and her words burned her lips. 'You wouldn't even have to die.'

Nurcia shook her head and said softly, 'No, that's not true. There are only two ways this can go. Kill me, and you'll have to get on with it soon enough.' She cocked her head. 'Trade me away, and you can't touch me. The Mansel won't want a beaten woman—look what you've already done to my face! The masters will not be pleased. How long do you intend to prolong this conflict?'

Magmaya was silent.

'You act like I don't know this, my chancellor. But I was the north, I ran the north—I cared for this city with more of a tender touch than your father ever did. Excuse me for killing my own creation, but when something breaks, you must toss it away.'

'Is that why you wanted us all dead?'

'Vargul wanted you all dead because he knew you would stand in his way. Had you let us take the city peacefully, we would have. Gods! The Tyla are the only victors in all of this—look at them, taking Orianne faster than the Mansel could've ever dreamt of doing.'

'We're not here to talk about them.'

'No?'

'No,' Magmaya started. 'I'm here to figure out what I'm going to do with you.'

'You're not going to execute me, though, are you?' Nurcia asked. 'You did that before, Magmaya. I was there, and believe me, I cleared up quite the scandal on your behalf. You can't do that to all of us, though. I'm sure there will be many more to come.'

'Us?'

'Anyone who breaks you,' Nurcia scorned. 'How do you think Kharon felt? He had ten enemies for each star in the sky. Could he execute them all? Could he torture the truth from every last one?'

'He tried.' Magmaya grit her teeth.

'And look where that got him.' She made a sour face and crossed her heart. 'So, what is it? Have you made your decision?' She made a sort of giggle. 'Are you going to kill me?'

'I was there when you attacked Rache.'

'I don't know what you're talking about.' She seemed frustrated. 'Can you stop with this nonsense?'

'I was sleeping in with him when he woke with broken legs,' Magmaya spat. 'Half the city accused me.'

'I remember.'

'I thought I smelled some hideous perfume when I awoke,' Magmaya remarked.

'I wasn't aware you wore any.'

'Don't do this,' she cried. 'For the love of the gods, confess.'

'I confessed a few times, I seem to recall.'

'Not to what mattered.'

'Did your false brother not matter?' Nurcia asked. 'Or Kaladeous? Would you prefer me to withdraw my confessions? I can always say I was a little dizzy—or perhaps you were... Besides, the girl who accuses me does have quite the tendency to drink while she's under pressure...'

'Enough!' Magmaya leapt up and drove her shoe into Nurcia's back. Her toes stung, but a rush of serenity rose through her, and she realised perhaps all she needed to do was hurt her.

But the turncoat just screamed in ecstasy, purring, 'Kick me! You can't trade a girl with broken ribs, no, no, no—not one beaten in the dungeons.' She crawled like a spider into a corner, limbs flailing. 'The price on my head is worth more than you'll ever be to this city.' She paused, smiling. 'Do it again, I urge you.'

So Magmaya did. And Nurcia laughed.

The guards called for her, threw the door open and tore Magmaya away. Nurcia laughed even harder then.

Don't let her see you cry, she cursed herself. *Don't let her see the tears, dammit.*

She slipped into the forest again and traced her path around the pond, and then to where she'd found *him.* There she could cry at least, and no one would be there to taunt her. She sat down in a bundle of leaves and sifted the snow through her hands until it burned her fingers. Her ears pricked up for a moment, as she swore she heard the calling of her brother; she heard his cries when she awoke that night to his broken legs.

Magmaya sighed and pulled herself up, wiping her eyes, finding them red. The day was drawing to a close, and she had a meeting with Rallun on the morrow. She heaved herself up and slumped back into her bed.

Council came and went in the boardroom, with no starry maps to gouge over nor even Siedous by her side on occasion, and Magmaya felt as if she was losing herself to the chancellor. She caught herself kissing bottles even more often than she did before the siege, and her dreams failed to turn to nightmares for they just started as them.

In time, they agreed (if agreed was the term she'd use) on a date for exchanging the prisoners. In two weeks, Nurcia would disappear, mocking her as she did. Not to mention, Magmaya's folly in the dungeons had cost them the price of another Mansel prisoner—the turncoat had been right—no one wanted a girl with broken ribs.

When she returned to bed each night, it seemed as if Rache always slumbered in another world, far, far away, and when she looked to him, the glint burning through his eyelids reminded her that perhaps he was sailing the cold seas and swimming with the fish-women—him against the world.

Each day, she returned to the pond in the forest's centre, and each day, she found it frozen over as even the heat of spring grew meek. And when she walked on its milky surface and eyed herself in its reflection, the seas didn't seem so big any longer. Orianne looked as if it was shrinking about her feet as the days passed her by.

But when she watched the stars, they didn't move an inch, save for glowing of the moon when it swam against the heavens or faded into the daylight. No wine spared her what loomed above. *If a day comes when the seas swallow the ice and only the tips of mountains remain, then I'll at least be able to depend on starlight*, she told herself.

It had been perhaps a month since she'd met the shadowed-eyed man, but Magmaya woke in a cold sweat all the same. She wiped her forehead clean with her wrist and sat up, bathing in the fumes of long-dead candlelight, while a myriad of rosy incenses carried through the halls and blinded her to the harsh light of the morning sun. It hurt to smell it, though; it had been there when she'd found Albany, and she feared it would be there until the day she dropped dead.

The morning was clear enough without the sun; she could even see through the fog from the tower tops and make out children basking in the freshly-fallen snow, eyeing the sky ahead. Strangely, as she watched around, she found others doing the same, forgetting themselves as they cried to the blue heavens in the west.

Whatever now? she asked herself and ran to her window, threw it open and stared out into the city. It was then her smile dropped, and her heart began to shudder.

There was a scar across the sky, hanging below the mountains and bleeding the soft skin of the seas as if it were still cutting, forever frozen in the moment the knife struck.

The shadow-eyed man hadn't quite been the fool Magmaya had thought; while the others stared in wonder, she did so in horror—a star was moving.

She made her way to the palace windows, finding a thousand scribes, each demanding her to explain exactly what was going on. And when she hazarded no reply, they came to their own conclusions.

'It is a sign from the gods,' one told her, hand twitching. 'When the world turns red with the blood of stars, the end is truly upon us.'

Who were the nameless gods anyway? Magmaya asked herself. *And why would they, at the end of all things, strike an orange smear across the sky? Was watching their people scream in fear so enjoyable that there would have to be an omen before the end?*

She watched as villagers chattered and children played, and the sky turned a cool red. The faint glow seemed to twist and twirl around the wound on the horizon as if it was broken and out of place.

'It was brighter this morning,' another scribe interrupted her thoughts. 'The sky is clearing. It's only a falling star.'

'I've never seen one so bright,' Magmaya whimpered to herself. She remembered escaping the palace to watch a rain of stars fall from heaven one night, but they lasted for seconds at best. This gouge in the horizon had persisted for hours.

'Aye.' One of the scribes smiled wickedly. 'It's a demon.'

Magmaya scoffed and ambled away, making her way through the winding, white corridors and up a complex of stairwells.

'My chancellor,' a voice crooned as she made her way into the boardroom.

Magmaya hadn't time to comprehend the others in the room before Siedous made his way to her. The night before, the palace had been empty. Now it was overflowing with Tyla, scribes and advisors she'd never remembering employing. She noted as well that the old knight was armed.

'We were about to send for you, my chancellor,' Rallun spoke grimly.

'The star,' Magmaya quipped, 'I thought I noticed something strange on the horizon.'

'You're acting callously, girl,' Rallun warned. 'It may be no blood of the gods, but it's lasting far too long to just be a falling star.'

'There's a woman in the city that tracks the heavens,' Siedous explained. 'I'm going to find her. Perhaps she can tell us something of worth.'

'Is that why you're armoured?' Magmaya asked.

'Orianne is not the place it once was.'

'I'll come,' she decided after a moment. *This is the most interesting thing that's happened in weeks,* she thought. *And the first thing that hasn't made my blood boil.*

'This woman isn't worth your time, Magmaya,' Siedous said. 'She's perhaps a maddened hag with a number of old maps. We're going to her out of desperation.'

'If she's so insignificant, why didn't you just summon her?' she asked.

'Her terms,' Rallun groaned. 'Like Siedous said, it's a desperate measure.'

'It *must* be the end of days for you to solicit an astrologist,' she said, turning to the old knight. 'I *shall* join you, my lord.'

'Very well,' Siedous mewled, and the pair left the palace together.

They found themselves out in the grey streets again, tattered banners beating against the wind. The snow fell softly, and Magmaya watched as it formed a barricade between her and the commoners. She was beginning to feel as alone and cold as she had that day when she rode back from the Sultide.

Siedous and her arrived in a small alcove, the crowds long behind. She swore she had been there before, but then again, much of Orianne looked the same at first glance.

'Through here.' Siedous gestured to a small entrance in the walls. It was flanked by a pair of leering stone gargoyles, sporting broken wings, buried beneath a thick layer of frost.

Without a word, they ambled inside and felt the cold fade as they were met with roaring fires and a great orange blaze. Bookshelves were pressed neatly against the brick-walled interior, alchemy jars were overflowing, and red rugs ran beneath their tread, trembling in Siedous' armour.

In the room's centre, a rather plump woman sat at an old wooden desk, near-impossible to make out beneath the heaps of sextants and globes. She was robed with a cunning smile, as the fire from the forked candlestick behind her shed its shell with each movement and reinvented itself anew.

'My chancellor,' the woman croaked. 'I thought someone might be joining us soon, but I never expected to be blessed by you. Could it possibly be that queer star?'

Siedous ignored her and said, 'My name is Lord Harluss, and on behalf of Orianne, we've arrived—'

'I remember you. You only enquired this morning,' she crooned. 'You never said you'd be bringing the chancellor with you, though.' Magmaya felt her spine go cold as a chubby finger was poked at her. There was something unnerving about the woman.

'Sit.' She gestured to a chair, as if bored. Siedous did as she said, and Magmaya followed, finding herself staring into her eyes. 'You like the candles?' She motioned to them.

'They're pretty,' Magmaya answered dryly.

'Aye,' she spoke. 'The pyromancers of the south claim that in the fires, there shall be truth.' She smiled. 'But I am yet to find it.'

'What's the star then?' Siedous asked, ignoring her. 'Does it mean us ill fortune?'

'It depends how one defines ill fortune,' she said. Magmaya cocked her head, and the woman laughed. 'But if you're asking if the gods have finally decided our demise,' the hag continued, 'then you might find yourself disappointed.' The woman's smile dropped, and she began to finger a globe on her desk, tracing the lines with blackened fingernails. 'I've tracked the stars since before you were born, my chancellor. And that's not a star.'

'Then what is it?' Siedous asked.

'It's the same thing it was twenty years ago.' The astrologer span the globe on its axis, and Magmaya watched it twirl before the realisation hit her pounding chest, and she looked up to the crone, eyes wide.

'It can't be,' she protested. 'The southern ships abandoned us!'

'Things never happen just once,' the woman said.

'The ship before was never so vibrant,' she persisted.

'The chancellor is right,' Siedous said. 'When that vessel came, it was quiet and cold. It didn't put on a light show.'

'Did the ship before not have torches at all?' the woman asked. 'Perhaps this one is of a different origin or different design. Still, I have no doubt—that is no star. The southerners are coming again to Ranvirus.'

'Well… how long until they arrive?' she asked with a stutter.

'Days, I would imagine.'

Magmaya found herself thinking back to all the times she'd gazed longingly from the palace, praying to see the same ship seep through the clouds again. She had dreamt of seeing the snowy mountaintops and brazen spires disappear so that she could be forgotten amid the waves. But it was always warmer when you wanted something, rather than had it. The thrill of the chase did something to her.

Now, though, she dreamt only of the warm, quiet nothing. Orianne, Rache and Siedous were a part of her; they always had been. She couldn't run now. She couldn't flee herself.

There was a scream of wood against steel as Siedous stood abruptly, his expression grim. As Magmaya looked to him, she saw that his armour was darker, despite the flames from the fireplace still raging.

'My chancellor,' he started, 'let's take our leave.'

'Going so soon?' the witch asked. 'Am I not privy to these matters?'

'You know as much as we do,' Siedous replied.

Magmaya stood and turned to the hag as the strange thing looked up with a crooked smile, cleared her throat and held out her palm.

'I've a family to feed too, my lord.' She looked to the old knight.

Magmaya sighed. 'Pay the lady,' she said, and so Siedous flung a silver on her desk and bid her goodnight.

They were back in the streets again without another word, and her heart was pounding, though she couldn't quite decide whether it was with excitement or fear. Her dreams never made her sweat so much.

Magmaya looked back up to the light as it bled across the sky. If the southerners were truly to be coming, then who would they be? Would Albany's mother return to the north only to be told both her lover and son had been slain? Or would they be far more sinister?

'Are they going to kill us?' she asked at last.

'I don't know if they mean us harm,' Siedous admitted. 'But all those years ago when they arrived, the north changed. I fear all will not be the same again once these travellers arrive either.'

'We should've stayed with her,' Magmaya said as they began to make their way back to the palace. 'Perhaps she might find more to tell us.'

'Perhaps,' he answered. 'Perhaps not. She can only make out little stars moving, not who is in them.'

'She might've not been exact,' Magmaya said. 'She could've been wrong.'

'Tell me, chancellor,' Siedous said, 'have you ever seen a star grow so close to the shore?'

Not for a hell of a long time, she admitted to herself and made her way to Rache's chambers.

There at least, she could just watch the candlelight flicker without any interruption. The warm glow soothed her as if it were a solid thing, rebuilding itself with every passing second. But in the moments it stayed still, Magmaya saw herself in-between the flames, and she couldn't help but watch as her skin was burnt to ashes, only then to be forced to dance again in the flowing white wax. The mirage was lulling her to sleep.

The night before, she'd dreamt about the temple for the first time in what felt like forever. This time, though, there had been a woman standing atop it, watching her and smiling. She was oh so red and oh so gold, but before she had a chance to speak a word, daylight struck Magmaya through the windows.

She turned to Rache and watched his eyes close and flutter with his beating heart, smoothed back his hair and left a kiss on his forehead before rising from the furs and out of the room. Magmaya looked back to him with a smile; while he lay in ignorance, the boardroom shrieked, and she stood in silence. She wished she could've joined him, closed her eyes to the world that threatened to swallow her whole and yet, the siege had laid waste to the old Magmaya that would have allowed herself that luxury.

When Vargul had come for her home, she had been broken and bleeding, without a choice. But now as she stood in leisure, the world seemed more strenuous than before. She had never felt more alive when she was so close to death, and she had never felt more dead than when she was living in paradise.

By evening, Siedous had sent for her, and again, she found herself in the boardroom. Maps flooded the tables, detailing Ranvirus' landscape: where the seas began and where the mountains stood tall and where the Deadfields continued on forever and ever south. Rallun looked down at her as she studied, eying her every move as she traced the map, his cold stare unflinching.

'The vessel is still making its way east,' the Tyla announced after a short while.

Magmaya looked up. 'How many men can we afford to send?'

'Enough to boast our strength,' Siedous replied. 'It matters not how many arms we bring, though. If they want war, this broken city will be shattered in a moment's notice. We're nothing to them.'

'Neither of us are anything compared to this frozen hell,' Magmaya said under her breath. 'Whatever that vessel disgorges, I shall be there to see it.'

Siedous nodded. 'When they make land, they must meet truly the best of us.'

The chancellor smiled warmly, stood from the map and announced, 'Orianne rides.'

Nine

The night before they left was the coldest she had ever felt. Usually, her mornings were lit with starlight, but the coming of the southerners had blinded Orianne with something of a fire.

It was making Magmaya restless. The mere thought of it was exhausting her, yet the day insisted on forcing her to get up again.

And when she did, the corridors seemed to tremble beneath her. Even her summer furs were failing to protect her from the cold of the cells. She just had to remind herself that an hour later she would march to the star on the seas, and maybe then she'd be able to quell the feeling of nausea that had been building in her.

'I was beginning to think you'd forgotten me,' the traitor said when she entered.

'Almost,' Magmaya lied.

'I dread to think what would've happened to me if you had.'

'It doesn't matter,' she said. 'It's been decided.'

'Oh.'

She ambled across the cell and eased herself onto a mound of broken cobblestone. Magmaya thought for a moment before deciding to look down at her, some wretched thing grazing on the floor. No longer was she huddled up, though, but sprawling, nude and pressed against the wall, her sheet tossed away, along with her modesty. She was still beautiful, Magmaya realised, despite her scars, and she caught herself still wishing she looked like her; she wished she had such rounded breasts and ripe thighs. She almost shied away. And Nurcia noticed it.

'Am I making you uncomfortable?' she asked.

Magmaya ignored her and said, 'We have made an agreement to have you and another of our captives exchanged for our men held by the Mansel.' She sighed. 'You will be marched there in a short number of days, but until then, you're a prisoner of Orianne. Is that understood?'

Nurcia closed her legs and stood, confused. 'What?' Her lips curled up into a ghost of a smile. 'I almost feel sorry for you,' she said, looking to the ceiling. 'My prayers have been answered! Vargul Tul watches over me still.'

'Vargul Tul is dead,' she snapped.

'I was waiting here,' the turncoat continued on, ignoring her, 'waiting for the day you would come and gloat about how you were to take my head off.'

'You have a committee to thank.'

'A committee? You've been doing less as chancellor than I thought.'

'*I* had the final say.' She was losing her temper already. A voice inside of her kept telling her to leave—but she couldn't yet; she had something to prove still.

'And that say forced you to agree with the others, no doubt.' She nodded. 'You wouldn't want to make your situation worse after all. The masses disliked your father, but they'll hate you if you're to keep your pride over your own men. It *is* difficult for us women, I suppose.'

Magmaya tried her best to ignore her, but her words were nestling themselves in her head. 'I have something else to tell you,' she said.

'What?'

'Do you know what happened twenty years ago, Nurcia?'

'Many things, I might imagine.'

'The Kytherans came.'

'Yes,' she said. 'Well?'

'We do believe they've returned.' Magmaya smiled.

Nurcia's battered face contorted. 'Why are you telling me this?'

'They have larger armies than us,' Magmaya said. 'They're better armed. They have more allies.' She paused. 'I just want you to know that if Vargul Tul did take Orianne and even thought about heading south, they would've arrived and wiped him clean off this earth.'

'The same may yet happen to you.' Nurcia shrugged.

Magmaya almost laughed at that. 'What?'

'The southerners may be all-powerful, but they're not gods; they're not the right or wrong in this world,' she explained. 'They may come to see Orianne as more of a threat to their power than the Mansel could've ever been. After all, Orianne is chocked full of demagogues and aristocrats. What's a bigger threat to peace than dogmatism?'

'You're foolish to think that,' was the only reply she hazarded. Her threat hadn't even left a cut. Sometimes, she felt as if her every word had been stolen from her.

'Perhaps,' Nurcia began. 'But that's beside the point. What I care to know is when I'm being brought to Mansel.' She frowned.

That frown stripped all the strength from her. *She doesn't care, she doesn't care,* she reminded herself and forced herself to spit, 'Confess.'

Nurcia groaned. 'I've confessed time enough already. There is no more truth this world needs from me.'

'As chancellor of Orianne, I beg to differ.' Magmaya grasped at air. Her title emboldened her, but it had no effect on the turncoat.

'What I confess doesn't matter now, I am already incriminated,' Nurcia said.

'It matters to me!' she roared. 'It matters to the old books. It matters for your legacy.'

'Now you are sounding like Kharon Vorr,' she said. 'Legacy this, legacy that. Talk to me again about legacy once you've met the southerners.'

'No.' Magmaya shook her head. 'We shan't be seeing one another again.'

Nurcia nodded and began flaunting her nudity about the room, catching the gazes of the guards.

Magmaya sighed, turned away and said, 'They say you bowed to Tul when your village was taken.' She paused. 'Why in the world...?'

'My father was a cock,' she remarked. 'And his cock was all he thought with. I was glad when Tul killed him.'

'And you were glad when your village was sacked?'

'I remember not being pleased at first,' Nurcia admitted. 'But once I found Vargul, I understood why. Perhaps you will too one day.'

The chancellor slapped her for that, and the traitor's cheek glowed a deep red.

'You think you haven't cut me enough?'

'There's still time in the day.'

'It's a shame you don't have all day then, isn't it?'

'If I were you, I'd quiet down,' Magmaya's voice was fire. 'I've a few days left. I might yet change my decision about what I'm doing with you.'

'I invite you to.' Nurcia smiled. 'Let it be known, though, I have watched you for as long as I can remember.'

'Your time watching me has finished.'

'My time watching you was long enough,' she said. 'I've all your secrets hidden away. If I happen to be displeased with this decision of yours, a slip of the tongue might make one spill.'

The traitor leaned forward, so close to Magmaya that she felt consumed by her. The guards leapt forward as Nurcia pressed her mouth to her ear, rasping as she was torn away, 'Your false brother was a quiet boy.' She moaned, 'The same was true when I was plucking his eyes out, vein by vein.'

'Get her away from me!' Magmaya screamed, and the guards pinned Nurcia against the back wall. 'What kind of god would want *this*?'

'My god.'

'Your god would have you murder them?' Magmaya scorned. 'Kill Albany? Try for Rache?'

There was silence for a moment as the guards began to bind her in chains, fastening her to the wet walls, but Nurcia still had some talk left in her, it seemed.

'Yes, he would,' she said after a moment and shrugged. 'And I did.'

The snow spilt from the sky like it really was the end of days; it had started slowly, but by the afternoon, it had littered the Deadfields with an ocean of orange-red ambience.

The falling star ripped across the faraway seas faster and faster as it grew closer and closer, clawing its way east. Occasionally, it would catch the light of the moon or the white of the sun, and streaks of molten silver would rush across the mountaintops. The star had become so intertwined with the horizon, it had become part of Ranvirus itself.

And beneath it, the chancellor's company thundered on wearily. The Deadfields were beginning to reek like something feral again, and she couldn't help but shake the idea that something terrible was closing in on them. Then again, it had been a day like this when Shalleous and her had ridden to die. One of them had even succeeded in doing so.

'We're walking into certain danger,' the old knight said as he reared over to her, but Magmaya just sat high in her saddle. While she was still deathly afraid, her fear of the cold had become more bearable. The ice was melting all around her.

'Of course, we are,' she said, her gaze not leaving the knight. 'But we've been alone for too long, Siedous. We ride on.'

They carried onwards across the glittering skyline. Magmaya turned, noticing small waterfalls breaking through the ice from the Sultide beyond and across to the Deadfields. She watched crooked trees bend from the cliffs at impossible angles, gasping for a taste of the sunlight high above. She watched their gnarled roots claw from the soil, frozen in opaque mounds of ice.

The old books told that when men had first travelled to Ranvirus, there hadn't been an inkling of life; there had been no grass, nor geese, nor trees that chimed; there had been only ice and ruined pyramids made of glass and stone. Perhaps buried beneath her they were still there. Perhaps they were the answers to all her problems; perhaps there was a cure for Rache, a poison for Nurcia, and ship that would take her south. All she had to do was give herself over to the cold again.

By the time she crawled out of her daze, Magmaya realised her deer had begun to clamber up the mountainside; the company was already a quarter of the way up the precipice. Hooves clung to the ground beneath them as if they were embedded in it, riders peering on into the snow. But all the chancellor saw was an endless curtain of white upon a mountainside that had been skewered so much by the incline, she could hardly figure out which way was up.

The chasm on Magmaya's left grew deeper as they ascended, and the path thinner. The company were forced to split duly into ranks of two or three, but soon enough, the path was swallowed by a wall of stone, and from then on, each man rode without a partner.

Magmaya spared a glance down the abyss below, eyeing the trees which might have well-been needles from where she was. A single misstep would send her tumbling a thousand feet downwards, but as if by some miracle of the nameless gods, the deer drove onwards, relentless to the unpleasant lashings of rain.

The higher they climbed, the more Magmaya felt the warmth of candlelight beat against her back as if it was calling her to stop, to turn back and ride home. With every breath, she thirsted to draw the silver blade from her hip and strike at the shadows of Nurcia around her. But without borrowed light, Moonbeam had no shine, and Magmaya reasoned it wouldn't even cut its way through the sleet. No longer did the warm, red glow of the falling star guide their way, but instead, cold spears of white light beckoned them to nowhere.

And with each upturned stone, Magmaya's belly still throbbed like something putrid was festering inside, and every strain resounded throughout her like a hurricane. All the old knights had been incessant on passing down stories of their battles and tales of their scars, but Magmaya dreaded the day she'd be telling the world how her greatest trophy had come from a misplaced kick.

The racket of crunching ice beneath the deer ceased as the icy path met the rigged mountainside that had hung above for so long. It seemed, at last, the end was in sight as she spotted a thin silver crag, spearing the shore below.

And that's when she saw it: a crooked shadow cast across the valley. The vessel was a hulk of brass and iron, pearls and rubies, seeping through the mist and dwarfing the mountainside. Tendrils of cold steel rained down into the ocean like entrails from a beached whale, while the red fires from its braziers bellowed up into the heavens.

The chancellor's heart pounded, and her stomach ran warm with anticipation; it was no pearly mass of the gods' reckoning, but it was a human thing fashioned from the same metals she herself wore. And though Magmaya hated to say it, it was undeniably beautiful; it was undeniably beautiful and undeniably ancient like the Age of the Technomancer made flesh.

'Gods,' said Magmaya as her eyes began to water. A cacophony of gasps and whispers erupted from the men behind, but they were nothing; they were less than insects in the sight of something so colossal.

'In all my life, I never convinced myself I would see such a thing again...' Siedous told her, trailing off.

'I want to meet them.' She gestured to the shimmering figures that stood alone on the shore, stumbling from their landing boats. Magmaya couldn't quite make out what they looked like, though; she could only watch on with intrigue as they marched on the ice like shining pearls.

'They don't know we're here,' the knight whispered breathlessly. 'Don't act hastily, my chancellor. They may be dangerous yet.'

Magmaya nodded, and yet, she still couldn't tear her eyes from it all. Her passage to the shore seemed to have taken an age, but only the nameless gods knew how long the starry men had travelled to get to Ranvirus. What lives had they lived upon that barren metal craft?

And who even were they?

A gust of wind tore about the mountaintops, sending the deer reeling and screeching. The company retreated out of sight and rallied by a fallen tree. The snow howled and battered their flanks, but all Magmaya could think of was the armada of pearly men standing stoically about the water.

'Siedous,' she started again, 'we did not travel halfway across the Deadfields to stretch our legs. We must ride to them with goodwill.'

'When I see armoured men spilling down the mountains on horseback, I'm likely not to see them as friends,' he remarked.

'And what did the men of Orianne do upon the southern-people's arrival all those suns ago?' Magmaya asked. 'Did we run and hide then?'

'They walked to us,' he answered, 'we gave them meat and mead, and in return, we got a bastard boy.'

'These southerners seem different,' she asserted herself, but Nurcia's voice was ringing through her head: *the same may yet happen to you.* She shook the thought away. 'Besides, have you forgotten we're still at war? Fighting on another front is the opposite of what the city needs. We've little meat left to share, I know, but we have no means to turn these people down.'

One by one, the deer and their riders trickled over the mountaintop like an army of ants on a canvas, the vessel looming overhead, blotting out the glaring sun above. In the distance, across the thick, white plains, the strange men grew larger, yet no more discernible as their armour looked as if it was changing from green to blue, and blue to purple with every passing moment.

The clatter of hooves thundered through the mountains, throwing up snow and dirt with each step. Magmaya felt the wind rush out of her soul and for a moment, she rather quite enjoyed feeling nothing at all.

As they approached the shore, she was able to make out a few details on the vessel: crinkles and intricate murals plastering its broadsides; it was an articulate configuration of brass scarcely wrought by human hands.

This isn't at all what I remember the last ship looking like, she thought. *Then again, I was only a child then...*

Siedous rode on ahead for a moment, before she saw him slow and followed suit. Soon enough, the columns before them began moving as the strange intruders turned from colourful specs to people, standing in rank about the haze. The entire company became sheathed in the shadow of the mountainside, and yet, the men before them weren't; they were seemingly glowing against the darkness of the snow.

Silhouettes danced across the ice as they approached, and it quickly became clear the southerners were heavily armoured—rainbow light glistened off their breastplates as they stood solemn and faceless against the snow. They clearly numbered in their hundreds—a block of armoured might against a horde of unkempt cavalry. If conflict broke out, Magmaya's men were to be no match.

Siedous edged a little farther forward, bracing himself from the storm. 'Make yourselves known!' he called; his face was grim and broken as if had fought a thousand wars. By the state of him, hc might well have done.

A silence took to the world, and with bated breath, the Orianne and Tyla waited. Magmaya felt her stomach twist and her heart break as finally, the veil of snow fell between them, and the ranks stood forward, letting the onlookers revel in their divinity.

Their faces were nowhere to be seen, though, encased behind flowing masks and towering headdresses, giving the illusion they stood two heads taller than any man the north mustered.

And then, their ranks parted slightly as two more of their kind stepped through to face Magmaya, silent.

One removed his helm with an elegance she might've heard of in a faery story, as the handsome prince stole a fair maiden from a blazing tower. And this prince was not to disappoint—he was perhaps the most beautiful man Magmaya had ever seen. He had amethyst pools for eyes and swords for cheekbones which cut her when they caught the light, all while burning silver hair ran long down his neck, lashing against the snow. Yet at the same time, there was somewhat of a homeliness about him; in those pearly eyes, there was violence.

She watched as he moved his gaze furtively from Magmaya to Siedous, and from Siedous to her men. He took a step back and looked to the taller man beside him with a tenacious nod, emotionless, before readjusting his helm.

And then, he stepped forward with a certain elegance too, although there appeared to be an unspeakable weight resting upon his back as he did. And as he approached, the chancellor could make out a large, sweeping falchion fastened to his hip, flaming with angel's wings and talismans.

He reached nimble fingers to his helm and unsheathed it, and in that moment, Magmaya had never been more mistaken. For *this* was truly the most beautiful man she had ever seen. His flowing locks were as shimmery as the snow, and his eyes were like obsidian; glassy and black. His fur cloak snapped against the wind, and he beamed with kind lips like he'd stepped out of an age-old painting.

'Who are you?' Siedous called through the storm.

'We're *the truth.*' His words seemed to melt away as he spoke them.

'And who is *the truth* to Ranvirus?'

'Fabius Uliana, Lord Commander of the Divinicus,' the angel replied. 'Castellan of Inamorata. And the south.'

The truth, Magmaya's mind raced. Nurcia had said there was no right or wrong, but here it was, standing before her—with a cloak! She thought back to the cramped girl sat alone in her cell and remembered how she'd decided what was to come of her. She was beginning to change her mind.

Ten

Something like lightning had run through Magmaya as she'd watched the shadow of the pearly vessel cut through the horizon, scattering lights from its burning braziers across the snow. All those years ago it had been so much colder, and the rain had been unrelenting, but the wonder was all the same.

She remembered how the books which had given her height had tumbled from beneath those little feet, and how she had clattered to the floor amid a heap of trinkets and papers, elbows raging and back stinging. There had been footsteps as she struggled to stand, but Magmaya found no such luck as the papers insisted on sliding beneath her again and again, bruising her fingers as scrawny, yellow hair fluttered into her eyes. Her face had glowed red, and footsteps had rung about the corridors.

'Gods,' a voice called, *'Magmaya!'*

It was the tall lady Kharon had spent so much time with, shrouded by the light of the moon. She was pretty, Magmaya had remembered thinking, but she looked different to everyone else—different to Orianne. She was an intruder.

'I fell,' Magmaya stuttered, and a huge hand reached down to steady her.

'It's all right, girl.' She'd taken it, got to her feet and bent down to dust off her dress. *'What were you doing?'*

'Trying to look out,' she answered with a dribble. *'The... the ship.'*

The woman smiled. *'It must have been quite the shock, seeing it come here.'*

'Angels.' Magmaya ignored her and pointed out to the vessel. It was nestled beneath the mountains, balanced on a crystal sea as if the winds would capsize it at any moment.

The woman's smile faded. *'No, no. No angels. Only us.'*

'Kharon says that angels come down from the heavens,' Magmaya had insisted. *'Like you did.'*

'We came from the seas.' She cocked her head nimbly. *'We ran away from the angels.'*

'Where did you run from?'

'The Silver City,' she had said. *'Well... it isn't quite a city. And it isn't quite made of Silver. But the angels have disappeared from there now, anyway. Soon, we'll be going back.'*

'The priests say we have to pray to angels. Not run away from them,' she'd groaned.

'We don't pray to those angels, girl.'

'*Why not?*' she asked. '*Don't they love you?*'

'*No. They aren't real angels.*' She had whispered to herself, '*None of them are.*' But Magmaya had heard her all the same.

These *were* angels, though. And it was the truest thing she'd ever known as she watched them stand about in the snow. Magmaya could scarcely believe the whole ordeal wasn't just another dream. Sweat pooled around her fingers where she tugged at the reigns until, at last, she found the courage to loosen from the saddle and dismount.

She found herself looking up to the Divinicus as if she was a child again, their grinning yet vacant faces bearing down at her with perhaps the deepest condescending she'd ever been witness to, and yet, somewhere in her, she found the strength to speak.

'Lord Commander Fabius, it's a pleasure to meet you,' she said, a hint of weariness in her voice. 'I'm Magmaya Vorr, chancellor of Orianne.' Magmaya paused. 'What brings you so far north?'

Silence took the shore as the first man to have stepped forward did so again, and like before, he loosened his helm and stared them down with those wrinkled, beady eyes.

'Magmaya Vorr,' he began, his voice coarse and elegant all at once like two people were speaking in unison. 'I'm Lord Legatus Kurulian, Chief Advisor to the Lord Commander.' There was another pause as he reached to his hip and produced a bound scroll. He began unsheathing it, until Fabius raised a hand.

'Legatus,' the Divinicus ordered him, 'there's no need for such a formality. We're not at war with these people.'

Kurulian nodded quietly and slipped the scroll away.

'The question goes unanswered,' Magmaya grumbled.

'I said, we are the truth—' Fabius started but didn't quite finish.

'We've little patience for such niceties,' Siedous snapped.

'Oh?'

'We scarcely have anyone travel to our shores,' he said. 'My chancellor deserves an answer.'

'Of course.' Fabius nodded sympathetically. 'Twenty years have passed since the Kytherans arrived here, no? Twenty years is time enough. Inamorata has long been due a trip north.'

'Do you normally wait this long to make new friends?' Magmaya asked. She remembered it now—some story Kharon's lover had told her of how above Kythera, there stretched Inamorata—the land of false angels and aristocrats.

'My lady,' Fabius began, 'we've travelled for almost two weeks to reach—'

'But for what?' she cut in. 'Territory?' *Why do I expect something so shallow from a man dressed as an angel?*

Fabius' eyes widened, and a deeper, darker smile spread across his face. 'We want your allegiance, not land. Our colonies are rising against us. The continent must unify against them.' He paused. 'We've been studying the north for many weeks now. It seems you too are in trouble. You need our hand also.'

'We *were* in trouble,' Magmaya said.

'If Inamorata holds the north, we can coerce the southernmost reaches into compliance,' he said, ignoring her. 'Isolated, we're no use at all.'

'The north isn't held by anyone,' she said. 'Except me.'

'So, you're turning us away?' Fabius asked.

'Orianne takes no commands from pearly men,' Siedous scorned.

'No, it doesn't,' Magmaya said. 'Though I suppose we can at least listen to them.' She turned to Siedous and whispered, 'I'm no happier with this arrangement than you are. But we shan't just turn them away.'

'Thank you,' Fabius crooned. 'We come to the north to bring peace and to vouch for the chancellor of Orianne. We would not travel a thousand icy seas out of folly.'

Magmaya nodded and turned to the others. 'Then let them share our wine. Let them tell us of the south,' she proclaimed.

'Mag—' Siedous protested, but she ran a finger across her throat.

'We would be honoured.' Fabius nodded.

'Bring only as many men as you need,' the old knight instructed glumly. 'The city is beyond the mountaintop. It's a hard ride.'

Despite their lack of cavalry, the Divinicus were resolute as they travelled. Fabius had, of course, insisted on bringing half of his company with him, as well as his advisors. And as they began to scale the mountainside, Magmaya couldn't help but wonder if her bitterness was playing into Fabius' hand. Even through his headdress, she could see those black eyes move from dead tree to dead tree, weighing up her home. Perhaps he had conquered a thousand lands and killed a thousand girls like her along the way. How many others had he struck down with that shimmery falchion of his?

'My chancellor.' Siedous reached her, panting. 'I've good faith in you,' he said, but then, he frowned, and her heart sank. 'But we were warned of angels by the Kytherans, Magmaya. We can't dare trust them.'

'I know,' she answered quietly. 'But what alternative do we have? We can't turn them down—they outnumber us vastly. Besides, we're in ruin, Siedous.'

'When angels fall from the sky, most drop to their knees and pray, Magmaya,' he said. 'But there's one thing they always forget to do—look to the heavens and ask *what's in it for them?*'

'How do you mean?'

'*We are the truth,*' Siedous reminded her. 'In all my years, I have never known anyone so self-righteous. And I knew your father.'

'Neither of us have been to the south. We don't know what they're like.'

'Just tread carefully, my chancellor,' he warned. 'You may think you know what this faraway land is like, but I fear these men are as selfish as we are.'

'I know, I know,' she admitted. 'I suppose any angel that dresses like that must be compensating for something.'

Siedous smiled warmly. 'Take them to the boardroom and show them a girl who isn't afraid to love where she lives,' he said, and then her heart must've broken in two.

Rallun and perhaps a hundred Tyla stood stoically at the city gates when Magmaya and the angels returned. His expression was as ambiguous as ever, but the strained faces of the raging crowds behind him proved clear enough to interpret.

The commoners parted as they rushed into the cobblestone streets, shattered edifices and spiralling towers encasing them. And above all the noise of the city, her people were shouting, that much was certain; she was feeling sicker by the minute.

'A warm welcome.' Fabius must've caught up with her because a moment later, he was without his helm and whispering in her ear.

'The city is afraid of people like you,' Magmaya remarked. 'Strange men from far away have shown us little kindness of late.'

'You were invaded?' the Divinicus asked.

'Betrayed,' she admitted. 'Besieged.'

'I see.' Magmaya felt her stomach curdle as he spoke, his voice like warm silk against her neck. 'Have you been their leader for long?'

'A few months,' she said feebly.

'A few months is time enough for a young girl,' he said, sighing.

'Quite,' she agreed and rode on through the city.

The boardroom had become an increasingly familiar sight over the passing weeks, and on each occasion that Magmaya sat at its head, she felt as if she was losing another part of herself. With each new query came a verdict to pass which stemmed a new tree of rulings and obligations. Perhaps in a few days, she too would be maddened like her father, and not a high lord would be able to stop her.

But now, angels sat before her with smiles that could've burned hell, and something else in her had changed. The snow fell like a storm of blazing moonstars, while their shimmery vessel (she had heard it was called *The Golden Damnation)* lingered beyond. Their shadows engulfed hers, and their mere presence seemed to light the candles in the room.

And when a girl sat face to face with angels, she could do nothing but spend her every word praising them. It didn't matter whether they were truly made of stardust or not, she hadn't a choice in the matter of how she treated them. They were angels with haloes, and she was an unkempt girl atop a ruined city. Perhaps it really was the end of the world.

Scribes fluttered in and out, clearly in awe—and so they should've been. The small, pale men were nothing in the wake of the towering angels; they were shimmering like stars and sported silky tunics which seemed to flow off them like silverwater. And every time a scribe approached, they did so with greater trepidation than they ever had around Kharon, staring up to their towering heights in some vain hope to describe their likeness.

'If we may begin,' Kurulian said with that voice like twisting leather and silk all at once. 'I can hardly believe these men are privy to our council, my chancellor.'

'Each meeting is recorded,' she heard herself say, 'as was the last, as the next will be.'

There was silence for a moment as paper was tidied. Then, Rallun addressed the angels, droning on for a little longer until he finally asked something of substance:

'May the Lord Commander make clear where exactly his host travelled from?'

'Of course,' Fabius replied. 'The Divinicus hail from Inamorata, a great power south of Lumiar—'

'Lumiar?' Magmaya asked.

'South of your Silver Mountainside. Desolate and uncontested, save for several terrible death cults. Only a fool would travel so far north, especially by land.' He straightened himself. 'Anyway, twenty years ago a similar vessel journeyed here, no?'

'Yes, but smaller.' Siedous answered, to Magmaya's surprise. When she had fallen from that pile of books, it had looked as if it were the biggest thing in the world.

'From Kythera?' Kurulian asked.

'That's where they claimed to be from.' Siedous nodded. 'But they were not like you. They were no host of armoured angels.'

'Have you a problem with armoured angels?' Fabius cocked his head.

'No,' Rallun said through gritted teeth. 'We certainly do not.'

'They were low-born pilgrims, that's all I mean,' Siedous said. 'They wanted nothing but warmth and a haven.'

'I see,' Fabius said. 'You didn't let them take advantage of you, though, did you?'

'How do you mean?' Magmaya asked.

'You really think they travelled *here* for warmth?' The angel smirked.

'This isn't about them,' she said, growing irritated.

'I fear it is, my dear.' Fabius turned to Siedous. 'How long did the pilgrims stay for?' He pursed his lips together.

'A year? I couldn't tell you exactly,' the old knight murmured.

'Though you did say the meetings were recorded?'

'Yes.' He nodded. 'But they're to be found in the archives.'

'Then so be it.' Fabius said with the wave of a hand.

'The archives are vast,' Magmaya found herself saying. 'It might take hours.'

'I am happy to wait,' Fabius said, seemingly unperturbed.

'Then we'll adjourn this meeting until the morrow,' Rallun announced, turning to the angels. 'We can offer your men hospitality until then.'

'Very well.'

Magmaya stole a deep breath, turned to one of the serving girls and stuttered, 'Bring me something to drink.'

A moment later, the boardroom was silent, and she found herself on the balcony again and staring out into the endless cold. The angels had gone (for now), but her council persisted like they were demanding something from her. It was suffocating.

'I can't stand this heat any longer.' Magmaya fanned herself and headed to the doors.

Siedous tried to say something, but it was just a whisper to the wind. And so, she left the room alone, only to find one of the palace's sentinels following her. She turned back, dismissed him and ambled through the halls, sparing a glance at Rache as he slept and carried on until she finally felt the cool of the frost against her skin again.

The wind that cut at her face was refreshing and the thought of escaping the boardroom even more so. But with every passing second, she found herself drawn to the far-off mountains and to the light of the vessel that hummed beyond. It might as well have been a falling star; perhaps one of those would've brought less distress than the angels had. She wished she could've just curled up beneath the wrath of a fireplace and allowed Kharon to tend to it; perhaps then she could have forgotten about Nurcia, forgotten about everything.

But Orianne was a different place than it had been when he was alive. Whether it was the Mansel or the falling angels, it was different. And it was difficult. The only constant was the light crunch of wet snow beneath her foot, and even that had thawed a little as the summer sun reached its peak and beat down on her with endless silver passion.

Her stomach was grumbling, but she was forced to remind herself it would be a while until she'd sup again— she had time to kill and no place to find herself, so she strolled around the outskirts of the palace and across the broken bridges that led out into the mountainside. They were caught somewhere between prosperity and ruin, easy enough to scout across still, given the right tread. Rushing water cut through the snowy banks below, threatening to swallow her with each misstep, but she had come too far to die from falling. Then again, she had heard that the greatest of kings drunk themselves to death.

Soon enough, the foot of the mountain would appear, and with it, she could look out for miles across the city below and down to all the tiny people and rows of spires that stretched out into the Deadfields. She smiled and took a deep breath, letting the cold, empty air fill her lungs. That was before she heard another pair of footsteps in the snow.

'My chancellor,' a grim voice called, and she turned, half expecting to find Siedous coming for her again. But instead, there was Kurulian, braving the snow with a face sterner than the snow itself.

Magmaya curtsied awkwardly. 'Forgive me—'

'No need.' He waved the thought away, but his voice was cold, and she thought for a moment it might have been sarcasm.

'Do they want me back already?' she asked. 'I didn't think the food would be ready yet. I wanted a little break before the... talking started again.'

'No, not yet,' he answered duly. 'I too am bored with talks, though. Don't I deserve to see the mountains? There aren't mountains from where I come.'

'There aren't mountains in Inamorata?'

Kurulian shook his head as if he were deep in thought, but his eyes lacked the truth that everyone else's always spilt. 'Inamorata has many mountains, remnants of long ago. But I'm not from there.'

'Kythera, then?'

'No,' he said. 'All my men are of the south. Fabius too. But I'm not.'

'If not the south, then where?' she asked, growing impatient.

'Somewhere across the seas.' He shrugged plainly. 'Far enough to be a stranger. Close enough to be a slave still.' He paused. 'And the less said of that, the better.'

'Oh.' Magmaya fell silent, irritated. 'So how did you find the Divinicus then?'

'I travelled, I bargained.' He tossed his head from shoulder to shoulder. Sometimes, a man must kill to survive, and killing impresses the angels.'

'Keep your killing away from here,' Magmaya said. 'We've had enough of that.'

'Lord Rallun spoke of a siege,' he started. 'It was recent then?'

'Yes,' she admitted. 'I bloody fought in it.'

Kurulian frowned and asked, 'Did you...?' He dragged his finger across his throat.

She nodded.

'There's a certain knack to taking someone's life,' he replied. 'Some people wouldn't wish death on their worst enemy.'

'A knack?' she asked. 'It's this talk that makes me afraid of you.'

'Good,' he said. 'Our reputation wins half our wars for us.'

'I do hope this isn't one of your wars,' she mewled.

'No,' he said. 'You'd certainly know if it was, girl.' Kurulian smiled for what felt the first time, but as he did, his face seemed to twist, displaying an army of scars, hidden behind the wrinkles in his skin.

Magmaya wondered for a moment before stammering, 'If you're so good at killing people, then maybe you can help me.'

'How so?'

'There's someone I've set my sights on.'

'Oh?'

'We took prisoners after the siege,' she explained. 'One of them—well, there are personal stakes.'

'And your council wants them alive, I presume?'

'They want to ransom her back to the invaders.' Magmaya's head was growing warm just thinking about it. 'She was a traitor. She'll get away with her crimes.'

'Ransom her for what?'

'A small number of our men,' she explained.

Kurulian nodded. 'And you have no other prisoners?'

'A few. None like her, though.'

'You're their chancellor,' he remarked. 'It's *your* choice.'

'Is that supposed to make me feel better?' She scoffed. 'It doesn't matter. Fabius said that you were the truth, though. I thought you might've been able to help me.'

'Half the south prays to their Maiden Gods, the other half prays to us,' he remarked. 'Does that make us the truth?' As if in answer, he shrugged.

Magmaya sighed. 'I thought you might have some insight into what I'm going to do, not riddle me.'

'What are you going to do?'

'I don't know.'

'Then I can't help you.'

She grit her teeth, annoyed. The morning had left her exhausted. 'Fine. What would *you* do with her, then?'

He paused for a moment. And then he said, 'Break her.' The Divinicus glowered. 'Have your fun. There is nothing more thrilling than revenge. But after that, you must do what is best for your people.'

'I don't understand...'

'How many captives are you trading her for?' he asked.

'Four.'

'Then there are five lives you can save.'

'What?' Magmaya exclaimed, miserable. 'I can't quite believe what I'm hearing.'

'Because it's not what you want to hear,' he said.

'I wouldn't be able to live with myself if I let her go!'

'Neither would those captives.'

He was infuriating her. If she hadn't known any better, and if she'd had Moonbeam in hand, she would've lashed out. 'I couldn't do that,' she persisted. 'I couldn't stay and face the fact that across the Deadfields, the woman who defaced my family still lives. I'd never be able to show my face in the north again.' Magmaya paused, frustrated. 'Where's the furthest place south? The Silver City?'

'I wouldn't advise going there.'

'No, of course, you wouldn't,' she spat. 'You southerners wouldn't see me do anything that makes this a little easier.'

'Fine then,' he said. 'Kill the girl. Go south. But when you get there, don't expect to want to stay.'

'Oh, and why's that?' She cocked her head.

'Because your precious Silver City is no more,' he said like poison, and with that, it seemed as if the world had indeed ended.

Rallun had arranged a great feast to hail the coming of the angels that evening, with twelve courses each and a dining hall lit with the pyromancer's magnificent green fires. There were only two courses in the end (both under-cooked) after the famine the Mansel had brought about, and it had immediately become clear to Magmaya that the whole event was just another way for the Tyla to investigate the Divinicus more.

She speared her meat again and again and thrust it down her throat; she wasn't sure what animal it once had been, but she didn't care—it was sour and dry and made her gag, but that was the least of her worries.

Magmaya had been placed at the top of the table, as the chancellor always was, and on her left was Rallun, Siedous and the rest of her court, and on the other, Fabius and his cohort of angels sat. Beyond them, flocks of other dignitaries carried on until oblivion, like an endless stream of mirrors devouring their food.

'My chancellor, my chancellor, my chancellor!' they all chanted, and her wine started to taste like water. Whenever she took the knife to her meat, and it bled a little, she could only think of the scars that flocked Nurcia's face as she sat alone, rotting like a corpse in that dungeon, her words chiming in her ears: *He had his breeches down, I had to shoo him away. He said he wanted to fuck me.*

'In Inamorata, we have feasts like this often,' Fabius said, cutting into her thoughts. 'A hundred courses which last all day, until we're merry and can't drink anymore.'

'What happens if you get full after two courses?' she asked.

'We learn to stick our fingers down our throats,' he laughed and downed a glass of wine, gesturing to the servitor for another.

'Are things much different in the south?' she asked.

'Different, yes,' Fabius answered, setting his glass down, 'but I'm surprised by how many intricacies remind me of home.'

'Like what?'

'Your board meetings, your courtesies; even some of your architecture reminds me of the shanty towns in the Ash Wastes,' he finished. 'Oh—I meant no offence, my chancellor.'

'It's quite alright,' she said dryly. It wasn't the first insult he'd spoken of her home. Nor would it be the last, she was sure of that. 'We've recently been under siege. We're not quite what we used to be.'

'You should come to see our palace cities,' he remarked. 'They span on for dozens of miles. Towers are made from glass and ivory. Spires and arches plaster the skyline. I do think you might appreciate it.'

'Everyone dreams of going south,' she laughed, remembering that girl who'd prayed all those years ago for an angel to take her away. Her life was becoming stranger than her dreams. 'It's a long walk.'

Magmaya looked across the room, and for a moment, she thought she saw him again—the shadowed-eyed man—standing in an archway. When she looked back, though, he was gone.

'Would you excuse me for a moment?' she asked, feeling a chill catch the air.

'Of course, my chancellor.'

Magmaya stood, feeling all the chatter stop and each pair of eyes turn to her. She saw Kurulian's stricken face and Siedous' confused expression; she saw Rallun gesturing her to sit down and Fabius sitting back with a smile. She stole a breath and clanged her knife against a platter of greens, reached into her pocket and took out a small note; they were words she had prepared, intricate and precise—words that as soon as she spoke, would turn a thousand tongues against her.

'Orianne, Tyla...' she stuttered, feeling sweat amass under her arms. 'Inamorata...'

'Sit down!' she heard Rallun plea, but she turned away instead, stole and breath and opened her mouth to speak.

He had his breeches down, I had to shoo him away. He said he wanted to fuck me.

'After some long deliberation about Nurcia Vyce's fate, and in light of her recent confession, I have decided that she shall not be ransomed back to Mansel,' the chancellor explained. 'Instead, she shall be executed.'

Cries rang out about the room. She could almost feel Siedous and Rallun's scorn lash against her back. *They* didn't concern her, though. Instead, she glanced at Kurulian, only to watch him scowl. Disappointed, she turned back to her papers.

'In her place—' she continued, the crowd's shouts eclipsing her, 'the Mansel prisoners will be exchanged for our men. If I were given another choice, I would take it— but I will not stand for a traitor going unpunished.'

The table erupted into screams, cursing her every breath, and her head began to swim. Nurcia had been right—they would hate her more than they did her father.

'Tomorrow—tomorrow noon,' she spluttered, taking a short drink. 'That is when Nurcia Vyce will be executed. I want this matter finished with.'

Magmaya brushed her hand against the table, and with it, plates fell to the floor and shattered across her feet.

She was growing dizzy. The walls were caving in. Her ears were burning.

'My chancellor!' she heard as Siedous jumped to steady her. 'My chancellor...'

Magmaya's head was pounding. Her palms had broken her fall, but they were weeping with blood. Grit pressed into her cuts. Silverware skewered her knee.

And then, another tower of plates collapsed on top of her, and the room turned black as pitch.

The next she knew, the morning sun was shimmering through her window. And so, she rose and faced the day once more.

Eleven

It felt as if years had passed by the time Magmaya faced the angels again. She had hoped the hours apart might've lessened the blow, but all her council and the Divinicus did was stare at her, vacant. It seemed her decision had managed to make everyone in the palace her enemy.

Fabius shuffled in his seat, still wearing his signature smile, as Siedous and Rallun sat, spilling seas of tattered papers across the table. The Lord Commander clawed a few to himself and began to pour over them, searching for something.

'I apologise for the clutter.' Siedous frowned. 'Our late chancellor made quite the habit of trying to forget these times.'

She and the old knight hadn't spoken since Magmaya readjusted Nurcia's fate, but she couldn't back down anymore. She had made a declaration of the execution's time—midday after their talks were finished. Then at least, she could get Nurcia out of her head.

'I see,' Fabius said. 'You truly did keep everything, no?'

'It appears so,' Siedous replied. 'But I couldn't tell you a thing about them. When the Kytherans came, I was nothing to our chancellor but a lowly spearman of the realm. Chancellor Magmaya was a child, and Lord Black was far away. I'm afraid you're speaking to men on behalf of the dead.'

'It is very satisfactory,' Kurulian said, but his manner suggested otherwise.

The chatter droned on for a while before Siedous began to sort through the papers, reading them aloud and covering them in such detail Magmaya could scarcely stay awake. The old knight passed up speaking about the chiming trees and the height of the mountainside, but instead, an empire of handshakes and bows, pleas and smirks. In none of the texts was there an account of the woman who had mothered Albany; there were only tales of high lords and aristocrats with smoking pipes, knives and cloaks.

In one the transcripts, the Kytherans had spoken briefly of the Silver City and of a woman with scales of pure gold. It was said she had a mask of cloth that shielded her white eyes from the world and had brought peace to the south. They had referred to her as the Golden Woman, and from then on it seemed neither of the angels were willing to speak.

'There is a final clause,' Siedous finished, showing the wad of papers to the board. Although the writing was in black, Magmaya spied a smothering of red in each signature—blood no doubt. The old ways had never been kind to wrists and palms. '*Upon the declarations of today, we find* Kythera *and* Orianne *to be one, united in conquest,'* he read with a shrill murmur and sat himself down. Magmaya just thanked the heavens she didn't have to listen to another word.

'As I said,' Fabius began, 'the Kytherans never came here for warmth. They came here to make use of you.'

'Well, what does the chancellor have to say?' Kurulian asked her.

Magmaya stuttered, 'I don't think there's a verdict to be made.' Her eyes narrowed. 'We pledged ourselves to Kythera, whether they came here for warmth or not.'

'Ranvirus has been long enough without claim,' Fabius said. 'The Kytherans abandoned you. You're free to pledge yourselves again.'

'What if my people are not to pick a side?' Magmaya asked, forcing her thoughts back to the angels. *They're beautiful, yes, but we were warned not to trust them.*

Fabius giggled as if he was sharing a joke with himself. 'My dear chancellor, to not ally with the south is a death sentence in the wars to come.'

'The wars to come?' Rallun asked.

'You *have* been isolated,' Kurulian remarked. 'Before that vessel arrived here, Kythera pled severance from us, and we granted it until they chose a wicked emperor to rule over—'

'In mercy,' Fabius interrupted, 'we killed their emperor. But in return, they sent the Golden Woman. Some thought her a goddess.'

'A goddess?' Magmaya asked.

'She started a religion,' Kurulian said. 'Is that justification enough?'

'So, what happened to her?' Siedous asked with a smirk. 'Gods don't just fade away. Gods do not *die.*'

'This one did,' Fabius said, and silence took the boardroom like a cold knife. 'They still worship the corpse as if it were anything more than a dead woman with a halo. And ever since she died, Kythera and Inamorata have been on the verge of war.'

'I don't want to hear about her.' It was a lie, but Magmaya was growing frustrated with the angel's lack of transparency. 'I don't know what to make of any of this.'

'If I may,' Siedous interrupted, 'we don't even know *who* we're allying with.'

Fabius nodded, stole a piece of paper from the table's centre and began scratching away at it with a small quill. The sketch looked awfully familiar; Magmaya had seen something like it before when a small falling star had struck a far-off bay and left a near-perfect ring behind. In the centre, Fabius drew another string of land, isolated against the concaving mouth of the earth.

'This is Halo Blue,' the Divinicus explained. 'And this is Astralica, where the high lords rule from. If one was to stare out from the highest point, they would see for miles across the waves.' He paused. 'When the winter comes, the seas freeze over, and many pilgrim across from the Free Islands to my lands, just to revel in it all. Inamorata is made of a thousand shining cities, a hundred beautiful lands and countless loyal men. But far away, all alone and lost in the snow, there stands Orianne.'

'Don't be fooled by my Lord Commander's poetry,' Kurulian spoke up. 'Inamorata isn't a land of aristocrats. It's a beacon.'

'I'm not fooled,' Magmaya said. 'I want to know what would happen if war is to come.'

'The Divinicus would take levies,' Fabius explained. 'The Custodians of the Reaches are already marching farther south on outlying cities, but given enough time, they will come north. We hold a fragile balance in the continent, and Ranvirus isn't exempt from that.' He smiled.

'We already have our own war to fight,' Rallun remarked.

'If you do not ally with us in due course, the Reaches or the Kytherans will take the north with force,' Fabius asserted. 'In return for your loyalty, we will serve as a barrier against any further invasion.'

'We've got a barrier,' Siedous said. 'Hundreds of miles of mountains and ice lie between you and me. Why do you think we were never able to travel south?'

'Have you forgotten the seas?' Fabius asked.

'I don't care. I won't be forced to fight in someone else's war,' Magmaya protested. 'We can scarcely hold our own ground here.'

'So be it,' Fabius purred. 'Sit alone in the cold—it's no matter to me. The fire will take you all in the end.'

Magmaya wasn't quite sure who fired the first blow, but a moment later, it seemed as if all hells had broken loose. Shouts and roars were lurched across the boardroom, as Siedous and Rallun began to call profanity at the angels. In response, Fabius' eyes blazed, all while Kurulian sat back and watched as if he were bored.

She turned away, sparing glances at the scribes who looked frightened and intrigued all at once, desperately trying to scratch away the happenings before them. She looked back to the stoic knight beside her, not so stoic any longer, as his face burned deep red. And then she glanced at Fabius, the fiery angel, clawing at the very paper which he had so delicately drawn upon. The voices had begun to twist into something malign. The room became alight. The hail outside turned to rain.

'Enough!' Magmaya called, louder than any of them, something primal rising up inside of her. The room fell silent and, in that moment, she was above them all; she was the scared little girl turned snake. 'I've made my damned decision.'

The rain hammered down on the palace grounds and washed the freshly fallen snow into the gutters. It was just outside the forest where Albany had been found, where the earth was a mess of broken copper artefacts and muddied grass. Crooked stones encircled them, growing darker in the rain, all while the Orianne and Tyla banners snapped in the wind above.

All the palace had come to watch, but Magmaya hadn't allowed any of the common folk in—Nurcia had threatened to spill her secrets to the crowds, so the least she could've done was control who heard them. But there were still more than enough people present to ruin her, each unkempt and wet as if the wind was going to toss them aside at a moment's notice. The angels had taken their leave, but the rest of the palace just stood and stared, sombre faces paving a clearing through the overgrowth of weed.

Magmaya watched the rain fall as she stood under the shelter of the tent, her podium outside beneath the wrath of the storm. And in the puddles, the headsman stood in black, save for a mask of golden roses that covered his eyes, ears and mess of red hair.

There was an undeniable quietness about the air too, despite the hammering rain. Even the birds had fallen silent. That was until the screeching of geese turned the heads of several scribes as they looked about the grounds.

'Wouldn't it be unfortunate if one of them shat on her head?' She heard someone laugh a little too loudly. What *her* they were referring to, Magmaya didn't know, but the day was growing grimmer by the moment, that much was certain. None of her men were talking, and Rallun's men had withdrawn themselves, lurking away in the corners of the field.

'We'll all be drowned by the time this is done with,' someone else grumbled. 'The least I could ask for is the headsman to miss once or twice.'

'She's here,' she saw a warden mouth from across the yard. He nudged the sleeping Ceremonia beside him, who stirred and stood.

'Orianne and, uh… others,' he said. 'We bring forth the traitor.'

There was a squelching amid the mud and grass as the palace guard's armour shimmered through the treetops. There were three of them, Magmaya noted; three holding one chained prisoner, bruised and carrying that face she had taken so much pleasure in scarring.

Nurcia still looked beautiful, though; that's what bothered Magmaya the most. She was wearing a silk and white dress. Its hem was already wet with mud, and her shoes were blackened with soil. She had a silky blindfold across her eyes as well, as she stammered through the swathes of sodden earth where the milky-brown puddles swallowed her.

Slowly, they led the traitor to the centre of the field where the stone circle stood. Executions had taken place there for as long as Magmaya remembered—they had once been tombstones, weathered and forgotten by time. Now they were just remembrancers of all the widows they had made.

The scribes began to chatter among themselves; the scratching of their inks on their unwritten tomes filled the silence as they recorded each uneasy breath and each cough about the crowd.

A priest stepped forward and cupped Nurcia's back, making a short prayer to the nameless gods before deciding it was time. The traitor's handmaidens were crying, throwing themselves at whatever they could lash their tears upon, and though Nurcia seemed calm, as the headsman lowered her neck onto one of the stones, her lips were undoubtedly quivering.

'Vargul Tul was right to have come here,' Nurcia began, voice trembling. 'Look at yourselves—public execution? You know nothing of honour.'

'Your honour didn't save Albany,' Magmaya said as she stepped up to the podium, stomach fluttering. 'Nor Kaladeous, nor any of the others.' She paused. 'Bow your head, Miss Vyce.'

'There was no honour in murdering my life, my god,' she wept.

Magmaya ignored her and took a deep breath, coughed and read off the scroll before her.

'Nurcia Vyce of Orianne,' she said, and the rain filled her hair and drenched her furs, 'you have been tried and have confessed to the murder of Albany Moore, the murder of Kaladeous Garneth, conspiring against Orianne, coercion with the Mansel, and the desecration of Rache

Vorr. In sight of the nameless gods, your life shall pay the price for your crimes. Do you have anything to say?'

'Whatever happens,' she had said to the headsman, *'after her last words, you are to take her head off.'* Magmaya was savouring the moment he would.

Nurcia finished her prayer and said, 'My hearing isn't what it used to be, my chancellor. Would you repeat the verdict?'

Magmaya sighed, her heart drumming. *Just get it bloody over with,* she thought and said again, 'You have been tried and have confessed to the murder of Albany Moore, the murder of Kaladeous Garneth, conspiring against Orianne, coercion with the Mansel, and the desecration of Rache Vorr.' Her throat was aching. 'In sight of the nameless gods, your life shall pay the price for your crimes. Do you have anything to say?'

'Thank you, though I must apologise for the confusion,' Nurcia finished as the headsman crept forward. 'I never confessed to maiming Rache, my chancellor.'

Magmaya's eyes grew wide. Her stomach was twitching as she reached out her stiff fingers to the headsman. The officials about the ground were shuffling about, shouts of confusion echoing, but the executioner was still moving. *He can't hear her!* she realised.

The headsman raised the axe into the heavens and hammered it down through Nurcia Vyce's neck.

She could almost see a smile form on her lips when her head rolled away, and in Magmaya, a bottomless pit grew, and her vision glowed red, her head turned dizzy, and the world collapsed around her.

'What was due has been done,' the crowds said, confused, but Magmaya wasn't listening. She felt her chest grope at her lungs as she strode back through the mud, away from the bloody mess that had once been Nurcia Vyce and through the light of the braziers as they finally died in the rain.

'Siedous, I've made a mistake,' she cried.

'I know.' He stroked his chin, and she watched the small hairs brush about his fingers, grey and tattered. 'Most of the palace was there to see it.'

'What do I do, then?' Magmaya yelled.

'There is nothing more to do, the traitor is dead,' he said. 'Whether she confessed to maiming your brother or not doesn't mean she wasn't incriminated enough. It matters not.'

She looked out the window of the boardroom and watched the snow sail through the wind. At last, she was permitted to be alone again, but her stomach was in knots, and there was a ringing in her ears that just wouldn't cease. She couldn't have been alone if she wanted to.

'It does.' Magmaya scowled. 'I was meant to keep her alive until she confessed to it. Now she will never be remembered for what she did to Rache—she got away with it. As far as the world is concerned, the bitch is innocent. That bloody headsman!'

'*You* know she is guilty, my chancellor, is that not enough?'

'No,' she stammered. 'One day I will die, and with me, time will forget. Half of those I tell won't believe me and the other half will be forgotten too. The only way to remember her treachery is to record it—or gods forbid, live forever.' She laughed at the thought.

'Perhaps she is better forgotten,' Siedous suggested. 'Is that not a great enough punishment?'

'If she is forgotten, then surely Rache will be too…' she murmured. 'And with him, me, you, Albany. Gods, it feels like I'm already dead.'

'My chancellor—' he put his hand to her back, but she pulled herself away.

'I don't know what to do.' Magmaya sighed. 'I don't even know how to lead—I'm going to my quarters. I need to sleep.'

It was a lie, of course. If she ever managed to get herself to sleep, it would be a miracle. Whenever she closed her eyes, all she saw was Nurcia, and she feared it would be like that for a very long while.

'If you'd wait a minute,' Siedous said and started over to a drawing desk. He returned a moment later, hands full, and crouched beside her on the threadbare carpet, placing a wooden board down beside him.

'What are you doing?' she asked with almost a laugh. 'What's that?'

'Sit,' he said, so she did, and though she couldn't help but think of the bloodstains about the floor, they were becoming less real in her mind. It was getting easier. 'It's a playing board,' he said. 'The Kytherans left it behind for Nurcia but considering what happened…' he trailed off.

'And why are you showing me this now?'

Siedous produced a small velvet bag from beneath the board, unlaced it, and shook it about. A number of carved metal pieces tumbled out onto the floor, and one by one, he picked them up and began arranging them about the hexagonal squares on the board, sometimes second-guessing himself, but eventually satisfied.

'Apparently, this game is commonplace all over the south,' he answered after a while. 'I can't take you there, I'm afraid, nor can I take your brother to the Cold Seas. But I can give you this.'

'And what's this?' she asked, bewildered.

'An hour,' he said. 'An hour to see you laugh again, and then we can forget this ever happened. Not a damper on your pride.'

She smiled. 'Please stop, Kharon Vorr was never one for...'

'Emotion, I know. But I'm not Kharon Vorr,' he shrugged.

'A compelling argument.' She caught herself laughing—perhaps it was enough already. 'How do you play?'

'I'll show you,' he said and plucked a piece between two fingers, moved it four hexagons forward, and three diagonally. 'It's simple enough to start with,' he explained. 'There are two different sides: the *weeping veils* and the *laughing veils.* When my weeping piece moves, it can place it up to seven places however I like.'

'And whatever am *I* to do?'

'Copy me,' he said. 'I've spent years playing on my own.'

They carried on well into the evening, and the more she played, the more she understood. Each time she took one of Siedous' pieces, she was able to move another of hers; in time she found herself manoeuvring around his backlines and taking his *weeping lord.* Half of her pieces got knocked down in retaliation, but she carried on until the conversation strayed.

Siedous began telling her of the first woman he'd kissed before his father had thrown him out and he'd clawed his way to the palace. She'd been seventeen and him fifteen, and her tongue had tasted like sugar, he told her, and her neck even more so.

He told her how not long after he'd come of age, the chancellor had held a great feast and even the commoners had been invited. He told her how a nameless shadow of a man had appeared, slept with half the guests, and disappeared.

He told her there had been another great feast under Kharon to welcome the coming of the southerners all those years ago, and how between meals they had played the same game. He told her how it was that evening he'd been made a knight and how it had been the last time he'd ever drunk. He told her he'd been so happy then—happier still when a maid across the moonlit hall had told him how bold he looked in his tunic. Happier still when he'd gone home that night, tired and weary and warm.

Though after all of it was said, he'd been happiest when he'd given Magmaya her first wooden sword and watched her strike down that metal scarecrow again and again into the frozen cornfields. She caught herself laughing at that.

It was only once the stories had stopped that the game did too, and Siedous counted up his pieces, and Magmaya hers.

'Beginner's luck,' he said as she stood, and began clearing the game back into the bag. 'I bid you a good sleep, Magmaya.'

'Thank you,' she nodded. 'And you, Siedous. I'll see you on the morrow. Maybe then we can be free of these angels, and I'll be able to think a little clearer.' She paused for a moment. 'You never did tell me what the game was called—?'

'*The Lamentation of Fates,*' he said with a smile and put the board away. 'Invented by a man who just wanted to laugh at the world. I'll see you tomorrow.'

On her way back to her chambers, she kissed Rache and hummed him to sleep as he lay, unbeknownst to the day's happening. But no matter what she did, no matter the game, Magmaya couldn't forget. When she crawled back under her sheets, they were cold and wet, and in all the shadows that sprung across the walls, there was Nurcia, kneeling and denouncing her confession.

It was then she realised she'd been wrong—the Divinicus weren't the truth; they hadn't a clue what to do. But then again, perhaps they just didn't care for any northern matter. How many more would insist on coming to her home and leaving her in the dark?

As if in answer, as she tossed and turned, Magmaya felt something prickle her ears and scratch at her neck. Her heart was ringing with fear as if someone had come for her, but as she dragged herself up in a cold sweat and ruffled her hand beneath her pillow, she found the culprit, sharp and icy.

Magmaya curled her fingers and tugged it out, finding herself with a tattered paper, old and torn as if it had been weathered by all of time. She unfurled it and poured herself over its contents, feeling her hands tremble against the cold.

> *My chancellor,*
> *Meet me alone in the forest after dusk.*
> *Don't tell a soul.*
> *Xx*

Magmaya tossed it aside, but her mind insisted on racing. Who could it have been? Rallun? Siedous? But why would they need to meet her in secret? Fabius or the Divinicus? The angels were under strict supervision; Magmaya had assured they were under curfew. She could hardly fathom going out alone to face some horror of the night. In the pit of her stomach, she imagined seeing her father there, or Albany or Nurcia, growing from the rose thorns and throwing her into the pond.

But then, a moment later, Magmaya found herself out of her nightgown and sporting leathers and furs. She stole a glance out her window, and as expected, found a pair of guards striding back and forth amidst the falling snow. Beyond that, she could make out nothing, save for a few burning braziers lit in the city below, where merry men would steal themselves an ale and a sell-maiden, and travel back to the pleasure houses in the Seventh Quarter. Farther across, the mountains stood tall, and an army of trees waited, swaying softly in the cold wind.

She slunk to the corridors, tip-toeing as she closed each door with a whisper behind her before moving to the sculleries. Magmaya turned away from the rows of wine which besieged her from every direction, wrestled herself beneath columns of ribbed spoons that shimmered under the thin candlelight, and stole towards the door in the corner.

A single key hung lank from beside it, so Magmaya pulled it from its place and drove it through the keyhole. She had to remind herself that guards rarely patrolled at the back of the palace and low and behold, she found herself alone as she stepped out beneath the moonlit sky.

She found the Silver Mountainside humming above her like the goliaths of old, and she felt a shiver cross her spine before retreating to the sculleries.

Magmaya ruffled through the drawers, like a bird pecking at its own feathers, until she found a large carving knife and forced it through her back pocket. The weight in her coat and the cold in her hand reassured her—enough to find the courage to carry on.

And as the chancellor did, she followed the trail into her forest as she'd done a thousand times before; trees sprouted from the ground like wraiths at her throat, their spindly fingers reaching for the moon. But the farther Magmaya found herself from the palace, the more they became one with her, and their hailing became her calling. Roses tickled her bare ankles as she walked, and the crunching snow beneath her feet began to calm her so that she loosened her grip on the knife and traced her way through the intricate dark, smiling.

But then, a voice called out from behind, and Magmaya Vorr froze.

Twelve

It wasn't the first time she'd reached for a weapon in the forest. But it was the first time she found one.

It bit at her hands as she struck at the trees and moonbeams, drawing not a drop of blood, save for the silence of the night. And the night remained silent until footsteps echoed from behind her—a heavy crunch amid the skin of the frost.

'Who's there?' Magmaya called, though her voice was faltering.

'Put that bloody thing away,' the voice said.

'Kurulian.' At last, she recognised the voice, but she found herself gripping the carving knife harder still.

'Drop it,' he said. 'And I'll do the same.' He gestured to the blade at his hip. He was fully armoured, and despite the lack of light, Magmaya was able to make out a myriad of terrible trinkets pinned to his breastplate. 'Drop it.' He gave her a sideways glance.

The chancellor did as he demanded, and the carving knife fell into the snow with a light thump. And as promised, Kurulian followed suit.

'I know I shouldn't have had you come out here,' he said curtly. 'And I know it's cold but—'

'How did you get out? You're under curfew,' she cut in. 'My heart nearly burst...'

'No guard is as sharp as their master boasts.'

'Then I suppose I'll have to find new guards,' Magmaya remarked. She paused for a moment. 'So *why* are we out here?'

'It's quiet,' Kurulian admitted. 'I began strolling about the grounds earlier today. You can hear every whisper, every chime. But I presume you already know that.'

'This isn't your place,' Magmaya spat, 'your kind isn't allowed here.' *Only I am,* she reminded herself. She'd heard terrible stories of what her forest had once been a hundred years ago—a witch's place—a cursed place. That didn't matter to her, though.

'My kind?'

She ignored him. 'Why are you even armoured? I do hope you're not going to kill me.'

'No.' His answer didn't much relieve her.

'So why *are* you here?'

'You wanted to talk to the Divinicus.'

'What?'

'I heard you tell Lord Black. After you returned from the execution.'

'I remember,' she admitted. Magmaya *had* said it; the Tyla had been pestering her and well… Her thoughts trailed off. 'There's a better time for this.'

'There's no better time than when the moon is ripe with colours. People tend to be more honest at night.' Kurulian gazed up. 'Is this about your decision in the boardroom?'

Magmaya smiled and shook her head.

An animal shrieked through the night—something between the call of a bird and the low baying of a wolf. Magmaya shuddered, and even Kurulian began to look around with a sort of trepidation. He fingered the snow and found his blade, though he seemed hesitant to sheath it.

'In truth, I did have a request of you,' Magmaya admitted after her heart had stopped trembling. 'I was going to ask your Lord Commander, but I think I know what his answer will be.'

'I feel like your rejection of our alliance was enough to halt any goodwill he might have had for you,' Kurulian said. 'But go on.'

'You're not like him, though,' she grumbled. 'But I'm scared your price will be an extortion.'

'There's only one coin of worth,' he answered plainly.

'I've heard about your Blood Sovereigns,' Magmaya said. 'I'm not a bountiful chancellor. I have little in the way of money to offer you.'

'Money isn't what I want,' Kurulian groaned.

'Well, I'm not giving you my body.' She covered herself.

'I don't want your body, either,' he said. 'But do go on. Soon enough, the sun will rise, and we'll be two fools standing about in a field.'

'I tell myself I don't want it.' She sighed. 'But I know I do. And I'm scared that soon I'll need it more than anything in the world.'

'And what's that?'

'You have to take me south.'

'The only coin of worth is *information*,' Kurulian explained. 'And even that isn't sufficient for what you want.'

'I thought as much.' Magmaya looked away. There was an ache in her chest telling her she was about to cry. 'I just wanted the soft grass between my feet,' she said, frowning. 'Do you know how cold it is here? I wanted the sun to beat down on my back, and I wanted to feel the warm sea against my skin. I'm trapped in the north. I need you to help me escape.'

'These people are yours to govern,' he reminded her, 'and they need you far more than you need any warm sea. Rallun has already declared for your city against the Mansel, no? Then you must lead them.' He paused. 'I'll be on my way.'

'I can't,' she called. 'All my life I've been told it is not a woman's place to rule—they're right. I'm only the chancellor before my brother because of his damned legs. Besides, you probably heard what happened today at the execution.'

'Yes, we all did.' He nodded. 'I presume you wish you hadn't killed her now. You made the mistake of not listening to me. Don't worry, you'll learn in time.'

Magmaya fell silent and watched him saunter away, holding the blade tight against his hip. Soon enough, he became a shadow amongst the trees. The strange animal sound called again, and she sighed, dropped to her knees and picked up the half-buried carving knife.

But then, a sudden strength rose in her.

'Kurulian!' Magmaya called, and her voice echoed about the mountains, sending a small flock of birds flying from the trees and into the embrace of the moon.

'What?' he replied duly.

'I have information.' She made her way over to him, pleading. *I can't remember the last time I pleaded,* she realised. *What a pathetic thing I've become.*

'I've heard much of what you people have to say.' Kurulian turned. 'And much of it bores me half to death.'

'Then what *do* you want to hear?' she asked.

'When I say information, I mean there is a chain of whispers that spans the world,' he explained. 'The chain acts as the eyes and ears of anyone who needs it. Fabius' handmaidens use it, the children of Rallocier use it, and I do too.'

'I don't understand.'

'Allow me an example. There are a hundred people dining together,' he said. 'One of them wants to kill you—which one?'

'How would I know?'

Kurulian shrugged. 'As you dine, you notice one of the more drunken guests at your table has switched places with someone at the bottom of the court. In the place of one of your advisors sits some low-born you've never met. What now?'

'He's the killer?' she asked. 'He made my advisor drunk so he could get closer to me?'

Kurulian shook his head. 'The advisor who left simply had an upset stomach, and the low-born saw an empty seat and took it. But there is a man two seats across from you wearing chain-mail.'

'So, it's him?'

'He's one of your knights.' Kurulian grinned. 'Anyway, the first course starts, and you're served your food; the meat is a little raw, and the vegetables are dry, so you wash it down with...?'

'Wine?'

'Wine, white wine.' He nodded. 'Vintage from the Summerlands, sour and perhaps even drier than the food. But that's the least of your concerns. By the end of the first course, you're dead.'

'That's not fair,' she grumbled.

'Of course, it's not. Now how did you die?'

Poison?

'Poison.'

He nodded. 'Your advisor *did* have an upset stomach.'

'So, who killed me?'

'It's a little late to be wondering that now.'

She shook her head, irritated, and asked, 'What does all of this mean?'

'Information is a peculiar form of currency, but a just one,' said Kurulian. 'When the children of Rallocier want to know which slaver they're about to be auctioned to, they look to the chain of whispers. Perhaps they find out they can escape to the north—to a faraway land called

Ranvirus. Where's Ranvirus? What's it like? Not a soul knows, it seems. I thought you may be able to help with that.'

'Why me?'

'Because you're the chancellor of this bloody place.'

Magmaya sighed and perched on the stump of a small tree. It stung to sit, but she hadn't an ounce of strength left to stand. The day had worn that from her.

'The least wine ever did was poison me,' she heard herself say.

'Your father was the last chancellor here, no?' Kurulian asked.

She nodded.

'Tell me about him.'

Magmaya felt something rise in her—a desire to spill all her secrets at once. She was disappointed in herself; she'd worked so hard to preserve them; she'd killed a man to keep them.

No, she was forced to remind herself. *That's not why you executed him.* It didn't matter why, though, anymore. She was becoming deathly afraid of what dawn would bring if she wasn't to speak another word.

'I never liked Kharon Vorr,' she said at last.

'More,' Kurulian barked.

'He never liked me.' She was flustered.

'More.'

'I was there when he died.'

'More.'

'He wanted to kill me.'

'*More.*'

Don't say it, she told herself, *don't you bloody say it,* but her mouth was betraying her. 'I killed him first,' she sputtered at last, and then it was done.

Not for Kurulian, though. When he leaned forward and asked, 'Why did you stop?' her heart must've shattered again.

Don't say it! She wished she could've screamed, but that bloody broken heart was betraying her. She could almost feel it already: the warm grass between her toes, the sun lashing at her back, the salt-water in her hair. She was already going south, she just had to finish her plea.

Magmaya stole a breath and felt the words spill from her mouth. She let them spill a little more and didn't let them finish until she saw the quicksilver in the Divinicus' eyes. She didn't finish until the birds flocked back to the trees to nestle their young. She didn't finish until she'd confessed her every last sin, both that she'd committed and had been committed against her.

She didn't finish until the moon inside her began to rot.

Yellow clouds faded across the mountaintops. The newly broken waters were illuminated with streaks of shattered light.

It was the time of year that Ranvirus didn't seem desolate at all; it was the time of year Magmaya could watch the sunrise for as long as it permitted her. But she hadn't any time now, it was leaving her as quickly as the colours were drained from the skies. The angels were going, and so was the moonlight, but perhaps worst of all, Rache was sitting with her at the foot of the mountain, watching the river swell beneath the broken bridge with a smile that could've melted the stars. Second worst, she hadn't died in her sleep.

'I love you Rache,' she said and pulled herself away. She didn't dare watch the bronze light shimmer in his pupils.

'You too.' He beamed, though after a moment his smile dropped. 'You look sad, Magmaya.'

'No, no,' she replied, 'of course not. What makes you say that?'

He shrugged. 'Your eyes. You look tired, too.'

'I am,' she admitted. 'I wish I could sleep forever.'

But if I did, the world would pass me by, she realised, and a gnawing in her stomach began eating at her, threatening to never leave.

'Perhaps sleep isn't the answer,' she murmured, 'perhaps I just need time alone.'

Rache looked to the horizon, and she followed suit. There was a light glow from beyond the mountains that could've only come from one thing, and Magmaya's eyes began to water at the thought of it. Streams of tears cut at her cheeks. The sunlight was hurting her eyes, but she didn't care. Time was fleeting, falling head over heels. It was running through her fingers like sand on a shore.

At last, the sun rose, and daylight broke across the heavens. The moon faded from a great, pearly goliath to a thin reminder of the night, and the orange beams of newly born light became one with the blue-grey clouds.

Birds began to chirp as if an invisible symphony had arisen around the pair and engulfed the mountainside in something of a boreal cacophony. She thought back to Siedous, wishing her well as she groaned to him, and realised it was the last time she'd see the old knight. *It's for the best*, she told herself. Besides, there weren't any words she could've strung together that might've been able to say 'goodbye'.

He had fathered her, and she had left him, though, but it was as all offspring did. It was the legacy of fathers to give their blood for their children, and maybe her time leaving was long overdue; that's what she told herself anyway. Maybe Siedous had buried his duty and given his blood long ago.

Neither she or Rache spoke a word as Magmaya carried him back to the palace, past a thicket of guards and into his cradle. The candles that had once hung above had melted to thick yellow stumps, and it seemed that after long last, the leaves he'd collected had turned to ash and strewn themselves across the bed. She laid him there and left a final kiss upon his cheek before taking her leave without so much as another glance.

She buttoned her jacket, strung her satchel and made her way across the balconies which ran along the city's prow. There, she was able to make out the chatter from the early risers, wipe the dew from her eyes, cock her neck and carry on across countless flights of stairs and through columns of prying scribes as they begged for some kind of detail of the angel's departure. But Magmaya just let them brush past her and ambled onwards, through the fog-stricken streets and over the broken bridges that made her home.

That was when she found Kurulian, sheltered by the broken draping from an abandoned kindler's stall. He was armoured again, but this time he wore thick crème robes atop his iridescent plate, inscribed with delicate angel's wings.

'You're late,' he barked with that leathery-silky voice of his. 'No later than daybreak, I said.'

'I had people to see.'

Kurulian grunted and gestured her away.

The chancellor of Orianne followed him through the streets as a new sky began to form overhead. She watched as the common folk emerged from their homes, beginning their usual tedious routine, and Magmaya covered herself with her furs. But they weren't interested in her.

Despite moving in guise, it didn't take them long to clear the inner city, but the journey ahead threatened to go on for half an age, and the thought of it was making Magmaya's eyes shrill. It was a sickly morning, in truth.

Quickly enough, they reached the outskirts of the city and then the gate. Every few hundred yards, a sentinel stood tall and silent, looking across the Deadfields and into the cold beyond. Once they reached a gateway, Kurulian struck his fist against the stone, catching the attention of one of the guards.

'What?' he spat.

'I want to return to the shore,' the angel replied.

'And the girl?'

'Mine.' His voice almost made her shudder.

'Will you return within the hour?'

'No.'

The guard licked his lips as if deep in thought but sighed all the same, raising the gate enough for them to step out into the cold. And as they did, Magmaya felt a chill run through her like Kharon's ghost was still forbidding her to leave. She found herself sparing a glance back to the city and felt almost as if it was yearning for her. But she was too far gone to be swayed by a breeze.

Magmaya sighed wistfully and looked up for a moment. 'I am craven?' she asked the angel. 'For doing this?'

Kurulian frowned. 'You're bolder than most,' he admitted. 'Now eyes down, head up,' the Divinicus commanded, and she did as she was told, bowing before him. 'We've a long walk ahead.'

The angel's departure had been almost as revered as their arrival. Hundreds had gathered in the streets so they, at last, had a chance to shout their praise or hatred (it couldn't be for sure unanimous). Siedous and Rallun had stood together at the city gate as the chancellor had reported falling ill in the early hours of the morning, taking to the mountainside for quiet air, all while the roaring of the crowds and the shimmering of the Divinicus' armour carried on into the skies. Before long, the angels strode from Orianne and back across the mountains.

The girl watched as Fabius and the angels made their way into the entrails of *The Golden Damnation,* and as they did, the custodians and slavers worked tirelessly to tend to their every need, rearranging the clockwork in hope it would ignite the craft's ancient furnaces.

A flurry of men rushed around, but Kurulian and Fabius lingered behind as another pair of Divinicus arrived before them, garbed in lavish robes.

'Lord Commander.' One of them bowed.

She watched Fabius nod and pass the pair, wandering off to find his solitude. Kurulian, on the other hand, murmured something and turned. He made his way back over to her and closed the grimy doors behind him.

Magmaya pulled herself from her cupboard in the corner of the room and turned to him, brushing back her hair.

'Take a step outside, and Fabius will open you from hip to throat,' he thundered. After she looked to him, perturbed, he sighed and said, 'A halo doesn't make you an angel.'

He left without so much as another word, and Magmaya groaned, threw herself back against the cold, iron floor and listened to the hums and whirs as they drummed beyond.

She peered out again, finding the hall to be empty, save a few slavers, and without another thought, forced the doors open. None of the workers hazarded anything more than a disdainful glare, and Magmaya caught herself smiling. She quickly found herself in the belly of *The Golden Damnation*, ambling through a string of chambers and examining the seals and mirrors.

There was a burst of steam, and then there was a jolt as the floor seemed to give way beneath her; but in truth, it was Ranvirus that did. Magmaya found her footing and scampered across the cabin, clinging to the walls.

She escaped into an annexe, to a pair of arched windows complete with broken glass and flickering oil lamps which hung over her like waiting vultures. Patchwork clouds fluttered above, swallowing up the vessel's broadsides. She began to feel atop the skies, flying, flying, faster, faster.

There was something nagging at her still, though—some grim reminder to stay true to the girl who had prayed in the forest that day. But how could she be anything less than an angel here? Less than a goddess?

A worker rushed past, murmuring something of furnaces being ignited, 'Blazing greater than before,' and Magmaya turned back to the windows, and through the dark silt and black ichor that clung to the glass, she saw the vessel rumble about the waves and heard it groan beneath her.

It was as if a cathedral was carving its way through the seas, complete with spires and brass domes like a swelling painting. And in it, there was a choir of angels singing about the waves.

A halo doesn't make you an angel, Magmaya was forced to remind herself; she knew the words were true. And as the world disappeared behind her, she felt herself smile. It felt as if everything was to fade away from around her: Orianne, the mountains and even the Divinicus. *A halo doesn't make you an angel, no,* she thought, but the Divinicus might've well been.

Magmaya turned and watched the seas lap up the land, the clouds devour the sky and the sun eclipse the stars. And then she saw it: a faint shimmering in the corner of her eye. She forced her gaze back to the mountains, and then to the trees as they chimed and called and sang for her to come home.

~*Part Two*~

Thirteen

Small balls of lint rose to the surface of the white broth, but Magmaya downed it all the same. Dying from poisoning felt preferable to dying from hunger, and besides, it was the eleventh ration Kurulian had brought her—she could only presume she was safe now. Coincidently, her meals were the only way she was able to count the days on *The Golden Damnation,* for the light was bleak and broken, and the sun seemed to be hiding from her.

The food reeked of oil and grease and tasted like it too—but that was becoming the least of her worries; the instant Kurulian had found her at the windows and locked her away again, she had convinced herself he was trying to kill her. Silver glimmers shot around when she dozed, and golden faces faded the moment she awoke.

Sleep was a strange encounter to come across too; occasionally, it permitted her in waves and troughs, but once in a blue moon, when the sun was burning bright, she felt the world settle beneath her and the warmth flush against her skin. Being awake was equally as strange, though; it was a flash of colours and heavy nausea. None of it made any sense.

Orianne had become a dream, and she hated forgetting her dreams; Magmaya was beginning to fear more than ever that perhaps one day Rache would fade from her memory too. Once, she could've never imagined a day without him, but here she was and though it hurt her to remember, forgetting would kill her. There was no looking back, no up or down; there was just the bleak silence of whatever lay beyond those thick iron walls, bleached with rust.

That was until one morning, light came trailing through small cracks in the door and burned away the dark like fire to a curtain of insects. Magmaya looked up from the corner, from where she had keeled over like an unborn child, and found an angel standing before her.

'Kurulian...?' she stuttered and found her voice hoarse and dry. She traced the outline of his flowing garb and shimmering hair, but the figure didn't reply, save for the shake of a head.

Quicker than she could comprehend, a pair of things (she called them that for they had no faces) rushed forward from the wall of light. She screamed as a nest of arms grappled for her own and pulled her to her feet, metal giving way beneath her blistered toes. The *things* were the only reason she found the strength to stand, though; her newfound body was weak and broken. And by the time her head was forced up to face the light, there was Fabius standing tall in the warm glow.

'You?' He was entirely unimpressed, that much was obvious.

'You...?' she spat back.

'Why did you say my Legatus' name?'

'I thought it was him.' Magmaya coughed. Her head was pounding with visions that weren't hers, and when they finally faded, a chill forced her to face the Divinicus again.

'Who brought you the food?' It was clear the angel was enraged, and yet, he kept a temperament about him like unbroken water. He was beginning to remind her of Vargul Tul.

'I... I....' she spluttered some more, desperately trying to untangle her words, 'stole it.'

'Lies.' Fabius' voice came like a knife to her lips, threatening to cut her where her skin was weak. She almost felt herself fall apart before him.

'My lord,' a third voice cut through the veil of light, and Magmaya's ears perked up. Fabius spared a glance back and watched Kurulian amble through. 'Who's she?' he asked, and Magmaya froze, cold with fear.

'The chancellor of Orianne,' Fabius explained, raising an eyebrow.

Kurulian nodded to himself, looking to her as if she was nothing but some distant memory. 'She's of no consequence to me, my lord.' He curtsied and turned, and Magmaya felt her blood boil.

He left me for dead! After everything, he hadn't stood for her?

'What are you doing here, girl?' Fabius asked at last.

Magmaya was too unsettled to reply; words were foaming at her mouth and dribble was abandoning her lips. She felt her palms quiver.

'I came here the morning before you left,' she pleaded. 'No one knew, I was alone, I—'

'Don't play me for a fool,' he cut in. 'Nothing you did in the north was without cause. The same here, you think you stowed away without some ill intent?'

'I—'

'Get her a drink,' Fabius interrupted, and the thrall things obliged, dropping her to the floor.

They returned rather quickly and forced a glass between her fingers. Its contents were black like unbroken pitch, but she drunk it all the same, wincing as she did.

When she was done, Magmaya tossed the rest aside and looked up to Fabius with the eyes of a lost child. 'Am I in hell?'

'Perhaps.' The angel shrugged. He folded his arms into his chest. 'Depends on your sins, girl.'

'If I confess them, then can I leave?' she asked. Her head was dizzy. She felt as if she was going to collapse.

'You're black as soot.' He ignored her, but whatever was in place of an answer came with the smile that looked like the angel that had come all those lives ago, when he had been but a dream, rising from the seas.

'This place has been rather unforgiving,' Magmaya admitted.

'You were a fool for coming here.'

'I couldn't stay there any longer,' she protested. 'I'd made a mistake. I'd made too many mistakes. I couldn't go on like that, Fabius.'

'We've had people like you before,' he groaned. 'Stowaways, merchants and the like. You've abandoned your people, chancellor.'

'They'll govern better without me,' she said. 'They're safer now.'

'You chose to distance the north from us. What makes you think I will vouch for you after you renounced my people?'

'I don't need you to vouch for me.' The mere suggestion was making her uneasy. 'But there was no other way to escape—I—'

'I'm not taking you back,' the angel asserted.

'I didn't expect you to,' Magmaya murmured. 'I did—'

'Then you shouldn't have expected safe passage south,' he thundered. 'It is not a wench's right to stowaway. I still don't understand exactly what you hoped to find here.'

Neither did she, in truth, but her mouth answered for her. 'Anything but the cold,' she stuttered. 'I killed a woman I shouldn't have. I was in no position to carry on there.'

'You wanted to represent your people here, then?' he asked. 'Take our land instead?'

Magmaya scoffed. It was all she could do not to laugh. 'I don't want to rule over anything,' she wailed.

'I once thought like you.' He smirked. 'But I embraced what I did. I was not craven.'

'I couldn't do that,' she murmured. She wanted to hit him. 'I couldn't misguide my city any longer.'

Much to her surprise, Fabius nodded, and she caught him staring her up and down, from her ashen feet to her black nails. Even more to her surprise, he said, 'My men will see that you are bathed and cleaned. I will not have anyone coming from the Divinicus smelling quite as shit as you do.'

'Excuse me?' The light was playing a trick on her, she was sure of it.

'Your skin will be fresh, it will soon forget this place, forget the north. You'll start again under my curfew.'

'I can bathe myself,' she snapped but found herself backing down. She'd come too far to lose everything in a petty spat.

Fabius nodded to himself. 'I'll have someone escort you to suitable quarters.'

'Here?'

'No,' he said. 'I will send you to men who will work you. Perhaps then you can discover what you wanted here. Have it known, girl, if you were some low-born child, I would not be so understanding.'

A moment later, he was gone, and Magmaya's eyes began to sing beneath the dirt and dust that plagued them. And when she stood, her feet shook as if she were a fool balancing on a spire.

It was fear that woke her from a midday slumber and forced her to follow blindly through tattered, rusting passageways, damp with copper-blue and silt. The passage inland had lulled her to silence and yet, a burning anxiety nested in her like an old friend—Fabius truly couldn't be so merciful, could he? An angel like him wouldn't allow a damper on his pride, and she was exactly that.

'Highport,' one of the Divinicus told her and pointed across to the shore. It was still miles away, though. They hadn't cleared the black waves yet.

Behind her, the shadow of *The Golden Damnation* lingered, and before her, there was Inamorata at last. And upon its banks, there was a crumbling edifice, throned with countless towers and spires, wrestling itself free from the sea.

'It looks like it's half sunk,' Magmaya remarked.

'It is,' one of the thralls replied, but for all she knew, it might have been a drowning man rasping.

'As Highport was built higher and higher, it sunk it farther and farther beneath the shore,' another one of them explained. 'So, time and time again it was built higher to compensate. But that only made it sink even more. Now there's as much Highport underwater as there is above it.'

Soon enough, though, Magmaya couldn't see any of it as the world around her become choked with fog. But when she looked up, she saw the same sun as there had been in the north; there was the same sky, the same moon, the same stars. It was as if she hadn't travelled a mile.

It reminded her of a dream she'd had once—a dream that the world had woken up to seventeen suns glimmering in the morning sky, and that she had been a priestess, draped in brass and blood. What it had all meant, she hadn't a clue. Kharon had never let astrologers pick apart her nightmares in fear they'd curse the palace. It seemed they hadn't needed an astrologer to be cursed, though.

Soon enough, the crumbling towers reappeared from the mist and with a shake in her legs, the angels led her onto the sodden black shore, into an iron cavern and through a network of worn corridors beneath Highport.

Shortly after, several of the Divinicus left her for another turning, and so found herself stumbling alone amongst the horde of strange thralls with only a single angel in sight. There weren't even any windows; it was as suffocating on land as it had been on the ship.

She shook herself free of the daunting haze to study the walls as they walked, finding complex spider webs of wires and pipes crowding them, broken with rust. Was this the kind of place the Golden Woman had once stood? Was she now walking in the footsteps of a goddess?

But there was nothing holy here. Save the blue-green stains that dulled the copper-red walls and a lightless complex free of warmth and voice.

As they turned a corner under the dim lamps from above, a group of locals appeared and approached the surrounding thralls; they wore strange metal contraptions across their mouths and spoke in a strangely rigid manner as if they were automatons talking. Almost all the others sauntered off then, leaving a single angel and a few thralls to march her forward, shake hands and begin what appeared to be an immortal conversation, which she could only shy away from by hiding in the shadows.

The chatter continued on until Magmaya's heart nearly burst with fear, as without warning, a local tore a sharpened baton from his hip and levelled it to the angel's face.

The remaining thralls around her collectively shuddered and hid away, but she found it in herself to stand and it seemed the Divinicus did too. He took his falchion from his hip and Magmaya closed her eyes, heart pounding before she disappeared into an alcove. The thralls fled while the assailants seemed to pour forth from every crack in the walls.

But then, there was a burst of light from the corridors beyond, and Magmaya braced herself—but there was no clatter of blades, only stunned silence. She opened her eyes.

Footsteps beat through the corridor like each one was a falling god, crumbling to its knees. And then she found Fabius standing over her, looking to the locals with an expression of absolute calm. She would have hazarded to say he was even enjoying the attention. And with him, another Divinicus joined the fray with a blade outstretched, dazzling in the dim light and blinding the room.

The fighting ceased almost immediately. The locals stepped back and surrendered, but the Lord Commander paid no heed. He raised his finger, and his Divinicus' falchions rang out. The locals began screaming, and blood lined the gutters.

Magmaya winced, but Fabius was there to comfort her—her noble knight, standing above her with all the eyes and subtly of a wise god.

'Get up.'

Magmaya did as he demanded, avoiding the stares of the corpses, and looked to Fabius. The angel motif that swept across his shoulder must've cowered in his wake— if she had been none the wiser, she would've dropped to her knees and prayed.

'Fabius,' she caught herself stuttering.

He turned away and looked to the other angel, standing tall among the grimacing dead. 'What happened?'

'They claimed they never agreed to harbour a girl,' he replied, and Magmaya realised, *even here they don't want me to rule.*

'They had notice enough,' Fabius groaned.

'What kind of place is this?' Magmaya cut in. Heat was rising in her forehead.

'Highport.'

'You say that,' Magmaya sneered, 'but I can't see anything; there are no boats; there are no seas, except maybe that black foam we sailed on. Only bloody corpses.'

'You know this place better than I?' Fabius spat. 'If you don't like it here, your options are scarce, girl. The seafarers have little use for a child like you, and I need not another handmaiden. And I assume you don't want to be a refreshment for the older men, no?'

She shook her head.

'I thought not,' he said. 'There's someone else here who can harbour you. Be gone.'

Magmaya nodded, Fabius disappeared, and without another word, she followed on through the corridors as if the slaughter had never happened and blood did not still stain the floors. After a moment, she plucked up the courage to ask one of the thralls, 'Who am I going to now?'

'Spider,' he replied. 'But you will call him *sir*.'

'Sir,' she whispered, 'Sir,' she hummed as she chanted the name of her new owner.

He was a stranger man than Magmaya had expected—nearly seven foot, she guessed, sporting a thin, white beard and eyes like small, black beads. Spider had been a revered blacksmith at Highport, but she'd heard the years had taken their toll and he could scarcely turn out a hammer now. It looked as if he still liked to surround himself with all manner of furnaces, though, likely stolen from some archaic craft that might have travelled the Cold Seas a thousand years ago.

The Divinicus had left Magmaya at his doorstep, deep in the cavernous honeycomb of the port; there was no sunshine or warmth, save for the few kindles of Spider's daily labour and the candles which prided themselves on going out far too early. Outside, there were a number of tin bowls strewn with flayed chicks and cubes of meat where half-clockwork cats would scrounge and paw. The strange man referred to one of them as *Dreadbitch* before ushering her to her chambers.

The room had a delicate quality about it as if it was to fall apart at a moment's notice; a crooked bed frame and broken porcelain bath seemed to be the only things of note. But Magmaya didn't care; she threw herself down against the tattered sheets and watched a cloud of dust erupt up around her like it was the most interesting thing she'd ever set her eyes on.

A heaviness was pressing on her forehead still, so she closed her eyes for what began as a moment, then a minute and then a night. But she felt as if hadn't slept at all when dawn arose with a great pounding, and the door was thrown open—and for a moment, it felt as if the world was falling apart around her.

Spider barked something, and Magmaya dragged herself up from the bedding to face his dark eyes. He tossed a dirtied garb on the bed and left the room as quickly as he had come. She sighed and found the will at last to stand.

It was a dress, plain, frilled, and slightly too large for her waist, but she wasn't in the mood to argue.

After changing, Magmaya turned to her satchel, reached in and found a small knife. It shone in the dim candlelight, and a tide of warmth crashed through her; it was Rache and Siedous, it was Kharon and Nurcia, but above all else, it was her fear. It was the carving knife she had taken when she'd met Kurulian that night. When she'd made the decision that brought her here.

No. She held back tears. *I have to forget. This is my life now. I chose it.*

A murder of crows plucked at the trailing eyes of corpses as they swung steadily from the rafters above. The dead men had rusted contraptions strapped across what was left of their mouths, while yellow-black robes flailed from their limp bodies as if they were the only things in Highport that were truly alive.

Under the brick and clockwork arches, hundreds of stalls had emptied as the crowds flocked to grimace, and Magmaya only found herself doing the same. The market (which was more of a towering complex) would have largely overwhelmed her if it hadn't been for the unsavoury attractions that hung above.

Dead light bled from shattered windows, and a stale breeze tore across the courtyard, sending the bodies into a perpetual swaying. A moment later, though, the crowds were gone as if the limp things had never been there. But Magmaya stayed—she had recognised them immediately.

There was no doubt in her they were the ones the Divinicus had slain the day before—and it showed. Their entrails were dangling out of their bellies and dripping with gross ichor, and when the crows fed, the corpses burst into fountains of mucus. Magmaya had to turn away before a sickness came over her.

'Move on, whore.' A salesman waved her aside, and so she carried on.

The commoners would dare call me a whore in Orianne, she grumbled. *But I'm not in Orianne anymore.*

The other marketers weren't anymore warm; she asked at every turn where she might find a way out to the seas, but it soon became clear that there was none. If she could've at least had a breath of fresh air, the place might've been bearable.

She passed an elderly fisherman selling all kinds of sharp shells, black shells and poisonous shells, and begged of him to tell her where she could see the ocean. But he had only threatened her and warned her to beware the waves. Another merchant tried to offer her a playing board for a *Lamentation of Fates*, and she would've been half tempted if it wasn't for the snotty handprints all over the wood.

The day passed in an instant, and Magmaya returned with the same basket of metals she had started with, and slumped before Spider, her eyes bleached and grey. He was hunched over a workbench, fingering a deck of colourful tarot cards, but he quickly scooped them up and faced her with something of a disdainful frown.

'There were bodies in the market, sir,' she said numbly. 'No one seemed to care.'

'Aye, and it seemed people had little care for your iron too,' Spider hummed, his greasy hands paving through the rusted ornaments.

'*Dead* bodies,' she insisted.

'Often are, girl.'

'People were staring.'

'Looking for things to pawn if anything. I say you're a fool if you die with your purse.' He scratched his cheek. 'Go and get rest.'

'The Divinicus killed them.' She stared into the fire and saw them die and scream and die again with each remoulding flicker. 'Were they the ones to string them up?'

'The angels aren't savages,' he said to her surprise and took a sip of ale out of his flagon. His stomach growled. 'I wouldn't know, anyway. I only take their heathens; I don't… chatter among their pearly wings.'

There was silence as the fire burned the gap between them, and Magmaya heaved a sigh. 'Did they tell you anything about me?'

'Only that you were from somewhere far—not often do the arks come to these parts. They're as rare as good ale.' He shook his head. 'What business you have here is none of mine; only that you follow by my rules.'

'Have you cared for many of the angel's friends?'

'Few,' he admitted. 'They seem not to be too abundant. Men like them aren't what they seem, girl. They're pretty and the best pretty you'll ever feast your eyes on. But I wouldn't trust them alone with me for a moment.' He frowned. 'Whispers say they eat souls, but I don't believe whispers; they're as human as you and me, just a little more shiny.' He paused like he'd said too much. 'No matter, you must be something special. Otherwise, a pilgrim like you would be strung up for the crows too.'

The thought made her sick to the stomach. Had she been a low-born girl, would Fabius have killed her?

'Were there more like me?' Magmaya asked.

'Like you? I don't know what you are.'

'I was the chancellor of a faraway city.' The words tasted so false now.

'No chancellors here, if that's what you mean. Many of the others were the Lord Commander's contacts.' Spider shrugged. 'One of them he told me to guard with my life, though—never has that happened again.'

'And who was he?'

'*She.*' He coughed, thumbing a shard of metal. 'She fled from Kythera, and for whatever reason, the angels took pity on her. She was beautiful—for a whore anyway.'

'Oh,' Magmaya exclaimed. 'Perhaps she sold herself to Fabius.'

He shook his head. 'No, no,' Spider said. 'I wouldn't think so. But he did care for her. She said she didn't sell herself anymore. Not after she met their emperor apparently.'

'The emperor of Kythera?'

'Emperor, king, archon, *my lord,*' he replied. 'They're different names for the same bastards. It's no matter, he's dead now, and so is the whore. Few moons later, she was found with a mouth of seaweed, caught in a fishing net.' He dropped the metal. 'And that was that, girl.'

'She found her way to the ocean?' Magmaya's eyes widened. 'But I was told they were—'

'Cursed.' He nodded. 'Anyone can get to the Winter Seas. But yes, it is true; they're haunted all the way to Belliousa.'

'*Haunted*?' She smiled. 'I once travelled across a land called the *Dead*fields. I know a lot about ghosts, and there aren't any.'

'Alright, if a girl says she knows, then certainly she must.' He smirked. 'But there are unspoken rules about this place, girl; don't go to the seas at night, pretend you didn't see the lights in the sky, don't touch the wishing stones. You may not believe in your god,' he said, 'or faery, or wisp, but you sure as hell wouldn't dare challenge it.'

Spider didn't speak much more after that, and soon, the ale soothed him to sleep in a pool of his own spittle.

Magmaya began to feel herself buckle too, and at last, stole the ale bottle from the strange man, slumped into her bath and wept, feeling her humble dress become one with the water and part of the night.

Her tears were shimmers of salt; the world grew quiet, and sleep came to her softly for the first time in what felt like centuries. Warm water rippled over her navel and kissed her neck, so all that was left was a swell of stars and silence and the gentle hum of a stained-glass moon.

By the time daylight had broken, Magmaya's eyes were sore with the cold. The privateer who begged her to purchase his forgeries felt half a world away, fumbling with runic beads as they trickled lank from his ears and lips. It seemed no matter how often she tried to bargain for the chisel at the back of his stall, he insisted on giving her all manner of memorabilia and false relics instead—so artificially bright they almost eclipsed her.

The man clearly didn't speak the common tongue; she was able to decipher one or two words, but when a girl couldn't even barter, it soon became clear *she* was the foreigner.

'Golden lady!' another merchant exclaimed, drawing botched circles around his nose with one hand, while the other thrust a shimmery mask in her face, eyeing her basket of metals.

'No, no.' She shook her head and carried on with a sigh.

Soon enough, she'd return with an empty basket and nothing to show for it. Again.

The basket wasn't the only thing she had that was empty—her belly was too. So, it was luck she found a fisherwoman lurking in an alcove that was willing to sneak her some white wine (after a little too much pleading). But not only was it vile, the bottle was musty and old as if it had been used as a toilet once. She carried on and got herself several sickly-green scallops for a pair of coppers, cracked them open against a nearby fountain (it was thick with rust, but she didn't care) and let the cold flesh spill down her throat and trickle across her chin. Those tided her over, at least.

'Hens for silver!' An overweight and slightly gaudy looking man pointed at her purse, holding a rather dishevelled looking bird under his elbow. It squawked at Magmaya, and her eyes turned wide.

'Tools for Spider,' she replied, for that was all she'd been told to say.

'Finest eggs you'll ever see!' The man ignored her with a smile of broken teeth. The feathery thing squealed again. 'I'll prepare it for an extra piece!'

'It's quite alright.' She shook her head.

There were several curiosities at each of the stalls; most of them were being described as ornate talismans or something of the like, but on closer inspection, almost all of them were stitched together scrap or broken jewellery. When she arrived at one of the markets by the windows, however, there stood a painting perhaps twenty feet tall, encased in a silver frame with a canvas that appeared to sparkle in the dim light. It was a full-body portrait of a woman, cloaked from head to toe in a thin veil of gold.

All around her there were praying saints and cast down demons; it was a piece of awe and majesty that Kharon Vorr might have died for. It was the Golden Woman, no doubt, and she was as beautiful as the stories had described. Magmaya thought that if she reached out and touched her, the painting might've come alive and taken her from this dreadful place.

'Seven Blood Sovereigns for the painting,' the old man at the stall croaked, but as Magmaya drew herself closer, she noticed that he wasn't quite as old as she had thought; he was just wrinkled by smoke.

'Seven?' she spat. 'I won't earn a single one in my life. Seven?'

'You're one of the angel's, no? They have friends in the Inamoratan Grand Banks, and they have friends in the brass presses. I'd wager you've a hundred hidden away in that purse of yours, girl.'

She stepped back and rolled her eyes. The Sovereign was worth so much that it had value across the whole world—they were called Blood Sovereigns after all, and they were often earned through the grisliest deeds. She *would* have killed for one, though—a single piece could buy you a small farm in the mountains, or perhaps a square metre of land in any capital.

'Painted by Lorde Lydia of the Chain Islands,' the seller interrupted her thoughts. 'It was said the Golden Woman posed for hours to allow her to paint the picture.'

'Did the demons pose too?'

'Even the demons, they say. But the woman's mere radiance banished them shortly after.'

Magmaya scoffed and continued on. She wasn't sure what she'd even do with such a painting anyway.

The halls twisted around her like a labyrinth as she clambered several stairwells where the downtrodden slept; half of them were scraping for coppers, and the other half were maddened, doing all they could to scrounge for opium.

The next storey had a balcony framed by marble arches, stained with smoke and green with rot, but beyond, there was nothing but an endless garden of smog, stretching out into oblivion.

She turned back to the complex and found it crowded with a maze of tables, each with its own suite of drunken gamblers tossing dice and beating down playing cards. Around every corner, there looked as if there was a different bard, dancer or jest, their sickly tunes overlapping into some grotesque melody. Magmaya passed one of the tables, and the gamblers raised their eyes in scorn, half-clockwork faces pumping away at cigars. She watched as they tossed silvers and golds onto the table, only for all of them to somehow lose. And one by one, they trailed away to the drinks stand.

The man serving there didn't seem any happier to see her either, but then again, he had a scar down his left cheek that seemed to turn his face to a permanent grimace.

'We don't serve wenches here,' he spat.

'Spider sent me—'

'I don't care if Cardel himself—no, I don't care if the Golden Woman *herself* sent you. I'll beat you bloody if you take another step closer t' me. You're lucky you caught me in a good temper.'

'I only want a drink,' she crooned. 'Three coppers.'

'Twelve, and after that, you leave.'

'Four.'

'Get this whore out.' He rose, and her stomach fluttered. 'Make sure she never comes back 'gain!'

Magmaya wanted to scream. The man was big and brutish, and the place was crawling with others like him. And each of them had her father's eyes—she was sure of it! Each of them had been watching as she'd killed him.

'Let her pass in peace, my good men.' One of the gamblers stood abruptly; he was tall and lank with a sort of disconcerting manner that reminded Magmaya of a vulture.

'Reed, she's ours to deal with, she's—'

'She's the Lord Commander's,' he said. 'Look, my men, the luck of the Maiden Gods has been with me today. I have gambled away every piece of lead I own into gold. I wouldn't test my luck any further. Let the girl go, she will not disturb you again.' He turned to her and cocked his head.

Magmaya's lips were stinging as she watched the complexes pass below, feeling her mouth grow dry and her legs buckle. Gods—how had she been so foolish? To ransom that much of Spider's money for a drink she didn't need? To bring all the gangers down upon her?

'My lady,' a voice called from behind, and she turned to see the same man again, standing tall in flowing garnet.

'Oh,' she started, 'I never thanked you—'

'I need no thanks.' He smiled and said, 'But you look thirsty, girl.' He produced a bottle of wine from his coat and left it in her palm. The surface was clear and shimmery, not at all like the one she'd had earlier.

'How did you know I was with Fabius?'

'I'm one of his court's own men,' he replied. 'By association, though, and only with good coin.' He giggled.

She opened the bottle and took a swig. It was warm.

'Thank you,' she murmured. 'What's your name?'

'Cheyne.'

'Cheyne—?'

'Cheyne Reed. You wouldn't have heard of me, my lady. I'm from no noble birth.' He shrugged. 'You, though? You're the chancellor who stowed away south, no?'

She nodded sheepishly. 'Magmaya.'

'Magmaya Vorr, yes,' he remarked. 'I've heard.'

'Am I that big of a story?' she asked.

'In truth, it's not often that some high-born travels so far south to play war,' he admitted.

'Play war?' she asked. 'What do you mean?'

'Don't you know? By coming here, you've entered our territory, our war, Magmaya,' his voice was crisp and smooth as he crooned to her.

'*Your* war?'

'*This* war. This never-ending war for the south,' he exclaimed, 'where each winner is shortly toppled by the next. Ludicrous affair, really.'

'I don't understand.'

'Why, like any good war, this one has battles we must all fight, Magmaya,' Cheyne continued. 'Not just with knights, heroes and swords, but with words, women and wine. Is this what you want, girl? I don't. I stay far away from these things.'

'I didn't come south to go to war.'

'No, I didn't think you did. They say all northerners dream of coming south for luxury.' He giggled again. 'If there's something you must know, it's that luxury is a commodity here, girl, and it's won through one thing and one thing alone. And I don't think a little Lamentation of Fates is suited for a girl like you.'

'Not suited...?' She coughed, remembering Siedous all those lives ago. 'I—I killed Vargul Tul!'

'I don't know who that is. That tells you enough.'

Cheyne looked around with a smile and breathed softly on the windowpane. She wished she could have punched him—how dare he insult her like that! If everyone here was playing war, then she would too.

'I must be on my way if you wouldn't mind,' he turned back to her. 'To be clear, don't go back to the higher complexes again. I won't always be there to help you.' He tossed a coin into the air. 'After all, today was my lucky day. I might not be feeling so generous tomorrow.'

He disappeared, and a moment later, it was like he had never been there. Despite his thin eyes and sharp nose, he was the kind of man she forgot about the moment he turned away. A prickly man, an *annoying* man.

Magmaya stole a breath and fastened the bottle to her bag. She didn't want anymore.

Fourteen

She continued back to Spider and the days began anew.

'Have you ever heard of a man called Cheyne Reed?' she finally built up the courage to ask him.

He was fumbling through the metals she had brought back, but he soon gave up, sighed and sat back.

'You're not great at this, are you girl?'

'Cheyne Reed?' Magmaya persisted. 'You've heard of him?'

'Seems you're the only one who hasn't,' Spider replied. 'One of the Legatus' men under Fabius—or so when he's paid enough. He's got a manner about him. It unsettles me. You didn't talk to him, did you girl?'

'Uh…' she stuttered.

He groaned. 'Don't make that mistake again.'

'He was kind to me,' she murmured, tasting the wine again.

'He's kind to everyone,' Spider said. 'Next thing you know, there's a knife in your back, and he's the heir to your castle.'

'You know him well then?' Magmaya asked. She was unsurprised to hear that Cheyne wasn't to be trusted, but it didn't worry her any less.

'I know him as well as any sod,' he said. 'And any sod knows well enough to stay away.'

She set out again the next morning with barely two hours of sleep, and despite the rising of the sun, the farther her legs carried her, the darker and damper it got. As the day dragged on, the lights grew dimmer, and despite the rushing of diseased pipes overhead, she felt farther from the oceans than ever. She couldn't even guess what the time was, though it was surely late, and she had little to show for it but an empty belly again.

'Tools for Spider.' She passed a hag at a stand, but as she grew closer, it became apparent that the woman was dead. Maggots were spilling from her eyes, and her mouth was sobbing with spit. Spider had indeed been right—bodies were commonplace, and the worst thing was, she didn't care. When she'd found Albany all those lives ago, it had left her frozen with fear, but now, she passed the corpses like they were old friends turned strangers.

The last few days had been turning her into a native, and she was beginning to forget herself; her life as a chancellor had vanished and now she couldn't even find the sunshine in her own home. And where was Fabius in all of this? He had promised her to be cleaned, but he had disappeared—and as for Kurulian? He had turned a blind eye once they had arrived. She thought to the weeks before where she might have called him 'friend'—what a fool she had been.

The air around her was growing heavy, so she found herself clawing at the windows. The clearest view of the outside appeared to be right near the sex houses, though, from which over the past hour, all she had heard were bursts of giggles, moans and shrieks. Every few minutes, a new sell-maiden would enter, drag someone in, and with the passing of the sun, the same fool would leave alone, dishevelled and red.

Magmaya turned her attention away, took out a small, dried leaf from her bag and pressed it up against the window, watching as the light gleamed through and struck the veins with a brilliant orange; they had never glowed so vibrantly in Rache's room. He must have realised by now that part of his collection had gone missing, but she had hoped her own absence might've outweighed that. There were thousands of leaves like that on the trees in the north anyway, but none at Highport. In Ranvirus, they were short and spiny, but at Highport, they stretched to the clouds and cast great, green fans about the air.

Magmaya took the leaf down and glanced a little too close to the right. For a moment, she could make out a throng of pink things pressed up against the glass walls and forced herself to turn away; if anyone caught her by the sex houses, Fabius would surely cast her out. But it wasn't like she had the intention of going in.

'That's a pretty leaf,' a soft voice sounded behind her. 'I've never seen one like that.'

The sell-maiden was wearing all yellow, from her corset to her thin leather tights. Even her hair looked as if it was dyed with the berry of some golden flower.

'It's from far away,' Magmaya stuttered, trying hard to ignore her.

'Oh—oh gods!' She clapped her hands together. 'You're the girl from the north? The one Fabius took here. I'm right aren't I?'

She stayed quiet and turned away, but the girl didn't lose her enthusiasm.

'I've never had one of Fabius' before, let alone someone from so far away.' She pressed her finger to her lips and giggled.

'I'm not one of Fabius',' she said, fondling the leaf. *And Highport is all I can seem to remember anymore, anyway.*

'You have pretty hair, north girl,' the sell-maiden said, ignoring her. 'What's your name?'

'Perhaps I should be on my way.' She motioned to another corridor, but the sell-maiden just tugged at her arm.

'Don't leave,' she purred. 'I had a bet with Qulaia that I'd have Fabius before her and you're the closest I'm going to get,' the sell-maiden squirmed. 'But enough about me—how do you like it here, huh? How would you even describe Highport? Is there another word for shit?'

'It's cold—everyone wants to kill me or fuck me,' Magmaya admitted, unsure of why she was still talking. Reality felt like a thousand miles away. 'I spend a lot of my time afraid.'

'Time will see to your fear,' the girl pursed her lips together. 'Even the most craven of us forget what's it's like to be afraid.'

Magmaya was silent.

'I take it you're not the fucking kind then?' the sell-maiden asked.

'Something like that.'

'So, what *do* you like to do, huh?' she asked. 'I know where you can get some great ale around here. Or perhaps some cards? I'm not any good at cards. In truth, I don't know how to play.' She paused. 'What's your name again?'

'Most people call me wench here,' Magmaya smirked. 'Or bitch or whore—oh, I mean no offence, I—'

The sell-maiden giggled. 'It's quite alright. They can't call you a whore if you're proud of being one.'

An oily breeze carried through the street, and a voice called from behind, 'Are you done?' The pair turned.

'I'm busy,' the sell-maiden said to the man, tall and draped in brown leather; he might once have been handsome, a thousand years ago.

'If you're so busy, why aren't you in the cathouse, Malla?' He began to slip his hand around her waist.

'Give me a minute.' She slapped his wrist away playfully, but he only tightened his grip.

'I'm tired,' he crooned and ran his hand through that yellow hair. 'Let's go.'

She said a minute, Magmaya wished she had the strength to call, but all that came out was a murmur.

'What was that?' He raised an eyebrow at her. 'I don't want you.'

The man pressed himself against the girl and tugged at her breasts. Malla (if that was even her name) stifled a cough as he pulled her away, pawing at her. Magmaya's stomach was knotted, and no matter how much she willed them on, her legs wouldn't move.

'I'm not done with her...!' Magmaya stuttered, feeling the words spill from her throat.

'Oh, you're one of those girls?' He just laughed, and a moment later, they'd disappeared into the shadow of the sex house.

Magmaya's legs buckled again, and then there was silence as if it had never happened, save for the stench of alcohol that had clung to the man's neck.

She held herself, tight, and looked back across the other stalls, mapping out the path back to Spider in her mind. *Just down one street,* she told herself, *one right and one left. It'll take barely a moment to get back.*

But a moment later, she was inside the sex house, and the vile miasma of sweat and perfume began choking her.

Pink walls rushed her by, and a thousand naked bodies on red velvet reached out to her, begging her to join for a few measly coppers. But they all disappeared behind as she forced herself on through clouds of scented incense and over heaps of twisted limbs.

Stray hands clawed at her backside, and greasy fingers slipped through her hair, but Magmaya just hurried on through the maze of ecstasy and giggles, her head pounding. She could barely make out a thing in the low, red light; even the bundles of flesh and stained fur recliners seemed distant, let alone her own satchel as she clawed through it, waiting for the cold to scrape against her fingers.

At last, she found the carving knife and carried on through the kaleidoscope as it encased her, through tendrils and skin. Despite the urgency pounding in her chest, she wanted to crawl up in the corner and cover her ears. Maybe then she could finally be forgotten.

But then, she heard a scream from the corridor beyond and carried on.

She followed the squeals through another chain of corridors and linen until a row of doors confronted her. Magmaya traced the sounds to the one in the centre and pressed her ear against the wood; there was a racket of pleas and grunts, and so she readied the knife and pushed through the door.

Malla was pinned down against the chair in the room's centre. Her tights and undergarments had been torn off and scattered about the floor. But there were others in the room too, standing around and tugging at the bare breasts of some other girl.

Come with me, please, she wished she could've screamed. But before she could open her mouth, the man holding Malla began to tear down his breeches and press himself forward, fast, so Magmaya moved faster.

Next thing she knew, he was beneath her, and the room had come alive. The sell-maidens were screaming, and the others had sprung up. But it was too late. She raised the knife into the air and beat it down, again and again, until the back of the man's skull was a bloody pulp. He hadn't even found time to scream.

The other men threw themselves at her while Malla disappeared, but she screamed even louder than the harlots had and held the knife up to the light.

'You think that'll scare me, girl?' one of them barked. 'I've fought with rapier. You ever heard of Fleetfront?'

The man behind yelled something incomprehensible and lurched at her.

Her hair caught her eye as she rose. He swung again, cumbersome.

Magmaya threw herself aside, as she had done with Vargul all those years ago and put her knife in his throat. He spluttered and fell back, clawing at his neck, but lost himself in the clatter of the falling chair.

She turned to the other one and watched his chest rise and fall, holding the sell-maiden between two talons.

He dropped the girl and fled.

'Malla!' she must have shouted a thousand times before the hour passed. Magmaya's arm was red and swollen—she hadn't noticed the man behind had managed to hit her. The gash was warm when she held it, but at least the fire reminded her she was alive.

She plucked up the strength to call again to a hundred stalls that weren't listening, 'Malla! Malla. *Malla…*'

Was that even her name? Magmaya wanted to cry. *The other man was still out there—if she found him—if he found her…!*

Magmaya washed the blood off her carving knife at the rotting fountain. She could still make out shrieks from the sex houses, but this time they were fearful as the sell-maidens began stumbling upon the corpses she'd left for them.

The idea of killing the man hadn't even formed in her head; it just seemed to have happened. She had taken more lives over the last few months than she could've ever imagined when Siedous had first given her that wooden sword—it made her sick to the stomach. But now, she had killed someone from the south! She didn't even know who they were—perhaps sons of a high lord who would seek revenge, or knights or brawlers. Maybe elsewhere they were good men. But it didn't matter, watching them writhe had ignited some rush in her like a forbidden baptism.

She couldn't protect Malla for the rest of her life, though; she was a sell-maiden after all—something like this was bound to have happened before and bound to happen again.

Siedous would have known what to do. But he wasn't here, and neither was anyone else who could help her. Perhaps Spider would have to do. But after all that had happened, the Divinicus would probably be at her throat, and Spider wasn't going to prove capable against them. For now, though, she would just walk and breath and shiver.

At last, daylight surrendered itself to the cold lips of the moon, and she began to make her way back. She had little else to pawn (but her clothes) and nothing more to do than scour the world for oceans everyone swore were haunted. She hadn't dared to ask anyone any more about them—not even the more reasonable natives; they had claimed even a glimpse of its shimmer was a curse. But the more Magmaya became deprived, the more want she felt.

The south wasn't meant to be a market of the superstitious, nor an empire of liars and thieves and rapers but instead, green grass between her toes, a yellow sun lashing against her back and a new moon above the sea at night. She had sworn to herself that one day she would sail back to Rache, tell him of the fine wines and lush grasslands and humming seas—how her journey had been forged by a goddess and blessed by starlight and how he would walk again—walk back south with her.

But only the dim roar of a crowd surrounded her now—crusting pipes and shattered glass, hailing saints plastered with posters offering ransoms. Dying thickets of moss enveloped her toes from the red earth, but *that* wasn't the grass she wanted beneath her feet. Even the sea began to tease her as it crashed against Magmaya's ears, promising nothing but a haunted façade.

The dying of the light couldn't have come sooner, though as the day finally caught up with her. The corpses that had been left to the birds had rotted to nothing but lank bone, threaded together with lengthy red sinews. It couldn't be long until Magmaya's victims were to be strung up too.

It was awfully humid, and nausea began to visit her again. *It's time to leave and forget the girl pleading in your mind's eye,* she told herself and made her way back.

Magmaya hated to return empty handed, and if Spider was awake at this hour, it would only mean he would be disgruntled too. She sighed and raked her fist against the heavy iron door; once, twice, three times, until she became impatient and slipped in the key which she had watched the old man hide in the glass of a nearby lamppost. She turned it in the lock and watched the bulwark twitch and click under her fumbling until, at last, she wriggled inside.

Rusted spikes jutted from the furnaces like broken ranks of soldiers; all manner of spear tips and jagged blades stared her down from the flames. The fires of the workshop burnt in Magmaya's pupils as she looked around, forming spiels in her mind of how she would tell Spider of her shortcomings. She didn't quite expect him to lash out at her, but there were some chances she couldn't bear to take.

The purring of the flame broke the silence as Magmaya strode across the room, looking for evidence; for some sort of notice or anything at all to suggest where that damned blacksmith might have gone.

And then she saw him, wilting with a grimace against the back of the door, skin pale and fingers bloated. He was unspeaking and unmoving as he hovered about a head above the floor, for that was where he'd been nailed to the doorframe.

Magmaya didn't feel sick, but instead, a sense of infuriation skulked over her. She patrolled the chamber again, past her door, as a knot stiffened within her and grappled for her skin.

She'd done this! She had brought the wrath of Highport down upon him!

It wasn't until there was a clattering from her own quarters that a crimson heat flamed in her forehead and ears. She froze and looked to her door.

His killer was in her quarters.

She turned away and took a step forward, feeling the floor rasp beneath her tread; there was a malign fusing of wood and iron aching away beneath her. Magmaya stopped again and looked back to her door. No sound.

She let the seconds flow past her like a hailstorm before she took another step. The furnace's crackle thundered against her with each gone moment as if she was about to be eaten by the fires. One wrong step and she'd never forget it.

Move now or die.

Magmaya flung herself across the room and around the worktops. The fire began glistening in her eyes and eating away at her tears, and she felt herself fall into its embrace, closer, closer.

No, it's not time yet, she told herself, *there's still life left in me.*

She stole a piece of trailing leather from a workbench and ran her hand through the flames, producing a red-hot poker the length of her arm. She still had her carving knife, but that wouldn't do if her enemy was armed with anything longer than their finger.

Despite the fear of it all, she couldn't help but be enamoured as the newly born blade wavered and glowed between her broken fingertips. It was gold and orange and blue all at once with the hiss of gods long-dead. If she'd known any better, she'd have thought it was an art piece.

Magmaya turned and felt the heat beat down against her back; the burning poker was still pressed against her palm. She threw herself against the door of her quarters and forced herself in.

The man wasn't the survivor from before—that was all she comprehended before he lunged at her.

A splatter of blood sullied her clothes, and steel slashed across her collarbone. But that was before she ran the brand forward and thrust its quivering tip through the man's chest.

It was over in a moment, but the smoking of the blade seemed to last a lifetime.

She dropped it as its fervour began to dwindle and toppled to the ground in time to watch the man die. He'd curled up like a babe as the red blade fell between them with one last sigh.

Magmaya cradled her palm, blistered and pink. The leather hadn't been enough! She released the scarred, putrid thing and heaved her head back against the wall, but her heart didn't stop racing until the man's stopped beating.

There would surely be more coming for her, though. The man that had fled from the sex house had only alerted the cavalry!

Her fighting arm was burning like all hells, and she would undoubtedly be outnumbered. Impatience was driving Magmaya into a crazed spin, and the room was shaking, moving, stirring. She could feel the cold floors embracing her and see the corpse staring back.

And then there was a pounding against the metal of the door. They were at the walls!

Several more knocks followed, closer to the entrance than before and Magmaya froze, her mind screaming at her to run, run back north. But instead, she lay still, unflinching until the pounding grew again. Why would the attackers be taunting her so? If she had to die, why couldn't it be with all the grace of a danseur and the chivalry of a knight? Instead, she found herself weeping, holding herself as her cheeks flushed red.

'Spider,' a voice called amid another tempest of thumping.

Magmaya stood from her cradle. Surely, they would know Spider was dead? Why did they have to insult her?

'Spider!' the voice roared again with all the subtly of a prophet, and then silence ate away at the room. That was before whoever stood on the other side forced their way through the door.

Before she could think, the charred poker was hot in her palm again, and the distance closed between herself and the intruder. If she was to die fighting some fiend, then so be it—it was what she deserved after all she had done.

She opened the door to Spider's home and yellow light spilt in, haloing the three angels in the glow of the burning furnace. There was a rush of cloth and silver before a prickly cold washed through her like nothing she'd felt since Orianne.

Magmaya dropped her blade in subservience and collapsed before them. And then something warm rushed through her, and she couldn't help but look to them with the eyes of the child that persisted inside her.

'Oh,' one of the Divinicus said softly, 'Magmaya Vorr. They did say you looked like your father.'

Fifteen

The dress was silk and silver; it was a sparkling memory of a better time like an ocean under the light of morning stars. It was too beautiful, from the clear jewels that shimmered across the bodice, to the thousands of perfect stitches articulated by the most gifted of artisans to make its boundless waves.

Magmaya had never quite seen anything like it, let alone wear, and yet, after she discovered it fit her to the inch, she couldn't shake the feeling that something wasn't right. Even after she had bathed amid the flowing red wax of dying candles and the stench of powdered incense, it hurt to wear. She looked back to the fish-headed men, scampering crustaceans and humming dragonflies as they stood sentinel over the baths, cast in stone; they were all for herself: the warm water, the soaps and salts and fetishes that Fabius had promised so long ago. It was only a shame she had to kill to get them.

Her eyes still ached with the rush of the strange powder she'd felt compelled to inhale, but it had taken the ache away from her chest and hands. A handmaiden had told her it was sometimes known as *Eliadur* or *The Dew of the Honey,* and she began to feel the way she had all those millennia ago when blood had frequented her face.

For once, though, there was no dirt beneath her fingernails; the salts had made her skin soft and numb; she had been made warm with steam and raised with the choking smoke. The dress was kissing her as she stood in it, but its soft lips whispered to her, *Just stay in the bath a little while longer.*

She was tempted to trust the voice; the baths *were* beautiful, from the strange plants that crowded every corner with their porcelain vases, to the flock of luminescent fish that swam eagerly about a tank in the wall, glowing yellow as they did. But by far the best aspect of the spa was the balcony. Unlike the boardroom in Ranvirus, it didn't lead her to a snowy hell but instead a light summer breeze as she gripped the white curtains, hard.

And at last, the ocean was glowing before her, caressing stone beaches at the foot of the rocky hill below. Magmaya could see the marble of the palace disappear into the golden sand, which in turn stretched out until it met the shore. The sky was alive with the stench of salty sea air and the brawn of tumbling waves. The view absorbed her, and the humidity lashed against her face. It was smelling like summer sex again.

Mere hours before, she had been trapped in a complex of blood and rot—now she was in a castle of angels! She couldn't remember the journey out of Highport, but when she'd awoken again, she had opened her eyes to ranks of opal statuettes and cherry perfumes.

According to the handmaidens, there hadn't been a man or woman at the bay that had stopped talking about her. Rumours were circulating that the north had declared themselves against the south and Spider's death was but the beginning of the war to come.

Surely the Divinicus wouldn't force her back, would they? There was certainly no way home. Perhaps the dress was her last rite before they finished with her and that's why it hurt so much to wear.

A figure lingered in the archway, and for a moment, Magmaya supposed it was one of the strange sculptures that didn't quite resemble a person at all. But this one moved. She was draped in lilac, but she wasn't wearing a headdress like a bird's cage which the other handmaidens seemed to have insisted on doing.

'My lady.' The woman bowed, her accent thick. 'Have you bathed well?'

'Yes, thank you,' she said to the handmaiden. 'I'm glad to be out of there. Highport, I mean.'

'That's good, my lady,' she replied. 'Are you hungry? Thirsty at all?'

'No,' she murmured.

The handmaiden nodded. 'After you are finished here, the Lord Commander wants to speak with you.'

'Oh.' Magmaya smiled, but then gestured to her hair. It had been soaking wet only a minute ago, but the warm sea winds had left it lank and salty. 'If you give me a moment.'

'No, please, my lady.' The handmaiden ambled towards her. 'Let me.'

'There really is no ne—'

'Please, let me.'

The girl ran her fingers through Magmaya's hair, combing away the black knots with such intricacy, she couldn't feel it untangle. She dried it with a small, grey towel, and her hands tugged back her curls with such a sweet caress, it made her scalp prickle. Then, the girl stretched her hair back and knotted it sharply before moving to dress it with all manner of hoary ribbons and pearly bows.

At last, the servant stepped away and stood before her with a satisfied smile, and Magmaya's eyes turned wide as she glimpsed herself in the shimmer of the windows. She half laughed. 'Thank you—I—it's more than *I* deserve.'

'I am glad you like it.' The handmaiden beamed. 'You see, I was a girl of the Summerlands, and it was said that if a girl couldn't use her fingers well, then she was no girl.' She shrugged.

'I see.' It was all Magmaya could do not to laugh.

'There's lots of talk about you, my lady.' The girl frowned. 'They say you're from far away. Kythera?' She looked at Magmaya's dress.

'Farther,' she replied. 'I lived in the north.'

'Goodness,' the girl said timidly. 'You've made quite a trip. From Lumiar?'

'From Ranvirus,' Magmaya explained. 'The city of Orianne. I doubt many of you here have heard of it.'

'My lady, quite the opposite' She shook her head. 'I've so many questions!' She took a pause. 'If you would give me a moment?'

'Yes...'

'You're so kind, my lady.' The handmaiden scuttled out of the room, her plume of coloured hair swaying as she did.

Magmaya reclined in her seat, felt the warm leather burn her back and caught her mind wandering; how did *she* know about Ranvirus, let alone Orianne? The Divinicus had claimed she'd looked like her father! It felt as if the south knew more about her than she did herself.

Footsteps clattered through the archway as the handmaiden returned, a smile creeping on her lips. She had something in her hand. Something delicate. Something red.

'Allow me.' She ambled around Magmaya and took her hair again. But this time something prickled against her left ear and ruptured her locks.

'What is it?' Magmaya asked, but she feared she already knew.

'A rose, of course, my lady,' she said. 'The emblem of your city.'

'Thank you.' Magmaya grit her teeth, but her heart was sinking. 'It's an honour you knew.'

'The Lord Commander travelled to your city not long ago, yes? We all heard about it,' the girl explained. 'Did he take you back with him, then?'

'Something like that.'

The servant nodded and rushed around to face her. 'One last thing, if I may.' She plucked a small, feathered brush from a table beside the baths and ran it through some greasepaint. She crouched to face her and swept it across her eyelids, black spilling down Magmaya's milky skin. She stepped back, nodded and said, 'Now you have the eyes of the Great Burned Lady.'

'I don't know much about your Inamoratan gods, but I can only hope that was a compliment,' Magmaya remarked.

'They're not my gods. Mine are from the Summerlands, far across the seas,' she corrected her. 'A woman grown without burning eyes was to be cast out and never courted—' Her face went pale. 'Sorry, my lady. I shouldn't keep speaking ill of the Summerlands. It is a beautiful place, truly.'

'I once thought that anywhere south would be beautiful,' Magmaya muttered. *Highport proved me wrong about that. Perhaps I should stowaway again and go to the Summerlands.* She smiled to herself and paused. 'I'm not still in Highport, am I? Where exactly are we?'

'Where are we?' The handmaiden looked shocked. 'We are in the Prism Manse.' Magmaya raised an eyebrow, so the girl carried on: 'At Hardingham Reach…? How little have you been told?'

'Less than you might expect,' she said. 'I haven't seen Fabius in a long while, and going by the size of this place, it's looking like I never will again.'

'The Lord Commander is a busy man.' She shrugged. 'But you're right, my lady; Master Fabius' abode does rival the palaces in the capital, even—there are hundreds of people here, if not thousands. It's where the angels reside and depart upon their great arks. Connoisseurs from all around the world make the pilgrimage here to drink, speak with or court the Lord Commander and his nobles. I presumed you were perhaps one of the latter, being a high-born girl and such.'

'I'm not here to court Fabius.' Magmaya laughed at the very thought. She could trust this girl, yes? Then what did she have to hide? *Have your fun. But after that, you must do what is best for your people,* the words rang in her ears. 'If I am here to speak with him, then I have to break him.'

The handmaiden led her through a complex of dizzying lilac halls, each more intoxicatingly vibrant than the last. Marble columns shimmered around her feet, dwarfing the pathetic monuments her home had insisted on erecting, all while she watched herself wander in the clear, checked floors. The servants and Divinicus alike stared down her dress; it was a flowing thing like a blossoming flower, and it was beginning to make her uncomfortable.

'They're staring at me.' Magmaya turned to the handmaiden. 'It's like they've seen a ghost.'

'It is the rose in your hair, of course,' she humoured. 'Eyes tall, my lady.'

'Forgive me for not asking sooner,' Magmaya started, 'but your name...?'

'Anclyn,' the girl whispered, groping her robes. 'Anclyn of the Water.'

Magmaya grinned. 'Now I've a name to curse if you let me come back talking like one of *them.*'

She smiled and turned, glimpsing a shimmer of broken glass from across the halls—and then she saw Kurulian, marching amid an ocean of acolytes. She caught his eye as he crossed her path and mouthed his name, looking for some semblance of the angel she had seen fall from the sky. But he just spun around, and a moment later, he was gone.

Magmaya looked back and frowned, stole a deep breath and carried on.

From beyond the great double doors she had been planted in front of, she could make out the pleasant chirping of birdsong and beating of insect wings; the sound soothed her like the suckling of honey or the glistening of freshly fallen rain, and for a moment, she was home again.

She took another breath as the guards either side dropped their staves and hauled the doors open, light spilling in from the heavens. She was met with a dazzling yellow and brilliant white as whatever lay before her let itself be known: a broken marble pathway submerged beneath a horde of flowers, sporting striking violets, reds and golds, all convulsing gently under trees as red as summer wine.

The stench of raw pollen bit her nose as she stepped out. And then a spray of water lapped at her neck from a pair of ornate fountains. She passed over a small stream as it ran clear beneath a tiny wooden bridge below—she was beginning to feel like a giant. It was only a garden but walking in it felt like stepping into a painting. The same fear struck Magmaya that had done as she had boarded *The Golden Damnation*—a vivid excitement she couldn't ignore. But newfound humidity engulfed her and, in an instant, sweat had soiled her forehead. The garden somehow felt more real than the inside of the manse— even the clouds were looking as if she could reach out and tear them from the sky.

Anclyn wished her luck before falling away behind the doors. They shut with a pleasant click, and Magmaya looked back to the glowing pathway; from somewhere beyond the purple skies, she swore she heard a swelling of music and chatter of voluptuous whispers. But when she moved, the voices stopped, and she thought for a second the whole thing might have been a ruse.

She had all the fear of the world in her, but she forced herself to keep on walking. A chiming of water from crinkling leaves made her shudder as she followed the winding trail, passing beneath candlelit arches and wicker houses. It was beautiful, all of it—but the flowers and trees were almost suffocating as they loomed over her, dragging her farther inwards until she was intoxicated.

That was when she found the chair waiting for her in a clearing ahead. It was made of ochre and lined with a velvet that would've suited royalty. The table was no different, nor the stone gazebo that hung over her, nor the man sitting on the chair across from hers.

And it turned out, it wasn't as easy to break a person as it was to fall in love with them. It was difficult to argue with an angel once you stepped foot in heaven.

'Magmaya,' he said, smiled and stood, gesturing to the table. His robes fell to the unending rows of platters, symmetrically arranged around a number of tall candles, burning bright. All around her there were herbs she didn't recognise, meat she'd never seen walk and silverware she wasn't sure what to do with.

Fabius plucked a grape from a basket on the table and pursed it between his lips. 'Pray sit.' He gestured to the empty chair. 'Help yourself to whatever you may please.'

'Thank you.' She did as he commanded and found herself staring into those starry eyes of his again. 'It's a beautiful dress,' she stuttered.

'A beautiful dress for a beautiful girl in a beautiful garden,' he said, laughing. 'What do you think, Magmaya? I had my landscapers import trees from the Summerlands and stones from Glassrock just to lay the foundations.'

'Impressive.' Bile began to build in her throat.

'Wine?' he asked, groping at a bottle and pouring her a glass before she hazarded an answer. 'The grapes in this were broken down to make this wine perhaps a century ago.' He set the bottle down, smiling. 'There is no finer gift I can think of to give back to this world than wine.'

'Perhaps grapes?' Magmaya suggested. 'Not everyone enjoys spirits.'

'No,' he agreed, 'but they miss out.' He raised his glass. 'You and I both drink, do we not? We've nothing to miss.'

'Nothing,' the girl uttered, chiming her glass against his. She downed the drink. 'To good health,' she said, wiping her chin.

'Good health.' Fabius smirked, lapping at his wine and wiping his lip. 'Look at you—chancellor of Orianne! How quickly you've again become a high-born woman from that dusty little girl in the depths of the Damnation.'

'Well, your baths are luxurious.' Magmaya felt sick complimenting him as if she was betraying herself with each breath. Perhaps it was his intoxicating perfume or the aroma of rich food, but she felt uneasy all the same. She almost wanted to go home.

'Everything is luxurious here,' he said. 'The north has long been isolated. You seem to have forgotten the finer things in this world. The commoners call it decadence. I call it living.'

'Oh,' Magmaya remarked, unsure.

'I can see why you would want to escape that miserable place.' Fabius smiled, then looked to her as if sensing her blood growing hot. 'Oh, I'm sorry. I mean not to insult you. It is only that the mountains insisted on casting terrible shadows and there were no stars to look upon—I love watching the stars, watching them move. You know the shamans say we used to travel across them? I doubt upon any of them there was ever a place as grand as my gardens, though.'

'Things fall from the sky, sometimes,' Magmaya said, growing annoyed with his arrogance. 'They did in Ranvirus anyway. The priests said it was divine punishment.'

Fabius laughed at that and asked, 'So is that why you're here, then? To get a better view of the stars?'

Magmaya almost laughed too. *If I looked up at the stars for but a second, I'd probably find a sword through my back.*

'Ranvirus wasn't the place for me,' she admitted with a sigh. 'I abandoned my people, yes, but... it's better that I disappeared. I told you, I made mistakes.'

'Not everyone's born to lead.' Fabius nodded. 'But you fought for your home, did you not?'

'My... Siedous taught me,' she said. 'I can swing a sword good enough, I suppose. But nothing like your angels.'

'I'd worry if you could,' he remarked, lulling the glass between his fingers. 'Knives on the other hand? You seem to be handy with those.'

So that's what this is about, she realised and looked down, half-embarrassed, half-angry. 'I know.'

'It was quite something that happened at Highport,' Fabius remarked. 'Spider was a...' he paused, '...friend of mine. It's unfortunate he had to die the way he did. He was a valuable asset to us.'

'I'm sorry,' she stuttered. 'I should've thought. But—'

'You were reckless.'

'There was a girl about to be raped.' She frowned.

'She was a sell-maiden. That's what they're for.'

'You weren't there,' Magmaya insisted. 'You didn't hear her scream.'

'A lot of screaming comes from those whorehouses—you think that was any different?' Fabius shook his head. 'There's a silent order in Highport; one which rules from the shadows, and I thought you'd have better sense than to piss them off.'

'I wasn't thinking.' She sunk into the chair.

Fabius nodded and took a deep breath, sat back and closed his eyes. 'You'll learn the ways of the south in time,' he said. 'But this whole escapade was unnecessary, girl.'

'It wouldn't have happened if your angels stepped in. You could end all the crime in Highport on your own,' Magmaya remarked.

'There's a fragile balance to these things, girl. You think you can shake a tree without the leaves falling off?'

'That balance can be changed,' she protested. 'If anyone in this world could change that, then it would be you.'

'You seem to have the wrong idea about us,' Fabius said. 'Has Kurulian been whispering to you?'

'Excuse me?' Magmaya asked, feeling a bead of sweat run down her flank.

'Look, the Divinicus Order was established long ago, Magmaya. And it was established under a single Lord Commander,' Fabius explained. 'But it was decided that a single seraph would not be enough to command all of the powers; there had to be cherubs and thrones and all ranks of us.' He looked to her with a smile like ice. 'You may eat, still.' He swallowed another grape before continuing, and Magmaya slumped into her seat.

'Anyway, three Legatus were appointed to command where their Lord Commander couldn't—an extension of his will, if you may. I have come to watch over Rael, Akanah, and my most exalted Legatus and perhaps the greatest swordsman in the world—Kurulian.'

'And why am I being told this?' Magmaya's voice was shaking.

'It seems you do not fear him as you do the rest of us, girl.'

'Fear?' she scoffed.

'*Fear.*' Fabius nodded. 'When a little girl sees a flock of angels descend from the clouds, she may stop for a minute to stare in wonder, but only before she runs away.'

'You're all terrifying,' she remarked. 'But what's your obsession with Kurulian? I only said his name! I was sick, I wasn't thinking.'

'My obsession is that this would not be the first time a Legatus has turned against his Lord Commander,' Fabius snapped.

'If your Legatus turns against you, then that's not my doing,' she said. 'I was just a girl who had lost her father. I won't be accused of... whatever you're accusing me of.'

'An accusation reveals one's true nature in time.' Fabius looked to the flowers around him as the last of the sunlight shed down on them.

'Your soldier said he knew me,' Magmaya remarked, breaking the silence. 'He said I looked like

Kharon Vorr. How would he know? I never saw him in the north.'

'Akanah.' Fabius nodded. 'Your home may have felt like a lonely place; it did to me. But you were far from alone. Your freezing royal cities weren't forsaken nor forgotten. They were maintained by favours from the south. While Kytheran ships ran to you, afraid, we may have well been your gods, keeping tabs on your folly.'

'If that's so then why did I have to stand alone against a warlord?' Magmaya grit her teeth, feeling anger boil in her. 'If your Legatus was watching over me, then why were we left alone for so long? It wasn't just Highport, was it? It seems you're intent on abandoning everyone.'

'I wouldn't get into a conflict that brought me nothing. I would expend none of my men for that.'

'To save others is nothing?'

'To save outsiders is nothing.' Fabius raised an eyebrow.

'Then why am I still here?' she spat.

The Lord Commander paused, pondering something before he turned back to her. It looked as if his façade was to crack in two. 'Allow me to tell you something, Magmaya.'

'I fear nothing can stop you from doing that,' she said under her breath.

'I once awoke to a great upheaval in my home too,' he started. 'I escaped what remained of my village and travelled to the altar which stood atop a nearby plateau. I had scarcely left the house before and the next I knew, the world around me was on fire and under the sunder of pirates—you can imagine how afraid I must have been.' He laughed.

'You can be afraid?' she asked, only half joking.

'Apparently.' He paused. 'But that's beside the point; I was half naked and covered in bruises, but I dragged myself up that mountainside, feet swollen with pores, white and burned. I stayed for the night once I made it halfway, where I swear I died. By the next sundown, freezing rain had lashed away half the skin on my back, but I reached the flat of the peak.

'And what did I find there other than a pair of Divinicus, heavy with the blood of the pirates? They guarded the plateau as if it had been their babe, but as I approached them, I fell at their feet like the helpless bugger I was. I cried to them, and I wept in the mud and ashes and asked those angels something I'm sure a girl like you might've.' He smiled.

'And what was that?' she said.

'What would any orphan ask?'

'*Are the pirates dead?*'

Fabius scoffed. '*Why did you not save my mother and father*?' he spat. 'Why, when two men from paradise above could ward off an entire raiding party, could they not spare a working man and his pregnant woman? Why did they save the cottages, the churches—the bloody whorehouses from the pirates, only watch them burn from the hilltops?'

'Why?'

'*Why* is the most dangerous question a man can ask,' Fabius answered, taking a sip of wine and swilling it around his mouth. He swallowed and smiled. 'They told me angels had no cause for the common man. They told me there were larger triumphs at stake, beyond me. Perhaps I didn't understand at the time, but if I were at that plateau now, dressed in pearly-white, I do think I would make the right decision.'

'The scriptures the Kytherans brought said that every man was a gift to their mothers and gods alike.' Magmaya frowned. 'I don't think I believe in any god, but if you really are an angel, then perhaps you better try to read a holy book.'

'Like the church does?' Fabius boomed. 'We make our own gods.'

'Your family died because the men you lead are heartless,' Magmaya scorned. 'What use is the bigger picture if the frame is burning?'

'Look. *I* didn't fall to the fires.' His teeth shone, and his eyes widened as he spoke. 'As Akanah studied the children of Ranvirus, I decided to let nature take its course. I stood by the teachings of those angels I had met, and I stand by them today.'

'What exactly did you call me here for?' she spat.

Fabius laughed to himself. The sun was beginning to set.

'Magmaya,' he started. 'I am willing to forgive this little delinquency. Don't we all suffer strife and rebellion?' He paused for a moment. 'I've one proposition for you, though, my chancellor.'

'Yes?' *Chancellor?* It had felt an age since she'd been called that.

'Sir Larjun Uliana has recently arrived back from council at Lostgarden. He's my nephew—a young lad, bold and handsome. Unmarried. To cement an alliance between Ranvirus and the Divinicus of Inamorata, I propose that you and he are betrothed.'

'What?' Magmaya exclaimed. Her face was turning red.

'All women must find themselves a political union of sorts. Besides, I'm offering you a second chance for what you decided in the north.'

'I don't represent the north,' she spat. 'I was a deserter—I'm not one of them anymore. Besides, I'm not marrying a soul.'

'You may not be the chancellor any longer, but whether you're a deserter, bastard, cripple or girl, you're still a high-born. And if you quit that temper of yours, you might still make good for my nephew. He's strong-willed, and I hoped someone might've liked to balance that.'

'This isn't why I travelled south.'

'No, you travelled south in an act of defiance. Now you must pay for that.'

'I travelled south because I was afraid of what I was already paying for!' Magmaya cried and thumped her fist down on the table, spilling her wine. 'I wanted to start again—to see the Silver City, but every dream I have is crushed before I wake up, *dammit.*'

'I won't hear any more of this,' he asserted. 'I'm showing you mercy. My nephew will meet with you on the morrow. Assure your handmaiden dresses you well.' He paused. 'Now is there anything else you want, girl?'

'I want to sleep.' She stood abruptly, threw the chair back and tossed the rose from her ear into her wine glass, not stopping to watch the petals swim about the red water. She skulked away, letting the garden fall behind her step, as her dress swept the ground once more.

Fabius smiled and finished his meal.

Sixteen

No matter how much she pleaded with Anclyn to make her look wretched, it seemed the handmaiden couldn't weave her into anything less than beautiful. So Magmaya made an effort to accidentally fray the edges of her dress and spill wine across her belly.

Sir Larjun Uliana, on the other hand, was as handsome as his uncle, and he was quite aware of it. He was a few hours late, of course, but Magmaya was thankful she had more time to make herself look a mess.

He wasn't as tall as any of the Divinicus, but then again, he wasn't one. All the same, he'd made a statement of riding to the ground below her balcony on a silvery-white mare, caped in thick lavender from head to toe. A dozen men rode with him, perhaps fools or comrades, scoffing and waving and cheering as he approached the palace, just like in the faery stories.

'Sweet Magmaya Vorr of Orianne,' he boomed. 'Would you come down to me, so I can see your face in the morning sun?'

'You *could* come up here,' she muttered to herself.

He appeared to have heard, though, and sneered, 'What was that?' Larjun cocked his head. 'I will have you know, Miss Vorr, that I have a hundred other high-born girls waiting on me to address them and you are but one. Now once again, if you would be so kind as to come down here and show me that beautiful face, as well as give my men a glimpse of your breasts of yours, eh? You do have breasts, no?'

If *she* had been a Divinicus, she would have dispatched of him then and there.

She wasn't, though, and reluctantly Magmaya found herself clambering down the trailing staircases, guards escorting her as she did. Before she even stepped outside, she could smell his wafting perfumes and sour incenses amid the warm breeze.

'My dear girl,' he crooned. 'It is an honour.'

'Lord Uliana,' she said, curtsying. He was even more distasteful up close.

'No, my lady, that's my father's name and my uncle's before him.' He scowled. 'Call me Larl, if you must.'

'Larl.' She nodded and began to walk alongside his mare. 'Have you heard much about me?'

'Only that you're a high-born girl my uncle insists on marrying me to.' He sniffed. 'Shoved you in Highport before he got the idea, though. I do hope you've bathed since.'

'A fair amount,' Magmaya remarked. 'So how do you like your girls then?'

He laughed. 'I like my girls to see to my needs, and I shall see to theirs, my lady. That's all I have to offer any woman.'

Magmaya began to realise how young his voice sounded, how childish he was. The way he pronounced 'woman' was the same way an infant pronounced 'mother'.

'So, what do you have to offer me in return?' he continued.

'I've been rather busy lately,' Magmaya said. 'I was chancellor in the north,' she boasted.

'Yet you ran away all the same, I hear.'

That hurt, she thought. 'Only after I won a bloody war.' She knew she shouldn't have said it, but the words were brewing inside of her. She wanted to punch him in that pretty face of his.

'I like my girls feisty,' he said, seemingly unmoved. 'Though uncle said you were a fair maiden?'

'How old are you?' She ignored him.

'Seventeen,' he replied loudly. 'Uncle says on my next name day, he shall take me to a joust at Nemesis Palace. Perhaps if you do me proud, I might take you along.'

Magmaya scoffed. 'So, have you ever even taken up that fancy sword of yours?'

'*Eclipse* is more than a fancy sword!' He reeled back, voice wavering. 'I'll have you know that I stabbed a halfling through the heart when he attacked a Divinicus.'

'A half—?' she stuttered. 'You mean a dwarf? With a feat like that, one of your men would better be suited for me, I think.'

His comrades looked around to one another with gaudy smirks, but Larl was growing red.

'Shut up!' he screamed. 'You know my uncle. He won't be happy about you talking to me like this!'

'No,' she remarked. 'Uncle won't be proud.' *But I suppose I'll have to suffer him later...*

'You'll regret this spite, wench,' he cried feebly, but then he turned to his men, cold, and said, 'Go and take her clothes. And then her tongue.'

Magmaya felt something of a red-hot fear course through her as Larl's men trotted over with curled fingers and crooked hands. Her legs turned stiff.

She stumbled as they swiped, and her neck ached as they tore at her, and all around her, there was Larl laughing as he sat atop his pompous horse.

'Leave me alone!' she cried, and a cold arm fastened around her wrist.

'Clear out,' the arm's voice called, and suddenly, the hands were off her. There were curses and taunts from Larl's men, then the wrinkled face of a palace guard looking down to her. 'My lady, did they—?'

She shook her head and dismissed him, catching her breath and buttoning her clothes. She could still feel a thousand hands on her, though, clawing and scraping at her skin. She wanted to be alone.

Magmaya looked back up to her balcony, held herself and sighed. But then, something caught her eye— Cheyne Reed, standing in the window above her own like a cat basking in the sunlight. He appeared to have been watching, she noted, with a grimace about his lips as he did.

He looked to her with a nod and turned away into the manse.

The next dress hung off her body the same as the last. But this one was either too big or too small, she couldn't tell, and it was clear it belonged to someone else; Magmaya was borrowing a life from another girl and dressing herself to fit a mask she didn't own.

Anclyn smiled at her faintly as she dressed from behind a column of decorative water, but there was no denying what she thought. Magmaya hadn't told her yet that perhaps she had thrown away her only opportunity for stability, so it came as a surprise when she had been told in the early hours that Fabius wanted to meet her again, and within minutes, the dress had been carried in by a pair of suiters. Her eyes were still sore with the anxiety of the day before, but Anclyn insisted on rushing her from her chambers and bathing her in so much incense that her lungs burned.

They were callous scents and calm scents, healing scents and herbal ones, but they all reeked of some other girl—the girl who owned the dress. She longed for the days where everything had fallen into place—that night in the forest—the night she'd told Kurulian everything she'd ever known and everything she'd ever been. But that was a lifetime ago. Perhaps it was an atonement for her sins—perhaps she should've taken Rache with her. It was selfish to have acted as impulsively as she did.

Perhaps she shouldn't have come at all.

'A rose, my lady?' The handmaiden held the flower out. 'It would suit the white of the dress. It is just as beautiful as the last, I think.'

Magmaya shook her head. 'I must wear only what he wants me to.'

'And your hair?'

'My hair...?' she paused. 'Has someone worn this dress before, Anclyn?' she asked after a moment.

'My lady, I...' she stuttered.

'*Anclyn.*'

The handmaiden looked defeated. 'How did you know?'

'It reeks of pipe smoke,' Magmaya said. 'And it's not quite my size.'

'I...' Anclyn stopped. 'I shouldn't be telling you this, my lady.'

'I figured enough for myself,' she remarked. 'Spider said there was a sell-maiden Fabius kept safe. It must've been hers.'

'I could get you a new dress, my lady.'

'No.' Magmaya shook her head. 'Perhaps acting like she did is my only opportunity to have Fabius actually pay attention to me.' *Perhaps he might even show me a bit of mercy after yesterday.* 'Did you know her?'

'No, I...' Anclyn started, 'it was many years ago. She was but a passing girl before the Lord Commander took her into hiding.'

'Was she from Kythera?'

Anclyn nodded.

'You should've told me.' Magmaya bit her cheek. 'So, you remember nothing about her? Not even her face?'

'I was young.' Her eyes were wide. 'But I remember her voice; it was warm, and I was very afraid. She was kind to me.'

'You remember how she spoke, but not what she looked like?'

'A Summerwitch once told me that nothing was permanent—not even death,' Anclyn explained. '*When a man dies, he is born again in the soil, in the buzz of the honeybees and in the song of the birds,* she said. So, what good would remembering a man's face be when the same man would come back with a different one?' she asked. 'Besides, I've cared for so many and—'

'Who were these witches?' Magmaya cut in, concerned.

'There were many,' she explained. 'They worked with unspeakable things: black arts, electrics, silverchange...'

Magmaya nodded and stood, finding herself on the balcony again. The sea breeze sifted through the air and filled her mouth with salt as she looked out to the beaches, following the warm dunes and queer trees and small harbours that ran across the waves to nowhere.

'Is there nothing you can remember about the girl?' Magmaya asked at last. 'Anything I can say—anything I can use to make Fabius at ease with me?'

'I must not betray the Lord Commander,' Anclyn asserted. 'A month we travelled across the Water under the toil of the old masters. The Divinicus liberated us. I apologise, my lady, I shall not speak ill of them. Not here.'

'No, no,' Magmaya said, 'I don't need you to betray him. I only want to understand. The girl drowned at Highport, no?'

Anclyn thought for a moment before exclaiming, 'My lady, I remember now—she loved the seas.'

'The seas?'

'Yes.' The servant girl nodded. 'I remember her telling me how she loved the tides and the trees and the beaches—she wore seashells and ivory I think. Perhaps I do not exactly remember her look...'

'It will suffice,' Magmaya said and ambled back from the window, setting herself down before Anclyn. 'It'll have to.'

She knew her way back through Fabius' garden but took her time even so. She made sure to gaze at each flower as if she was a paramour, high off her love, and bask in the low light as it bleached her skin from that new-born sun. Once she reached Fabius, she approached him with a grin, curtsied and sat without being told.

The table was laid out the same—perhaps exactly so for the candles flickered as if they have never been extinguished the day before. Her eyes didn't leave his as he gazed up her body—the dress against her chest, her hair at her fringe, running down her collarbones to the seams below her breasts. There were no flowers in her hair, for that was how *she* had been sculpted.

She nodded to the angel opposite and poured herself a glass of wine, beginning to drink without a thought.

'Magmaya,' Fabius started with a smile. 'I am most glad to see you again.'

She downed the wine (sour), looked up to him in agreement and said, 'I'm glad you invited me.' She reached across the table and grappled for a yellow fruit, flinching slightly as she realised she'd bitten into the skin. She gave it a disapproving stare and set it down as Fabius bellowed with laughter. Her heart sunk.

'You can wolf down the bitter wine but not what I grow in my own gardens?' He smirked. 'No matter. Another beautiful dress, don't you agree?'

'Only as exquisite as the last,' she replied. *He'd brought up the dress already,* she thought, *was now the time?* 'Whose was it?'

Fabius lowered his glass and licked his lips where the wine had stained them. He wiped his chin of violet and grit his teeth behind the draping handkerchief.

'What would make you assume it was anyone's but your own?'

'Where I came from, I did not have a new dress for each dinner.'

'This is not where you came from.' His voice was sweet, but there was a poison underneath that couldn't find guise in the wine. 'I can afford the finest trinkets, the finest garden and, of course, the finest drink at the mere snap of my fingers.' He pursed them together and smiled, knowingly. 'There is nothing beyond my reach, certainly not a shiny little dress.'

'You would waste a dress on me?'

'You're hardly a waste,' he said. 'You and I may have butted heads, but there is no denying you are an important woman, Magmaya. My nephew seemed to have thought so, anyway.'

'Really?' She was surprised, feeling cold again.

'I must admit, I am displeased in the way you treated him,' he said.

'He tried to strip me,' she scorned.

'He's a young lad, Magmaya.'

'That's no excuse.'

'*You* treated *him* unfairly,' Fabius replied. 'I was hoping to court the pair of you. We made a deal, remember? I would forget your delinquencies in exchange for you and him to be betrothed.'

'I made no such deal.' She cocked her head. 'I'm thankful for your hospitality, Lord Commander, but I wouldn't marry for it.'

'Then what would you marry for?'

Magmaya sat back in her chair. It was a question she had never particularly thought about; marriage had just never occurred to her. She didn't think there was anyone she would want to spend her life with, especially so if it was arranged.

'I don't know, but I'd have you pick out my wedding dress,' she remarked.

'Don't try and distract me,' he said. 'This isn't about dresses. This is about what I'm going to do with you.'

'Then why would you go through the trouble of giving me someone else's?'

Fabius' smile turned to something grim. 'Is this a game to you?'

'It smells like pipe smoke,' Magmaya explained.

'Must have been from some ship outside.'

'Not many smoking ships outside,' she bluffed.

'There are enough,' he shot back.

There was silence for a number of seconds. Then she asked, 'Did you love her?'

Magmaya hadn't meant to have said it quite so early, but the words rushed to her mouth from her gut in an instant as if she hadn't rehearsed them a thousand times before. A new kind of adrenaline washed through her, and so she didn't notice Fabius wave his hand, nor the pair of Divinicus guards emerge from behind and take her arms with their iron fingers.

Her mouth turned dry as they pulled her from her chair, and she stumbled into their grip.

'I meant no offence, Lord Commander,' she lied, and her heart seemed to burst from her chest, 'but you pitied *her*. Why not me?'

'And who was *she*?' Fabius' voice was like the sun and the moon, life and death all at once; he might as well have been a god.

'I don't know,' she admitted. 'I never wanted to act like this—'

Fabius cut her off. 'Is this the work of that damned servitor?' He motioned to the Divinicus. 'See to her—'

'No!' Magmaya shrieked, Anclyn dancing in her vision. 'Fabius, please.'

'Please? Have I not granted you asylum enough? Have I not fed you? Have you not supped at my court and drunk my wine, only to spit in the face of my family?'

'*Please.*' She sunk down. 'Don't throw me out, I have no one else. Please!'

He looked to her and bit his tongue. After a moment, he brushed his hand through the air, and the Divinicus released her, arms aching and throat sore. Her heart rose and fell, and for a moment, she felt as if she was going to be sick.

'Spider told me,' she admitted at last. 'Spider told me there was a woman you loved. But he's dead now! There's no reprimanding the dead.'

'We'll see.'

'I too have loved,' she said. 'Perhaps not the same as you and perhaps not as fiercely, but Fabius, I need you to just listen to me as you listened to her. You were the one who dressed me like this...!'

'Why should I not cast you aside?' He shook his head. 'I have shown you mercy for the last time.'

'And I'm grateful,' Magmaya nodded. 'Sometimes my tongue gets the better of me—'

'Enough!' Fabius cut in. 'Just tell me what you want and tell me quickly. I've little patience left for your kind.'

The gentle humming of a bee broke the silence, and Magmaya's shoulders fell. Holy beams of light cut across the peach skies, unbroken and unfettered until, at last, they died with the passing of the day.

'Let me join you.' Magmaya bit her tongue as a new sun rose within her. 'Make me an angel.'

Seventeen

We make our own gods, Fabius had said—then why couldn't she be one? Instead, he'd laughed and expelled her from the gardens without another word, the flavour of vile wine still clinging to her lips.

The night showered over Magmaya as she slumped against the windows, the hum of crashing waves from the seas outside keeping her awake. Shattered moonbeams struck the room like spears as portraits of pearly armour stared down at her, phantoms in the dusk. She had never been so unsettled, so far from home, and so unsatisfied with who she had forced herself to become.

She considered calling Anclyn; a dull ring of the bedside bell would do the trick, but she found herself deciding against it; it was no use disturbing her sleep for petty matters. Magmaya had chosen this life for herself, and if she was to end up cold and alone, then that was her doing.

The wind that whipped against her bare back was nothing compared to the icy nights she had spent in Ranvirus, though—nothing compared to the nights she and Rache had spent huddled beneath a mountain of wolf fur and the blazing of a dozen candles. He'd told her the stories he'd read from his books, and she'd told him the stories she'd lived; how Kharon Vorr had stalked the halls in a search for understanding before she'd disappeared to the lake in the forest where there had been roses and corpses and—oh.

Magmaya set herself up, sweating. Perhaps it had been in another life, or perhaps it had been just yesterday—it didn't matter anymore. She was at the Prism Manse now, and nothing could stop that—no estranged morning a thousand years ago.

As she made herself comfortable, she felt her shoulder brush against something cold beneath her bundle of lilac pillows. She straightened herself and yanked at it, finding a newly crumpled scrap of paper in her palm. She'd been a fool to have not noticed it earlier, but it didn't matter; her heart was rising in her chest, hands were shaking the way they had all those moons ago. It was his handwriting, there was no doubt, but it spoke to her the way a stranger did.

> *My chancellor,*
>
> *The balcony.*
>
> *Xx*

Her heart sunk a little, and the last light of the day broke across the room. But she forced herself up across to the window anyway, scrubbed away the scars of her breath, and peered through to the seas beyond. There was not a soul in sight, it appeared, save for the haunting of the waves crashing against the rocks. The buzz of a distant city roared on the horizon as smoke coiled up into the clouds, trees swaying as the winds kissed them. She was about to turn away—but that was before a glitter from somewhere below struck the corner of her eye, a thousand different colours at once.

She needn't have looked any closer—it was a Divinicus to be sure—an unflinching pearly mask staring back at her. And so, without another thought, Magmaya threw open the double doors and stalked out onto the balcony and into the moonlight where the figure stared up at her, faceless against the wind.

'Have you been waiting all night?' She laughed, a spring breeze toying with her hair. 'You weren't to know when I was going to open that letter.'

Kurulian shrugged, his armour crinkling beneath his bulk, and turned back to the shore. He plucked a stone from the many beneath his feet and tossed it out to the waves, losing it to the midnight gale.

'You're still armoured?'

As if in response, he moved his fingers to his headdress, and with a swift turn, lowered it to his elbow. His half-blemished, half-beautiful face stared back at her, and Magmaya found it was the same face beneath palm trees as it had been beneath pine. She watched as he threw another stone and made his way towards her—as close to the balcony as he was able to get while she could still make out those distant eyes of his.

'Voices down,' he commanded.

Magmaya sighed. 'What did you call me for?' she asked at last, and all the thrill was gone. 'I can't imagine it would be for a stroll along the sand.'

'Do you know where Fabius is sending the Divinicus next?' he asked, and she shook her head. 'There's a small island off the coast here called Belliousa. All the residents there are acolytes—fanatics of the First.' He scoffed as he spoke.

'The First?'

'A religion.'

'Ah, yes. Your kind are so above that,' Magmaya remarked.

'There was a coup about a decade ago,' he said, ignoring her. 'It was then the Cult of the First broke their treaties with Inamorata; their new High Priestess had a great disdain for our Lord Commander, it seemed. Anyway, in a few moons time, a small company of Legatus Akanah's men will sail there, and the isle will be ours once more.' His voice was but a whisper, though it carried through the night as if he were an inch away. 'Perhaps you've already heard of this in our talks?'

'I haven't been invited to your talks,' she remarked.

'You don't need to be invited to hear them.' He smiled. 'They aren't quite as secure as you might assume. One small favour for a servitor here, another one there, and a man can find out anything. That's what the chain of whispers is all about.'

'What if I don't want to hear about your Divinicus' dealings?' She was still angry with him, in truth, for leaving her for dead with Fabius. No glassy midnight encounter would remedy that.

'Well, I heard you don't want to distance yourself from us as much as you say.' He paused. 'Do you remember what I told you when your council in Ranvirus was adjourned?'

'We discussed many things.' She swallowed.

'I didn't *ask* to be an angel,' Kurulian snapped. 'I *burned* for them. Perhaps I've done things I regret, but all I've done has been in the eyes of the Lord Commander, and in the eyes of what is just. To become an angel, you do not ask the seraphim—you kill for the seraphim,' he said, and Magmaya felt chicken skin crawl across her neck.

'Fabius told me you're perhaps the greatest swordsman in the world.' She grit her teeth.

'*Perhaps*?'

'Well I can swing a blade, I chance,' she said. 'Fabius had no reason to dismiss me so.'

'No.' He shook his head in disapproval. 'A sword will not win you a war. At best, a sword will kill the right man and save you the war. But fire *wins* wars, girl.'

'Fire?'

'All you've ever known is the snow, I suppose,' he said with a laugh. 'Look, my chancellor, at this very moment, there's a resurgence of mercenaries at Fleetfront, a prince travels north to take my head, and there's the issue of *the damned blockade* as Fabius has resorted to calling the Reaches,' he scoffed. 'Those first two have driven the Lord Commander into a crazed spin, but the Reaches? They've driven him mad. For eight months now, four thousand Inamoratan troops have been trying to lift a siege against our spice imports in the east, but they've been met with nigh-endless opposition. Perhaps you could ponder on that.' He took a breath.

'I don't know anything about your politics,' she said. 'I barely knew my own. I don't know where the Reaches are either. I only travelled here by following angels…' *I'm not one of you.*

Kurulian sighed and hummed, 'You may have travelled here by following angels, but you're heaven sent to me.'

She stood back, unsure of what to say, so she plucked up the courage to ask, 'What about Belliousa then? Why are you telling me any of this?'

There was no response.

'Gods, I gave everything to come here,' she spoke again, louder, as she gestured to the seas. 'Everything! And you've spent half my time ignoring me.'

'Are you still breathing?' he asked.

'What—?' She paused, confused. 'Yes…'

'Then you haven't given everything, girl.'

She looked to the heavens, annoyed. 'Tell me what happened to the Silver City, at least,' she demanded. 'You helped me escape the north, now help me escape this fresh hell of… awful, awful wine.'

Kurulian's wrinkled lip contorted into something of a grin. 'Cyrel is the coldest place in winter,' he answered. 'That's all.' He turned and began to walk away.

Magmaya pondered for a moment about speaking, but then did so anyway. 'Wait!' she called through the dark. '*You* know why Fabius can't lift that blockade, don't you?'

His eyes narrowed, and he reached to his waist. White glass gleamed in the moonlight, then the air, and then she caught it, cool in her palms.

'Goodbye Magmaya.'

She didn't protest this time but looked to her hands instead. She found a small, clear vial, clasped with cork and lined with mercury. Inside, there were all manners of powders and strange leaves—no larger than her smallest fingernail; they were green and silver, brown and gold, and they shone even when the moon escaped behind the clouds. She raised an eyebrow and fastened it around her wrist, her heart warm and trembling.

And when she looked up again, the Lord Legatus was nowhere to be seen.

Later, she found herself falling. Or was she flying? Magmaya tried to tell herself it didn't matter which, but truly it did. In one version of events, she would plummet forever until she forgot what it was like not to. In the other, perhaps she would find some strength within herself to rise and scream and soar.

'I'm afraid of falling,' she tried to shout, but only a murmur came out.

'No need,' a watery voice answered from the shadows. 'You could fall forever, so long as you don't land.'

Streams of light burned from above before darkness reigned again. The stars swirled around her limp body like wet oil on a canvas, and after what felt an eternity, she fell into a well of mist, standing quiet and afraid. It formed a vast hall of mirrors, surrounding her from every possible angle—and then the voice spoke again, 'The man who loves you or the woman you love. Choose.'

'I can't!' Magmaya cried, and for the first time she realised, 'There's no one here I love.'

One of her reflections turned with a smile, and her visage swelled like the breaking of still water. Following a deep impulse, Magmaya felt herself step forward inside it.

Sand. It was in seeping down her back and burning in her eyes. She'd never seen a desert before, not in all those cold nights in Ranvirus, but a voice in her head told her it had to be one—the rolling dunes, the suffocating heat, the loneliness.

She turned to the horizon, and there she found three small girls walking, or rather leaping, towards her faster than any girl could. Under the beating of the harsh sunlight, she could make out bruised mouths stretching from ear to ear, stitched into a perpetual smile with eyes dead long before their time.

But a moment later, they were gone, and the dunes had turned to mountains, and the scorched orange sands had become snow. But it was still hot, hotter than before, even. She only realised why when she turned and found the ground had caught alight. From the heavens, fire was given birth, and from the icy grounds, oil erupted, until all of it was lost in the inferno. All except her.

'You can't kill us.' The voice was warm.

'You can't kill us.' Magmaya nodded, but all she could do was choke on the flames, choke and choke until she choked herself awake.

She rolled over onto her stomach to face the ceiling and found Anclyn watching over her. There was no sunlight streaming through the windows. The room was sheathed in shadow and night. How long had she been gone for?

'What man loves me...?' she stuttered, wiping spit from her lip.

'My lady?' Anclyn asked. 'I didn't mean to wake you, but you were out for so long, I—'

'Out? Oh. I had a terrible dream, I...' She looked to her wrist, finding the vial.

She hadn't told her about Kurulian—surely there was no need? Their meeting meant nothing, but she couldn't afford to spill those secrets—they were the only ones she had left in the world.

'Cyrel.' She rolled her shoulders back, remembering: finding a map, scouring every inch of it, and taking her leave for just a moment. Every minute felt as if it was only a dream.

'Yes, my lady,' Anclyn said timidly. 'But are you sure you're alright...? You were sleeping awfully heavily.'

'Of course,' Magmaya said. 'I'm fine.'

She sat up in the pale moonlight and looked to the handmaiden as she stood about her chambers. None of it made any sense anymore, though—not since she'd taken a sample from the small vial (just out of interest). It had been more than enough to knock her out for a while, and far more numbing than any Dew of the Honey. But Anclyn needn't know that either.

She followed the handmaiden drearily back to the map, finding the tattered paper sprawled about the floor. She traced the lines from the Ash Wastes to the Crownlands, and the Spires to Rallocier as they crept drearily down the continent's neck; it was all so much larger than anything she'd dreamt of. Above it all, there was the seemingly endless Lumiar Badlands, and above that, there was her home, so cold and far, far away.

'I do fear Cyrel isn't on here,' the handmaiden replied. 'Not on any of the small notes or anything.'

'It has to be.' She yawned, feeling sleep kiss her again. 'Are there any other maps?'

'Perhaps there are, but finding another at this hour will be a stroke of luck,' Anclyn admitted. 'I doubt there are any more stashed away behind drawers.'

'Fabius told me Cyrel was in the north,' she lied. If it was the coldest place in winter, she reasoned it would be somewhere close to her home. 'Well, not *north,* but north enough. So where is it?' She pressed her fists into the ragged thing. 'How old is this, anyway?' she asked. 'Must be at least thirty years.'

'Something like that.' Anclyn nodded. 'Perhaps it was discarded for a reason.' She thought for a moment. 'I've heard the Lord Commander speak about Cyrel—oh.'

'What is it?'

'Cyrel is a name, my lady.'

'I'm well aware.'

'No, forgive me,' she continued. 'Cyrel is the name of a man.'

The coldest place in winter. Magmaya mused. *These are cold men indeed.*

'No, *surely,* it must be a place,' she rasped.

'I don't quite understand,' the handmaiden said. 'If perhaps you could explain what this is all—'

'I can't,' she cut her off. 'Anclyn, if Cyrel is a man, then who?'

'The Lord Commander speaks of him sometimes,' she admitted. 'Emperor beyond the Reaches, Son of...' she trailed off and moved her fingers to an armada of crudely drawn mountains and a thin, snow-swept shore. 'Son of Faurgun, the Malignant King and Master of Slavers.'

Magmaya followed Anclyn's hands to the peaks and then to the inks scribbled beneath her pink nails— *Faurgun,* it said in the common tongue; Faurgun beyond the Reaches. Faurgun the city. Faurgun, the man.

'Each ruler must've renamed it after themselves,' Magmaya concluded. *Only in an empire of angels would a man be so arrogant.*

But then, she thought to Orianne and knew that wasn't true, a city and a community named after the heroics of Orianna Rel, the Liberator. Perhaps her home and this strange wilderness weren't so different after all.

'I've only a couple hours before sunrise,' Magmaya started. 'Is there any chance at all I can meet with the Lord Commander before tonight?'

'I can arrange whispers among the handmaidens,' Anclyn suggested.

'Whispers?' She thought back to what Kurulian had said.

'We share information,' she explained. 'And we can use that to look out for ourselves… and our mistresses. Anyway, your request will reach Fabius before sunrise. He seldom sleeps.'

She couldn't remember what she'd said next, but the Lord Legatus was dancing in her mind until the night had grown old. She thought and cried and cried and thought again until she couldn't feel her toes, nor the pounding in her head. But soon enough, daylight had broken and what was due had to be done.

By then she'd convinced herself to back down and to know her place; she wasn't royal here, she wasn't beautiful, nor a chancellor or a person at that; perhaps if she had been a whore she would've been given a little more respect—she wished she could've laughed at that.

Her eyes still bled with the rising of the sun when the whispers returned; the angels had agreed to meet her again, but further murmurings had quickly followed; it appeared she would find Fabius in his gardens, but not alone. His entire council would be there, as well as Akanah's and Rael's own, and a hundred more scribes and advisors, no doubt. Magmaya could only pray Kurulian would attend too, but there had seldom been news of him. Besides, from the way he had spoken to her the evening before, it seemed as if it would be a while before they would talk again.

The gardens had a sense of foreboding this time. The flowers no longer blossomed like gold and honey in the light, but instead frowned at her every step. She wasn't special any longer; no more would she be the apple of Fabius' eye. Perhaps once she had thought a pretty dress and a reminder of his past was enough to control a vengeful god, but now, she walked to his council as a sinner did to his priest.

No dress had been hung for her that morning; there were no fresh bath salts, nor anything to break her fast. Anclyn had scarcely said a word since she'd awoken either, but in hindsight, Magmaya might have just not been listening. Had she become so obsessed with each of Kurulian's whispers that she couldn't even listen to anyone else? Had he once told her he had been enslaved? Or had that been a dream? After everything she'd admitted, she thought they could've understood one another—but she had been wrong before.

Magmaya knew the way; a part of her spirit was embedded in the hum of the forest. But now, it appeared to twist impossibly like some wicked geometry had taken hold, and she swore she was walking in circles.

She was growing suspicious, but it wasn't until she arrived at the pillars beneath which Fabius and herself had dined that her suspicions were confirmed.

'My lady,' a figure bundled entirely in eggshell robes addressed her from where they had sat, the table bare, the feast finished. 'My Legatus wishes to see you.'

Legatus? she asked herself—would Kurulian be seeing her again? But if so, where was Fabius?

The servant led her up a series of steps and under pink-flowered arches where the morning sun struck her eyes with a malice. They didn't share a word until they reached the top and by then, she was out of breath.

Basking in the light from above there was a small hall, arched like a battlement jutting from the Manse's summit. Sunflowers raped at the clear windows, and weeds ate away at the broken coving fell apart before her very eyes.

'This way,' the servant commanded, and Magmaya followed, the shadow of the hall blotting out the harsh light from above and sheathing her world in shadow. She followed her through the open archway. The stench of raw fish assaulted her immediately, and then the heat of blazing candles. She looked around, finding much of the wall had been worn away to the bare brick, and what remained was choked with fractured paintings and antlers of long-dead bucks. *Like the one that kicked me in the gut*, Magmaya recalled.

The room was empty, save for her, the servant, and some strange figure hunched over a mahogany desk at the hall's end.

'Legatus Akanah,' the woman spoke, and there was movement from the desk. The hunched figure shooed her away and beckoned Magmaya forward, so she ambled over. The wood creaked as she did for what felt like hours of walking before she finally reached his foot.

Akanah didn't look up, though, quill in hand as he scratched away at a piece of weathered parchment. Among his cluster of papers was slightly nibbled on bread, vermillion prawns, a ribbed bottle (full) and a choir of candles singing praise before him. He wasn't as beautiful as either Fabius or Kurulian, but something about his greased-back hair and coy smile gave her the impression he'd have his way with anyone.

'Do sit,' he said curtly, and Magmaya did as he said, searching for some weakness in his façade.

She hadn't seen him since his abrupt arrival at Spider's inn, but he looked different now, like each time she'd remembered him before had made him a little more false. 'I must admit, I was expecting more people.' She looked around.

'No.' He ignored her gaze, still. 'This hall is mine alone until council.'

So, the whispers had been right, she realised. *But she'd been summoned earlier.*

'I was under the impression this was the Lord Commander's garden,' Magmaya said.

'His garden, my hall,' he muttered.

'Oh.'

'Where are my manners?' He looked up, at last, asking the question Magmaya had been all along. 'Would you like a drink?'

'No,' she said, though her hands were shaking. She hadn't felt so thirsty in a while, but she was afraid to take a gift from this newcomer.

'Shame.' He poured himself a glass. 'While the rest of the world is either drunk on wine or pride, I have a chance to think.' He caught her staring. 'It's water, I'm afraid,' Akanah said as he took a sip.

A deep silence broke out, and his chest groaned.

'You were the one watching me, then?' She sat forward after a while. 'Watching my family?'

'A name on paper, as was your father.' He shrugged, going back to his writing. 'Most girls like to believe angels are watching over them in one way or another, yet all seem surprised when they meet them. Strange, eh?'

'Angels,' Magmaya scoffed. 'They say it's an insult to call the Divinicus that, but you people seem to like it really.' She took a deep breath. 'So, *you* summoned me?'

'*You* asked for Fabius, and I was recommended you.'

'I'm sure he was happy to hear from me,' she remarked.

'As happy as you might imagine. So, what did you want to ask him that you're failing to ask of me, then?'

Magmaya thought for a moment and looked to the windows where the sunflowers ate away. She'd rehearsed a thousand times telling Fabius, but not this imposter. He was just as arrogant as the others, though, no matter how much wit he carried with him. Perhaps she could approach him with the same tone she did Fabius and the confidence she did Kurulian. But the first had cast her out, and the second had wished her goodbye.

'I want to bargain,' she said at last.

'Bargain?'

'Yes,' she admitted. 'I have heard of some trouble in the Reaches, and I thought I could offer you my own... suggestion.'

'The Reaches are Legatus Rael's territory,' he spat. 'You are aware, girl? You should be telling *her,* not Fabius. Nor me.'

'I was only offered you.' She shook her head. 'Look, I have studied your lands, and I think I can see what others have missed.'

'Insulting,' he remarked. 'Eight months we have tolled upon this matter and nothing. So, what would a foreign girl have to show for herself that we cannot?'

'If you cared to listen, you might know,' Magmaya answered.

Akanah sat back in his seat and folded his hands into his lap. She studied the wrinkles around his dull, green eyes, older than him and sullen beneath skin that seemed to stretch unnaturally over his skull.

'What could you possibly want from all of this?' he asked at once. 'The Lord Commander said you wanted to become one of us, but you defy us at every opportunity.'

'I want you to listen, that's all.' Her eyes were wide. 'Perhaps then, you can do your job as an angel and weigh up my soul. But just listen first.'

'I shall listen the moment you say something of substance,' he remarked. 'I have sat at this desk for far too long now, seemingly speaking to no one, and my back is starting to ache. So, I urge you to get on with it, girl.'

'Thank you.' She nodded but felt her stomach tighten all the same. 'I think you've been betrayed.'

'Oh?' Akanah asked. 'How so?'

'The only way an endless supply of troops could travel across the mountains to defend the blockade so quickly is by not having to cross the mountains at all,' she said. 'The troops came from the peaks themselves.' She looked away and wondered, not quite sure where she was summoning the words. 'Cyrel is the problem.'

Akanah shook his head. 'Cyrel is a province of labour and trade with the capital; they've even *helped* us with the Reaches. They're no military afoot.'

'Maybe not,' she said. 'But maybe Cyrel are positioning the Reaches' troops atop their mountains rather than sending their own.'

Akanah, to her surprise, nodded and pushed himself into his chair. She could almost feel the leather burning against his back. He lifted his ranks of fingers to find his platter and scraped at the rows of pink shrimp which were the furthest things from alive. He chose one and snapped the dead thing between his nails, sinews spilling out onto his lap.

'Have you heard of Belliousa, Magmaya?'

'You have juice on your chin.' She ignored him.

He wiped it clean with gritted teeth. 'An island ran by a church off the coast,' he explained. 'It's long been an allied state of Inamorata, but some time ago, they got themselves a new leader and have since become a threat to us.'

'A threat?' Magmaya asked. 'How?'

'Unlike Cyrel, Belliousa *is* militarised,' Akanah answered. 'Deih of the Water, their matriarch and supposed goddess, has thousands of crazed fanatics at hand to fight for her every gospel. She could turn on us at any moment.'

'Why would she?'

'She made herself an enemy of the Lord Commander's when we tried to make peace with her, and she's only been threatening us ever since. Now that the

Reaches are engulfed in civil war, the last thing I want are the Free Islands and an entire religion rallied against us.'

'Have you forgotten the armour you wear?' Magmaya scoffed. 'You *are* religion.'

'So was the Golden Woman, and then she died.' He frowned. 'Since then, the world has been desperately trying to make sense of it all. I know I have. People have turned to us.'

'So, what about her?' she asked. 'You angels are awfully secretive.'

'It doesn't matter. She's dead now, along with her disciples. Belliousa doesn't follow her anyway, nor us— they follow far older gods.'

'What about them, then?' Magmaya asked. 'Are you going to wipe these zealots from their island?'

'They're men crafted the same as you, and they'll die just as quickly.' He bit down on another prawn. 'But I don't want to cull an entire country. Like I said, they have allies in the Free Islands and Vavaria. They must be turned to our cause.'

'One look of the Divinicus was enough to sway me,' she admitted.

'One look will not be enough to sway a woman who thinks herself a goddess.' Akanah grit his teeth. 'She is arrogant, and some say she works with black magic.'

'So what?'

'So, Miss Vorr, we have come to the conclusion that you will speak with her.'

Magmaya's heart leapt into her throat, and she thought she was going to fall from her chair. 'You want me to go to *Belliousa*?'

'When Deih first took power, Kurulian led a force to Belliousa to discuss peace terms,' Akanah explained, 'but he was the only one she would spare a word with; not his Small Court, nor any of the other Divinicus. And do you know why?'

'Why?' she asked dryly, though she didn't care to hear his answer. The thought of having to go somewhere else foreign was driving her into something of a madness.

'Because he wasn't one of us,' he replied. 'Deih of the Water wouldn't speak with any of the angels, only foreigners.'

'But he is an angel.'

'He was scarcely one then. Unfortunately for us, Kurulian wasn't as inclined to talk as she was.'

'And what does that have to do with me?'

'You tried to prove something to me with your spiel about Cyrel,' he said. 'You held a small city. And most importantly, you're a foreigner. You don't know our customs. I'd wager if you'd talk to their demi-goddess, she'd talk back.'

'And she would acknowledge me because I'm not one of you?' Magmaya frowned.

'Because you're not one of us.' Akanah nodded.

And never will be, she thought. 'So, what about me then? Is this the reason I'm meeting with *you?*'

'You're meeting with *me* because of a recommendation.' He thought for a moment. 'The recommendation was if you sold your story to me, I'd suggest we'd take you to Belliousa.'

'I sold you my story?' She was almost excited at the prospect.

'Not particularly,' he admitted, 'but we're running out of options.'

She sighed. 'And after that?'

'Once you have spoken with Deih, and Belliousa is rallied in our image, you shall be free.'

'Free?' Magmaya narrowed her eyes. 'Free from what?'

'Free to take whatever the Lord Commander offers you. If all goes well, he'll give you a cottage in the mountains or something of the like,' he answered.

A cottage in the mountains? That was more than she'd ever expected. Perhaps then, she could forget everything—forget the cold, forget her father and forget the angels.

'I shall pass your... theory to Rael,' he continued. 'Until then, you bathe, you coat yourself with perfume, and you practice speaking to the High Priestess until we leave for Belliousa. A week's time,' Akanah concluded.

'But—' she stammered. 'What if I—?'

'Speak well, and you can expect a hefty reward.' He cocked his head. 'Speak out against us, and you'll find yourself at the mercy of Highport, I suppose.'

'And I have no choice?'

Akanah leaned in on her, exposing every pore of his skin to the sunbeams of the sullen windows. She felt his breath on her forehead as he spoke and sunk down. 'My dear, between your stowaway and your insult upon the Lord Commander, I fear there *is* no choice for you. In fact, I'm surprised Fabius has been so merciful.'

Magmaya could only nod and watch as Akanah sat back with a smile like he had never threatened her. He plucked at the bread (before deciding he was full) and leapt up.

'What about Anclyn?' Magmaya looked up to him, and her cheeks flushed with colour.

'Anclyn?'

'My handmaiden.'

'What does your handmaiden matter?' He grimaced.

'I want her to come to Belliousa as well,' Magmaya said.

'No,' he snarled. 'The Lord Commander's handmaidens hail from the Water in the Summerlands—the same as the High Priestess. Having one of them there would compromise our efforts.'

'Then I shall sit and wait until you agree,' she stammered.

Akanah roared with laughter. 'I'm very patient, dear girl.'

'Then the pair of us shall wait here forever.' She shrugged. 'But a girl must not always look a girl; there are powders and perfumes as you say. Hells, I might be my handmaiden now. Perhaps you just haven't recognised me yet. I wager Deih wouldn't either.'

'Then you would be the handmaiden with the quickest wit I've ever come across,' he remarked. 'For someone so patient, you seem awfully impatient to find an answer.'

Magmaya looked away, silent.

'Have the girl plaster herself with greasepaint, and speak with me again,' he replied, ignoring her. 'How much of a disguise could a girl with half a wit make?'

'We do fairly well,' Magmaya scoffed and stood to face him. 'I do suppose I'll be seeing you again soon.'

'Inevitably.' His voice was cold. 'See yourself out.'

Her chambers were quieter when she reached her bedding that night. But then again, she'd spent the past hours chasing aloof, screaming birds about the gardens with big yellow beaks that bled for their young. Everything was quiet compared to them.

She longed for an evening where she could be alone with her thoughts, but Anclyn was always there, quiet and nose-twitching since she had broken the news. Perhaps it was selfish to bring her, but she couldn't abandon the only friend she had. And what about Akanah? She hadn't heard from him nor from the other Divinicus since the morning, and she was beginning to wonder if the whole thing had been a ruse.

Before she'd retreated to her chambers, Magmaya had sought solace in the shade of an old tree outside the Manse, and she'd been half-tempted to pray to it. But instead, she had plucked at the grass tufts and wrestled them between her knuckles, all while the river flowed drearily around her with a wrinkled smile. She had imagined seeing for miles from where she had sat, but the lumbering hunk of the city blocked most of the view outward. She had even grown so bored, she had contemplated going to find Akanah in that hall of his, but she decided against it. Although in the end, he had offered her kindness, she couldn't be so sure he would again.

A gentle hum and soft breathing began from Anclyn's chambers and cut Magmaya out of her dream. And when she stepped out to make her toilet, she felt as if she were gliding, but never far from the alabaster floors.

Nameless gods, let me soar, she prayed, *let me fly away, dammit.*

When she returned to bed, she found it as equally difficult to sleep as she had on the toilet. Sweat was pouring down her back, and her skin was stinging with the moon's kiss, all while Anclyn's heavy breathing seemed to incessant on keeping her awake. *Does anyone manage to sleep in the Water?* she asked herself.

In time, her mind turned to Deih, the High Priestess—how could a foreign woman like her rise to such a position? If Deih became so powerful, why couldn't she?

But Magmaya wasn't a girl of the Summerlands or even Inamorata. She was a pawn from an icy wasteland, and now she was a pawn of angels.

She threw her head down on her pillow, and tiredness washed over her like a setting sun, a hundred heartaches across her body. The night before she'd been searching maps for a place that didn't seem to exist, yet now she wanted anything but. She writhed and wriggled amid the heavy heat of the night and the blankets—until her neck grazed against something sharp.

She sat up, sighed and looked to the pillow. And then to the letter.

> *My chancellor,*

It read,

> *You were right.*
>
> *Xx*

Eighteen

Magmaya found herself wandering about Fabius' gardens again the night before she was made to leave. Something about it reminded of her of the forest around her home; it was where she'd ran to when she was twelve and woke up bleeding for the first time. She hadn't understood it then; all she had been taught was when the blood began, she would be made good for her man. Magmaya had been so afraid, but she had been a different girl then.

She bled again today, but there was no fear left in her. Her shoulders had stiffened, and her stomach had swelled, but she just bit down on her lip and carried on through the dusk.

'I've never done anything quite like this, my lady,' she heard a voice call and turned to Anclyn beside her. 'The Lord Commander, he—'

'Isn't here now,' she said. 'Just walk.'

They passed through the ruined façade of a castle wall, overgrown with ivy and lit with a red glow, all while in the distance she swore she could make out some music playing. It was enticing, but sour still. Each call of 'hallelujah' made her feel uneasy, and the harmonies grew as if building to something disastrous.

Never mind that. She shook her head and looked out across a lake she swore was too large to fit atop the manse. The night filled its surface with pitch, but atop the water, there was an army of statuettes, each lit a different colour: a myriad of yellows and blues, greens and oranges. Their reflections were like crystals in the lake, still images that might have been real if she squinted.

'I don't understand this place,' Magmaya mused.

'Me neither,' Anclyn admitted. 'I've never been here at night. My lady, we should be going back.'

'No,' Magmaya called, perhaps a little too loud. 'We're not Fabius' anymore. Let's keep moving.'

Perhaps that's just it, she realised—no matter how beautiful the garden was, she found herself ready to move onto the next attraction. If she was a royal, she fled south. If she was dining with angels, she ran to the heathens.

Stay—some corner of her mind whispered. *Stay,* it said, but she shrugged it off and continued through another archway. It was a tunnel of yellow light, sparkling like a hall of glittery moons.

Magmaya looked to Anclyn, her made-up face bathed in the speckled lights, standing alone under the arches. She wished she was as beautiful as her.

'You've never been here at night?' she asked the handmaiden. 'It looks like you were born here.'

Anclyn blushed. 'My lady, a trick of the lights can do many things...'

Not everything.

Vibrant cherry blossom trees sprouted from the earth around them and formed the path ahead. As they carried on down the trail, the murmuring of music grew louder until Magmaya felt her chest tighten. When they arrived at the end, a row of stone braziers and black ponds awaited them. She felt drawn towards the fires, her face warped in the waters below. And as she reached out and caressed the heat, all the flames of Highport came back to her. She wanted to kiss them, love them, become them. If Anclyn was beauty, the fire was perfection.

Magmaya brushed her fingers back and forth through the fire, and her heart skipped a beat. A thousand colours rushed through her mind, so she did it again and again, feeling something reawaken within her until she had left her hands a little too long and—

'Magmaya!' She turned to Anclyn as the handmaiden pulled her back from the braziers. She took her palm, inspecting it. 'Your hand, you could have—'

Her skin hadn't burnt one bit.

All I've ever known is the cold. Magmaya smiled.

'The Divinicus are sure to be on the prowl again, my lady,' Anclyn insisted. 'If they find us—!'

'If they find us, I'll burn them.' She laughed. 'Have you ever seen the fire of a bleeding girl?'

They turned back anyway, though down the path they came across a pair of small statues, one on each side. On the left, there was an angel's silhouette with a chair beneath so whoever perched there could sit with a halo above their head. But on the right, there was the silhouette of a demon, also with a chair below, so whoever sat there would be bestowed with a pair of fiery horns.

They found themselves taking turns in each one, smirking as they did. When Magmaya sat in the seat of the demon, she was almost able to see the roaring crowds and horned apostles calling, but when she sat in the seat of the angel, she was blinded by the bejewelled eyes of fanatics and cheers of praise. *No one would sin if they had this,* she decided. She knew which side she would choose.

But then, she awoke, and there was sweat rolling down her back and a red wetness festering between her legs. The world came to her slowly—first as a haze, then as a room of shadow, the first lashings of sunlight at the windows. She had never felt so reluctant to face the day.

There was a knock at the doors, and Magmaya jumped out of her seat, papers fluttering through the air. She leapt up to gather them, bundling the scraps in her arms. Over the past week, Akanah had given her no short supply of doctrines to scour through. She had become numb to the words and the words numb to her until nothing she spoke or read had any meaning at all. But there was no time left to understand; Akanah had already sent notice to Belliousa to let them know they were coming. Soon enough, she would meet the High Priestess and sell her an alliance. The thought terrified her.

It hadn't helped that she'd heard a hundred thousand rumours of Deih over the past few days; 'She eats human flesh and wears skin,' they said, 'She's a succubus who cuts off the cocks of those she ensnares.'

Magmaya shook her head and turned away. *Faery stories*, she told herself as she'd always told Rache. If only she could believe herself.

The door stirred as she pulled herself to her seat, feeling the cool of Kurulian's vial against her wrist. Then her mind turned to another Legatus.

'You will represent my Small Court to Deih,' Akanah had instructed her. *'She is not to be told where you're really from. If word travels that the Divinicus are using some northern girl, we'll all be damned and you with us.'*

'Where from then?'

'You must still be a foreigner, of course. Cecalia is a small village south of Halo Blue. You've heard of it, no? Your accent is cold enough, yes, but your swagger... that might take work.

'Then what?'

'Then, Deih will question you about us. You'll just happen to have all the right answers.'

'But my skin's no different to yours,' she had said. *'My eyes are the same colour; my face is the same shape— so why do you expect her to choose me to speak to? She won't know I'm not one of you.'*

'She'll know.'

'How, if she won't be told?'

'She just will.'

Magmaya awoke from her haze as a girl entered her quarters. She had hair like silver and a face like snow; she had sunset behind her eyes and a net of ribbon stringing back her locks, all wrapped up in a dress like trailing pitch.

'Are you ready to be dressed, my lady?' the servitor asked.

'Who will be dressing me?' Magmaya asked back.

The girl laughed and twirled her dress; her orange eyes were illuminated with a shimmer of greasepaint as she flounced across to Magmaya's desk, outstretching her lank arms as if she were a dancer.

'No one,' her eyes were alive with joy. 'No one but a free girl.'

'Then are you sure you're bothering the right person?' Magmaya said, growing annoyed.

'Do you not recognise a lady?' she asked, disappointed. 'Do you not recognise a lady's eyes? Do you not recognise a girl named Anclyn of the Water?'

Magmaya sat back, her eyes wide. 'Anclyn?'

'Today is the day a girl is free!' she swooned. 'Yes, my lady, I did fear you wouldn't recognise me.'

'Your greasepaint—you look so different.'

'It's the eyes.' Anclyn shrugged. 'I'll do yours now, yes?'

'I need a little more time,' Magmaya protested. 'I still haven't got through half these bloody papers.'

'But the ships cast their sails today.' Anclyn frowned.

Magmaya nodded, but when she thought of the ships, her mind went to the great iron galleon that had come to her home. How could she sail farther away when she had troubled herself so much to come here? Perhaps nowhere she went would satisfy her need to flee.

Nevertheless, Anclyn began to tidy her hair and thread it with a handful of ornate, white flowers. She smoothed her fingers with a warm powder and ran them through her glossy locks.

Not before Magmaya had come to the spas had she felt so clean and settled and pure, as if she were a maiden.

If the Divinicus had granted her one heavenly gift, it was to be washed and clean and feel herself again amid an ocean of salt and steam. She had never felt asleep in the south.

The journey to Belliousa would take two days, though it would be a long walk across the island before she presented herself to Deih. If the matriarch was to choose her from the Small Court, she would have to look beautiful and proper; but she wasn't exactly used to that—it would be better if she wore it in a little first.

By the time she had been finished with, Magmaya scarcely recognised herself; she hadn't half as much powder on as Anclyn did, but her skin was clear and spotless all the same. Her eyes were no longer sunken beneath lilac grime, but instead alive with the night's sky. When she gazed into the looking glass, it was clear the girl she had once been was long buried. By a shedding of the skin, her face was new. But at the same time, she could still feel herself inside that body that frowned back at her—all her memories of Kharon, Rache, Nurcia—the greasepaint hadn't washed them away.

Magmaya tore herself away and looked to the balcony. There at least, the day was clear and the oceans still and calm. The horizon sparkled with scattered sunbeams as foamy green waves crashed against the pillars below, and then she turned to Anclyn, all eyes.

'I'll be at the docks within the hour,' she told the handmaiden before slipping away—there was something she had to do before she allowed herself to leave.

She began ransacking her own satchel just after noon had struck. The stench of the sea air swallowed her, beckoning her to Belliousa, but she couldn't bring herself to go. Not yet.

But her things had to; each glimpse of her new face in the windows that passed made her surer of it. By the time she reached the old library at the end of a small meadow, she was certain.

Rache's leaf was still glowing from last night's moonlight, but even that seemed to fade as she slipped it between the pages of the book he'd recommended her so long ago. Unsurprisingly, she'd never found time to read it between the disaster at Highport and the angel's rule. But perhaps when all of this was done, and she had that cottage in the mountains, she might just be able to.

She slipped the book behind one of the shelves in the library, where surely no one would find it, and carried on.

Magmaya had a few pieces of jewellery with her too: name day gifts or sparkly inheritances from an aunt or someone else she'd never cared to know. She left them in a fountain at the foot of a local High Lord's estate where she hoped a more deserving girl might make use of them.

Last came the carving knife, but, of course, it was the easiest to hide. She made sure to scrub off every bloodstain before leaving it on a tavern table and making her way back to the seafront. She just hoped no one would notice the northern sigils carved into the ivory shaft.

By the time she was done, all she had left were the clothes on her back and the vial Kurulian had given her. She would have never left Moonbeam in some tavern if she'd had it with her, though; that relic was a real weight in her palm, and with it, she had felt unstoppable. But that was with Siedous now, so far away. And in a couple of days, it would be even farther behind her.

Besides, that was some other girl's sword from some other girl's life. That was the sword of the chancellor of Orianne, and she was Magmaya Vorr.

The dockyard was larger than she had imagined and the galleon larger still. It had no name, for its hull had been ravaged by time and the kiss of the waves. Seabirds hummed overhead as they circled the angels on the peer; there were two hundred of them in total, an armada of faceless faces standing in uniform, hanging on their Legatus's every word.

Their presence was second only to their arrival at Ranvirus, but here the sun beat down so vigorously they formed a single kaleidoscopic blur of light, bending and twisting as they stood against the water. Even the shadows of the looming palace behind failed to hamper their glow.

Perhaps a thousand servants, nobles and scribes stood behind the countless marble rails too, tending to their angels' every need and scratching the sight into the histories. *If only Rache were here to see this,* Magmaya thought. *Damn those fish-women, for these were Divinicus at war.*

She and Anclyn (as well as Akanah's Small Court) had clustered around the Legatus as he looked over his troops. The most noteworthy of them all was Krel, his personal swordsman. From the stories she'd heard, he was less of a swordsman and more of a butcher, though; his two-handed blade was longer than most people were tall. Not to mention, he was probably the biggest man she'd ever seen. She wagered he could've taken Belliousa on his own.

'Deep in thought, I see.' One of the Small Court's men brushed past her. He had a greasy voice and stale eyes, and his name was Cheyne Reed.

Of course, Akanah would have chosen him *to go to Belliousa with them.*

'Lots to think about,' Magmaya shot back.

'What would a girl like you trouble herself with?' He chuckled to himself.

'Like *me*?'

'Perhaps I didn't make myself clear,' he said, and she was ensnared again as if he was offering her another bottle of wine. 'I mean no offence but how has the great chancellor of Orianne found herself in an administrative court? Last I heard, you were destined to live out your days as a Uliana.'

'I must admit, I'm not taken quite as seriously here,' she replied.

Cheyne nodded and said, 'I know that feeling all too well.' He brushed a flowery cape over his shoulder and leaned in so close he could've kissed her. 'If I were the Legatus, I would have made you an angel myself.' He tutted. 'Such a shame, my lady.'

He winked at her as he disappeared into the rest of the Small Court, and Magmaya felt herself shudder. *Not only had he been watching me from the balcony, but now this?* Did the whole world know her secrets? Did the whole world know about her and Kurulian's meetings? Was she playing herself for a fool?

She felt a chill run down her wrist and unfastened the vial, turning to Anclyn.

'Take this,' she said to the handmaiden. 'Put it in with your greasepaint or something.'

'Yes, my lady.' Anclyn stared at the vial. 'What exactly is—?'

'I'll tell you later.'

There was an achingly long roar, and the crowds turned their attention to a tower above where the squires and lords perched. There was a hustle among them and a shimmer from beyond the great pillars.

And then Fabius strode onto the balcony, his pearly breastplate shimmering where his eggshell robes failed to cover. He looked down at the ranks of the Divinicus with those striking black eyes and made the slightest of nods to Akanah—and then he caught her eye, and then she caught his, one robed fool staring at another.

But Fabius, the wise god, simply turned away, smiled at his men and disappeared into the arches beyond.

And so, the galleon began its course.

Magmaya's compartment was cramped, and Anclyn's even more so. Her tiny bed was built into the wall beneath a porthole, looking out to the endless seas; it might have been homely if the swaying hadn't made her vomit once already. Candlelight filled the space around her as she collapsed on her blankets, clawing at the covers until the gentle humming of the ship lulled her to sleep.

She awoke early in the morning with eyes stained, bleeding peach powder. Her robes were tattered and creased, and the groaning of the endless black waves was giving her a headache. At least when she'd been trapped upon *The Golden Damnation*, she was able to listen to the gentle hum of the furnaces and numb herself to the swaying, but here there was nothing but the stench of piss and dreary grey cloud as far as she could see.

Before she fell asleep again, the screeching of a horn startled her, and she rose, feeling bile rush up her throat. Magmaya changed as quickly as she could and rushed down the corridor.

She continued on to find Anclyn contemplating her reflection in the porthole of her compartment. Her robes sat flush against her body as they had the day before; her greasepaint was unmoved by the night. She noticed a frown in the glass.

'My lady.' Anclyn turned, smiling. 'Are the seas not beautiful?' She looked around. 'It is the first time in so many years I have not been blinded with Inamorata.'

'They're pretty,' Magmaya agreed. 'If you would come with me to the sculleries, they're beginning to serve food—hot food.' She couldn't wait, in truth; it had felt like forever since she'd eaten something that wasn't processed by 'the finest of cooks' or imported from gods knew where. Perhaps there would be some ale or cider not so poisonous to the tongue.

'Alright.' Anclyn smiled gingerly, and they set off.

'I must be back as soon as we're finished.'

'Oh,' she began, 'your greasepaint.'

'No,' Magmaya replied. 'I've more doctrines to examine, still.'

'For Deih.' Anclyn nodded. 'Do you know who she even is?'

Her heart sank—she hadn't told her where Deih came from. *The Water* was part of the woman's title! Not that Anclyn knew that, but it couldn't be long before she did. But Akanah had insisted the handmaiden wasn't to know.

'I know I must earn her respect,' she said. 'If I couldn't win an argument with Fabius, then what chance do I have against a High Priestess?'

'You're going to argue with her?'

'My conversations always seem to turn into arguments,' she admitted.

It was a minute before midnight the next day when the trumpet sounded again. Rain lashed against Magmaya's window, and she threw herself awake in a cold sweat; she found the window foggy with foam and the midnight ocean beyond.

The trumpet sounded again, and she scrabbled for the bedside chest, feeling for something that wasn't there. *We're being attacked*, she decided, but then it dawned on her that perhaps they were sinking, and she began sweating even more.

She threw on a pair of sandals and tossed a bundle of robes over her shoulders. The rain beat down against the deck above, and then the boat rocked until she was almost thrown off her feet, and all there was to light the path were the stray flashes from the thunderstorm.

Magmaya followed the impressions of the light to Anclyn's compartment. She found the door unlocked and pressed her way through, finding the handmaiden asleep still. She watched her chest rise and fall, greasepaint soundly kissed upon her eyelids. Even in her slumber, and then when she awoke, her beauty persisted.

'Trumpets are sounding.' Magmaya's voice was hoarse. 'The storm's getting worse.'

A thin slither of light from the moon guided them through the upper decks as they passed a number of sleeping servants. If the ship was sinking, then why weren't they doing something? Was it *her* duty to wake them?

The higher they reached, the more violent the storm became, and the brasher the shrill rain and louder the thunder. Once they arrived on the deck and stood against the night, the wind almost tossed them out into the smoky ocean, and it quickly became clear the sea didn't care for them at all.

Their robes and locks began to snap with the whipping of water, though the clouds above offered them no respite either. Magmaya waded her way through the lake that had gathered on the deck and fastened herself and Anclyn to the railings. It was clear enough the ship was not sinking, but instead quickening through the choppy black sea. No one else appeared to have even been startled—there was not a soul in sight amid the iron ropes and sodden crates as they tumbled from side to side on the cursed thing.

A third trumpet sounded through the rain, and the storms encircled the ship as if it was changing its course. Then there was a roar of thunder and Anclyn fell to the deck and then Magmaya. That was until a bolt of golden light ran through the heavens. It illuminated the black clouds and electrified the midnight waters, and for a moment, there was daylight. The moon was eclipsed with the white flash, and on the horizon, something peered through the veil of fog and rain.

A skyline—a skyline of arches and pillars, of trenches and towers; an empire of salt and steam.

'Belliousa,' Anclyn whispered through the gale.

'Belliousa.' Magmaya nodded, and a laugh crept to the corner of her mouth, the last of her greasepaint streaming down her face. They looked back to the buildings that lined the rocky shore and then to their centre where a mountain stood, cold and jagged against the darkness. And at its peak, there was a temple.

By morning, the rains had cleared, and yet, they hadn't been certified to leave; the ship still sat silent upon the waves, rocking gently as it stared down the wilted shores.

Magmaya hadn't slept since she'd awoken that night, and since the sunbeams had begun scorching Belliousa, she'd been able to make out a small gathering of people on the shoreline. They had come and gone throughout the morning, but no matter which of them left and which of them arrived, they all wore deep-red robes, forming something bloody upon the brown sand.

At the height of noon, several small landing boats were dropped from the flanks of the vessel, and the Divinicus spilt out from the ship and into the water. As Magmaya watched the servitors row them to shore, Anclyn finished dying the last of the greasepaint into her skin.

Though as the handmaiden stepped away to admire her handiwork, Magmaya couldn't help but turn back to the knot of red on the shoreline like a carrion bird did a carcass. She took Kurulian's vial from Anclyn's brushes and fastened it around her wrist.

But then, a hand clamped down on her shoulder, and she almost jumped from her skin.

'Magmaya.' She turned to Akanah behind her, resolute in his glittery plate. She hadn't seen much of him on the journey here, save for passing remarks and humble acknowledgement—but he looked quieter now, and far more alert. 'Try not to damn this for us,' he scorned and ambled away. 'My court's barge is this way. Make haste.'

As she followed him over to the starboard, she found Cheyne and the rest of the Small Court. Like Magmaya and Anclyn, they too had been rushed into creamy-white robes and thin opal breastplates. And then there was Krel, holding his enormous sword in such a way that if he turned too quickly, it would send the servants around him flying.

As the minutes passed, Magmaya watched as the cloaks on the horizon became figures and then people and then faces. Some fled as the armada approached, but in their place, others flocked to the water, and a few even waded through, dying for but a touch of an angel, screaming praise and hatred in anything but the common tongue.

Magmaya had been right—just a look was enough to sway them. But would it be enough for Deih?

As Akanah's own barge began to near the shore, the locals approached in something of ecstasy. They brushed themselves against the hull of their boats and began to scrape at Magmaya's robes with broken fingertips.

She flinched away and stared them down; there were children and elders, women and men, all sporting the red robes she had seen from the ship. Not one of them had an inch of hair across their scalps; in its place, they were inked with runes and lettering.

Krel stood tall in the barge and began to draw his blade, growling at the locals as he did. Soon enough, the boat hit the shore amid a froth of dead fish and half-drowned feathers.

The locals retreated from the shallows and back onto land as the Divinicus stormed out of the barges, holding their blades as they cleared the crowds and paved the way for Akanah. Magmaya, Anclyn and the other members of the Small Court scurried behind him as the Belliousans chanted, and the Divinicus shoved them aside.

Magmaya looked around, peering through the chittering crowds. What struck her first was the humidity; there was no summer breeze, no warm reassurance—just sweat and smog. She shook the feeling free and followed along the swathes of upturned mud and brown puddles, finding a number of crumbling stone arches and marble pillars jutting from rubble and sumps; there was not a piece of greenery in sight, no blade of grass, lone flower, shrub, nor tree. It looked as if Belliousa was dead.

'I've never seen a place so desolate.' Anclyn appeared to be able to read her thoughts. 'I've heard even the Ash Wastes has trees.'

Akanah barked something at the crowds, and Krel stepped forward, raising his cleaver into the morning sun. The Belliousans began to scurry away into the shadows until, at last, the streets cleared, leading up through the hills and to the summit.

'The First Temple,' Akanah announced, pointing to the mountaintop. 'That's where we meet Deih.'

The farther inland they walked, the more the streets began to reek until the stench of faeces became almost unbearable. The children didn't seem to mind it, though, as they looked up to them from beneath their iron huts, flies snapping around their bald heads. Magmaya noticed beneath their stretched skin, there was no meat, only bone—they were as dead as their island was.

Elsewhere, a younger woman eyed the angels with something of scorn as she carried a basket of brown water back from a pump.

And Magmaya could only watch in horror as Krel stopped his stampede and hammered a bloody fist down on her shoulder.

'That's not the face you look on a Divinicus with,' he growled, and she flinched, fell back, and cradled the bucket in her arms.

'Enough,' Akanah said to Krel, but there was no stopping the brute. The girl shouted something inaudible in defence, but the thing of a man only boomed with laughter.

'Whore!' he howled and groped at her lap, tossing the milky, brown liquid into the mud. He carried on walking while the woman began to cry and paw at the droplets, licking them like a kitten did a saucer of milk before they disappeared into the earth.

Magmaya looked to the handmaiden and felt heat rise to her ears. Fabius had said the Divinicus were protectors of the peace, but if their first instigation on foreign lands was to harass the already starving locals, then they were surely more akin to semi-demons.

From the corner of her eye, she saw Krel shake his head and amble away. They could only carry on, silent in rank—before a determined scream erupted behind them.

The Small Court turned as the same woman threw herself towards Krel, a glass bottle in her hand. And before he could react, she drove it forward, and it shattered across his skull.

He stopped and grunted.

For an instant, Magmaya almost thought he was going to ignore it. But a moment later, the cleaver was unsheathed, and the woman began screaming. The Divinicus splintered and drew their own falchions, pinning the girl down and trying to rally Krel. But he just burst from his clutches, stammering and roaring as he did.

There were protests from Akanah and yells from his advisors, but for every inch the woman was pulled away from him, Krel took a foot, hacking at the air.

'Stop!' Magmaya tried to call and waded over, forcing her way between the beast and the girl. But it was no use; Krel pushed his way through until it was only him and the Belliousan. He raised his blade, striking the sunbeams, and the girl cowered, her eyes either side the shadow of the sword.

And then, a voice called out, calm, and the bickering crowds turned to Krel, blade still hanging above the girl.

But between them, someone else stood. She was cloaked in the same crimson as the other Belliousans, and even though Magmaya might have been a mile away, her perfumes were intoxicating and enticing all at once; they made her head heavy and the world spin. Her body seemed to glitter too as a choir of copper trinkets fell from her hips, wrists and dangled from her chest where a nest of coloured plumes and flowers began.

'Whores! I'll kill you both,' Krel roared and hammered down the blade.

And hit the earth below.

The Belliousan girl was gone, but her saviour was omnipresent, turning to Krel with all the grace of a saint.

'You may think me a whore,' she said, smirking, 'but to Legatus Akanah of the Divinicus, I am Deih of the Water, Firstborn of Oquelia, High Priestess and Matriarch of Belliousa.' She paused. 'And so terribly pleased to meet you.'

Nineteen

At the height of summer, the gardens were no less beautiful than he remembered; each year outdid the last with flying colours as if all the ambience and divinity left of the world had been poured into one place. White alps filled the horizon beneath a striking blue sky, while fields of purple flowers littered the hills. The farther he was from the Waterborne Cities of Halo Blue, the more radiant and artistically complex the architecture grew, and the more he felt he was home again.

Fabius watched as faint blurs in the sky became marble pillars, and shimmers became arches made of starlight—and then, in the distance, there was *Forlorn Despair*—the palace of Astralica, the capital of Inamorata—he'd never thought a place could be so baroque, so frighteningly beautiful. How wrong he had been.

Despite how much he liked to think Astralica was a city of waterfalls and spires, the place seemed to reinvent itself with every step he took like the oceans were playing a cruel joke. But it was the most gorgeous joke Fabius could've dreamt of. He felt naked here, stripped of his rank, but it mattered not. None of his misdeeds, none of his false promises mattered—all that did was Astralica.

Out of the corner of his eye, he spotted movement in the flowerbed, and then there was laughter. From between the twisting stems, he saw a pair of naked bodies, embraced in something of ecstasy. *This is the Garden of Maids,* he reminded himself and rolled his shoulders back. He better not have been seen—it had been too long since he'd loved.

He turned his attention away as the couple giggled and escaped the flowers, making their way elsewhere. They made no attempt to cover themselves in front of the Divinicus, but it was no matter—an instant later, they were gone, and the palace was his again.

Seeing them like that had sent his mind to Larl, and how he'd thirsted after every last woman he'd ever met. While Fabius despised the way Magmaya had treated him, no high-born woman would have gladly accepted his nephew's invitation to strip while also making good as a lady wife. He made a note to never take him to Astralica, though. He'd jump right in the flowers.

Some shimmer of gold in the distance brought Fabius back to reality, and he looked up, finding a nest of bronze statues towering in the skyline. They were all of angels; not like his Divinicus, but the classical angels from the lore that intrigued him so greatly—angels with eagle's wings and rainbow haloes atop their heads. But for every angel, there was a demon too, cast in a reddish marble and sporting leathery bat wings and horns that pierced the clouds. Each time he visited, there appeared to be a new collection of monuments, and each was grander than the last ensemble.

And between the gods and devils, a third figure stood draped in a dress of liquid diamond.

And then, unlike the statues around her, she moved, and Fabius beamed.

'Lord Commander!' The girl bowed, shielding her eyes from the scorching sun. 'It has been far too long.'

Fabius grinned, but when she stood, he stammered, 'It should be me to bow.'

'No, I insist.' She shook her head, but he did so all the same. 'My lord, outside the palace, I am as much a girl as any other. But never mind that. It has always been Kurulian to visit. I have missed you, Fabius.'

He rose and took her hand with a kiss. 'As I have missed you, Zinnia.'

'You're all so busy,' she remarked. 'When I look at you, I see a heavenly man, but I suppose you're a soldier when it comes to it. You have a life outside of paradise.'

'I'd like to think so.' He laughed. 'It's never as exciting as the faery stories. Wouldn't want to upset the peace, would we?'

'Of course not, Fabius,' she said. 'With all this talk of not seeing one another, I don't suppose you have seen my father recently, no?'

'It has been a number of months, I must admit.'

'I swear it was yesterday. Every year is quicker than the last. Maybe next year will be only an hour.' Zinnia blushed, and her eyes glistened in the sun; she always had been pretty—not beautiful (no one from her father's loins could ever be beautiful), but she had luscious brown locks and a face like sweet cinnamon all the same. Besides, she was the crowning jewel of the empire, a symbol of prosperity. When little girls dreamt of being a princess, they dreamt of being Zinnia.

'An hour feels like a year if you've nothing to do.' Fabius grinned. 'Now about your father?'

'I do think the emperor has fallen ill,' she stammered at last.

'Ill?' Fabius exclaimed. He'd never known a ruler that wasn't Cardel Avont; not since the emperor was a boy-king everyone had laughed at. But he had become a fierce emperor, wise and just. He wasn't elderly, though his appetite had always gained the better of him.

'It's hard to explain,' she admitted. 'He scarcely wants to eat, and when he does, he can't keep food down to save his life. But you came to see him, I presume? Shall I take you?'

'Yes, thank you,' he said as the pair and his Divinicus guards began to make their way down the stone path, edging ever closer to the palace. 'How's your brother faring?'

'My brother,' she began, 'is only the second most beautiful child of my father's.' She sniggered, but suddenly, she was serious. 'He's been away for several weeks now, in truth. On some pilgrimage across the Summerlands. I hear he is doing well.'

'He ought to be.' Fabius nodded. 'He shall make a fine emperor someday, already doing his duties.'

'And I, a fine empress,' she said. 'Or perhaps that isn't quite how that works.' Zinnia laughed to herself.

'You *would* make a fine empress,' he said.

'And you, Lord Commander?' she asked. 'My father said you took one of the arks to somewhere far north?'

'Gods!' he laughed. 'Ranvirus. I've never seen so much snow—I've never seen so much nothing, rather. It felt as if there was not a moment of sun, and when there was a glimpse of light, a war was taking place.'

'A war?' she asked, almost excited. 'Did you intervene?'

'No, no.' Fabius shook his head, passing under a flowery arch. 'It's their duty, not ours. The only moments I spent there were those of doctrine. It seems I'm outgrowing my days of the blade.' He thought to Highport and the scoundrels the Divinicus had slain, the rush he'd felt as they had darted towards them. His falchion's calling was hardly outgrowing him, it appeared.

'What were the people like?'

'Dull. Or dead.' He laughed. 'Their chancellor, though.' He shook his head. 'A complication of sorts.'

'Is that what you've come to speak with my father about?' Zinnia asked. 'I'm afraid all of this quite goes over my head.'

'That,' he said, 'and something a little closer to home. Something in Cyrel.'

'Oh?'

'You wouldn't believe the mess they've dug themselves into.'

They carried on wistfully down the garden path and arrived at a large gatehouse, fashioned from stone and ivory, all while the shadow of Forlorn Despair bleached the sunbeams from their faces with every step. That was until, with one look from Zinnia, the gates were thrown open, and the group sauntered inside.

Beyond the first gate, there were several more, each grander than the last and each requiring several servants with large staves to pry open. But beyond the final pair of gates, a cold spray met Fabius' cheeks, and the crashing of water sounded through the grounds. It had been only a few months since he'd seen the sight of the capital, but each time he arrived, it stunned him as if it was his first.

It was a marvellous sight indeed—a terrace of foaming fountains, draping tapestries and braziers burning blue; for years Fabius had tried to sculpt his own manse in its likeness, but each time he came here, the comparison became bleaker.

'Lower your blades.' Zinnia smiled at the guards either side of the entrance, and the gateway came wide open. Astralica was an island in the centre of Halo Blue, yes, but there was something strange about seeing an open door as if anyone could just walk inside to the paradise beyond.

But he wasn't *anyone,* and neither was she.

The second they stepped inside, they found the court alive with chatter. There was no time for Fabius to admire the clockwork pieces that rested on their podia, the sculptures that lined the halls, nor even the dizzying checked floor, for a horde of jesters and aristocrats danced about them. Astralica was burning bright.

'It's busier than I remember,' Fabius said, and his voice echoed throughout the halls.

'I think father misses my brother,' she admitted. 'Surrounds himself with all sorts of people he doesn't care for.'

'He's a changed man, then,' he said. 'The emperor as I knew him couldn't stand the sight of anyone he didn't know.'

'Well,' Zinnia said. 'It *has* been a long few months.' She paused. 'There is some rather special news I think he'd like to talk with you about, too.'

'Then I shall find him right away,' Fabius said.

'Of course.' She blushed. 'Anyway, I'm never one for my father's gatherings. I do believe he will be around here somewhere, though. I shall see you soon, no doubt.'

'It's been a pleasure seeing you again, my lady.' Fabius bowed, and the princess smiled, slipping away into a corridor. The last he saw was the flash of a clear dress and flushed cheeks like polished pearls.

He was then met with a very different sight.

'Lord Commander!' a voice like sandpaper rasped at Fabius' throat and embraced him before he could fathom the sweaty palms clasped around his back.

'My lord,' he said, eyes wide.

The portraits around the hall showed a boy more handsome than anyone else his age, but this man looked as if he ought to have escaped from the gambling tables of Highport. His hair was long and unkempt, and wrinkles had grown beneath his cheeks and pressed his forehead into his eyes; his chin was unshaven, and the ensuing beard stretched wildly beneath his stained robes. If the chatter about the halls said Fabius was the best man at ageing, then Cardel Avont was definitely the worst.

'Don't bow, you bastard,' he boomed, but Fabius never had.

The emperor wrapped a wet paw around his wrist and pulled him over to one of the grand tables, throwing the crowds aside. Once they'd cleared, he was presented with three women, each of them handsome, and each of them baring their breasts; one to the air—and one to the suckling lips of a child.

'Move.' Cardel waved a pair of them away, leaving a blonde with wide doe-eyes behind. 'Is he not beautiful?'

Fabius looked to the girl, frightened in that green silk dress of hers, and then to the child cradled in her freckled arms. She covered herself, and the babe tore itself away, and as it faced the Lord Commander, he saw it was far from beautiful, or healthy at that. Its skin was a sickly blue, and its forehead looked as if it had been touched by some plague. Fabius smiled timidly and stepped back.

'Wonderful.' He nodded and outstretched a hand to her. 'I don't believe we've met?'

The woman said nothing, and the child began to cry. She hushed him, and without a word, she scurried away.

Fabius lowered his hand, slowly.

'Who thought I'd father another child, eh?' He laughed. 'Of course, you did! My seed is strong.'

'A bastard?' Fabius asked.

'Janai and I are to be married come autumn. Then he shall be an Avont, truly,' Cardel replied. 'No one need knows of my...' he trailed off.

'What's his name?'

'Vancel,' Cardel answered, beaming proudly. 'Vancel the Strong,' he said, though the child looked anything but. 'My eldest has not yet disappointed me either, of course. He's off in the Summerlands, you know?'

'I've heard.' Fabius nodded, noting there was no mention of Zinnia.

'What brings you here, anyway?' he asked at last. 'You didn't send word ahead.'

'I sent seven letters—' he started.

'Wine?' Cardel cut him off, holding out a shimmery, gold flagon.

'No, thank you,' Fabius said. Each time since the first, he had declined for the wine was sweet like none other. Once he started, he knew he wouldn't be able to stop. Besides, the emperor already looked merry enough, and he needn't contribute to that.

'Your first mistake.'

'I sent seven letters, my lord,' Fabius repeated. 'I must speak with you and your advisors if you will.'

Cardel's smirk contorted into a grimace, and he looked to the Divinicus behind him as if he was just noticing them for the first time. 'There's no need for them here.' He waved the angels away.

Fabius looked to them, begrudgingly, and nodded—the pair left. He turned back to the emperor, and his heart sank—this was not the proud man he'd once known. This was a shell.

'I'll be the first to admit, Lord Commander, that I've grown tired of political matters,' he grunted. 'I thought you were here to drink, but your Divinicus are an... unwelcome sight. Perhaps you should wait to speak with my son instead. He's the one to deal with these happenings now.'

Fabius felt as if his ears had caught ablaze; he could hardly believe what he was hearing. *A king without duty is not a king at all,* they had once agreed, but now, the man who had said those words trespassed them with his life.

'Your son does not command Inamorata. You do,' Fabius scorned. 'Your daughter said you are unwell. Perhaps you need to sit down, my lord.'

'I am not sick!' he spat but sat all the same. 'Whatever drool that girl has been pouring in your ear, I don't know. But that's women for you.' He paused. 'And my son? He is my life—'

'There is more than your life on the line.' Fabius raised stiff fingers in frustration. '*Your son*—the surrogate emperor of Inamorata—isn't even in his own land. I fear he shall be far more interested in the girls of the Water. He is not responsible.'

'He has long come of age!' Cardel protested.

'As have most boys. That does not mean they can rule. When my Larl comes of age, I'm not going to trust him with the Divinicus.'

'Neither can an old man rule,' Cardel said. 'I've lived through this monarchy for more years than I can count, and I would be lying if I said it had not taken a toll upon me, Lord Commander.'

'Then you *are* sick.'

'Have you come here to do anything but insult me?' the emperor asked. 'It's not too late for me to withdraw my support for Kurulian in the trial to come.'

'I know, and I am grateful for your support.' Fabius sighed heavily. 'Look, I came here to tell you the Seven Freeguilds have broken their contract with Lostgarden.'

'That's what a company of mercenaries and assassins are best at,' Cardel scoffed. 'Next, you'll be telling me whores get paid for fucking.'

'Akanah and his men are travelling to Belliousa as we speak.' Fabius ignored him. 'While Kurulian and I will soon travel north to Nemesis Palace—in the hope of securing an alliance to bolster Rael's forces in the Reaches.'

'Bolster your forces? So, you're here to ask for more? Seems you've already got much on your mind.'

'I came here to ask for permission,' he said. 'To hire the Seven Freeguilds. I'm worried for Akanah and his men. You remember that northern girl I sent you that letter about? She's with him, regrettably, and she has more of an influence than you may think.'

'But *you* are better than to allow her that influence, aren't you?' Cardel asked, though, in his words, there was something of a threat.

'I'm keeping her at arm's length, yes,' he said. 'But it's important we ally with the far north before Kythera do again, and this girl is our one chance of that happening. Anyway, Kurulian made the suggestion to show her worth—in Belliousa—by getting her to talk with their matriarch. After all, Deih prefers not to speak to the establishment. And this girl, being an outsider and such, might be able to help us.'

'If it's what you think is best,' Cardel said.

'I don't think it's best,' Fabius admitted. 'I told you I was worried, my lord. I fear she will royally piss all over this opportunity. There's a fragile balance in the Free Islands. All it needs is someone like her to come along and—'

'You don't trust your own decision?' he spat. 'I think I know which of us is getting a little sick.'

'I trust my decision, but I don't trust my ability to get there the moment something goes awry. I need the Freeguild to monitor Belliousa so that if something goes wrong...'

'The girl dies?' Cardel suggested.

'The girl dies.' Fabius smirked. 'And if rumours spread that the Freeguild are disturbing the peace on Belliousa and not us—the balance isn't broken.'

'You intend for them to disturb the peace?' the emperor scorned.

'I intend for them to do what they must,' the Lord Commander remarked, 'should the girl make a mistake, that is.'

'Well, *I* orchestrated the wars against the Death Cultists of Lumiar,' Cardel boasted, 'the Four Genocides, the Forgotten Bride... I have given permission for the most pillages, robberies, political rapes and murders than anyone in my long lineage. So, tell me, what is the difference between them and us?'

'My lord?'

'What makes you the saviour when you kill those who oppose us but makes our enemies fiends and irredeemable bastards, eh?'

Fabius threw his head back and took a deep breath. He looked back to Cardel with a smile, cold, as if mercy had never been a part of him.

'You *must* be sick, my lord.' He laughed. 'It's okay when an angel does it.'

Twenty

Her skin was silk and honey up close, and her eyes were like kaleidoscopic watery mirrors. The scarlet drapes that flowed across her body showed seemingly every inch of her beauty, for there was not an inch she was afraid to show. Save for perhaps, strangest of all, her hands which she sheathed with black calfskin gloves, and her belly where her drapes enveloped her. But Deih was a goddess, it was undeniable, and those who had suggested otherwise were fools to think so.

When Magmaya had first boarded that starry ship south she had imagined a little world of glass oceans and emerald lands with spires that reached the heavens. Fabius may have disappointed her, but Deih had more than compensated for him.

Once the angels had escaped the muddy sumps, it was as if they had stepped through a magic door. It was like something from a faery story she had never believed.

Even the Belliousans' robes were lined with heroics, from Deih's own to the Temple Guards' who stood at the mountain's foot. Beyond the red silk was copper and divinity, lettering and symbols in some language Magmaya didn't recognise.

'It's a pleasure to meet you,' the High Priestess said to each of the Small Court. 'Allow me to show you to the First Temple.' She had smiled, and then she was gone.

'The Water?' Anclyn exclaimed not a moment after. 'She said...?'

'Yes...' Magmaya could barely form the word in her mouth, but there was a paralysing tranquillity in her secret being spilt. 'Yes.'

Anclyn shot her a look of dismay and turned away. Magmaya's heart sank.

She sighed and peered forward. She could make out the silhouette of the High Priestess through the shadows of the Small Court as she strode by Akanah's side—him pouring glass words in her ear all while she smiled and nodded, taking no heed.

He'd been right then—Deih didn't care for the angels at all, Magmaya realised, but the thought only made her greasepaint heavier and chest tighter.

Fortunately, there weren't any more incidents on the two-hour walk, though Magmaya had grown tired all the same. Her legs had rallied against her, and it had become increasingly hard to breathe amongst the thick, oily air. But with each step, she at least knew she neared the First Temple; there she would assume her duties and get the ordeal over with. Besides, whatever temple was good enough for a goddess would surely be good enough for her. Anything was better than the slums.

As the path grew steep, they passed pillars of stone and iron, and then a hundred frowning faces looking to the Divinicus in scorn. *They've been visited by the angels before,* Magmaya remembered. *Gods, they're so afraid.*

With every passing second, the air became heavier with sweat and fog, and it felt increasingly so that Deih was leading them into a trap. The excitement of arriving in Belliousa was slowly turning to dread, and as they passed more half-submerged hovels, a haunted chill came over Magmaya.

And yet, the closer the Temple grew, the grander the buildings became; they turned to great houses and smaller temples in their own right, all while walls inscribed with murals of the High Priestess led off into a network of sprawling streets, stretching on beyond reason. Instead of mud-coated fanatics huddling in their huts, there were aristocrats in silk, sporting countless brass trinkets in a vain attempt to mimic Deih.

Soon enough, the alleys and streets disappeared behind them, and the climb became nigh-treacherous as they clambered up a thin crag. But then, as if in answer to their woes, a single glorious stairway emerged from the haze, carved from ivory and brown stone as if the mountainside was leading them into the heavens. At increments, there were arched watchtowers, each boasting a pair of Temple Guard. They were fearsome things indeed, though their faces weren't quite right as if they'd been torn by a thousand years and stitched back together by a blind seamstress.

'As you can see,' Deih proclaimed at last, 'the First Temple is near impregnable. Not many from the continent can claim they've stood atop this mountain.'

It is impregnable, Magmaya reasoned, gazing up to the bastions that stood resolute in the cliff-side, and then down to the winding gorges below. At some points, the path grew so thin that one misstep would end in a terrible fall into the misty ravines either side of her.

Orianne was built into a mountain, though, and that hadn't stopped Vargul Tul. Then again, she couldn't see any gaping entrances below the First Temple that might've led into a sewer or thermal. *They don't need thermals here,* she decided. If it was any more humid, she might have melted.

A few the watchtowers were so obscured by the rain and fog, Magmaya wouldn't have even guessed there was a soul about. She could scarcely see ten feet before her, or behind for that matter, save for perhaps Deih as she shimmered through the cloud ahead.

It was then she realised she'd become distracted—the cliffs were dancing around her feet, threatening to toss her to heavens knew where; she'd been spending all her attention staring at a glittering red robe! Magmaya just hoped the journey back would be a little less insufferable. How the founders of Belliousa could have decided it was a good idea to scale the mountainside and settle at its highest peak was a mystery to her. Orianne's heights had never made her afraid, but for some strange reason, Belliousa breathed new fear into her. There was no sky, no ground, no road ahead and no trail behind. She could only move forward and pray she didn't fall.

But as the minutes passed, a breathlessness washed over Magmaya, and she found herself faltering. She spared a glance back to Anclyn and could tell she felt the same.

In time, she felt her lips and mouth turn dry, and her ears began to ache as the climb turned to a crawl, yet it looked as if they were no closer to the summit than they'd been when they had started. Even the once numerous outposts were dwindling in number, for in their place, thorny trees tore across the dead soil, and a violet ivy coiled up the steps until the path became nothing but a grim reminder of the grey wasteland Inamorata had become. And still, the mountain felt so very alive; Magmaya almost felt claws scratching at her ankles as she passed, like those who had fallen prey to the climb in ages past wanted to drag her down with them.

And Magmaya almost wished she *was* lost amongst them, where the weight beneath her feet meant nothing. And yet, the more she wished, the closer the First Temple grew until the bastion of a mountain disappeared behind them, and all that remained was an endless column of marble beckoning them into oblivion.

'The First Temple is atop these steps,' Deih announced proudly. 'Welcome to divinity.'

Divinity was still a hard climb away, it seemed. Anclyn refused as much as sparing a glance, so Magmaya could only clamber onward. And the farther she climbed, the more disciples of the First appeared. They too were draped in silk and little else, and they dropped to the ground in rapture beneath Deih as she passed, begging for an inkling of her to grace them.

But while they knelt beautiful and near-naked, Magmaya couldn't help but notice something strange about each of them; clockwork bulged from their arms as if they were automatons from lore, and their faces sported all manner of inks and irons. Where they should have sprouted breasts, there were instead ribbons of copper beneath their skin, running down their hips, fusing bone to flesh and flesh to metal.

As the climb droned on, bannisters emerged from ruined stumps and disappeared into the mist. Candles littered the steps where they descended to ruin, most having fallen prey to the rain, while a small number persisted like yellow eyes in the dark. The trails of light became less sporadic the higher they climbed, clustering together around small shrines, laced with flowers, reliquaries and memoirs.

'Many who have seen the light of the First pilgrim here from across the world. Sometimes generations pass before they arrive.' Deih looked to the shrines. 'You can only imagine how these last few steps feel for those who've travelled a thousand leagues.'

Gods, I can, Magmaya grumbled.

They carried on past a growling hunchback who could scarcely sustain his own weight on his cane, acolytes with blazing candles melted into their hair, and handmaidens with tattered aprons like sprawling dresses which trailed farther down the steps than she could see. She even passed by a bloated individual who was more sigil than man; an array of orchestral pipes and totem poles emerged from cavities in his blistered spine. The more she saw, the sicker her stomach grew, but Anclyn just looked enraptured with the ruin and grandeur. That was until they caught a glimpse of the Temple.

It peered through the mists like something holy unearthing itself from the soil. There were spires without number, enchanting her as they pierced the skyline. Angels descended to form the arches—a complex of stained glass and milky marble. It was so much larger than

Magmaya had imagined when she'd first seen it from the ship.

The First Temple was a veritable fortress and monastery all at once; shell-shaped fountains framed its height, all while streaks of water hung above like cuts in the air. It was as if Deih and the First Temple had been formed in the womb together—a woman made in the image of her own worship. And yet, whatever miracles she had performed in the decades before were truly no comparison to the indomitable city of carved stone and divinity.

Anclyn wasn't giving anything away, but she must've been enchanted too. And as for Krel and Akanah? Who knew what went through their minds. It must've been jealousy, surely. Not a soul could look upon the First Temple and feel arrogant still. When Magmaya had travelled with the angels, she had thought herself to be a goddess. The thought was laughable now.

'Repent!' The serenity was gone with a screeching, as a horde of preachers stormed towards the Divinicus, and pearly swords were raised faster than Magmaya could acknowledge. The robed followers shuffled back, but they kept on screaming, 'Repent! Repent to the First and your souls will be saved!'

'Stand down. These men are guests,' Deih scorned.

'Priestess,' they protested. 'Those false angels have contaminated blood. Each step they take on Belliousa is blasphemy.'

'It is not for you to decide what makes blasphemy,' the High Priestess thundered. 'Return to your families and thank the First *you* have been saved. In good time, these angels may be too.'

Through the crowds, Magmaya watched as Akanah raised an eyebrow, and the disciples disappeared with a hiss. Deih muffled an apology to the Divinicus, and they carried on without another word.

With the protests behind them, the First Temple (at last) was in walking distance. Magmaya found herself thinking to Kurulian—how had he felt in the shadow of such a thing?

After what felt like a millennium, the steps levelled out onto a patch of broken earth, and the grand entrance to the Temple appeared. Before the Divinicus, a thousand Belliousans must have crowded, draped in red silk and brass. They outnumbered the angels vastly, but they were disorganised and scattered about the hilltop, and the angels towered above them.

The entrance itself was an arched bastion, shimmering yellow even when the sun failed to shine. The stone was carved into flocks of fiery birds, stretching their wings across the spires, all while their trailing tail feathers haloed the First Temple with grandeur like none other.

The High Priestess looked to Akanah, aloof. 'This way, please.' She gestured to the doorway, and all the Legatus could do was nod and bow and walk.

Magmaya turned to Anclyn with a fretful smile, but the handmaiden's attention was drawn elsewhere. She looked away with a sigh, and an instant later, they shuffled inside the Temple, and the Divinicus were lost behind them.

There was a hint of summer inside the walls that she hadn't felt in what seemed like a lifetime; Magmaya *was* a summer child, after all—born during the greatest thawing Orianne had ever felt. But there hadn't been anything like it since, and she'd once feared there wouldn't be again.

How wrong she had been! The First Temple had come alive once the light reached it; it was a maze of pillars, each inscribed with a thousand hieroglyphs so that not an inch of the original stonework was visible. And where the sun showered down, there was revelation within the carvings. The runes in the floor were a little more sinister; by the looks of them, they had time before been flowered with the blood of virgins. Now they were stained bronze and copper—echoes of sacrifice. There were statues and shrines about the halls too—effigies of men and women too pure to reason with.

Magmaya turned her attention to a flock of harpists lingering around fountains. They had grins like pearls on their lips as they played, and she found herself ensnared. There was no escaping the monks either as they shuffled about the corridors, curtsying to Deih before moving on to tidy their shrines.

Hanging cloths were stitched into glorious tunnels, and it appeared as if the passageways they lined would stretch on forever until the motifs they carried no longer had any meaning. How Fabius had forsaken Belliousa for his 'higher order' was quickly becoming a mystery; if only he could've seen for himself the marble arches, the sprawling ivory and hovering bells, then perhaps the Lord Commander would've submitted to Deih at last. Perhaps if he'd seen the truth, none of this would have been necessary.

'Welcome to the First Temple.' Deih turned sharply to the Small Court as they gazed up across the halls. 'The First have blessed your coming here.'

'You have my thanks, High Priestess.' Akanah bowed. 'I do hope we can arrange a union that will benefit both of our peoples.'

'For too long, Belliousa has been at odds with Inamorata,' she remarked. 'Your last Legatus didn't seem keen on changing that. I do hope this time will be different.'

'As do I,' Akanah replied curtly.

Deih nodded and looked away from the Legatus. And then her eyes fixated on Magmaya.

She froze.

'You were the girl who intervened earlier, no?'

'Yes, my lady.' Magmaya bowed. There was something cold growing inside of her; there was a sickness between her lungs. It was fear she was feeling, she was sure of it. No excitement could've tasted so rancid.

'And you're part of Legatus Akanah's Small Court?'

She found herself nodding.

'Then I am grateful,' Deih said and looked away to the others. 'Upon notice of your arrival, we have prepared a great feast for all of your Court, as is the tradition of Belliousa. If you would come with me.'

The High Priestess led them through a series of doorways like each was a portrait framing the next. They arrived quickly enough at a large hall, where the roof concaved, and candles lined the cavities, flickering with a ghostly ambience.

The hall was cut in half by a black wood table that ran from its head to toe. Strangest of all, it was barely a foot from the floor, and instead of chairs to perch on, there were striped cushions dyed pastel that could've hidden a thousand years of dust, she reckoned. Several of the table's places were already filled with all manner of bizarre looking people; half had vases for heads, while the other half appeared to have no heads at all. They spoke in tongues Magmaya didn't understand and traded coppers and incense across the dining table. But they all stopped their chattering once Deih entered.

'My lords and ladies,' she began, 'we are joined tonight by the representatives of Inamorata—the Divinicus of Hardingham Reach. They have come to discuss a truce and all sorts of dogmatism I shan't bore you with.' They laughed at that, and the High Priestess beamed. 'But first, we will allow our guests a feast.'

While Magmaya's dinner for the Divinicus had offered twelve courses, the Belliousans' actually delivered. She found her place next to Anclyn among the other members of the Small Court, with Deih at its height and Akanah by her side. He spoke at her while she just smiled all the way until the first meal arrived: a platter of crabs which looked as if they'd scuttle off the plate at any moment. To eat them, each diner was offered a small, barbed spear.

Magmaya fondled the food for a little while, until she looked to Anclyn in confusion. But the handmaiden was already eating, impaling each scrap before moving onto the next.

'Let me help,' a Belliousan pushed by and pursed her hand around Magmaya's. She furled the spear between her forefingers and steadied it with the rest of her palm. 'Like this,' she said and swallowed the crab whole, smirking. 'Now you won't get any juice on your lap, girl.'

'Oh, thank you.' Magmaya tried a number of times, but she dropped her food more clumsily with each attempt, and her cheeks began to flush red. The Belliousan just laughed.

'I think everyone should try a Belliousan dish at least once,' another of Deih's servants said. 'People are more appreciative of forks after that.'

'Do you all speak the common tongue?' Magmaya asked, confused.

'Many of us do, but it's easier to ignore you if we pretend we don't,' the girl who helped her said before smiling and kissing Magmaya's cheeks. 'I'm Keriah,' she pointed to the other Belliousan behind her. 'That's my brother, Zoiln—we're High Priestess Deih's... advisors...' she explained. 'I'm sure you angels will be seeing us around a little more.'

'I'm Magmaya,' she replied. 'And I'm glad someone's telling me what's going on.'

'It is an honour to meet you, Maggy,' Keriah said.

'Magmaya,' she corrected her, but the pair had already disappeared.

Maggy, she thought. *Kharon had called me that once before Rache had been crippled and he still had hope of a boy heir.* Sometimes she wished she'd been born a man.

She looked to Akanah and found that *his* food had already been neatly prepared for him, and he had his own dining robes too. They reminded her of what Kurulian had worn around Orianne and the story he had told her about that feast. Chills began running up her spine. Was there a murderer at every meal? Was someone going to try and kill her here? *I better be cautious of my wine.*

Magmaya sighed and turned away. 'You look comfortable,' she said to Anclyn at last.

'This is how we eat in the Water,' the handmaiden replied for what might have been the first time in hours. But her relief proved short as she glanced at Deih and asked, 'You do know she's from the Summerlands, Magmaya?'

The next course was a boiling pan of small tentacles, orange and ringed like they'd been severed from a miniature kraken. Even worse, they still writhed about her platter, even detached from their body.

Krel tore into them straight away, ripping apart each tentacle with stubby fingers before grinding them apart with his teeth. At the top of the table, Deih ordered a servitor to stop Akanah's food from moving, while Cheyne, on the other hand, appeared to enjoy watching it wrap around his utensils.

Anclyn cried out as she bit into one of them, blushing. 'I've never tried anything like this.'

Magmaya smiled and felt a knot in her stomach begin to unravel. If only Anclyn admitted her a little more. But she had lied to her, and nothing good came out of that. All she could do was try to eat.

It didn't taste like anything, though, and the texture was another matter altogether. It was wriggling about her mouth, and when she swallowed it down, she felt it trying to crawl back out of her.

'*Ahaha,*' Keriah laughed from across the table, and opened a small vial, pouring its sugar-white contents over her meal. 'Look- it dances, Maggy,' she said, and it did; the food had found life again, and Magmaya gagged.

The next course was less of a course and more of a sample. It was the kind of thing commoners clawed at as they scoured the streets at night, but Magmaya looked to it with pity. It had started out colossal, in truth: a green fish with mirror-like scales bigger than even Krel. Strangely enough, the Belliousans began to pray over it, but only until a servitor brought a carving knife to the thing and all that was left were confetti-like sinews. Everyone at the feast was given a scrap, and though it tasted of oil and barely touched her sides, Magmaya was at least thankful she didn't have to embarrass herself in an effort to eat it.

The offerings of food continued well into the night, until Magmaya was very much full, and even past then, when she could hardly move anymore. She ate strange meats she had never known in life, from razor-edged whalebone to pastry filled with sheep's eyes. It would have perhaps been bearable if someone had spoken to her, but Cheyne was too concerned with what way he would eat his next meal, Akanah too concerned with Deih, and Anclyn too concerned with ignoring her concern. From time to time, Zoiln and Keriah would smile or make a jest, but above all the noise, there was silence.

Magmaya was glad when the whole ordeal was finally over, and the Court was allocated its quarters for the night; the talks were proposed to begin early on the morrow—when she presumed the High Priestess would summon her—and it looked like they needed her. Akanah had been talking to Deih all night, but she'd scarcely said a word in return, though Magmaya was beginning to doubt she would speak to her either. To a bystander, she might have well been one of the angels anyway. She could only pray the night would heal all her worries.

It seemed the night would never come, though. Even as Deih led the rest of them to their quarters, and as tiredness washed over her, the voice of the High Priestess ran through her mind and only became real again when someone drew her attention to it. 'May I have a word, young lady?'

Her heart sunk, and she glanced at Akanah. He nodded, and so she turned back to Deih.

'Of course.' Magmaya smiled, and Deih thanked her.

'If you would be so kind as to give me a moment,' the High Priestess said, and a number of robed monks swamped Akanah and the others. 'My loyal men and women will tend to your every need,' she said to the angels. 'Make yourselves comfortable—drink, eat, listen to the harpists play.'

Krel spat something vulgar, but Magmaya couldn't quite hear what as Deih laced her arm with her own; her skin was cold through her robes, while her lank, black gloves were nimble like spider legs as she flexed her fingers. The pair disappeared down a corridor together and into a maze of pillars.

'What's the matter, High Priestess?' Magmaya looked to her at last.

'In truth,' she began, 'I have not been able to stop thinking of you. You saved the girl from that *brute*.'

'No, you did, truly—'

'Would you care to tell me your name, girl?'

'Magmaya,' she answered, but it didn't taste like her name anymore. The syllables had become all wrong since she'd entered the First Temple.

Deih nodded to herself. 'Magmaya—?'

'Vorr, my lady.'

'Are you of noble birth?' the High Priestess asked, raising an eyebrow.

Magmaya winced at the question, but she just recited in her head what she had been taught to say: 'Somewhat, High Priestess.' She shrugged. 'You probably wouldn't have heard of me, though.'

'Oh,' Deih exclaimed. 'Akanah spoke of you at the dinner. He said you were a well-regarded royal lady, and I'm inclined to believe so.'

'Thank you, High Priestess,' Magmaya said proudly, though her underarms had become slick with sweat. 'It is an honour.'

'Where are you from, girl?'

'I grew up in Cecalia,' she replied.

'Cecalia?' Deih nodded. 'I've not heard of any *Vorr* from Cecalia. How is the weather that far south?'

'It's very...'

'Yes...?'

'Hot,' Magmaya lied, using every inch of her being to sound convincing. 'I can scarcely weather the summers,' she said but began cursing herself the moment she spoke. Deih's perfumes had clouded her mind—she hadn't learnt a thing about Cecalia's weather—only its doctrines and customs.

'Yes, I see.' Deih looked to her skin. 'And the trees—there are none like them here in Belliousa, no?'

'The palm trees line the streets for miles.' Magmaya nodded. 'Or so I remember, it has been many years.'

Deih smiled and stopped as they reached the end of the hall, and Magmaya found herself atop an ivory balcony. She gazed forward, finding a hall below and then a chandelier above which was little more than a blazing kaleidoscope, lighting the room for the rows of

Belliousans as they kneeled in a perfect circle upon the cobblestone floor below.

In the centre of the circle, where their red robes ended, Magmaya could make out some sort of face engraved in the stone. It was a skull to be sure, but its eyes wept with fire, and its teeth were jagged like cutlasses. There were whispers from the crowds as they prayed, and when Magmaya looked at them, she spied the faces of children and elderly alike. But no matter their age, their frowns were weathered by an age of grief.

At their foot, a preacher stood and echoed their words through an iron bell; his voice was distorted to the point of absurdity, and his gospels were more hellish than heavenly.

'You must forgive me, girl,' Deih whispered amid the prayers, and Magmaya turned back to her. 'For everything I do is for my people.'

'I don't understand,' she said. The hall had gone cold.

'I've heard worse lies than yours.' Deih smiled sympathetically, and Magmaya's head became ablaze.

'Oh,' was all she could stammer, but The High Priestess had scarcely begun.

'Why did you lie to me?' she asked.

'I—' she stuttered, on uneven footing. 'I don't know what you're...'

'Enough.'

'I don't—!'

'Drop the act, girl,' Deih said. Her voice was like a cold knife.

'Legatus… Legatus Akanah said you would tell I was a foreigner a mile off,' she spluttered, and a weight lifted off her back.

'He probably put you up to this, didn't he, my dear?' She tutted. 'You must never believe the lies of those angels. You should never have come here.'

Magmaya stayed quiet. She wasn't sure whether to be afraid of Deih's rage or grateful for her understanding. She was beginning to fear either choice would kill her.

'Cecalia *is* south of Halo Blue, but is it warm?' The High Priestess boomed with laughter. 'Heavens, no!'

'I'm sorry,' Magmaya frowned, ashamed. 'I never meant to—'

'I don't care what you meant,' Deih interrupted. 'You see, I was born and raised in the Water, girl—a coastal gathering. And as you might have expected, my sisters and I were stolen away by raiders.'

'I don't understand,' Magmaya said. 'What does that have to do with Cecalia?'

'Well,' she continued, 'that's where we were taken. I had thought my voyage there was the greatest hell the gods could have punished me with. Oh, I'll be damned, once the storms hit, the bodies of my sisters stacked up on the decks—the maidens once so beautiful and fair had become mockeries—'

'I'm sorry to hear that—' Magmaya crooned, but Deih cut her off.

'Our supplies ran low in time. I've never felt hunger like it—there is no thought, Magmaya, except the lust for food.' She stopped for a moment and laughed solemnly to herself. 'The only ones who didn't starve were the rats. They grew fat, big as hounds, until we heard them eating—festering, while we huddled at night. By the time we reached the shore, there were only two dozen of us left.

'But Cecalia you say?' The High Priestess gripped the bannister. 'That *was* hell, Magmaya. Once the slavers tore us from the ships, we had to make the trek to the Grandmasters' mansion through a short icy valley—and then through Cecalia.' She pressed her finger into Magmaya's cheek. 'Your skin is fitting for the summers there,' she remarked. 'But this was a terrible winter, and the only warmth we found was the shell of an old oak, but that rotted after a day. The next night, we huddled in the corpse of a bear. But sure enough, the fur was pillaged. And then,' she said, 'the corpses of our sisters allowed us the only warmth at night.' She paused. 'I would have given everything to have gone to the Cecalia you knew, girl.'

It's a sad story, Magmaya might have once said, but if anything, it made her fear the Priestess even more, not feel sorry for her.

'I made a mistake,' she admitted. 'I should have never lied. I was arrogant, I was—they said you were a succubus—they said you ate human flesh!'

Deih laughed. 'That's only half true, girl. We'd been made bloodied by the end of it all; our bodies were no longer any use for the pleasures of men.'

Magmaya stammered. *Perhaps she's lying,* she considered, but something in Deih's conviction told her that her words were gospel. It was clear that attempting to mislead her had been a mistake. Perhaps Akanah didn't know the world as well as he'd thought.

'Where are you from, Magmaya?' Deih asked. 'If that's truly your name.'

She frowned. 'I'm from the north,' she stammered. 'And I apologise.' The words felt hollow as she steered her gaze away.

Deih shook her head. 'This is none of your own fault, I imagine. I understand Legatus Akanah or perhaps even the Lord Commander himself planted you with me in an attempt to speak of terms, no?'

Magmaya nodded.

The High Priestess sighed. 'They assumed too much of Kurulian,' she proclaimed. 'I didn't speak to him because he was an outsider, I spoke to him because not everything he said was a bloody lie; not every word out of his mouth was advocacy or shit disguised as courtship.' She frowned, and Deih looked vulnerable for a moment. 'Why on the First's ashen soil did they ever think having you lie to me would help with some alliance?'

'As long as you thought I was from somewhere far enough away and not part of the Divinicus, you'd negotiate with me,' she trailed off. She had said too much.

'Cecalia may not be under the liege of the Divinicus, but it isn't that far away, girl.'

'It couldn't be too far,' she admitted. 'If the angels were caught using a northern girl without notice…'

'It would be treason.' Deih nodded.

'Akanah… he… he,' she stuttered, 'he just wanted the best—he just wanted to convince you.'

'He couldn't have done a worse job at it.' She sighed. 'I don't like being deceived. There shall be no negotiations of peace today.'

'But—'

'Look down to the prayer hall, Magmaya,' Deih instructed. 'Do you see my people? They have come from all over Belliousa in the wake of the angels, and hundreds more travel as we speak. But not in gross reverence, but in *fear*,' she explained. 'When the Divinicus came north, perhaps you looked to the heavens in wonder. But when they came to Belliousa, they struck at our wounds and cut our throats. We pray to our angels in fear of yours, can't you see?'

'Then there has been a grave misunderstanding!' Magmaya felt a chill run through her bones. 'I'll return to my Legatus. I'll inform him, like you said, there will be no negotiations. We'll return to Inamorata.'

'I fear they will not accept that so willingly.' Deih frowned. 'I suppose you have only been with them a short while?'

'A few weeks,' Magmaya admitted.

'That's why they thought you would be able to vouch for them,' she scoffed and began whispering to herself, 'I speak to Kurulian once, and they get some idea about me—'

'We misunderstood...'

'You may return to them, of course,' Deih said at last, 'but you may indeed want to hear more from me.'

'Why?'

'I don't think you're a fool, girl,' she said. 'I can see you do not blindly trust these angels, which is good. But I think you still might need to see something—hear something.' The High Priestess' eyes became alive as she reached out to take Magmaya's shoulders. 'If you listen to me, you will learn not become a pawn of the angels. I will teach you how to run, girl.'

'And what are you going to show me?' Magmaya asked, quivering. In her, the same fear persisted that had when she'd seen Vargul Tul in the boardroom. But this time, it was even more primal. Something about it made her unwell.

'The world.' Deih shrugged. 'I don't allow false angels to distract me from the truth. And neither should you.'

'I don't.'

'Then, by all means, go back to them,' she said, and Magmaya sighed.

'Why me?'

'If I can save just one person from them, the First will be pleased.' Deih smiled a motherly smile. 'If I can have one moment more with you.'

'They will suspect something if I am gone any longer,' Magmaya stuttered. 'I'm as scared of Akanah as you are.'

'I'm not scared of him. Not anymore,' she said. 'And I can assure you, it will be as if no time has passed. Once you return, petty politics will be of no consequence. Once you return, you'll know how to run.'

'I must be going.' Magmaya ignored her, eyes wide. She back turned to the corridor, but whichever way she looked, Deih was there as if a thousand mirrors of the High Priestess had been scattered about the halls. 'I already know how to run!' she cried. 'I've done it a thousand times before.'

'Please,' the High Priestess mewled, motioning away from the exit. 'Let me just show you the Temple. There's no need for worry; the First have spoken to me, and they are wiser and older than all of us, child. They have the power over the sun and the moon, the light and the dark, the life that inhabits you and the death that will become of you; they are the *cure,* Magmaya.'

As the goddess looked to her, for what felt like the first time, a fire ran down her spine, and she began dreaming again—dreaming the temple dream.

Through the kaleidoscope of colours, she saw Ranvirus and her deceit which had beseeched her, and her selfishness and lies which had brought her to Belliousa. They poured like golden honey from her eyes and into Deih's fingers as she felt the hairs on her scalp stand.

The cure—? That was what she had prayed for all along, no? To save her brother.

Magmaya shook her head and turned back to the hall; she could just about make out the silhouettes of glimmering Divinicus standing tall against the crimson of the Belliousans.

And then she looked to Deih, the comely priestess, as her memories left her in a cloud of heavy perfume. She was almost too beautiful to describe as she carried herself in those red, red robes with that whimsical frown as if her silver soul was looking down on her and—

Magmaya nodded.

Deih smiled and lowered her palm into the candlelight. Her leather glove was a darker black than she had first thought—blacker than the starless nights at home, blacker than the bottom of the pond in the forest and blacker than the ponderous eyes of Kharon Vorr.

But, as if her palm was haunted by Cecalia itself, nothing in the world could have prepared her for how cold it felt.

Twenty One

Anclyn could remember her first heavy rainfall in the Water; she remembered how the sky had turned black like a coiled monolith, and how the seas had been drowned of all their colour. She remembered how the leaves and the trees had swollen like spilt ink, and the mountainside had disappeared into the fog, swallowed up by the encroaching storm.

Then had come the first rumble of thunder—quiet yet cunning as if it were a predator giving its game away. After that was the first real clap: a sharkskin drum roaring from the heavens. Then it had seemed as if the earth itself had moved.

The rain had begun slowly, picking up par until it eventually drowned out the sounds of the maidens' mumbling prayers. The storm continued on for almost a week, and when Anclyn finally emerged from her hiding, half the shoreline had capsized into the ocean. The Water's boats had become spears of driftwood upon the shoreline, and the trees had been born again as broken barricades of sodden timber. Half the maidens lay dead in their huts, holding themselves like the day they were born. On the mountainside, the crop had been devastated, and even the highest points that hadn't been flooded had been struck by stray bolts of lightning.

'It is no matter,' one of the elders had told her in a grey, croaky voice. *'The storm will surely scare off any raids for a few days.'*

The rain that lashed out against the First Temple was child's play—a whimper of what she had known, what had crafted her. It was an insult to even call it rain but even more to hope it would give. Some of the more heathen members of the Small Court had even begun praying to the Maiden Gods that it would, but as if in defiance, the storm only grew worse.

She watched Akanah slump down on a desk in the small study they had given him, a thin veil of tapestry between her and him. He was the only one with a bed—the rest of them had made do, huddling around the great fireplace that turned the room orange.

'Hells!' she heard the Legatus curse, 'I'd sooner drink the storm drainage.'

It's not a storm, Anclyn wished she could've said. *It's a pitter patter.*

Cheyne slithered over to his chambers and tapped the Legatus feebly on his shoulder. 'Is there anything I can do, my lord?'

'Gods, you know I don't drink wine,' Akanah replied, moved to a window and poured the flagon right out of it. 'I need water, but none that was washed up with those fish at the shore.'

'Shall I send for some, my lord?' Cheyne asked.

'No, no. The rain will suffice,' he scoffed. 'Where's Magmaya's handmaiden? She can do it. Keep her busy.'

Anclyn's heart sunk, but Cheyne appeared to be on her side.

'The handmaiden wouldn't know where to go. She could get into all kinds of trouble, my lord.'

'There was something in that Belliousan food.' He ignored him. 'I'm not full anymore.'

'I can send for a platter of something too,' Cheyne suggested.

'Get the girl to find some dry food and water,' he said, looking to her. 'You know the way to the dining hall?'

She nodded.

'On your way then.'

Anclyn couldn't have been more nervous about having to navigate the First Temple on her own, but as she left the room, each member of the Small Court seemed to look to her with a longing to leave. Life under Fabius had been difficult and unpleasant at times, but Akanah had all the pride and wrath to match it. She supposed she was glad to get away, but the moment she stepped out of the chamber, she was confronted by an endless row of corridors that hung over her like a forest of tortured trees.

From someplace below, she could make out a conclave of prayers resounding through the halls—like a finger creeping up her spine. Their chants were unnatural and grating; obviously, the only similarities between Belliousa and the Summerlands were Deih and her food.

Nonetheless, she remembered the path back to the dining hall, and from there, she could find the scullery. If only she could remember what Legatus Akanah even wanted.

The Temple had become a maze of pillars—an impossible labyrinth of mirrors. There were no landmarks to guide her, no grandmasters to direct her forward. Nothing but shadows and eerie reflections across the stained-glass walls.

Occasionally, a flash of light would rush through the corridors and make her jump. And each time, a servant would reveal themselves shortly after, carrying a lamp or fiery candle. And each time, she would attempt to ask for directions, but they would just shrug and say something in a tongue she didn't understand.

The people here were even stranger than any she'd known before; in the Summerlands, the tribes had their own rituals and fetishes of sorts. The Iaol used to surround themselves with apes and cover themselves in their faeces to ward off demons. The Karlas used to replace their left arms with skeletal bird wings and wore crowns made from deer skulls. Luckily, the Water had been mostly exempt from all of that, but on Belliousa, everyone dressed in something strange. At the dock, there had been a dozen skinny dogs, but in the First Temple, priests wore necklaces made of their teeth, while the pilgrims appeared awfully well fed. Was it all for their gods? Her god certainly hadn't fashioned her that way, so why had theirs?

Down another corridor, she made out a rushing of water as the fountains burst to life around her. She was back at the atrium—she had come full circle! At least here, though, she was able to listen to the gentle tapping of the rain in peace and peer through the grand archways in wonder. *I may end up back late, yes, and I may be beaten for it,* she realised, *but I can suffer that for a glimpse of freedom.*

But then, there was a shadowy movement against one of the great windows, and Anclyn's heart nearly leapt from her chest. For a moment, the sound of the rain and rushing water had gone. A figure turned to face her.

'Stranger,' a voice sounded, 'don't I know you…?'

She felt herself smile, but the fear hadn't left her yet. 'You scared me half to death…' she exclaimed. 'You're…?'

'Keriah.' A figure appeared from the dark, and shortly after, another followed. 'You've met Zoiln, no?'

'Yes,' Anclyn found herself stuttering. 'You were talking with Mag—I—'

'What are you doing here?' Keriah asked her at last. 'You're Maggy's handmaiden, aren't you? Shouldn't you be with the others?'

'What's the name, girl?' Zoiln croaked.

'Anclyn,' she said. 'The Legatus sent me for water. I must admit, I got a little lost.'

'Looks like you've travelled half the Temple—First have mercy,' Keriah said with a laugh. 'Let us at least take you to the kitchens.'

'Us?' Zoiln asked.

'Us.' Keriah nodded.

Anclyn didn't recognise the way back, but Keriah insisted it was where she must have come from. It was as if the paths had shifted around her; the corridors and stairwells were turning like the Temple was one mass of clockwork.

'How long have you been her handmaiden?' Keriah asked at once.

'Not long,' she stuttered. 'I was the Lord Commander's until she came.'

'Is she good to you?' Zoiln asked. 'Women—they're not all pretty faces. Some have a real... callousness about them.'

'Of course, she is,' Anclyn trailed off. 'Deih's not callous, though, is she?'

'If Deih was like that, we wouldn't be serving under her,' he replied.

'If it isn't rude of me to ask,' Anclyn began, 'why are you serving under her? If you had a choice, then you could be free, couldn't you?'

'She came to us in a dream,' Keriah remarked lovingly. 'A dream we both had—a dream in which the First spoke to us. We weren't even on Belliousa, but they showed us a temple and showed us Deih, and she showed us salvation. We came to her willingly. We were enchanted, I suppose.' She giggled.

'Do you have any gods of your own, Anclyn?' Zoiln asked at once.

'I pray,' she admitted. 'I don't know who to. I suppose to my old gods—'

'How can you still believe in *them*?' he cut in. 'You met a real goddess today.'

'A goddess?' Anclyn exclaimed. 'I thought she was the High Priestess. She can't be a goddess—goddesses aren't—'

'Aren't what?' Zoiln asked.

'She's the High Priestess, alright,' Keriah said before Anclyn could hazard a reply. 'But she works miracles, she stops wars—she heals the sick! Not only that, but Deih cannot die! The First have brought her back to us before. And if she is to die again, she will be reborn from smoke and rain as the Angelica.'

'The Angelica?'

'The fiery angel that will save the world, as legends would have it,' Zoiln said. 'Some think it's only an allegory, but I know it in my heart to be true.'

'Did you ever meet the Golden Woman?' Keriah asked.

Anclyn shook her head. 'Even if I had, I would've been too young to remember.'

'You missed a lot then, dear girl,' Keriah remarked. 'She outshone the sun, and she was a false goddess. Think of what a real one can do.' She smiled, and her voice chimed. 'You may be unknowing of the ways of the First, but not for long. In time, they will reveal their true plans for you.'

What true plans? She wondered. *I never had a plan other than to serve.*

'How many are there?' Anclyn asked at last.

'How many what?' Zoiln replied.

'How many gods make up the First?'

'Could be a thousand. Could be two.' Keriah shrugged. 'All we know is there are precisely as many as there are. That's what they told us in our dream.'

'It doesn't matter anyway, Anclyn. When the Angelica is reborn, the anti-heroes and false gods of the world will unmask themselves,' Zoiln said gleefully. 'The First will show us their faces, and we shall be liberated at last—whether there are a thousand or two of them.'

'Are the Divinicus false gods?' Anclyn asked.

'Do they claim to be gods?' Keriah smiled pitifully.

'I suppose so,' she said. 'They dress like angels…'

'Then the First will rain down judgement on them,' Zoiln scorned.

'What about me?' Anclyn said.

'You'll need to be a little more specific, girl,' he replied.

'What if I don't come to believe in the First? In the Angelica?'

'Then you—' Zoiln started, but Keriah cut him off.

'You will,' she asserted. 'You will.'

After what felt like an age, they returned to the dining hall and arrived in the kitchens, still warm from the banquet. There were mounds of seafood and bloodied meats scattered across the countertops, and each dead eye seemed to stare down Anclyn as she passed by.

'What exactly are you looking for?' Zoiln asked.

'Water, I think,' she remembered, 'and some dry food of sorts.'

'Was your Legatus not happy with the refreshments Deih had left, then?'

'I don't think he drinks wine,' she admitted. 'He seems a little distraught.'

'Shame,' Keriah handed her a pair of clear flagons, both cool to the touch. 'The First were having a good day when they made wine.'

The group set off again in silence, chasing the candlelight back to Akanah's quarters. Deih's servants had offered to carry the food, so Anclyn just sauntered back empty-handed, fingering the crimps in her dress.

'So, where's Maggy now?' Keriah asked after a while. 'Has she yet to return to the others?'

'She was still gone when I left,' she said. 'I do hope she returns quickly; she needs some sleep. It's going to be a busy day tomorrow, I fear.'

'Knowing Deih, she'll be gone all night,' Keriah said. 'She can cast a spell over people, that woman can.'

'Oh,' Anclyn remarked. 'She's from the Water, isn't she?'

'Yes,' Zoiln said. 'Never been there myself, though. I've heard it's as haunted as Vavaria.'

'It's not haunted,' Anclyn said. 'I was from there.'

'You were?' Keriah asked. 'Your face—I would hardly believe it. I'd sooner guess Cyrel.'

'A trick of the lights can do many things,' Anclyn said, shrugging. 'Please don't tell anyone, though. It's only—I didn't know about Deih until I arrived. I didn't know she was from... and she's not supposed to know...' she trailed off.

'You secret is safe,' Keriah said. 'So, you didn't know her from the Summerlands?'

'No,' she said. 'Apart from Fabius' other handmaidens, I've yet to meet another girl from the Water.'

'Well, this is the Water's second home,' Zoiln said.

'How so?' Anclyn asked.

'Inamorata stole many of its inhabitants away and planted them here to work,' he said. 'When Deih came to power, she released all the slaves that had been taken from the Water. After all, there's no one she cares more for than her own kin. She's a forgiving woman—a loving one. You would find no one better to be the avatar of the First.'

'Anclyn,' Keriah began as they turned a corridor. 'If you wish, I can introduce you to the High Priestess tomorrow. You may not remember her from the Water, but she might just remember you.'

'I—I don't know,' she stuttered. 'I don't want to get in the middle of these politics. Besides—you said she's a goddess! I wouldn't know how to act or what to say.'

'I wouldn't worry about that, girl,' Keriah giggled. 'As Zoiln said, she is loving. You must never lie to her, though. Somehow she always finds out the truth.'

Anclyn laughed to herself. *That sounds like a woman of the Water.*

'And if Deih likes you,' Zoiln said, 'you might find a way to disappear.'

'How do you mean?' Anclyn asked, almost concerned.

'You would never have to see the Divinicus again—you'd be a whisper to the wind,' Keriah said. 'She might take you under her wing, provided you would commit yourself to the First, of course. Never again would you wait on an army of arrogant warmakers.'

'I...' Anclyn exclaimed. 'I don't know what to say.'

'This life of false angels and tending to greedy men shouldn't have become so ingrained in you, girl,' Zoiln said. 'Liberate yourself as Keriah and I did. We too were slaves of the Reaches, freed by Deih. You can be too.'

'If you want to meet her, come to me before the sun rises tomorrow,' Keriah said. 'The First shall be joyous in your embracing of them.'

Anclyn felt herself grin as they made their way back to Akanah's quarters, but her thoughts turned to Magmaya. She may have lied to her, but there was some warmth in her still when she thought of her. A warmth she couldn't just let go.

'I don't know,' Anclyn stuttered, turning to the pair.

'What do you mean?' Zoiln asked.

'I don't know if I can do this,' she said. 'I don't know if I can leave Magmaya behind.'

'She's just another angel,' he scoffed.

'She's not—she's only been with them for a little while. She's different; she's only a girl.'

'It doesn't take a while to become one of them. All it takes is a choice,' Keriah said, frowning. 'Anclyn, if you don't at least try and speak to Deih, then you'll be making a mistake.'

'It would feel like betrayal,' she exclaimed. Though her mistress had often drunk dubious amounts around her, things would be different soon once they'd finished with Belliousa. She knew it. 'After all of this is over, Fabius will give her an estate, and we will both be happy. I will look after her as her handmaiden, and I will treat her well, as she will me. I know it.'

'And give up Deih?' Zoiln asked. 'Give up the First and serve false angels instead?'

'I can't force this on myself,' she squirmed. 'That would be lying.'

'Just consider it, girl.' Keriah smiled warmly.

The pair said their goodbyes outside Akanah's quarters and left her with the food and drink. But Magmaya still raced through her mind as she scoured the room for her, finding no one but a dozen faces she didn't want.

'Is she still gone?' Anclyn asked.

'You're late,' was the only reply she got.

'I'm sorry, my lord,' she bowed, handing over the food and pitchers.

She watched his face contort, and finally cave, as a hand reached forward and took the food.

'You're dismissed,' Akanah sighed and waved her away.

Anclyn perched back down by the fireplace, yet she could still hear echoes of the siblings' footsteps outside. She was half-tempted to run back outside and follow them.

But... but Magmaya...?

When the room finally grew quiet again, it was as if the whole affair had never happened. In mere moments, all the food and drink she had stressed herself so much to find was gone, and all that was left were the flames.

As the night dragged on, Anclyn realised she wasn't the only one who wanted to huddle by the fireplace; the others from Akanah's Small Court were there too—strange faces and wise lips. She wished she could've told a jest or sang in tune to the flames as the choirs did, or even just weep at the notion she once thought she was free.

Occasionally, Cheyne would look to her from his secluded corner of the room with a moody grin, and she'd turn away, cold. She had often seen him creeping about the gardens of the manse but never had gone so far as to talk to him. He appeared to have a strange obsession with Magmaya, though—the thought made her even more sick than she already was.

As the night began to draw on, there was only silence and wind until, at last, someone spoke up.

'I served under Legatus Kurulian when he came to Belliousa, you know,' one of the old men croaked in that tortured voice of his—Yalsus—that's what she had heard Akanah call him. Anclyn wondered why the Legatus had cared to take him with them; perhaps it was ceremony. He seemed fairly useless otherwise. '*His* meeting with the High Priestess didn't go too quickly either, but at least we'd left by the dawn,' he giggled nervously. 'Perhaps Deih of the Water hasn't taken so kindly to the girl, either. Should we pray for her?'

'Prayer is for the hopeless,' one of Akanah's handmaidens said, spitting into the flames. 'You've seen the natives—that girl is the least of our problems. Keep your ancient spells to yourself old man,' she finished, and Anclyn looked away from the flames, realising she was being stared at. 'What about you, handmaiden? You're one of hers—is there anything you know that might get us out of this limbo faster?'

'I—' Anclyn began, but the handmaiden cut her off.

'You know this place is haunted, girl?' she snapped, and Anclyn felt a terrible chill run down her spine. 'The furthest reaches of this place will cast you over with witchcraft—it is known. Don't you want to get out of here?'

'Don't bother her,' Yalsus snapped, the fires lighting each crevice in his forehead. 'She knows as much as we.'

'Tell me,' the other handmaiden growled, 'Yalsus, your mother married into the Fultons, did she not?' She paused, and the old man nodded. 'I wouldn't bother talking, then. You've probably got webbed toes too.' She looked back to Anclyn. 'Drop the silence and keep your head up. Allegiance to your mistress won't get you anywhere.'

Anclyn didn't look up, though. She traced the flames instead and watched them move, watched them breathe.

'I'm talking to you, handmaiden!' she snapped again. 'How so I haven't seen you before, anyway?' She paused. 'Oh… You're one of Fabius' bitches, aren't you? You must have something to spill, then.'

'I don't spill secrets.'

The handmaiden laughed. 'Secrets are worth more than Blood Sovereign here—learn how to spend them,' she said. 'So, what about Magmaya then? Is she *really* from…' she trailed off and lowered her voice, '…the north?'

Another of the Small Court's maidens shook her head. 'Those pilgrims travel for months on end and give the clothes off their backs for a glimpse of the continent, only to be rewarded with a square metre of dirt—and that stowaway joins the angels? Perhaps we should just leave her with Deih.' She fingered for a whalebone pipe at her hip and lit it. The flame joined another in an empty glass on the mantlepiece.

'Shut up.' Anclyn turned away with a frown and whispered, 'She's as innocent as a rose.'

Yalsus giggled to himself again, and the handmaiden grinned wildly. Even the others who couldn't have paid less attention appeared amused, and Anclyn's face flushed with colour, despite the layers of greasepaint.

'She's not innocent.' The old man smiled. 'All my life I have preached for the Maiden Gods and taken in their chosen, but never have I come face to face with anyone truly free of sin. Nearly half the continent fought at Fleetfront, and the other half in the campaign the

Lostgarden—now that was a true war of knights of old, but that didn't make it any less dreadful. The High Lord of Emeralds, Illysis Doladerio, the purest prince and his purest paramour both bloodied their hands there. And if they hadn't done it then, they would've done it some other day.'

'What about children?' Anclyn asked. 'Don't you think they're innocent?'

'Do you see many children around here, girl?' he croaked. 'They either get their fingers dirty or die. *Heh,* perhaps you're the exception to that by the looks of things.'

'She probably still has her maidenhood,' one of the others goaded. 'I'm surprised you haven't already sliced her throat, Yalsus, in exchange for the night to pass a little faster.'

'That would get you nothing besides a flogging,' the girl pointed out.

Anclyn smiled, but she felt no joy in her; a mere number of days before she had been declaring herself a free woman—what a cruel jest that had been! Now she had laughed away her chance at escape for a girl who never cared for her. It had been her duty to protect Magmaya, but she was nowhere to be seen; it was a disaster. She feared she couldn't hide her shame anymore.

'My gods are kinder than you give credit,' Yalsus replied humbly. It appeared the conversation was still going.

'What about when the world was plagued with a Red Star?' the other handmaiden asked. 'Didn't your Virgin Priests try to ward off the moon by burning children?'

'That was the Dark Age of Transmutany, long before even me,' he said. 'Times have changed and so has the will of my gods. The times of holy crusades and flaming swords are long over. All we have left is prayer.'

'And the Golden Woman?' Anclyn summoned the courage to ask.

'Not one of ours.'

'Quiet,' Akanah hushed the court from across the room, and they all turned to watch him. 'I hear something.'

'What is it, my lord?' Cheyne purred.

The Legatus didn't answer, but forced himself through the door instead, looking about the corridor. The Divinicus followed him out, and a minute later, one returned.

'Come with us, all of you,' he crooned with a voice which wasn't quite fit to be human. Without another word, they shuffled forward and joined Akanah in the hallway.

She tried to wish it all away—to find herself not in some forsaken temple, but instead in a castle with a handsome monarch, watching over ashen beaches and lying on the warm shores of Inamorata. She would pluck peaches and berries fresh off the trees and follow the lines of birds into the sunset. But all the old castles were haunted; everyone knew that—and she was terribly frightened of ghosts. It felt as if every ambition she had was dismissed by someone at some point; she was even beginning to dismiss them herself.

At the end of the corridor, Anclyn watched as a cluster of robed things tried to keep the Divinicus at bay, but the angels just tread through them like wolves among pups, throwing mortals aside and carving a way for Akanah and his Small Court. She had always watched from afar as the Divinicus marched off to a distant land, but it was different to be among them. She wanted to crawl up in the corner of the hall and wait for it all to be over, but whatever was happening was bigger than her. And besides, there was someone else to consider.

'She'll be back soon,' she heard a Belliousan call. 'Return to your quarters.'

'All you hear is the wind,' someone else insisted.

She looked longingly to the spires and arches in the light of the moon, the stained-glass window bleaching the Temple in a terrible crimson.

Somewhere out there, Anclyn realised, *a girl is forsaken by the very angels she's praying to.*

Twenty-Two

No matter how many lefts Magmaya took through the winding corridors of the First Temple, she didn't reach the room she began in. Perhaps it was a malign trick of the light or impossible act of geometry, but each step she took made her more nauseous. She could only look to Deih once they reached a new passageway, to which she would always reply with a knowing nod.

Magmaya's head was growing light, and her shoulders burned where Deih had held her as if each step she took brought her farther from the ground and closer to the heavens. But still, the thoughts of the High Priestess' stories lingered in her mind—the taste of flesh and fur— the brisk cold that had made itself her enemy. With every passing moment, she felt herself become less Magmaya Vorr and more Deih of the Water. It had felt like mere seconds had passed since she had joined the High

Priestess, but deep inside, something screamed to her it had been a matter of hours.

The pair passed a small shrine as they walked, and the High Priestess stopped to bow to a man who kneeled at its foot. 'My condolences to the loss of your daughter,' she whispered, and the man blushed and praised her before turning back to his grieving.

That was until, in the reflection of his trinkets, his gaze caught Magmaya's, and he looked to her, mouth agape. Even from where she was standing, she could make out the terror in the Belliousan's eyes, and in them, she saw the shimmer of her pearly plate beneath her robes.

She tried to cover herself, but the damage was already done.

'He was paralysed.' Magmaya frowned, and they continued through the hall; it was black as pitch as if the sun had neglected it. 'Just a glimpse of my armour and he was frozen.'

'The reasons to fear the Divinicus are likely the same as those to worship them,' Deih remarked as they entered a thin hall, lit only by hanging candles from the wiry walls. 'I wouldn't worry about that, though, child. Where I'm taking you, none of that will matter.'

'And where are you taking me?' she asked, feverish. She felt uncertain, but something within her yearned to hear it. She had travelled through the First Temple so far already; she could only let a little more poison in. Perhaps in it, she would find the antidote she was looking for.

'Actually,' Deih said, with a flash of embarrassment in her voice. 'I suppose it's not where I'm taking you. It's who I'm taking you to.'

'Oh,' Magmaya remarked. 'Who then?'

There was a beating of clockwork, and the halls fell silent; an empty ticking followed their footsteps as they descended a flight of stairs. Then Deih spoke.

'You see, after Cecalia, we actually met the Grandmasters in that mansion we were taken to,' she started, her voice chiming through the damp of the corridor. 'I didn't know their names then, but I have since learnt them. The first I met was an old aristocrat called Nurmian Claerg who seemed to be on the brink of death himself. He had a wife and eleven children, I was told, and he fed and clothed them by selling girls like me to gaudy men like him who didn't know where to put their cocks.' She paused. 'He scared me the most. After him, I was shown to Fasorn Vedrick, Lord Commander of the Divinicus before our friend Fabius—selling slaves, would you believe it?'

'I would.' Magmaya thought to Anclyn with a frown. *How many others had there been?*

'He was a handsome man, dressed in that pearly armour I had for so long dreamed of,' the High Priestess continued. 'He was everything I expected of the angels, and his voice lured me in like a trance. Though underneath his façade, he was the type of man who paid his cohorts to keep quiet about his dealings in slaving. They were hardly quiet around me, however; even less so when they beat my sisters and me.' She scratched her cheek and blinked. 'Sorry… I heard he was slain at Fleetfront anyway. No matter; he wasn't the man I was destined to. That man was Torth Fulton. And he's who I want you to meet today.'

'Oh.' Magmaya nodded. *I don't want to meet a slaver!* She thought. What had she got herself into?

'Torth, and his brother, Karth, had received quite the inheritance from their late father, you see,' she said.

'He was perhaps the only preacher of the First left in Inamorata... and he was heir to Belliousa. His brother had made a different life for himself, though; Karth married into Nemesis Palace—a grand estate upon the Ash Wastes of Inamorata where he still uses the Belliousan sciences he adopted from his father to practice his—well, whatever he practices.'

'But Torth?'

'Torth used his inheritance for gambling in the Sumps,' the High Priestess explained. 'If you're with enough coin, a trip across the Kytheran border is as simple as an afternoon stroll. He made quite a name for himself at the playing tables and quite a reputation among the Inamoratan High Lords. But on one fruitless day, he lost everything: his wealth, his reputation—the clothes off his back. So, he turned to the only inheritance he had left in the world—the crumbling island of Belliousa. Here, he rallied the scattered devout of the First and brought a forgotten religion back from the ashes. Not that I knew all that as I stared him down that day—they were only faces then.

'Anyway, Nurmian dismissed me before I had a chance to learn his name. He looked to my frostbitten neck and threatened to throw me to a whorehouse or back to the cold of Cecalia. Fasorn didn't look at me twice—but Torth Fulton,' Deih said, smiling, 'there was something in his eye—some miracle by the First with which he found cause to pity me.'

'And he brought you here? To Belliousa?' Magmaya asked, frowning.

'Yes,' she said. 'But when I arrived, already bewitched by my saviour, I was surprised to find the island was plagued with maidens from the Water like me—

others he had saved from Nurmian and Fasorn. But I soon forgot about them. He told me I was perfect; he told me the First had sculpted me in their likeness.

'I hadn't heard of the First then, though. Before I came of age, I pledged myself to the Goddesses of the Long Summer. But when I arrived on the black shores of Inamorata, all the castellans and kings alike were devotees of the Maiden Gods—every action was taken in their name, only to be broken a moment later.'

'The north had its gods.' Magmaya nodded. 'But they only existed so we had something to blaspheme about.'

'It's not much different here, girl,' Deih said. 'It is the nature of men to place their doubts and blames in the hands of someone else; each step they make is justified that way—and when it can't be, they change the scripture.' She paused. 'I'd been taught to kill for my gods and kill other people's imaginary gods to prove ours weren't so.' She shook her head. 'This world was bloodied by angels long before the Divinicus came to power.'

'So where does that leave the First?' Magmaya asked.

'They were the only gods to speak back when I prayed to them,' Deih explained. 'I let go of my fear, and they banished it. That led me to become engrossed in the old stories of Belliousa until I finally summoned the courage to tell Torth Fulton that his—our gods—were speaking to me. And then it didn't matter how many maidens he'd had—I was his favourite. He told the world I was a gift from the First and gave me the seat closest to him on the Belliousan council; he dined with me, and he spared me from any work, while the others drowned in it because their heathen gods hadn't saved them, Magmaya. But the First had saved me.'

'You were Torth's lover?'

'Something like that,' Deih said. 'A peculiar type of love, though; he was better versed in the Belliousan sciences, like his brother.'

'How do you mean?'

'When we did not share a bed, he worked on me— he told me I was made in the image of the First, but my likeness was not perfection enough. So, it was with his hermetics that he made me, Magmaya. He fished the weak bones from my body and replaced them with brass and copper. He—'

'I don't understand...' Magmaya cut in, shuddering. If what Deih had told her about before wasn't witchcraft enough, then this certainly was.

'The doctrines of Belliousa dictate that we were crafted as imperfect beings,' she explained. 'Only with the removal of our weak flesh can we be made strong again.'

'So, he cut you open and...?'

'It was no matter,' Deih said. 'His clockwork didn't change me half as much as his seed. Mere months after I came to Belliousa, I was bestowed with new life itself.' She lowered her hands to her abdomen and cupped her navel with an empty smile. 'Three children, we discovered quickly—his seed *was* strong indeed. I treasured them inside me, mothered them as if they were in my arms, and prayed to the First they would live prosperous lives.'

That didn't much surprise Magmaya; since she'd met her, she'd thought Deih had a motherly look about her. *Mothers do dangerous things for their children, as gods do dangerous things for their people,* Magmaya was forced to remind herself. *Be careful, dammit.*

'But as if overnight, Belliousa had decided they had had enough of being ruled by an outsider,' the High Priestess continued, and Magmaya turned back to her. 'They took to the streets with torches; the hillside bastions weren't enough to stop them as the Temple Guard joined their ranks, and the First Temple was overrun. They proclaimed Torth a whore from the summit and burned his portraits. What of this did I know? Nothing—he had sheltered me from it all—so you can imagine my surprise when I awoke to a host of strangers setting light to my home.'

The closest someone ever came to taking my home was Vargul Tul, Magmaya thought. And there had been something unnerving about the way he had stood in her father's boardroom, invading her space. She could never imagine waking up with him at the end of her bed.

'There was no time to protest,' Deih carried on. 'I remember screaming and tossing about as they stole Torth from my bedside and drove a hot dagger through his mouth, but my pleas did no good. They stabbed him again in his heart and then his loins and then his eyes, and by the end of it, there was nothing left of my love but a bloody pulp.' To Magmaya's shock, Deih half-laughed at that. 'I screamed so loudly then I couldn't even hear my own wailing, all while they continued to defile whatever dead thing remained of Torth Fulton. That's when they turned to me.'

'And...?' The High Priestess' words had ensnared her.

'And I can scarcely remember what happened. There was steel, and there were flaming knives, but I only felt the cold. All I could do was writhe and splutter like an ensnared hare.' She frowned and looked to Magmaya, caught in the moment. Without another word, the High Priestess lowered her robes, exposing her belly, and Magmaya looked on her in horror.

What had once been the body of a fair maiden had become a tortured thing. Where there should have been divinity, there was a scar, black and wretched like a canyon across her navel. It was bloody and ruptured still, twisted with broken veins and shattered with skin like ash. And as she covered herself, that alabaster smile like a porcelain doll became hollow and cracked, and as she went to speak, her voice was hoarse. 'The last thing I saw,' she said, 'was a knife in my swollen belly. But by then I had no voice left to scream.'

Some string of incomprehensible words lingered on Magmaya's tongue—some sentence to validate her lamentation. But she couldn't say a thing. Before she could speak—or drool—they turned a corridor and made their way down a set of stairs, finding themselves before a grand pair of clockwork doors, flanked by a myriad of Temple Guard.

Deih motioned to them, and they stepped aside. She fingered a small, brazen key from amongst the many on her wrist, and the door opened with a hiss as if whatever behind it was drawing an age-old breath.

Magmaya felt her blood turn cold and spine begin to ache, but once the Priestess led her forward, it became clear there was no beast to be found, but instead there was a chamber of endless stone pillars, hanging chains and glass. She looked to Magmaya, softly, and held her belly, tight.

'The First made *us*,' she whispered. 'And I made them.' She gripped her womb. 'But who made me?'

The chamber flickered to life with an orange glow from a mountain of candles beyond. There were bundles of flowers about the room, alive and ripe with colour, and despite the dust and grime, it was clear the place had been visited often; *someone* would have had to have lit the candles and kept the flowers fresh. But this was no tomb of the living, nor shrine for Belliousans.

It was a secret; Magmaya could tell from the High Priestess' swift and hushed movements across the grey, oval floor—the whimper on her lips only served to seal her suspicions.

Magmaya felt drawn forward as Deih stopped abruptly by a small mausoleum where many of the wreaths and candles stood. She smiled to her and pricked her fingers against one another, unlacing those woeful black gloves as if everything evil was to be unleashed once her skin was.

'Where are we?' Magmaya asked, her low voice still loud enough to echo throughout the chamber.

Deih shook her head and pressed a finger to her lips. And then, with a movement like a ballerina's stride, she courted Magmaya closer, closer to the mausoleum so there would be no return.

'I died that night,' she said, still unlacing her gloves. 'I felt it within me—I felt the life slip away until there was nothing left. Nothing, except for a dream of coloured lights and stars that melted in my palms. And then the darkness and the cold.' She drew a breath. 'I was dead for eleven hours and nigh on five minutes, and during all of it, *he* was there.'

'Torth Fulton?'

'Torth Fulton.' She nodded. 'Every step of the way, he walked with me as I died, speaking of things I couldn't understand, nor remember. His face was fresh and young, though—younger than he'd been when I'd first met him. But he was afraid as if he too feared what would happen at the end of my dream. For so long, the last thing I thought I'd ever see was the First as I kneeled before their divinity, but in fact, the last thing I remember is his smile—oh gods that smile.'

Deih froze and unclenched her fingers from the lace. The gloves began to slide down her fingers, slowly, and then all at once, fluttering to the ground like birds taking flight for the final time.

But the gloves were no longer of any interest; all that concerned Magmaya were those hands. Where little, pink fingers should have been, there were only wretched, bloated things, translucent and stained beneath the skin— below that, an inky black mass had spread like a nest of veins below her flesh.

'I died that night,' she said again, spearing the gloves from the ground with shaking fingertips. 'And when I died, my body forsook me. My skin grew frail and cold, limp and heavy as if I'd never been inside it, all while my blood escaped to my fingers and feet. Perhaps when I saw him in my dream was the best time to forget—to drift into the arms of the First and into the endless sleep beyond. But what kept me awake was a ticking, Magmaya—a ticking that never began and never ceased.'

She moved over and pressed her chest to Magmaya's ear. And she heard it! There was a timepiece against her head—a metronome hammering on which threatened to never end.

'What...?' Magmaya asked, but her voice was wavering.

'The ticking never did stop, save but for a second when I awoke. At first, there was only the cold. It enveloped me like nothing else; no matter how warm the fireplace before me was, the cold wouldn't leave.

'I couldn't see, and I couldn't pretend to; there were only formless faces and splashes of colour like a painting gone awry. But there were words—I could hear at least. And then there were the red hoods of Belliousa, chanting—chanting that I was their saviour. They showered me bouquets of colours I had forgotten existed and words which had long escaped me. Escaped me so that the only two I remembered were Torth and Fulton. But he was a tyrant to them, and they'd killed him.' She paused for a moment. 'And *he* did not wake up.'

'But you did?' Magmaya stammered, her head growing light.

Deih nodded with half a smile, running her hands across the roof of the mausoleum. 'This is what I must show you,' she said and trickled her delicate, black fingers against her trinkets on her hips, finding a key amongst the treasures. She slipped it into a crevice in the tomb and heaved it open.

As if in response, darkness spilt out of the mausoleum like it was a solid thing—like an inky blackness made of thorns and granite. It extinguished the candles with an otherworldly breath yet coated the room in a tantalising warmth.

And within it all, there was Deih standing tall and scarlet in the rushing smoke, chanting some whisper of the ages.

She outstretched her dead hands and beckoned Magmaya forward; fingers ran through her hair, and blood rushed from her head as if her very life was slowly being drained from her. The tomb engulfed them both until the darkness fled, and all that remained was a flickering light above, marble pillars, and an armada of ivory draping from the ceiling.

Magmaya found a bed of stone in the centre of the mausoleum, and on it, a casket of glass. Past the shimmer, she could make out all manner of bubbles and inks in the sepia foam, swelling as the light touched them. And as she approached, it became clear there was something amid the darkness—a corpse within the endless amber; there were bleached bones, a few lose sinews of flesh, half an eyeball—a remnant of a face.

'Torth Fulton,' she couldn't help but stammer.

'My love,' Deih whispered and rushed to embrace the dead man's liquid sarcophagus. After she was finished, she went about tidying the flowers (roses), and then the tattered books and prayer leaves that were scattered around him. Seeing her do that almost broke her.

'You died.' Magmaya felt a throbbing rise in her head. There was almost no point in trying to make sense of it all; her strength had left her with her sanity. 'You said you were dead—you showed me your scars—I've seen your hands.' Her fingers shivered as she pointed to her. 'You died!'

'Magmaya—' Deih started, but she cut her off.

'You're worshipping a corpse!' she shouted. 'Calling him *my love*?'

'My girl,' Deih started, 'if you'd too seen what I have...'

'You died!' she repeated, but the High Priestess just took her hand with a warm smile. 'Let me go. Let me go! I'll—I'll go back to the Divinicus. I've heard—no! I've *seen* enough of this!'

'Please, Magmaya, let me finish.'

'There's nothing more you can surprise me with.' She pulled herself away. Her head was spinning—no, the room was.

'It's not about surprises, it's about the truth.'

'The truth?' she spat. *That's what the angels had said!* 'What do you want from me?'

'Listen, Magmaya, please.'

'Why?' Magmaya exclaimed. 'Why me? I can't stand here any longer—and—and—take advice from a dead woman.'

'Then what about a dead *man*?' The High Priestess gestured to the casket.

'It's the same damn difference!' she screeched. 'Your lover is bones and sleeps in formaldehyde. And you? I don't even know what you are. I can't be part of this any longer.'

Deih sighed as if disappointed and offended at the same time; there was a wistful frown about her. She reached out and pressed her dead, black finger to Magmaya's own lips and dragged it down to her chin with a soft hush.

'I did die—I died as equally as Torth Fulton did.' She shrugged. 'But thanks to him and the First, my heart continued to tick and click and whir, and it hasn't stopped since. It kept me dead until my wounds had closed, and it brought me to life. But Torth—when I look at him, I realise I'm living on borrowed time—*his* time.'

'Spend it wisely then,' Magmaya said. 'I don't need to hear any more about him.'

'For over a decade I have watched him bathe in bleach and waited for those eyes to snap open,' she said, half-crying.

'And you chose to lead the people who killed your love?'

'What would you do if you couldn't die, Magmaya?' Deih asked. 'If no mortal blade could touch you?'

'I don't know,' she stuttered. *Perhaps I would sit, I would think, I would rest. Maybe I'd even live long enough to forget all of this.* 'It doesn't matter, I—'

'But it does! The gods forged us with lives like candles to the stars,' the High Priestess remarked. 'Our world is ripe with famine, rape and murder. I have outlived my lover, my children were ripped from my belly, and I've slept in the corpses of my sisters—I can only live to suffer more. And now, those who killed my love worship me as a goddess—the Angelica, born again from the ashes of Belliousa. And I believe their worship, in truth, for the First have not stopped their whispers. They tell me secrets, riches; they speak to me still of my daughters. But I would give it all a heartbeat to hold him in my arms again.' She looked to the casket in despair.

Magmaya thought to Rache alone in his crib, half a world away. What she would've given to be back with him, but this was what she had chosen—to give herself to a witch.

'Rumours spread,' Deih continued on, 'that it had been *I* who'd killed Torth Fulton and declared war against the Grandmasters and against Inamorata. Perhaps those rumours saved my life from Belliousa's rage, but it seemed half the world worshipped me, and the other half wanted to string me up.'

Maybe they should have done, Magmaya thought.

'They made me their leader when I wanted to run and hide, and they made me rule with a heart I didn't have,' she sung. 'And after several months, I heard my children had been sold. I had been replaced with a clockwork belly as the traders had passed them through the Ash Wastes. My children were commodities sold to the highest bidder—triplets of a goddess taken before their first breath. Would you believe it? Trophies on some sick man's mantle.'

'Yes.' Magmaya stopped, drawing a breath. 'I've heard it all today, it seems.'

'It is my duty to the First for you to know.' Deih smiled softly. 'And in due time, you will need to know. You see, there are three truths you must learn. One for Mercy and one for Faith, and lastly, one for Death.'

'I don't understand.' Magmaya narrowed her eyes. 'I know those truths... I have fought for my home—'

'Not yet.' She shook her head and looked to Magmaya with a face more radiant than the ages, and once again, there was a palm held out, black and blistered.

'You want my hand?' Magmaya asked, and her voice trembled. Though beneath it all, she was infuriated—infuriated with herself that she hadn't left yet. 'Is there more I have to see?'

'Much more—for you've yet to open your eyes.'

When she touched Deih's skin, Magmaya felt herself grow limp, and a sickness washed over her. The world faded away like ink in rushing water, and then the High Priestess was gone.

There was a moment of peace and sincerity after, as Magmaya looked around the chamber. Still, Deih's words hung over her head like a curse, and her head grew lighter and lighter until it looked as if the mausoleum's roof had collapsed in on her.

She looked around for a way out—there had to be some way, somewhere she could escape from the madness of this lullaby. *Perhaps this was how Albany had felt in his final moments,* she realised—a helplessness and despair like none she'd ever known. It was the sort of thing that drove a woman mad.

As she turned away, some fragile whisper lingered in some part of her like a watery kiss, growing larger until it engulfed her. The dizzying sounds ran through her head like unbound colours until softly and slowly, they subsided, and she was left alone to study the monotonous thumping of a clockwork heart, raging against her chest.

And then there was a coldness against her palm again, and she looked up to find the omniscient face of Deih; her hand was in Magmaya's, although she could've sworn she'd never taken it. She watched as her palm, still swollen by the infernos of Highport, was engulfed in Deih's talon, thin and veined. They became intertwined like comet's tails—a malign tendril stretching from one corpse to another.

'What have you done?' Magmaya exclaimed, tugging at her hair. 'You've cursed me with witchcraft! You promised me the cure...'

'There is no witchcraft here, there is only truth,' clockwork spoke in tune with Deih's blossoming lips.

'One for Mercy, one for Faith and one for Death,' Magmaya spat. 'I know, I understand!'

'No,' Deih said. 'You must face them yet, girl.'

A sinister white glow washed through the Temple like a rain of hot needles. Magmaya was blinded in an instant, but not quickly enough to watch as Deih and the mausoleum slipped away into an aether, their hands unfurling at last.

And after all of it was done, all that was left was silence—in her head and all around her—an impenetrable buzz which kept her awake. In the back of her mind, Magmaya could still see glimpses of reality seeping through, but whatever spell Deih's words had cast over her was too strong. Before her, there was the First Temple, but no longer was it grand and shining; it was hallowed and shattered amidst a mountain of ash, twisted in the moonlight.

Magmaya felt a rush of fingers through her hair, and a chill joined her hand as if Deih was still holding it, though there was nothing to suggest the High Priestess still lingered. Perhaps it was what she had intended for her: a dream or vision of something she was supposed to be—but as her head swam, she couldn't even begin to understand.

She glanced about the room, frantic as a haze drifted across her vision. It hurt to stare, but it was agony to turn away. And in each corner of the chamber, she found a fresh horror growing; in one, there was a splintered tree with a woman's likeness carved into the branches, embedded from the rafters, while snow fell upwards all around it. In another, a maiden stood naked, facing the wall, but when Magmaya looked closer, she turned and revealed herself. Her breasts were savaged by the pecking of crows, her body bloodied for their picking. Flowers had attempted to grow and die from the sockets where her eyes had been, and a rib cage was working its way through the skin like a jagged sabre. In time, a fountain of birds arrived to begin the feast anew.

As she watched the girl bleed, Magmaya felt the same wetness grow between her legs. *It's the hour of the moon,* her mother had once told her, but this was surely the hour of some hell.

In the opposite corner of the chamber, a woman dressed in a red gown stood tall like a statuette, smirking as she stumbled forward, a knife in her back as she bled and smiled and bled and grinned.

Magmaya looked onto the final corner in horror and saw herself standing upon a charred moonstar, while a black sun rose behind her head. She was naked and bruised, and her eyes were alive with crimson—as were her thighs; it hurt her head to look, but it was no use trying to shake it free.

A vibration ran across her skin, and she pried her eyes open to face the Temple again, watching as it rebuilt itself around her. A wave of mist formed a petite cloud overhead, as a number of Temple Guard appeared before her, each raising a spear and shield to catch the moonlight above. They were faceless in rank, and as Magmaya turned, more of them arrived, standing atop the broken battlements. If her dream was over, then why did her reality seem so false?

In time, each of their shields became a mirror. They were a circle of reflections—a hundred distorted faces staring back at her—empty echoes of her own likeness. Sometimes, she wondered if it was the same girl in there—if the same girl was staring back. Sometimes, she wondered if Magmaya Vorr had been a girl from some story she'd read.

In one of the mirrors, she spotted herself crying to the nameless gods at the foot of her tree—a young blonde face, reddened and sore. She saw herself about the forest, all while looming trees formed grotesque patterns in the snow.

Don't follow the roses! she urged herself, but the old Magmaya wasn't listening, and she found Albany there again, as red as the day he was born.

When she looked in a few of the mirrors, though, there was nothing where her face should've been—not even an echo or silhouette—just a pool of white.

That was until one of the Temple Guard sprang towards her, making its way to the centre of the Temple. In the place of a helm, a face like bark sprouted, chittering and lapping at its lips. Magmaya felt some deep urge draw her closer and force her to touch its thorny façade, but the thing's putrid breath drooled like brown ichor, warding her back.

The chittering grew louder until it became a vile screech, bleaching the Temple with sound. Magmaya winced as she drew her hand closer, watching worms glisten as they burrowed in and out of the thing's face. She felt the grooves in its wooden cheeks and the orifices beneath her fingertips. And then she watched as it dissolved around her hands into a fountain of clear, snapping wings.

Magmaya screamed as the swarm rose out of the Temple Guard like a wave. It surrounded her and swallowed her, and then she was lost in them until there was nothing but an endless thumping that seemed to cut the air in two. She felt her lungs burn and beating heart rally against her as the insects festered upon her cheeks, nestling themselves into any cleft they could find.

They kept burrowing until her skin was torn from her, and she lost herself to the dark. She sat in silence, formless, until the insects had gone and the buzzing in her head was drowned out by her sobbing, and her skin was made new with her tears.

But something far worse remained in the corner of her eye: a culmination of the insects and shed carapace of the Temple Guard. It was an abomination; it was a hulk of smouldering pus like some terrible half-human thing. Even its skin (if she could call it skin) was red-hot with disease.

It reeked through the First Temple and washed away the incense and the song of the flowers. She couldn't bear to look at its face as it changed from glimpse to glimpse; one moment it was Deih's, the next it was hers. And where a mouth should've been, there was a black hole. And underneath, on the underbelly, there was something festering.

She sat, frozen, as with movements more intricate than a seamstress, the abomination outstretched a pair of arms from its belly, the skin withered to the bone. But they were human to be certain, and on their tips, human hands were born with rotten fingernails. It stretched, withdrew its arms, and reached it quill-like fingers inside itself.

A sickness caught the air, and Magmaya felt herself vomit. She could only watch as those fingers like diseased ivory pierced in and out of their owner's flesh, a wetness sounding as if it was rearranging its own entrails.

And at long last, it unearthed whatever it was looking for. The abomination lurched forward and screeched like a dying animal, ripping its fingers from itself. And amid a baptism of milky water, it offered her a child.

It was perhaps hours old as it cradled in the putrid, brown fingernails of the beast. It held it with a grace only a mother knew, but Magmaya couldn't bring herself to look. It was silent and calm like still water, but as the child slept, it wept inside her head.

'Get away from me...' she cried, but her voice was broken and coarse. She kicked out and screamed, but the abomination only dragged itself closer in some desperate hope she would take the child. But the closer it grew, the more Magmaya resisted, and the more she resisted, the more it began to grip the babe in its putrid, yellow fingers.

'Leave me alone!' she continued, and after a couple more attempts, the thing obeyed and slowly retreated away.

It looked at its creation in dismay, and its fingers tightened. In one moment, the babe was in its hands still, and in the next, it was not, as they turned to fists around the child, and from them, a serpentine coil of wings erupted, and a new swarm engulfed her.

Magmaya could only cough and splutter as she fell to her knees, overcome by the horror as the girl who'd slain a tyrant died inside of her, and the forest fire that ran through her veins was extinguished.

An instant later, it appeared as if the First Temple had been restored. The Temple Guard seemed to have slipped away into oblivion. Even the abomination had vanished.

She pulled herself up and out of her dream, but whenever she closed her eyes, the thing was still there, worming its way through her mind.

But she could run again, at least—run until her legs gave way. But it felt as if for every metre she left behind, the First Temple grew a mile. And for every mile the First Temple grew, the clearer it became she could only wait, wait until morning or whatever came next. Her mouth had grown dry, and her gums were sore with vomit, but worst of all, there was silence.

She waited for seconds, minutes, hours until its echo left her. But when it finally did, she had forgotten when exactly, like when one tried to remember falling asleep.

Twenty-Three

Up ahead in the dwindling darkness, Magmaya found a fork in the corridor. Through the arch on her left, there was a column of twisting stairs leading up to a glimmer of white light. Through the other archway, somewhere in the darkness, there were footsteps as light as a honeybee's kiss.

The High Priestess had made it clear enough that there was no turning back, and in the impulse driving her closer to the heart of Temple, there was something alluring; it was like there was an ecstasy hidden beyond every closed door. So, she turned to the darkness, and soon enough, it was as if the fork in the corridor had never existed.

The journey out of the mausoleum was perhaps more confusing than the journey there, though. The eerie masks and symbols of the First which lined the walls seemed to come to life with violent snares as she made her way through the shadows; their eyes were like black wells tracing her every move.

Occasionally, the corridors grew so chokingly thin, she couldn't help but be reminded of the hallways below Orianne she'd frequented a lifetime ago when Inamorata was just a dream, and a witch's curse was something Siedous had talked about to scare her to sleep. She hadn't believed for a minute that the fortune teller had used witchcraft to tell of the Divinicus' arrival, but had Deih told her the same thing, she might have believed it. The magic in her whispers wasn't something she could explain away.

Soon enough, the light began to fade, and Magmaya stumbled, snatching an invisible step and tasting blood. She felt for the wall in the wet humidity and pulled herself to her feet, stole a deep breath and carried on.

The silence that plagued the corridors was ringing through her ears and eating away at her head. She had left the dark a new woman, though it felt nothing now would raise her from despair.

The light could at least try, though, and a moment later, a new branch of corridors awaited her as if they were the sprawling legs of a spider stretching into nothingness. Around each corner, there were hieroglyphics in the stonework she couldn't quite decipher, while floating candles on clockwork plinths lit the way forward like a trail of blue wisps.

She glanced around, stared down by the frowning infant-faces sculpted into the walls, and followed the lights onwards.

It was as if some mysticism held the Temple in its bare grip; no longer was she in a fortress mountaintop, but it was as if she had ascended into the heavens. The weight of Magmaya's plate had drifted off her shoulders, and her chest felt as if it was swaying above her in the open air.

Magmaya felt a whisper call to her from the corridors, and she lashed out at the air, cursing, 'Get a hold of yourself!'

But her heart rebelled against her words, and deep in her, she knew there was no leaving the Temple now. Part of Belliousa had become ingrained in her, and any attempt to leave would've been sinful—a heresy against all she'd been told. The thought was filling her with dread.

As she entered the next chamber, candlelight lashed out against her eyes. She was blinded until the distant chanting of preachers below took over; their humming drowned out the silence in her mind, but when she opened her eyes again to face the light, it was almost worse.

Magmaya found herself in a chamber; it was a pocket of light amid a labyrinth; the curving walls were lined with the carvings of priestesses, stricken with bloody runes, and the ceiling was plastered with intricate paintwork depicting angels amid clouds of gold. In the chamber's centre, there was a table made of precious gems, shimmering blue to purple to red in the dim light. Beyond that, there were vases of porcelain and crowded bookshelves overflowing with holy books and drooping scrolls.

She followed the cobblestone floor until it met a veil of crimson silk, weaved with veins of ivory. Magmaya paused, stole a breath and traced the creases in the fabric as they reached a pale neck and a head of curling hair, fastened with a pin of polished brass.

She was intoxicating—her aura, and everything she was—and when she turned to Magmaya, it was like she had been born anew.

The High Priestess grinned and swilled ruby wine around the glass that lulled between her fingers, the trinkets on her wrists singing as they kissed one another. She set the glass down beside her and outstretched her hand. 'This is Elysia,' she said like honey. 'I must apologise for leaving you in the mausoleum, but I pray you will join me now.'

Magmaya felt drawn to a brass stool beside the shimmering table, but a red fear grew in her blood as she sat.

'You look pale, girl.' She frowned. 'Well a little more than before, anyway.'

'I don't know what to say,' Magmaya rasped. 'You wouldn't believe me if I tried.'

Deih shook her head and ambled across the room to a small stained-glass window. In it, there was a playing board—long discarded and overgrown with branches of candles—extinguished. That was until the High Priestess brought a kindling to them and they came alive with a green-blue flame, bathing Elysia in a cool glow.

Magmaya looked around in desperation as the colour absorbed her, but found no escape, save for the door she'd come through, spiralling into a world of black shadow. She turned back, ears pricked, as the High Priestess spoke again.

'I believe in many things some consider strange.' Deih nodded. 'I fear little you might say will surprise me.' She looked to Magmaya and tapped her fingers on the window, a whimper of sorrow about her. 'Are you thirsty?'

'I'm quite alright,' Magmaya answered stiffly.

The pair sat in silence for a few moments, allowing the air between them to soften, all while Deih supped slowly on her wine, and Magmaya sunk down low into the chair. The kaleidoscope of light that framed the room submerged them until Deih finished her drink, and then Magmaya looked up, eyes sore and cheeks red.

'This is the heart of the Temple—cold and hard to reach.' The High Priestess smiled to herself. 'Say what you please; there is no one around to hear and think you a fool.'

'I don't know, I can't—'

'Then don't speak another word,' Deih said. 'If you can't, then you can't.'

'But—'

Deih raised an eyebrow.

'I, I saw things in that chamber,' Magmaya found herself stuttering. 'They were... terrible... *things...* and all over me, there were swarms of insects and...'

'I see.'

'You have to believe me!' she pleaded. 'They were burrowing into my skin...! I know it was all in my mind, only colours and noises. But it was happening like it was right in front of me—not just in my head.' Her fingers were quivering as she moved. 'I feel—I don't. I don't know. But... I have to leave.'

Much to her surprise, Deih nodded, poured herself another drink and said, 'I would be more surprised if you didn't see a thing.'

'What?'

'Torth's resting place is a vessel for the First,' the High Priestess explained. 'They've shown you what you needed to see.'

'No.' Magmaya stood, feeling some fear burn deep in her. 'No, no! It was in my head. Nothing—nothing so terrible could be real...'

'Is that so?' Deih asked curtly. 'You see, girl, the First will channel themselves through their believers in this world. We are their advocates, their avatars, and what they showed you was no less real than you or I. If you were to ask the Lord Legatus Kurulian, he would tell you he saw the same. When the Divinicus first travelled to Belliousa, they didn't find an alliance, but instead some truth.'

'And Kurulian never wanted to come back,' Magmaya spat.

'He was awfully silent after he left the mausoleum,' Deih admitted. 'That was until he called me a witch and threatened to burn me. *How archaic,* I had thought.' She paused. 'But I can still remember the tip of his blade against my throat, and that was enough. I dare say the angels haven't quite liked me since, trying to starve out my island with their embargoes and taxes and the like.'

'So, what did *he* see?'

'Same as you: what he needed to see,' she explained. 'And that is no witchcraft, nor trick of the lights, but perhaps a placement of trust. I can't explain it, but maybe you can *feel* it, girl.'

Magmaya nodded, but then she thought she heard the child crying again. There was blood boiling in her chest, screaming at her to submit to Deih—to give herself to the High Priestess and forget all that had brought her to the First Temple. But her words were spun like a thread of warmth, and they lulled themselves through her mind— they were far too good to be true.

I can't go back to the Divinicus either, though, Magmaya realised. *I've been gone too long to return.*

'The angels weren't always like this,' Deih began again as if she was reading her thoughts. 'Not until *Auna'Iara;* not until the Golden Woman.'

'I keep hearing about her,' Magmaya said. It felt as if ever since she'd first been told her bloody name, her life had become more hellish.

'Of course, you do. When she took her first step on this world, it was as if the sky had fallen,' Deih hummed. 'For centuries, we clung to our holy books and prayed the heavens would send one of their own. But once she stood before us, there was no answer. Half the world dropped to their knees in prayer, and the other half took up their swords against the false goddess.' She smiled, knowingly.

'False goddess?' Magmaya asked.

'Well, some believed she was sent by the enemies of the Maiden Gods to blemish this world,' she replied. 'But after all of it was done, it seemed she had been masquerading as an angel rather than a devil of the pit.'

'You liked her?'

Deih shrugged. 'I'm not sure if she was the catalyst of what began or just a symptom, but she did good for this world, Magmaya. She revealed the Divinicus were not without stain.'

'I know that,' she said. 'Time and time again I have been warned about them, but when I see them, I'm… blinded.' She almost laughed.

'And that's a demon's greatest disguise,' Deih insisted. 'I was still a maiden of the Summerlands when the Golden Woman emerged, but her footsteps resounded far across the seas. You see, the Divinicus had been a force of holy crusaders wrought to watch over both Inamorata and Kythera unchecked, but Auna'Iara challenged that. The children of the Summerlands had been imprisoned for years by fear of a Divinicus raiding party or crusade—but the Golden Woman scared them away.'

'So, who was she?' Magmaya asked.

'Your guess is as good as mine, child,' Deih remarked. 'Some say it was because of her, the angels left Kythera. Others say she came to finish off the angels after they left—she *was* a warmaker, that much was for sure— the struggle between the Golden Woman and the Divinicus lay waste to much of the land.'

'I never heard about any of this,' Magmaya exclaimed. *The Kytherans that had come north all those years ago had been fleeing from angels— Albany's mother had never mentioned a Golden Woman.*

'Well, you have her to thank that the Divinicus didn't bring their conquests north,' Deih said. 'Hundreds— no, thousands died, Magmaya, and all the war did was draw country lines in the sand. After the Divinicus routed, they brought down every bastion and every monument Kythera had forged until only the Silver City remained. And you must know what happened to that.'

'I know about the treachery of the Divinicus,' Magmaya insisted. 'But I read nothing about this in their doctrines.'

'Then their doctrines have done their work,' Deih remarked. 'But for you to understand why I've brought you here, you must learn the follies of these men.'

'I am aware of them,' Magmaya said, growing impatient.

'Then you will know how the Aureate Reign came to an end, no? A gaudy, young Divinicus took it upon himself to kill the Golden Woman, and if by some miracle, he came back with her corpse.' The High Priestess sighed. 'They still sing of her blood; they say it was like oil laced with gold dust, and it shone like burning salt. One ounce of it would make you a man with more coin than coin there is.'

'Which gaudy young Divinicus was that?'

'The First... they do not tell me.' Deih frowned. 'In my dreams, they show me only a corpse—it must be hers, but it's not bleeding oil and gold dust—it's bleeding wine.'

'They don't tell you?' Magmaya exclaimed, confused.

'There are some things the First have me know. Others not,' she said. 'Her death, though, they tell me of that—it might have well been something you've read in a holy book—it sealed the fate of the Divinicus, too. From then onwards, it was as if they couldn't resist committing crimes against the world.'

'Like what?'

'Perhaps you should ask the Legatus Akanah about the songs the children sing of how he staked his own mother—right through the heart. The villages the Divinicus have burned, the children they have killed out of mere spite! Each Lord Commander seems to have committed a greater deviancy than the one before him.'

'So, what has Fabius done?'

'Fabius shall burn forever for his sins,' she said. 'But your friend, Legatus Kurulian?'

'*Friend*?'

'I can see the vial on your wrist, girl.'

'My vial...'

'His vial,' Deih said, and Magmaya sighed, losing herself again. 'There's only one of those, though. It's his sins which are perhaps without count.'

'You told me I had all the time in the world,' Magmaya asserted. 'You can start counting them. I can wait,' she said, but even as she spoke, she knew she was betraying herself. She had assumed from the start that the Divinicus were quite far from the gods they claimed themselves to be, but she had never expected such an intricate thread of travesties.

'Very few of his infidelities would mean anything to you,' the High Priestess remarked. 'And I fear he would strike me from the heavens if I dared to mention one.'

'I told him everything about me in exchange for passage south.' The girl looked to her feet. 'I made a mistake...'

'Perhaps,' she said. 'Perhaps not.'

'He told me...' Magmaya started, feeling something stir in her stomach. 'He told me that the Silver City was no more. Is he the reason it's not on any of the maps of Kythera anymore?'

'Yes, well...' she started. 'The city wasn't only a bastion against the Divinicus, but it was perhaps the only reminder of what the south was before the Transmutany.' Deih grit her teeth. 'When the Golden Woman arose, many cited her as a new renaissance, where man could walk arm in arm with their maker upon the soil—but she was slain at the hands of those who revered her. And in honesty, when she died, it was only inevitable the Silver City would fall too. Just not at the hands of an escaped slave who barely knew the ways of the south.' She paused as if contemplating her next words very precisely. 'They call him the Lord of Quicksilver, girl. I feel that'll suffice for an explanation.'

Her head was swimming. *It had been him?* All along, Kurulian had been the one to take the Silver City from her?

'But why?' Magmaya asked, feeling a string of dread spiral through her. 'Why did he do it? Why did he join the angels?'

'I suppose he was always one of them, girl. He only burned the Silver City to impress them. They're all the same,' she spat. 'They serve their empire with the majesty of heroes and prostitute themselves as mercenaries the next.'

Perhaps Kurulian is no different to the others. Perhaps what she had fallen in love with was the hazy reflection he had left in the ice that night in Ranvirus. She felt betrayed and frustrated. A sickness began to gnaw at her stomach.

'They're vile,' Magmaya heard herself say, but she didn't know from where she had summoned the words. They felt like fire in her throat. 'So, tell me how to leave them, then. Tell me how to run back north.'

'North?' Deih asked. 'I said nothing of you going back north.'

'Well I'm going,' she protested, sweating. 'I made mistakes there, yes, but I'd rather return to the war than suffer this.'

'You came here to escape war?' She looked concerned. 'You've brought the war to us.'

'If I can somehow take it back north, then I will finish it there.'

'I told you, you can't go back there, girl,' Deih pleaded.

'Then why have you told me *any* of this, if not to scare me away?'

'Because when *I* hear the First, I take solace in that it doesn't matter what they tell me,' Deih said. 'But what instead they show me—and what they've shown you.'

'Me?'

'They've chosen you,' Deih said. 'And they need you to do something for me,' she admitted.

They needed *her*? The First were foreign! Besides, she'd never really believed in any gods—Deih's or her own.

And yet, as Magmaya looked to her with all the fear of what she'd seen, she found herself yearning to know why. If she were to reject Deih, perhaps she would never understand. At last, she found herself asking, 'What is it?'

'I think you came south for a reason,' she explained. 'This conquest of Belliousa is a sign of things to come. The Divinicus' negotiations are control, and under them, my people will never know peace.'

'I understand.'

'Then you understand I must do what is best for them, no matter the cost,' Deih asked. 'You know that, yes Magmaya? Because to save my people, Fabius Uliana must die and the Divinicus along with him.' The High Priestess paused. 'And I can't be the one to kill him.'

Magmaya looked around the chamber as the realisation set in; the sparkling of the bejewelled table had drowned out her vision. Deih had been right, there was no running back north. There was no running anywhere.

'You know I can't,' Magmaya heard herself cry. 'You're conspiring against those who have raised me here! I can't...'

'They care nothing for you,' Deih said. 'You yourself admitted your disdain. They will use you as a puppet to speak to me and discard you as they please. And as for conspiring?' The Priestess laughed. 'You can't speak of conspiring against *him*; it was Fabius himself, once granted his new title, who commissioned the Abominable Sisterhood to bring an end to Belliousan sciences. For months,' she crooned, 'I watched as assassins arrived at my doors and slaughtered those I loved.'

'I—!'

'Look, girl, once Fabius finds a flaw in *you*, he will see to your dispatch,' the High Priestess explained. 'They will make an example of you, Magmaya, as you are hanged before the starving crowds of Inamorata, fed to them as *traitor*. My request is mercy—a way out of this before it's too late for you. In the name of the First and yourself.'

'Even if I tried, I could hardly best him!' she protested. 'And what then? My fate would be worse than hanging. If this cause is worth dying for, then you should be their martyr.'

'I can't.' Deih shook her head. 'They will not allow me within an inch of the Lord Commander. But they will let you meet with him, no?'

'Deih—!'

'Fabius will not die by the blade but by his own greed,' she explained. 'I will supply you with a potion. It will not be quick, but they will not suspect you. You will leave the manse a free woman. Both of us will be free, Magmaya.'

'I won't betray them.' She clenched her fists; she wouldn't have anything else poured in her ear by a woman she barely knew, no matter how noble the intention. She couldn't get caught up in more conflict. No matter how much Fabius had condescended her, she couldn't bring herself to kill him. He'd put all the fear of the world in her.

'Please,' Deih said softly. 'There are none as able as you to do this; I was a fool to ask Kurulian all those years ago—he was already one of them. But for you, Magmaya, it will be easy. The poison will merely have to touch his lips, and he will be dying. Think of all of those Fabius has left downtrodden—you will be a liberator from just cutting the head off one angel.'

'And then another will take his place,' she protested. 'I will not do this, Deih.'

'You will not, or you cannot?'

'Take your pick. But—' Magmaya tasted bile.

'But what?'

'I feel faint,' she admitted. The feeling had worsened the more the tension had built in her. She was bleeding down her thighs still, and the strange smell in the air wasn't helping the pain. 'But I can't kill him to escape this.'

The High Priestess nodded and made her way over to a cabinet lined with several flagons. 'The angels walk as church, government, judge, jury and executioner,' Deih remarked. 'No longer can we go on oppressed. I fear you've made a grave mistake.'

'So did Kurulian in your eyes. And he walked out a wiser man.'

'He threatened me.' Deih shrugged. 'A girl thinks differently with the tip of a sword at her throat.'

'I still don't understand,' Magmaya said. 'What did the First show me?'

'They showed you the truth.'

'Which was?'

'They gave you the knowledge and the courage to do this for me,' she said.

Magmaya shook her head. 'I can't be caught up in this. I'm going home or far away, at least, until someone will accept me without bloodshed. I want nothing to do with this—not with the Divinicus, not with the south.'

'I once thought like you.' The High Priestess returned with a glass of cherry-red wine and set it down on the table with a gentle clink.

Magmaya nodded, keeping her eyes on Deih, and forced herself to drink. She felt the strength return to her with a sour yearning and made herself stand, despite the grinding in her stomach, and looked to her.

She sat opposite, but it was like there were a thousand mirrors of the High Priestess projected throughout Elysia, blocking every exit. She may have been a witch, but Magmaya needed to leave. If she could somehow find a way back to Ranvirus where she understood the rules of the game, she could at least be at peace with herself.

She would take Anclyn with her and offer a thousand apologies for her deceit and beg Rache and Siedous for their forgiveness too. She would live in a palace upon the ice where no one would bother her, save for the whispering of the wind, where she wouldn't have to suffer any pearly armour ever again.

And if Kurulian had escaped by threatening the High Priestess, then so could she.

Magmaya found the wine glass and gripped it hard. She smashed it against the shimmering table, leaving a jagged rim behind. A chiming of broken glass resounded through the corridors, and she felt a fire rise within her.

But the High Priestess just sat still, swilling her wine about her glass with an unpleasant demeanour ringing across her lips.

And then a coldness ran through Magmaya's chest and pricked the back of her legs like a fistful of needles; her knees betrayed her weight, and she met the floor with the brunt of her cheekbone. The broken glass spiralled out of her hand, and she watched as Deih stood, lithe like an uncoiled serpent.

The poison will merely have to touch his lips, and he will be dying.

Magmaya could almost taste it creep across her mouth and looked to the wine as it seeped into the lines between the cobblestone like a river of blood. She wanted to scream; she had been foolish—she had been deceived! There never was a choice; the High Priestess had her wrapped around her finger from the beginning; she either killed Fabius or died.

'Deih!' she shrieked, but her voice was broken and blue. Each syllable burned her lungs as she spoke until each ounce of energy she'd gathered was drained from her. The Dew of the Honey; she could taste the kiss of Vargul Tul, the weapon of the Summerlands—she'd lapped it up like a dying man in a desert.

She felt her fingernails tear for the vial at her wrist in some wild hope it would overpower the poison, but any whimper of strength left had been washed away with the moisture in her eyes.

And then, as if to insult her, Deih's silvery sandal hammered down and shattered it across the stonework.

The High Priestess looked at her with a regard that she might have once mistaken for concern—the same concern an inquisitive child might've had as they watched an insect writhe and struggle in its death throes.

'This wasn't necessary.' Deih frowned. 'But you must understand, girl. With or without you, Belliousa will thrive.'

'You can't do this,' Magmaya spat, the roof her mouth lighting on fire. 'They'll know it was you!'

Deih shrugged. 'Be it a minute or a year, the poison will take you all in the end.'

The words slid off her tongue like quicksilver, but to Magmaya they were the grinding of salt. And yet still, her name couldn't escape her mouth, even as she opened it to curse. 'Deih!' she screamed and writhed about in the shards of glass, the wine dying her robes a sickly crimson.

The High Priestess watched for a few seconds more and appeared to grow bored, ambling around in disgust. She made her way back to the window, a kaleidoscope of colours washing over her eyes, and with a gentle hush, blew the candles out.

Deih looked back and sighed until finally, the incessant screaming grew hoarse, and the will of the First seemed to smile upon her, drowning the girl's dying sentence out.

The prayers of the Belliousans below echoed through the room and eclipsed the rising crescendo of their heartbeats, all while the wine on her lips began to taste sour again, like the sickness of sound in the chiming of silverwater.

Twenty-Four

She'd called out seven times in the last hour, and each scream was more fearful than the last. And each time, she'd stare Anclyn down with crystal eyes, alive and burning, and slump back down into the white of the bedsheets.

Magmaya found her robes bundled beneath a brazier (in a vain attempt to burn out the wine stains); her plate had been impervious to the alcohol, but it had cut into her skin—thin, red incisions ran across her neckline and circled her hips, cool in the light of the window.

'Anclyn!' she said, and her voice brought the handmaiden back to life. At once, Magmaya was awake, and the world had descended into chaos. Her eyes were burning, and her greasepaint had worn away as she stretched out stiff fingers, groping for Anclyn's neck.

It hurts! She wished she could've screamed. *Everything hurts!*

'My lady...' Anclyn pulled herself away, gasping. Realisation was flooding through her.

'Deih!' Magmaya spat, but her retching had turned to a whisper. 'Deih...'

Anclyn scurried to tend to her, pulling apart the bedsheets and combing through her hair, but with every movement, Magmaya undid it. After what seemed an endless game of back and forth, she sat back, defeated.

'One of Deih's Temple Guard's brought you here.' Anclyn began bundling her clothes up in her arms. 'They told us you had been drunken! That you'd threatened the High Priestess, my lady. I didn't believe them, but the angels, they're—is it true?'

Magmaya's eyes widened. She could still taste the Dew of the Honey on her lips and feel the smashed glass beneath her fingertips. She *had* threatened Deih; that much was true—*but she was her enemy!*

'She poisoned me,' Magmaya said. 'I need help, I need—' She stopped. 'Anclyn, we have to kill her; we have to kill that whore! We have to kill her before—'

A voice speared the air, and a cold breeze took the room, cutting Magmaya off. She felt helpless again, ensnared by the words she spoke.

Deih was standing in the doorframe, alone. The dull rain illuminated her body as she stood tall like a beautiful caricature of stonework, and as Magmaya fell back to her bedding, even Anclyn looked as if she was bowing down to her in rapture. With one breath, she owned the room—perhaps her vanity was understated.

'Handmaiden,' she spoke softly. 'May I have a moment alone with your mistress?'

Magmaya looked to the handmaiden with wide eyes, but whether through the poison or a misunderstanding, Anclyn nodded and left the room without so much as another word. The door was closed behind her, and at last, Deih and her were alone again.

The High Priestess ambled forward, admiring the braziers as she did. Each step she took seemed to cool them until the fires grew weak and the room was plastered with smoke.

After what felt like an eternity, Deih made room for herself and perched on the corner of Magmaya's bed, as a mother did to comfort a child, and said, 'You were very foolish yesterday.' The High Priestess tutted through bared teeth. 'This has become far more complicated than it needed to be.'

'Please.' Magmaya tasted the poison like bile in her throat. 'You need to help me.'

'I will help you with nothing,' Deih scorned. 'You have rebelled against the First, and they have judged you and found you a heretic. They will strike you down.' She nodded to herself. 'And as for your handmaiden? Do you care for her? Perhaps the First should judge her too, my love.'

Magmaya felt her cheeks glow red. That pleased Deih.

'You didn't kill me, though,' she spat. 'Perhaps the First abandoned you.'

'Are you so simple to have thought I would have killed you?' the High Priestess asked. 'If I were to have done that, then the Divinicus would've had ample reason to burn my island.'

Magmaya grunted and shook her head. 'You've still time to let me go then, Deih,' she said. 'Lay one finger on

Anclyn or me, and I'll tell them all what you planned for Fabius.'

'Tell them what you want,' the High Priestess said. 'Do you think they'll believe the words of some drunk slut?' She shook her head, and all of a sudden, Magmaya found it terribly hard to breathe. 'The only question now is—where do we go from here, dear girl?'

'You let me go,' Magmaya said. 'The angels and I take off, and we never see or speak of one another again.'

'You know things aren't quite as simple as that,' Deih said, sighing. 'The Divinicus won't leave without Belliousa under their thumb.'

'Kurulian left.'

'Kurulian had other allegiances to keep him at bay,' she explained. 'Besides, the First made us girls all the same, and I know how our clockwork hearts tick. I fear even if no one believes your story now, you'll find a way to convince someone in time. If I've learnt one thing, girl, it is that us women have the most convincing weapon of all, and it lies between our legs.'

'It doesn't matter what's beneath my belly,' she spat. *I don't want to relive last night again,* she decided, *cock or not.*

'Well,' the High Priestess remarked, 'if a girl says she knows, then certainly she must. Though I am tempted to believe otherwise.'

Without warning, she raised her dead, black finger into the light. And before Magmaya could react, Deih drew it down her chin.

'You will tell your angels you're a foul heathen, will you not?' She frowned. 'Provided you make this easy for us, it will not be any harder for you. The First shall decide your fate.'

'Fuck the First,' Magmaya said and collapsed back down into the bed; a sickly warmth began coursing through her that she knew all too well.

Much to her surprise, there was no retaliation. Instead, Deih nodded.

And then, she could only watch as the High Priestess leaned forward until her face was but inches from her own, that dead smile ensnaring her. And with those spindly hands of coal, she peeled back the bedsheets, revealing Magmaya's breasts to the frigid air.

She felt the urge to scream rise within her, but only foam brewed at her lips. Deih shrugged in an indecisive manner and went back to jerking at her sheets. She stopped at the scar on her belly where that bloody deer had kicked her into the snow, and a smile formed on the High Priestess' lips. She studied it for a short number of seconds before pressing her stony fingertips into the ruptured flesh.

There was a moment of blinding pain before a dull ache rose inside of her. But when she didn't scream, Deih looked disappointed.

So as if to compensate, High Priestess tore the bedsheet from her legs, and Magmaya's body stiffened. The witch's eyes settled below her navel with a prickly grin. They stayed there for a little while until Deih decided she was done staring and began tidying the bed, deciding she was content.

She leaned in close, and for a moment, Magmaya thought she was going to kiss her. But instead, she sighed and said, 'I think I'll allow you to explain to the Divinicus what happened yesterday.' Deih tucked a lock of hair behind her ear. 'Be sure to tell them your weapon is broken.'

Magmaya watched on in agony as the High Priestess made her way over to the door, tugged it open, and watched the Divinicus flood in. Akanah and his warband came pouring over her, carrying an endless supply of empty questions.

But from across the room, through the small, pearly crowd, Magmaya found the High Priestess, standing and smiling with a grin as cold as brass.

'What did you say to her?' Akanah's voice was fiercer than she remembered.

The others had left the room, though it had felt like mere seconds since they'd stormed in. But then, she noticed that the rain had stopped and that the fires had been extinguished—hours had passed. *That's the influence of the Dew of the Honey,* Magmaya reminded herself, *its subtle warmth will betray you—that's how the poison eats away.* It had dragged her unconscious back to Orianne, and heaven knew what it would do to her now.

Magmaya covered herself and looked up to the Legatus, chasing the lines across his brow until they disappeared behind his ears. If she had ever thought him or any of the angels to be gods, then she had been gravely mistaken. What the First had shown her was no one in pearly white armour would sit above her and dictate the laws of angels and men.

'I did what I had to,' she said, her voice brittle, 'for you, for the Divinicus...' she caught herself trailing off.

She could never tell him about Deih's proposition, of course; no matter how much she would've loved to flaunt her loyalty, she could almost feel her prying eyes still watching her. Each step she took was balanced on hot coal, and one misstep would burn her alive.

'Was drinking in the best interest of the Divinicus?' His eyebrows had contorted into something sinister, but Magmaya didn't care. Even as the back of his knuckle forced its way across her cheekbone, it was of little consequence. Even as a terrible heat rose inside of her chest and coursed through her neck like a thousand tiny kisses, it was all lost amid her fear.

'Have you forgotten Highport already?' the Legatus continued on. 'You made a grave mistake by pissing off the gangers there, because when you return, there will be no Spider, nor me to protect you. If your intent was to prove something to that witch with a drunken display, then perhaps Fabius should've kept you as chancellor in the north or wherever they breed you whores.'

'Akanah, please—!'

'Your actions are a disgrace to our kindness.' He ignored her. 'I just hope you know that none of your damn interfering matters; none of your plotting or anything of the sort.'

'I never—'

He hushed her. 'None of us will forget you betrayed our trust, but chiefly neither will you. Let it be known that even the humblest of Divinicus could have killed the Golden Woman, so a meek girl such as yourself is of little issue to us. Whatever fate Fabius decides for you, be it exile to Highport or an ashen waste, I will make sure to defame you in a way that spells *traitor* to the whole of Inamorata.' He took a breath, and she watched the tension roll off his shoulders as if the world was being moved like a weight.

'There's nothing more your people like than a good traitor, is there?' she asked after a moment. 'Makes you look better in the mirror.'

'Perhaps you should glance in yours more often, Magmaya. You won't have those doe eyes forever. Not after all of this is done.'

As he brushed back his hair and began to fasten his helm, she decided he could threaten her as much as he pleased; Deih and Akanah's curses were all the same; it felt as if nothing she did would change her fate. All she had left to do was die.

The second he left, Magmaya breathed a sigh of relief and raised her palm to her cheek, feeling a wetness. She wiped the blood into the bedsheets and stood, throwing a towel over her shoulders before making her way to the window.

All she could make out was a barrage of creeping mist along the mountainside; it was steep and merciless, and it ran down farther than she thought possible. If she found a way out, then perhaps, at last, she could rest.

Magmaya pushed the thought to the back of her mind and turned to the door, finding it locked. She could just about make out a whisper from whoever lay beyond, but it certainly wasn't in the common tongue. She sighed and turned away.

She stirred to the drumming of wind against the window and then to the night crawling in from beyond. Perhaps the passing of time did indeed elude the First Temple—surely it couldn't have been an entire day since Deih had poisoned her? Magmaya was half tempted to wave it away as the kiss of the Dew; it was easier if she did.

But it didn't matter either way; she only had one ally left in the Temple, and soon enough, she would be gone.

Magmaya had been the one to request that Anclyn came to Belliousa, and it wasn't hard to imagine that she too would be punished because of what happened with Deih. The thoughts weaved themselves through her head, and she grit her teeth in frustration—how had she been so foolish as to have found herself ensnared this way? Even now, she wouldn't have made a cunning chancellor, that much was for sure.

As the seconds passed, she paced about the room; the rumbling of her stomach was killing her, though it was becoming increasingly likely she wouldn't taste food ever again. *What was the last thing I ate?* She couldn't even remember now. How quaint the notion of food had been before she'd been without it.

She traced the stone floor and marble walls, searching for anything she could use to turn the tide in her favour. But apart from the braziers which were far too heavy to lift, there was nothing—they weren't even lit. Them, and the remains of Kurulian's vial which Deih had surely left to goad her. It would do her no good to escape, but she fastened what was left to her wrist all the same. After all, it was the only reminder of that northern girl she'd once been.

Occasionally, she'd find herself wiping the windows clean of condensation, only to see herself staring back in the fog beyond. The frame was far too small to escape through and even then, where would she go? It seemed the farther the sun dropped beyond the horizon, the slimmer her options grew.

Magmaya found herself thinking to Siedous and Rache and all the people she had left behind. And then to Kurulian. It was a cruel jest in hindsight; he had taken her south, told of her of Belliousa, and prompted her coming here. Perhaps if they had been together, they could've found a way out, be it by arranging whispers among the handmaidens or forcing the door down. Or maybe he would've just pretended not to know her.

As the dark of the moon rose into fruition, Magmaya grew aware of her restlessness. Amidst the silence, the sinister acoustic of prayer rose up from someplace below, and Magmaya decided she must've been placed in a kind of tower. She began wondering what the Divinicus were even doing—perchance they hadn't left already. The thought shook her core; the mere suggestion of being secluded with the disciples of the First made her deathly afraid. The angels may have been cruel and arrogant, but they were predictable at least. Blind faith always found a way to surprise her.

Were the Kytherans cruel too? She had read in the Divinicus' doctrines of their Empress, the Bastard Mother, and how their general, Sir Atthes Garcel, had deserted them for a witch from Vavaria. It was told no one knew the true heart of the Mother and her armies, but to meet them in the open field was to meet hatred incarnate. Though it appeared whatever faced her now would give her no respite either.

About an hour later (halfway through a doze), Magmaya leapt up, startled. There were scratches at the door, and then a jingling of metals and brass. It was opened a foot or so, and a robed claw pushed a wooden tray through. A moment later, the door was snapped shut again, metal was rustled, and there was silence.

Magmaya waited for the servant to disappear and made her approach, her heart rising in her chest. It had been what she had hoped for, but never in a thousand years had expected; while there was nothing on the tray save for a bowl of sickly, green broth, it wasn't the food she cared for. The fact that they had bothered to feed her at all gave her relief—they wanted her alive. Not only that, but they had given her a weapon. Neither the tray nor bowl were metal, but the wood would suffice—it would have to.

Despite her best intentions, she felt a bestial hunger rise within her and pressed the broth to her lips. It turned to a stream of thick salt and milky oil as it rolled down her lips, raw meat bubbling to the surface. Even though her stomach was as empty as it was, she couldn't bring herself to eat, and so, she tossed the contents into the corner of the room—they reeked of vomit.

Magmaya sat down, stole a breath, and felt the world rush over her. She looked to the discarded broth and watched as a rat (as large as a hare) scampered out of nowhere and began to feast on the uncooked meat. As its tiny razor teeth tore each scrap apart, she began to wonder if she might be next. Perhaps even the merciless Mother would've shown her more mercy than hunger would.

A chill took the room, and Magmaya glanced back to the window, peering into the blackness of the fog and eyeing a pair of stars above. She had dreamt of one day standing in the Silver City, hand in hand with Rache, and pointing up to the white north on a silvery globe. 'There's home', she wished she could've said, but they wouldn't have needed it anymore. Now all she could do was stare into the emptiness between the stars and wonder if any of them hurt the same as she did. And as always, there was no reply.

And as always, she went back to being a puddle caught amid a rainstorm.

After a short while, she crossed the room again and pressed her ear to the door. *It was time,* she had decided. *If I don't move now, each moment will slip into the next, and I will lose my chance.*

Magmaya worked quickly, driving the rim of the bowl into the brittle edges of the window sill. It was made of hard stone, but the fog had turned it damp, and so after a few swift strikes, a small black crevice opened in the rock. The rim of the bowl had found a way to splinter too, but Magmaya just found cause to ram it harder into the stonework.

And at last, she was rewarded as a small fountain of stones broke free, leaving her in a hot sweat.

She dropped the bowl and dove to the floor, gathering the shards in her shivering fingertips. She settled on one about the length of her forefinger and then began to work on that, running it again and again over the grooves in the walls until it was as sharp as Moonbeam had been.

It was heavier than Magmaya had expected, and she could scarcely move her legs, but she summoned the strength to stand all the same. She moved to the end of the bed, the bowl between her knees, took a deep breath and nodded. *Now it's time,* she repeated, *it's now or bloody never.*

Magmaya unravelled the bedsheets between her teeth and bit down hard, feeling her tongue lash out against the satin as her head betrayed her muscles. Still, she found the strength to steady her arm over the bowl, shimmering naked in the dim moonlight.

She could only hope that an ounce of the Dew of the Honey still surged through her. And with a whimper, she drove the stone into her arm. She bit down on the bedsheets as her blood began to flow—in thin lines at first, but then in heavy black swathes. *If I pretend not to feel it, I won't,* she decided, but the lie only lasted a moment before it coursed through her, relentless.

She spat whatever bile clung to her throat and watched her blood rise in the bowl. But it wasn't enough; the dish was slick and red, but it was far from pooling. Magmaya felt her arm grow limp and heavy but reminded herself to keep on moving.

Whatever would my father have said? He probably would have laughed. Or have told her not to get trapped in the first place.

She gathered another bundle of bedsheets and fastened them around the cut, watching the scarlet bleach through and the agony ignite in her eyes. But there was little time to dwell on her pain. She found that her cheek had long stopped bleeding, and after some short deliberation, wasted no time to unfasten her gown and move to her belly.

Even in the dark, she was able to make out the grooves and bruises where she'd been kicked by that deer in her past life. She traced the wound with her fingertips, drew one final breath and took the chiselled stone in her sweating palms—it was heavy and warm, and every instinct and every voice deep inside of her screamed at her to toss it as far as she could throw. But she had already begun; it was too late to turn back now.

The stone seared through the red gash in her navel like a white-hot wire. Her ripe skin began to contort and glow, and then her blood began to spill again. It was a trickle at first, but soon enough, it became a torrent running down the creases in her skin.

But it still wasn't enough—the blood dried on her fingertips the moment it touched them, and she still needed more—just a little more.

Some other part of her was still bleeding, though. And it had been for nearly a week.

Magmaya dropped the chisel and threw away the bedsheets, finding the skin between her legs already wet and red. *With a little spit, it'll run thick like butter,* she told herself, but she was growing weak and tired at the sight of it, and every instinct she knew told herself to collapse and drift off to sleep once more. But she knew she couldn't stop yet.

She couldn't stop bleeding until the First had been bathed in her blood.

It was quarter-past midnight when one of the servitors began roaming the tower block; all the prisoners convicted of a heresy of sorts were stored away there, and it was always down to the luck (or rather lack) of the draw that decided which of Deih's low-born maids were to patrol that night. The tower was usually crowded by the screeching of lunatics awaiting trial, but things had been different recently; word had travelled fast of Magmaya's drunken assault upon the High Priestess.

And that would only mean the patrols would be more frequent outside her cell.

As she'd expected, the sounds of her cries had echoed through the Temple so that even Deih heard them. The High Priestess still wanted her alive, and that was her lone weapon—perhaps she had learnt Mercy after all.

It was near half-past midnight when the servitor finished scaling the stairwell and arrived atop of the tower—Magmaya could hear her footsteps grow closer.

But it wasn't until half-past that the servitor approached Magmaya Vorr's cell, and when she did, she could almost see the sickness wash over her; there was a desperate groaning coming from behind her door, after all. As the seconds passed, the groaning grew louder like the mewling of a wounded kitten, until there was a chime of wetness—and then a scream.

Magmaya watched from underneath the door as her blood seeped into the intricacies in the servitor's toes, sprawling like a nest of tortured limbs across the cobbled floor.

After the scream, the groaning turned into a mumble. 'Help me,' Magmaya called, and then louder, 'Help!'

There was a nervous chattering from the servitor before a jingle of clockwork rang out, and the door opened to a trail of blood, cutting the cell in half.

The servitor followed it to its source: a small wooden bowl which appeared to have leaked the last of its contents. She followed it through the dim light of the window, and then to the girl in the corner, holding her bandaged stomach.

'Prisoner! What is happening?' she wailed in a crude attempt at the common tongue.

And that was her cue. Magmaya lurched forward and drove herself into the servitor's chest. She pinned the poor thing to the floor, but she just wouldn't stop screaming, no matter how many times she put a finger to her lips.

'Quiet,' Magmaya hushed, her eyes wide and bloodshot. 'Please…!'

The servitor was struggling, though; her screams were echoing through the corridors and setting the tower alight. It wouldn't be long until someone noticed, and then all her bleeding would've been for nothing. Even in a temple as large as this one, one misplaced shriek wouldn't go amiss.

There was a tangle of crooked limbs beneath as Magmaya reached back, feeling something sharp prick at her fingers.

Then an arm jabbed at her belly, and a knee found its way between her legs as if the servitor somehow knew where she had been bleeding. The pain came to her quickly but threatened to never leave. Magmaya toppled back, screaming.

The servitor pulled herself up, blackened with blood, but Magmaya forced herself up quicker, her fingers groping at something she couldn't reach. Crimson handprints spread across the walls as the Belliousan tried to steady herself, but she was too late—and too loud.

Magmaya forced herself forward and drove the chisel into the servitor's chest. The robed girl clattered to the ground like a statue pulled from its plinth, and her screams died out at last.

She was a pitiful thing to watch die, but Magmaya didn't have time to mourn. She had to keep moving.

She scoured the remains for something—anything which might've helped her, but she was forced to settle on bundling the cell keys between her knuckles. She decided to take the servitor's cloak too, but by the time she had snatched the bloody thing up, there was little else left of use.

As she left the corridor, Magmaya felt a sense of euphoria rush through her like a terrible sin. The girl was dead now; there was nothing else she could've done, surely?

But what if someone else confronted her? It wasn't like she would be able to find the strength to swing a sword any longer—perhaps something as pathetic as a ring of keys was the right weapon for her, after all. Besides, it was better than nothing if she wanted any chance of escaping.

The corridors and stairwells disappeared behind her like a swift breeze, and she thanked the gods no one found her on her way, save the troubled scuttling of a rat beneath her step. The path grew thin at some intervals, to the point where she had to crawl through sodden alleyways no wider than her hips.

In those precious seconds of darkness, where no stray light could taste her, she at last found the chance to breathe. To her dismay, the air reeked of vomit, piss and pathetic attempts to conceal the former with flowery perfumes.

The lower in the tower she reached, the larger the floors became; cell blocks sprung up around her, mostly empty of their heathens and heretics, and judging from the cobwebs, they had been for quite some time. But as Magmaya passed them, the occasional prisoner with stitched-shut eyes would throw themselves at the bars and yell something she didn't understand. Some of them were murderers, heretics or rapers. Others had committed different sorts of crimes; they were men who loved men or women who loved women or some other combination of the two. There were a lot of laws about love, she realised.

Magmaya could feel the weight of the keys in her hands as she passed them, but she still couldn't decide which way would be best to use them. She felt her arm drawn towards the lock, but despite it all, she couldn't bring herself to move an inch. Soon enough, Magmaya had left the prisoners behind her.

She couldn't hold on much longer—the cold of the tower was numbing, but the heat would burn her alive.

The corridors of the First Temple quickly became recognisable again; the architecture returned to veined marble and prestigious busts of people who never mattered. But still, their lips were sculpted to such a perfection, she was half-tempted to reach out and kiss them just to feel warm again.

After scouting through a myriad of halls, a grand corridor opened before her, complete with a checked floor shimmering with unbroken candlelight. Magmaya forced the red cloak farther over her eyes as she heard footsteps. And then a servitor passed, holding out a lamp before him.

It became clearer with each encounter that the simple disguise had worked. Yet still, it gave her no inkling of where the Divinicus might've been, let alone Anclyn. She scurried across the hall in an effort to remain composed and stole a glance through the window.

It was difficult to see anything at all between the fog and the staining, but Magmaya could just about make out the Temple's battlements disappearing into oblivion below. She followed the crevice farther down until she found a lone star in the darkness: a Divinicus standing tall against the wrath of the night. The angels had once been beacons of beauty—what had they become? What had changed in her so quickly to feel so much fear when gazing into the eyes of those who'd fulfilled her prayers? Perhaps all gods desired to be feared; Magmaya certainty couldn't see herself coming to love the world so artlessly.

She couldn't see anything more in the darkness, though, except for when it was too late as another face joined her own in the reflection of the window.

Magmaya looked up to face him, his endless robes overflowing with holy books. A few moments passed as she waited for him to apprehend her, but after a while, nothing came. In the end, she was the first to bite.

'The angels?' She bit her lip, attempting a thick accent that ended up sounding nothing like the locals. 'Are they leaving?'

'Are you blind, girl? They're swarming the Temple like flies,' he tutted, slurring each syllable. 'Their diplomats are in the quarters where they've been all night—may the First watch over our souls when this is done.'

'I was ordered to their quarters by the High Priestess,' Magmaya croaked. 'Where can I find them?'

'Is that some jest?' he spat. 'Why aren't you at the communion? The First need each and every soul they can muster in these times of trepidation. We are oppressed from all sides.'

'Where's the communion?'

The priest gave her a look like thunder, and it seemed for a minute he was going to lash out at her. It wouldn't have mattered if he had, though; she could've bested him even in the state she was in. The priest's arms were bundled with books, he had a belly spilling from beneath his robes, and he looked as if he could barely move those chubby fingers he wore. He muttered something under his breath and traced her body down to her hips, staring in horror.

'You're bleeding,' he said, and the colour fled from his lips.

Magmaya pressed herself against him, so her blood kissed his gowns, and forced the keys into his flowing belly; for all he knew, she could've stabbed him, and from the look in those bloodshot eyes, she might just have.

'Where are the Divinicus?' she asked softly.

'Black Quarter,' he choked, swallowing hard. But it wasn't enough, so she pressed the keys farther into his gut. 'Cross down the stairwell at the end of the corridor,' his voice rasped, but when she released him, his posture became stern again like he'd never been threatened. 'May the First have mercy on you, girl.'

Another priest pushed past, and Magmaya disappeared into the shadow of his cloak, forming a map of the Temple in her mind. She ducked beneath a dozen stone pillars and skirted the history books as she went, passing a hundred memorials to the times man stood in fields of wheat with no bronze bells to aid him. She crossed the Age of the Technomancer as a storm of angels descended from the heavens with horny masks of gold, though they all looked like the Divinicus to her.

She carried on down the hall, passing a row of chieftains cast in bronze, faces fearful as if frozen by their sculptor; there were good kings and wicked kings and lusty kings alike; there were kings with endless beards, and there were kings with hooks through their eyes. Occasionally, there would be a queen, always fretful but never afraid, and so Magmaya found the strength to dance through the Age of the Imposters and then through an ivory archway, losing everything in a series of betrayals and empires. A murder of crows chased her through a crowd of nobles as she carried on, escaping the crooked pages until all that was left was her.

Once she made her way out the other side, she discovered a chill in her palm; as she had passed through the flock of preachers, she had managed to swipe a ritual blade from one of their bony hips. Sly theft wasn't anything she had quite perfected, but her newfound desperation forced her to do things she would never have quite believed herself capable of. Besides, it was just the same as when she had stolen the Free-People's blade from that scribe she'd condemned all those years ago. The same knife she'd used to kill her father.

This new blade was as long as her forearm, though, and its shimmer in her palm had given her confidence she didn't have before. She slung the keys across her wrists as the servitor before her had and carried onward.

At the end of the corridor, Magmaya caught a glimpse of the Black Quarter. A glimpse proved enough— the hallway was lined with the Divinicus (Magmaya counted eight in total). Each guarded an iron door as faceless as the next, but in the shadows, she could make out the silhouette of Krel beneath his armour. He was helmed, but his muscled frame gave himself away in an instant. It was surely the Legatus' door he was guarding, and with him, there would be Anclyn.

The beast of a man looked around, and Magmaya jumped, praying he hadn't caught her eye. She slipped back into the darkness again, contemplating the impossible and letting the hymns from somewhere far mask the rush of her breathing.

She couldn't make out the words in their songs; they were clearly in the native tongue of Belliousa, and yet, the same phrase persisted at the end of each prayer and filled every chorus: *'Angelica, deliver us.'*

Was it the same 'Angelica' Deih had claimed to be—reborn from the First Temple? They were calling out to her for salvation, that much was certain. It was as if their fear had become song, destined to resonate throughout the island forever.

'Angelica, deliver us,' they sang again, before Magmaya turned and knelt, feeling beads of sweat spill across her eyebrows. She was beginning to fear she couldn't fight from the shadows any longer—she was far too wounded to see the night through. But if Kurulian had taught her anything, it was that there was another way to win the war.

At the end of the path, she found a shrine nestled into the wall, overflowing with flowers and prayer candles in reverence to the First—an ecstasy of colours. But in her chest where she had bloodied herself, Magmaya felt the weight of something missing rise within her: a deep emptiness that reeked of rancid cries and starless nights, and the warmth of something cold in a mother's arms. She shivered and turned away, feeling ice flutter through her.

As another horde of squabbling preachers passed, she dragged herself over to the shrine, the last of her energy leaving her. She tugged the hood farther over her eyes and stared into the candles, watching the wax disappear into itself and reanimate with each passing second. And as if in response, her eyes came alive and died again with the coming and going of the heavy white glow.

Magmaya wrapped her fingers around one of them and broke it free of its plinth, brought it to her eyes, and took a deep breath of the grey smoke. It was warm and lithe and soft as it spiralled in her lungs, nestling there, and giving her one last surge of strength through her loins and in her head.

There was another way to win the war. *Fire* won the war.

Twenty-Five

She watched the fabric take aflame with a ghostly white glow and spread to the ceiling where the tapestries fluttered down. She closed her eyes and let the loose embers rain into her shimmery black hair until it became a molten river of gold. Smoke filled her mouth like sweet salt and kissed at her dimples. There was screaming, but it was all one with the white noise; it was all one with the rasping and kissing of the flames.

Magmaya was a lunar eclipse caught amid a firestorm.

At last, she allowed herself to drop the candle from which it had all began before she watched it eat away at the carpets. The girl smiled and let the blackness fill her lungs; all around her were maddened Belliousans desperately tried to waft out the flame—the drunken ones even tossed their wine into the fires, only to watch in horror as it grew larger. But no one suspected her—a mere servitor afraid and tearful. No one would know who started the inferno, or even when. No one save the whispers of the wind would know the truth.

She was even more joyous when a new flock of Belliousan preachers arrived in horror and stared as the fire crossed the beams that held the hall aloft, bringing down the ceiling. All the bronze busts and ancient scrolls were turned to smoke in the wake of the white embrace, but Magmaya just looked down to the preachers and smiled, letting the words take her lips before she conjured them.

'Look at your temple,' she called like an apostle. 'The Divinicus have brought their fire on us. This is the doing of those false angels—they will bring death to the First!'

It was clear several the Belliousans couldn't hear her, and the rest didn't understand, but those who did appeared to spread the word, eyes blazing beneath those crimson gowns. The heat was becoming almost unbearable, but it only got worse as the natives set light to their torches and began the cycle anew.

Magmaya stepped away, feeling sweat rush down her back, and disappeared into another corridor, finding herself in a five-sided room with antique floors and ceilings stolen from oil paintings. While a number of Belliousans fled through, she heard a light rumbling beneath her feet; it was heavy vibration which grew and grew until it engulfed her spine and became as real as the fires around her.

And then, there were Divinicus at war, glowing orange in the fire—a blur of shimmering pearl.

Even with his helm firmly nestled in his gorget, Magmaya could've recognised Akanah from a mile away;

after all, mesmerising patterns carved from ivory spread like veins across his armour—he wasn't a man, but something heavenly. His plate wasn't for protection, it was a display, his blade wasn't a weapon, it was a loving kiss, and his word wasn't a mumble, it was gospel.

The Belliousans toppled and trembled in his wake, and as the angels drew their falchions, many of the preachers and servitors threw themselves to the floor in reverence of their newfound gods.

None of them appeared to have noticed Magmaya, though. She turned and skipped to the corner of the room amid the frantic prayers and screams, and she watched as the silent idols thundered onward.

And like how the heathens would follow the demons at the end of days, the Small Court trailed in, slow and disorderly, as if bound to one another by an invisible chain.

They weren't afraid—that much was clear, but then again, they must have seen this chaos a thousand times before. Who knew how many temples Akanah had burnt in his wake, how many preachers he had struck down while they prayed. What was clearer was that Anclyn had never seen anything quite like it, though; she had told Magmaya of the rainstorms in the Summerlands and the abuse from her slavers, but she had never faced anything like this; her eyes were alive with fear and flame, and her greasepaint was weeping with her too.

By the time she turned back to the room, there was a violent gout of fire as the tapestries above turned to ash and rained to the ground like falling stars. While the Divinicus glowed in its embrace, the red cloaks of the Belliousans burst into flames. Screams encased the room, but as the smoke began to rise from the burning men, Magmaya felt herself leap up.

The Divinicus stood quietly and watched the fiery Belliousans fall to their knees. They'd become spectres of light, clawing at the air and calling in a tongue none of them had cared to learn. The angels looked on in intrigue (or perhaps amusement), but their callousness was enough to mask Magmaya's movements across the halls. She fled from corner to corner until she found Anclyn and pulled her aside.

The girl of summer was worn and tired, and her greasepaint wasn't hiding that any longer. It swam down her cheeks in the glow of the flames while black ink ran from her eyes like the oily tears of a harlequin. But between the light of the burning Belliousans (whose screams were finally fading) and Magmaya's own bloodied visage, there may have well been just one girl with a silvery pond before her.

'Mag—!' Anclyn began, but she clasped her palm across her lips and tugged her away, the Small Court seemingly fixated on the burning corpses. At last, while the others were a corridor away, she unhanded her, and let the fire fill the silence between them.

It took them a while to catch their breath, but Magmaya couldn't remember feeling so tired a minute before. Her feet had turned to lead and her knees splintered wood. But between the roar of the flames and the heat of the moment, there was no time to think—no time for an idle confession.

'You were in the tower,' Anclyn exclaimed. 'Deih was—'

'We have to run,' Magmaya said softly, and the handmaiden looked up with a distant nod. When those tearful eyes stared Magmaya back, they were a watery shadow of what they should've been. 'The angels want me dead. And they'll want you too if we aren't careful.'

'What about Deih?' Anclyn asked.

'I don't know,' she confessed. 'I can kill her if I must—I *will* kill her if I must.' Magmaya opened her gown, and the ritual blade hummed in the light of the flame.

'She's one of my own,' Anclyn protested, too loud. 'She's one of my blood!'

'So was my father, and the world is a little better off now,' Magmaya whispered.

Anclyn stared her down, eyes wide. 'Someone hurt you.' She looked to her bleeding navel. 'Let me help.'

Magmaya shook her head. 'I know a way out—Anclyn, none of this—' She motioned to her stomach, 'none of this matters if we can just get out of here and away from these people.'

'The Divinicus were going to put you on trial,' Anclyn said. 'I didn't know what to do, what to say. They kept us in these chambers... I!'

Magmaya nodded and looked around the hall—it didn't matter what the angels *thought* of her; she might as well have been dead to their cause anyway.

'These fires?' the handmaiden asked, looking to her with dismay. There was a sadness about her that Magmaya hadn't noticed before—a sadness that once she saw it, couldn't be caged. 'It... who did this...? Do you—?' She trailed off, and Magmaya stared her down. Her head was pounding with the crackling of the flames and the dying hymns beyond.

'None of this matters,' she groaned, 'if we can just get out.' Her eyes grew desperate like the moon at dawn. 'None of it, Anclyn.'

She nodded slowly, and a moment later, the Divinicus had become a distant dream. The stone corridors were racing by as if they had never existed, but Magmaya could only pray to whatever gods were left on her side that Anclyn's absence had gone unnoticed.

As the walls of the First Temple unfolded around them, the heat seemed to grow worse. Though the fire was nowhere in sight, its kiss was omnipresent. Magmaya's robes were only clinging to her with sweat and blood, and Anclyn's greasepaint had spilt something devilish down her face. The bronze statuettes were hot to the touch, and it looked as if the whole Temple was melting away.

A group of priests ran past with flaming swords but paid them no heed, and Magmaya realised, *They're looking for the angels*. It had gone as she had planned with that rousing speech of hers, but it was different to be amongst it all, amongst the fire. She knew the Divinicus would overpower the locals with ease, but she could at least keep the conflict brewing for as long as it took them to escape. They turned a sharp corridor and carried on.

'Where exactly are you taking me?' Anclyn asked after a short while.

'The atrium.' Magmaya's voice was trembling. *It hurts,* she thought, *it hurts to admit I'm on the losing side.* 'Through there, if we can escape the Divinicus, we can leave this cursed place.'

'Can we risk that? If we cross the path with just one...'

When did you stop calling me my lady? Magmaya asked herself, ignoring whatever the handmaiden had to say next. Her petty squeaks couldn't help them out of here. Only she could. There was no other choice than to escape.

'I'm not letting Deih or Akanah get to us,' Magmaya cut in. 'They'll string us both up.'

It was partially true, at least. Both of them wanted *her* dead, that was for sure, but she had to keep Anclyn moving. It was clear she was still conflicted about who to follow—the Divinicus had been all she'd known for so long. Not only that, but she'd deceived her about Deih. Girl of summer or not, the High Priestess was her enemy—she had to understand that! *She* was the best choice for Anclyn... *wasn't she?*

'What's happening?' the handmaiden asked her as she stopped to catch her breath. 'This fire, what happened with Deih; there are too many things I don't understand.'

'You have to trust me.' Magmaya clenched her bloodied fingers. The words felt hollow as she spoke them; she wouldn't have believed them if she was on the receiving end. 'None of it matters—'

'None of it matters if we just escape—I know, I understand!' Anclyn protested. 'But at least I have the decency to admit I'm afraid. Let's throw ourselves from the tower at least so we can die in the light instead of some fiery pit.'

'I'm sorry,' Magmaya wheezed, but she could've pleaded forever. The desperation was deep in her bones. 'We have to keep moving. Think faster than the fire.'

Despite her best intentions, the end of the hall met them with a violet inferno. The corridor beyond had forked into three tails, but one was engulfed in flame; dozens of tapestries had been transmogrified to ash.

I don't recognise it here, damn it! Magmaya wiped the sweat from her brow. It appeared with every step, the Temple's walls shifted to outsmart her.

But Anclyn was still and smiling, her eyes alight as the inferno grew closer. Magmaya glanced over and watched her: a girl in rapture as she herself had been at pearly ships—so little, a lifetime ago.

'It's like…' Anclyn started, 'art.'

Magmaya shook her head. 'It's death,' she said. 'The Divinicus and the Belliousans will kill those who trespass them, but this will kill us all.'

'They say fire only kills the unworthy…'

'It doesn't care who it kills, only that it does.' She wasn't sure where she'd summoned the words from, but it was if Kurulian was nagging in her ear. *Fire didn't win this war,* she wished she could've screamed at him. *It's started one. And soon, they'll be no air left to breathe.*

Anclyn stumbled, but a moment later, Magmaya felt her palm in hers. She beckoned the handmaiden into the corridor ahead, shed her cloak behind her and watched it catch fire in the dark.

At last, Magmaya found herself somewhere she recognised, but it was hardly the same place since it had taken aflame. Divinicus plagued the room, soaring above the Belliousans like birds of prey, slitting throats, searing hearts and beheading with delicate grace. Truly they were unmatched by anything Magmaya had ever witnessed; they were above the brutality of Mansel, the stoicism of Orianne and the cunning of the Tyla—they were angels given form.

'Magmaya!' Anclyn screamed, and not a moment later, there was a Belliousan throwing himself at her, flailing knives above his head.

The girl ducked as metal cut the air above. She found the ritual blade at her hip, drew it, and parried his next blow. Limbs became entangled with limbs, dust amid dirt, before Magmaya forced her blade through the Belliousan's shoulder and then clumsily through his neck.

It was only after he turned limp that she was able to wrestle the blade free from him. She looked back again to Anclyn, expecting some sort of horror, but her face was still, and her frown gave nothing away.

It felt like a dream; the world was slipping through Magmaya's fingers. *Keep a hold of yourself,* she insisted. *You're chancellor of Orianne, slayer of Vargul Tul and the girl who did what everyone else was too afraid to do—you travelled south.*

The marble of the hall had once been intricately detailed with scripture and verse, but by the time Magmaya was done with the Belliousan, it had been stained with blood. Gone were the Divinicus and ancient majesty, and in their place, there were red corpses, hanging from every iron spike and crooked brazier like grizzly trophies, a string of flesh and crossbow bolts. And against perhaps three dozen Temple Guard, not a single angel had fallen.

'They might have well had already taken this place,' Magmaya remarked. She shook her head. 'The atrium isn't far from here.'

'What if it's already on fire?'

'Do we have another option?' She wiped her blade clean against the dead man's tunic. 'Perhaps I was wrong about the fire, though. The Divinicus may just be worse.'

'I know,' Anclyn grumbled. 'And if they're already by the exit, waiting for us?'

'Please!' Magmaya shrieked. 'You have to trust me.'

The corridors that led to the atrium were as complex as Magmaya had remembered. Still, it was more beautiful in the glow of the flame; the fire had illuminated the darkest crevices and sharpest corners, sending black shadows fleeing from the white glow. The heat of it all was unbearable, but at least there was no one else around unfortunate enough to suffer it. Perhaps the Divinicus had already made themselves scarce and left them in this fiery tomb.

Her thoughts were cut short. A maddened scream echoed through the hall, and Anclyn yelled. Another pack of Belliousans appeared an instant later, waving their magic staves and flailing burning tapestries.

Magmaya raised the knife again and struck down the first attacker, nestling the blade beneath the arm. But before she could pry it free, another pair were on her. She ducked as a torch spiralled above her head, and her assailants reformed.

Magmaya threw herself aside and kicked one of the attackers away. While the other Belliousan reached out, she parried his blow and lunged forward, driving the blade through his throat and feeling a warmth fill her mouth.

Much to her surprise, the last Belliousan got on her knees and began to plea in some language she didn't understand.

'*Mercy, please,*' Anclyn translated. '*My son is dead, and my left leg is burnt to a stump. Mercy.*'

No sooner had the Belliousan's body hit the ground, Magmaya turned and asked, '*You* know the tongue of Belliousa?'

'No.' Anclyn shook her head. 'She was speaking *Arykyr.'*

Magmaya raised an eyebrow.

'From the Summerlands,' she said.

Anclyn mumbled to herself as they crossed the corridors, but it was all just noise against the crackling of the flame. 'Whenever there was a tree-fire in the Water, the crones would bring pails of sand from the beaches to put it out,' she began. 'The elders wouldn't let me venture close to the flames, though—*it'll burn your soul out,* they would say. I always thought that explained why they were so damn crass.'

Perhaps once Magmaya would have laughed at that, but the thought of anything other than the First Temple overwhelmed her. Perhaps the fire had taken *her* soul from her. And if it hadn't, what had she allowed to become of it?

'Remember when it rained on the ship?' Anclyn pestered. 'I would pray for a little of that now.'

Magmaya shied away. She had brought the fire down upon the First Temple but had never meant for it to consume the entire mountaintop! And despite her efforts, it appeared they had been the last to escape; the Belliousans must have already died or followed a secret passageway out, and it wouldn't have surprised her if the Divinicus were able to walk through the greatest gouts of flame. But even if she had a pail of sand, she would've sooner found herself building castles in the sky than throwing it at the fires.

When she opened her eyes again, she found the Temple crumbling around her like ashen wood falling to pieces in her hand. When she was a child, the morning after the great fires were lit, she had made a habit of stealing wood from the fireplaces and teaching herself to draw with its chalky residue until it fell apart between her fingers. Siedous would have scorned her for that, '*It's dirty*,' he had said. '*But it isn't a live fire*,' she had always spat back.

But this very much was, and Siedous wasn't around to scold her any longer.

It was then a flaming stone broke loose from above. The ground shook, and the earth became broken with glass and shattered marble. It wasn't until the dust had cleared, Magmaya realised the debris were blocking the corridor.

'We should have stayed on the ship,' Anclyn started, tears welling in her eyes. 'No—I should've stayed in the Summerlands and you in the north.'

'I would rather die than stop moving.' Magmaya backed away. 'We'll have to take the long way around.'

'We're never going to make it, Magmaya.'

Each corridor was a ghost of the last, but in time they found an archway, a memory of a lifetime ago. And at last, there was the atrium.

Despite the flames having dyed the stonework a sickly black, the fountain was very much alive, but it seemed no amount of water would've set the inferno right. The harpists who had once intoxicated Magmaya with their music were sprawled around its basin; the spray of the water had bleached their wounds a rosy pink; they'd become even more beautiful than they'd been when she'd arrived. Other corpses flocked the flames too, their mouths agape as if still calling for aid which never came. They weren't Temple Guard or even armed preachers; they were low-borns or pilgrims who had travelled across

Belliousa just to look upon their goddess—a look that had killed them.

A pillar of flaming timber had cut the hall in half, though—the only way into the atrium was through a wall of fire. The ceiling above rumbled and sighed, finally giving up on itself as the angels began to flock the corridors.

With any luck, they'll seal themselves in, Magmaya mused, but then, the handmaiden spoke.

'She's there,' she whispered, and the whole room seemed to freeze.

She was the High Priestess, Deih of the Water, the Matriarch of Belliousa. It had felt as if they had met a hundred years ago, but in the time since, she had grown more radiant. Her eyes were oceans of ruby, her cloak was a rich scarlet that outshone the moon, and yet, all around her, there was chaos, beauty and fire, and it outshone them all.

But there was a stutter in Deih's step, and Magmaya squinted, making out a shimmer that she held below her shoulder. *She's been struck by a crossbow,* she concluded, *but it'll take more than that to kill a goddess.*

Despite the fiery blockade, Deih's eyes locked with Magmaya's, and the world fell away around her; an icy twitch rushed through her veins.

'Girl.' Magmaya tried to duck, but the High Priestess looked as if she was following her every move. 'You were in the tower, you—' She wiped sweat from her forehead. 'No, you started this fire—what gives you the right?'

'The right?' Her lips trembled.

'The right to kill my people?' Deih scorned. 'The right to set my home alight when you couldn't do the same to Fabius'? He was the reason behind this—he brought these semi-demons down upon us!'

'You know I couldn't have done that!'

Deih cackled. 'You could've tried!'

'I was afraid.'

'You don't know the meaning of afraid,' she said, and tears began streaming down the High Priestess' face in some vain attempt to extinguish the flames. 'I should have never trusted a foreign whore to do my dealings. She doesn't know her own principles, let alone someone else's.' She shook her head.

The fire raged behind Deih, higher and higher until she was a beast aflame, undeniably divine. Perhaps Magmaya had been serving the wrong gods all along; maybe she should have prayed to *her* to take her south. Maybe she would bring her fire and ruin once this was all done.

'You started this?' Anclyn looked up to her. 'You started this fire?'

'Anclyn...' Magmaya faltered. She couldn't summon the words any longer.

Footsteps thundered through the room behind the Priestess, but Deih didn't move. She simply locked eyes with Anclyn and watched her greasepaint weep like broken water.

'A girl of summer.' She frowned. 'It has been too long since I've met one of my own. Tell me, do you remember the rain—no—oh, on the First's ashen earth—tell me you knew me before I became *this* haggard goddess all men must fear.'

'Yes, I did,' Anclyn lied and wiped the powder from her cheeks. They watched as the High Priestess smiled, and the flames seemed to dance to her every whim.

She was still smiling when the Divinicus blade entered her back and left it through her womb.

Twenty-Six

There was another way out.

Magmaya would have rather been dreaming, though; the world around her had become a fiery hell. Its touch was without mercy, and just looking at it too long threatened to leave her blind. At least if she had been dreaming she could've forgotten the fire, but then again, even the sweetest daze would have surely become a nightmare in time.

She wished she was back at Ranvirus and watching the snow fall with Rache by her side. *Don't go,* she should have screamed, but the girl wasn't listening; she was travelling south with the angels. *Don't go!* It was too late to call; the girl was at Highport with a palm that blazed like hell. *Don't go...!* It was pathetic to keep trying; the girl was in Belliousa, and the First Temple was burning around her.

'Magmaya,' a voice called, and she was awake again, the shimmery face of Anclyn staring down at her. 'Magmaya, which way?'

There's a chamber beneath the Temple, she had told the handmaiden, *and from there, a path; it splits in two, and one of the forks leads off into the light of the sun.*

It was her last hope—she had gone too far to give in to the angels. She could still hear Akanah's voice as he stormed the halls with his men. '*Traitor*!' he had screamed. 'Foreign whore!' he'd rattled on, but when he had looked to the limp corpse of Deih, the world had been transmuted.

The High Priestess had been more beautiful in death than she had in life; even as she'd lain in a pool of her own ruby blood, she had still been grinning, wiser than them all.

'*Gods do not die,*' she remembered Siedous had said.

'*This one did,*' she heard Fabius reply.

There had been cries from the Belliousans and screams from the heavens, and it had felt like the sky was going to fall on them, but it had only been the angels that did. Magmaya had watched as Akanah had torn his great sword through one of them—an unarmed preacher, still a boy.

A halo doesn't make you an angel. It doesn't even make you a man, she realised.

Anclyn had remained silent ever since, and whenever Magmaya caught her eye, all she saw in the handmaiden was a watery pool of despair. She may have saved Fabius, but she had killed everyone else.

Anclyn, Anclyn! She almost heard herself call; she was supposed to be her friend, but now, it seemed she was gone too. It was fruitless trying to talk any sense into her. All she could do now was escape; otherwise, all of it had been for nothing.

It didn't even matter half the paths had been blocked by flame, it seemed to do no harm to walk through them. The burning wouldn't hurt until after she died, so what was the use in trying to avoid it? *In death, there will be a cure for everything,* she decided. *In death, it won't matter what happened here.* Whether or not they escaped the winding corridors of the First Temple, it would all be the same.

But Deih had died! *Now nothing will be the same,* she told herself.

'Magmaya—' the handmaiden began as they neared the bottom of a stairwell.

'I hear it too,' she said, cutting her off.

All had been silent since the clash at the atrium, save the crackling of the fires, but now, something else was growing amid the flames. Footsteps.

'We're going to die,' Anclyn stammered.

'No, we are not.' Magmaya clasped her hand over the handmaiden's mouth. 'Stay here.' She tugged the ritual blade from her cloak and shuffled up the stairwell.

Once she'd reached the top, she hurried across to a small alcove and stood, silent as the wind. But even there, the fires insisted on burning the water from her eyes and her soul from her body. Soon there would be nothing left but cinder.

Magmaya could still hear Anclyn mumbling at the bottom of the stairwell, but then, there were footsteps again, louder, and that's all that mattered. *Don't give up now,* she told herself, but she was feeling her legs tremble all the same.

A moment later, the footsteps stopped. The alcove was gone. A red cloak was darting at her. Magmaya parried the first blow, but she wasn't so lucky with the second. It was like her shoulder had been set alight as the Belliousan's knife seared through her skin. She watched herself begin to bleed again.

Then, the knife was out of her shoulder and coming for her neck. She ducked beneath the first blow. Parried the second. But there was no third—the Belliousan appeared to have wedged her weapon in stone of the wall.

Magmaya threw herself forward. The ritual blade was at her head. The Belliousan was sidestepping.

And then there were hands wrestling her own; different perfumes, different sweats were pouring over her. Brittle nails were forced beneath her skin, while wrists twitched like a pair of intertwined lovers, neither inclined to finish. Not until there was a knee between Magmaya's legs and she was staggering back, holding herself.

The pain was like a crashing wave, up her legs and through her throat, but she hadn't a moment left to think. The Belliousan was advancing on her with her own blade, the flames rushing around her, and Magmaya hadn't a choice but to pull herself up. She felt an elbow beneath a rib and a wrist against a collarbone, and then the knife was on the floor, ringing out like something sickly.

Magmaya's back was burning. It might have been on fire, but she didn't care—she couldn't care. Her elbow tensed. Then her fist was in the Belliousan's face, once, twice, three times. There wasn't time to relent; Magmaya grabbed her by that red cloak and forced her into the wall; cheeks were gashed by stone; blood pooled in the hieroglyphics.

And then something strange fingered at her teeth; she was pressing the Belliousan against the wall still, but there were fingernails burrowing in her lips like a thousand tiny knives. Then, she had no choice but to turn to the floor and watch their blood spill.

It was there she saw the ritual blade and dove to the ground. Hard stone and brittle metal cut her fingers as she cupped it, but she found some strength in her to stand. And when she did, the Belliousan struck her again, somewhere. But not before Magmaya pressed the bloodied steel through her arm.

And then there was a scream—a little girl's scream, but for all Magmaya knew it might have been her own. And with it, there was something hard against her shoulder, and she found herself on the floor again, head spinning and knife clattering away.

The Belliousan was lying against the wall, holding her shoulder and bloodied face. But there was someone else above her, reaching timidly for the ritual blade. A handmaiden.

'Anclyn...!' Magmaya felt herself call. 'Get... Kill... She's still alive. Anclyn!'

'No!' The handmaiden waved the blade around, forcing herself between her and the Belliousan. 'She's my friend—Keriah! Keriah, you're hurt... Where's... Zoiln... Zoiln...?'

The Belliousan's eyes began to well, and she glanced down sombrely to her lap. Magmaya's view of the First Temple had become thick like fog, but through the sound of her empty breath, she saw Keriah's broken face turn to rage.

'My brother…' she turned to Magmaya. 'You killed him!'

'I never,' she exclaimed, coughing. Her heart was aching at the notion, but she almost didn't have the energy to care anymore. 'I don't…'

'You failed Deih.' She spat blood. 'You let those false angels roam free, and now she's dead! You killed her, and you killed my brother. Nothing ever good comes from you shits coming south!'

'Keriah.' Anclyn tried comforting her, but she was pushed aside.

'No!' Deih's servant said. 'The High Priestess will be born again as Angelica. You will regret leaving the north, you filth!' She turned back to Anclyn and cried, 'Run away, dammit! That girl's a wildfire.'

'I did what I could,' Magmaya pleaded, feeling the life drain from her. 'I never wanted your brother to die, but—'

'But what, *Maggy*?'

'We're getting out of this cursed place,' she said, the smoke choking her lungs. 'The angels are holding the atrium, but there's another way.'

'You think you know this place better than I do?' Keriah smirked and turned to Anclyn. 'My offer still stands, girl. You need not follow this wench anymore.'

'I…!'

'Stay away from her, handmaiden,' she warned. 'She would sell your soul to get out of here.'

Magmaya felt tears well behind her eyes—she didn't want this! She had met this girl once—how had this happened? The last thing she would have given up was Anclyn. She would've sold her *own* soul for the handmaiden to escape.

'If you want to die here, then so be it,' Magmaya said and forced herself to stand. Keriah did the same, but her knees were trembling, and she toppled back down to the floor.

Anclyn was screaming. Deih's servant was in a fit of tears. The First Temple was on fire.

Keriah looked to the handmaiden with one last plea. Her hands were making the wall bloody, and she was tripping up in her own sweat. But a moment later, she was gone.

Magmaya sheathed the blade in her robes and crossed back over to Anclyn, holding her as she wept.

'What was that?'

The handmaiden was silent.

'What did she mean?' she insisted. '*The offer still stands*...?'

'It doesn't matter.' Anclyn shook her head. 'I'm not dying today.'

Magmaya bandaged her shoulder with a piece of charred tapestry and picked herself up again. After that, the corridors seemed to go by silently, though the smoke was quickly becoming suffocating. She hadn't expected such ferocity from Anclyn, but she had been wrong to underestimate her. Now she was striding ahead, following an imaginary guide as Magmaya coughed and spluttered behind.

'I wish I had killed Fabius,' she said, but the handmaiden just kept on walking.

'What about Kurulian?' Anclyn asked after a while. 'Would you have killed him too?'

'The Legatus?'

'Don't play me for a fool,' Anclyn snapped. 'That vial you put in my greasepaint— it's the same one he wore. You don't serve those bastards for all your life and forget these things.'

'He was kind to me,' Magmaya protested. 'He helped me leave Ranvirus. He wasn't like the other angels—he was aware of their mistakes. Anclyn, I never wanted to lie to you.'

'Mistresses lie to me all the time,' Anclyn scorned. 'But if you think what the Divinicus do are mistakes, then you are blind. Did you see the boy Akanah killed? He wasn't even a man grown.'

Magmaya found herself grow quiet and carried on slowly. But the corridor ended all too fast, and they soon arrived at a stairwell, leading down into an inky blackness. She wished she could've stayed for a second longer, scrape another footstep, or just have one more moment before she had to forget. But she found herself taking another step and another after that. It hurt, but wouldn't it have been worse to sit alone in Ranvirus and watch the stars go by, wishing she was one of them?

The clockwork doors appeared before her as they had a lifetime ago—but a halo of fire encased them now. The rows of Temple Guards had seemingly stayed valiant until the end, but all they were rewarded with were burning red cloaks as they slowly withered atop the stonework.

'Here?' Anclyn asked.

Magmaya nodded, fumbling about the remains of one of the Belliousans; she found a ring of keys, swept them up in her fingers and pressed them into the doors. She pushed them open with her feet and stumbled over the corpses until she found herself inside.

The candles had been extinguished, but the light of the inferno outside kept the chamber warm and bright. The room was untouched by the flames, however, and there was a chill about the air that made Magmaya question if the fire was even real. The chamber in the heart of the First Temple was a different world and would surely be the last place the heat would reach.

'It's damn cold.' Anclyn held herself as she wandered in behind. 'I don't even know what we're looking for.'

'Torth Fulton.'

Magmaya left Anclyn by the entrance and scurried over to the mausoleum in the chamber's centre; the once vibrant flowers had wilted, and the incense had died to a sickly wisp. She hauled open the door to the tomb, but this time the darkness didn't bombard her—the silence did.

The dead thing was still there, soaking in a yellow ocean, unwatching. Atop his memorial, a single candle still glowed. As she stepped back, another world unearthed itself, and a sickness groped at her chest. *The less time I have to spend here, the better,* she decided.

'Where are we going?' Anclyn asked from across the chamber. 'The angels will find us if we take any longer.'

Magmaya snatched up the candle and remembered, *Time doesn't pass here, that's what Deih had said.* But Deih was dead, and now, the seconds appeared to tick by in the chamber—had it all been a witch's trick?

'This way,' Magmaya said and led her by a curtain of winding pillars and down a corridor that seemed to grow an extra mile for every step she took. Grimacing faces in the walls stared them down, but they were all quickly banished by her candlelight. The glow of the inferno was gone, though—all that remained in the ocean of black was a single orange pinprick, enough to ignite their eyes.

The hallway should've been lit from the exit beyond, but Magmaya couldn't make out a thing in the distance—perhaps a door was closed, or something was blocking it. But the corridor was too dank and cold—there was no sign of fire. Perhaps the way out wasn't so engulfed in flame as she feared.

'Deih took me down here,' Magmaya said, her voice echoing off the tight walls. 'There was a fork in the corridor—one path led up into the light, and another led deeper into the Temple. She led me to a chamber where she poisoned and framed me.' She paused. 'I should have gone the other way.'

'She's dead now, and you're alive.' Anclyn shrugged. 'Maybe you made the right choice.'

'I can't be sure of that,' Magmaya said. 'We haven't escaped yet. The Divinicus will hang us for deserters if they find us.'

'The mainlands and their obsession with deserters,' the handmaiden mocked. 'In the Summerlands, if we saw a bear, then we turned our tails, and we were better off for it.'

'I don't know about you, but it's been a while since I've met a bear,' Magmaya joked, but the smile that came after seemed to hurt.

It won't be long now, she told herself. She could at least remember Anclyn was smiling; there would be light up ahead soon.

But much to her horror, as the path continued on, there was no sunlight streaming in. She could make out the twist in the corridor where the fork should've been and the path that led to Elysia, but there wasn't an archway or stairwell leading up into the light. In the dim shadows, there was nothing but the grime of the First Temple's underbelly.

No! she cursed herself. It couldn't have been so simple—she deserved to be thrown to the flames! Her heart was sinking faster than she felt it fall, and the coloured lights were blinding her.

She couldn't help but taste her tears—even they felt far realer than the light had. The passageway had been too heavenly and convenient; it had been a wash of a white and warmth. There was no way out—the other path led to a dead end in Deih's Elysia. The way back led to fire and entropy.

Magmaya wanted to fall to her knees and scream, but she couldn't find the strength in her to take even one more step. Instead, she just stammered and crooned the handmaiden's name, her eyes beginning to water. She wanted to let the tears flood from her, but what would Anclyn think then as her valiant saviour fell to the floor?

'I've made a mistake,' she said at last.

'What?' the handmaiden half laughed. 'How do you mean?'

'There was a staircase here, I remember the staircase!' she screamed. 'There was light shining down from it, and it was right *here*!' She beat her foot against the stone where there should've been an opening. 'It was right—bloody—there!'

'Magmaya, there's no door.' Anclyn shook her head. 'There are no stairs. It was farther on—yes! It was farther on… yes?'

'No!' Magmaya spat. 'It was here; it was right in front of me, carved into the wall as real as you are now. There was light coming through, I swear to you! We could've escaped through it… we could've run away from the angels and we—we could've started again. You'd never have to be a handmaiden to another mistress ever again—'

'But why?' Anclyn's voice trembled. 'Why would you imagine a *door*?'

'I told you—Deih poisoned me,' Magmaya stuttered. 'She touched me and I—she must have had a needle on her finger! I thought it was some magic, but it was a—a poison, and it made me see things—things that weren't there,' she cried.

'I don't believe it.' Anclyn wiped her eyes.

'I'm sorry, I…'

'Why, you *were* drunken, you mad, damned fool!' she shouted. 'You imagined exactly what *you* wanted. It doesn't take a genius to figure you stole yourself a bottle of wine from the High Priestess.'

'Anclyn—!'

'Is that why you started this fire?' she asked. 'You were off your head? This whole thing was inside your little mind while people bled and died out there. You've killed us both, you—you whore! You've damned us both to hell.'

'Please!' Magmaya tugged at the air and found herself on her knees. 'Anclyn, you have to believe me. She poisoned me! Please—trust me. I bet there's still a vial of poison on her corpse!'

'Trust you?' Anclyn backed into the shadows with a cackle. 'When I first met you, you spoke to me like a person, not some sewer rat. But you've been leading me through hoops and playing me for a fool—you've been lying at every turn!'

'No—'

'Is it because I don't speak the common tongue as clearly as you? Or is it something else?' She paused, shaking her head. 'It's not just me, though, is it? You left Keriah to die too. You left your family behind. Gods know how many others you've abandoned. So why not me, I suppose?'

The words were at her jaw like a kick to the teeth, and they were grumbling in her stomach. She cursed and turned away, but the world had crumbled by the time she looked back again.

And then there was silence.

And then there were voices.

They were cold and stern, and with them, there were heavy footsteps, as the chamber and the corridor lit up in a pearly glow.

'Anclyn,' Magmaya whispered. 'Anclyn!' The girl stirred and looked. 'The Divinicus are coming.'

She shrugged. 'It doesn't matter how we die, now. Only that we do.'

'No, no, no,' Magmaya insisted. 'It's not too late for you—plead to them, Anclyn; tell them I stole you away from the Divinicus. You tell them you knew nothing of my defiance—you plead until they believe you and give you the tallest castle in Inamorata as an apology.'

She backed away. 'But...'

'Just...' Magmaya clenched her fists. 'For the love of...' she paused. 'Just do what I bloody tell you!'

'I can't,' she stammered. 'I can't go back with them.'

Magmaya nodded and clawed at her hip, drawing the ritual blade. It caught the light and shimmered like something wondrous in the glow of the angel's armour, but it was heavy with blood, and it was pointed at Anclyn's throat. 'Go,' Magmaya insisted until her name no longer fit her face. 'Go!'

Anclyn gave her one last look and scampered away with all the fear of the world in her, eyes the size of the moon. She turned back for a moment and whispered, quietly, '*Were* you drunk?'

'No, but I damn well wish I was now,' Magmaya said with a laugh and disappeared into the fire.

~ ~ ~

Anclyn felt her legs drag behind her before she collapsed into the grip of the Divinicus. The flames started to rush up around them, and she slipped into the darkness; it was all so bizarre, like none of it had happened—like it had been a fever dream.

I didn't know, she rehearsed the words in her mind, *she stole me away.* But she couldn't bring herself to speak. The cold arms of the angels had paralysed her tongue— and she wasn't alone; as they escorted her out of the corridor, she found a crowd of captured Belliousans huddling from the fires beyond.

'The handmaiden,' one of the Divinicus said to the other before they tossed her into the pile of Belliousans, bloody and fearful.

The fire had cut the chamber in two, and soon enough, the corridors were in flames. It ate away with terrible fury, and the sight of it burned her soul.

Anclyn felt needle-like fingers caress her back, and then a sudden warmth as something brushed over her. She looked up to the lank silhouette of Cheyne behind, his flowery cloak draped over her shoulders. He pressed a finger to his lips and turned her attention back to the flames.

'There's something out there,' he said softly, and there was—hardly.

Each of them watched, from the lowest Belliousan to the most exalted Divinicus, as Magmaya Vorr swam about the chamber. There was silence as she tossed and turned and finally collapsed into the mausoleum.

'We better be off,' Cheyne scoffed, and a moment later, the chamber was gone.

Anclyn found herself re-treading the same ground, eventually trampling over the corpse of Deih of the Water, until the First Temple and all its infernos were behind them.

The angels had clustered outside on the mountaintop and had begun making their way down the ivory stairs with Akanah at their head. There appeared to be as many Divinicus as there had been upon arrival, plus the two dozen Belliousans they had taken hostage and the captured banners they were burning. There was no sign of Keriah amongst them.

It would be a long night—that much was certain.

'You were Magmaya Vorr's handmaiden, no?' Cheyne caught up and put a cold arm around her.

'Yes.' She shuddered.

'And you were her friend?'

She shrugged and upped her pace. Anclyn felt an ache grow in the pit of her chest, a hole she so desperately wanted to fill. But all around her was the bombardment of the night and the glittery armour of the Divinicus blotting out the stars, and the hole just seemed to grow wider.

'Good,' she heard him whisper from behind. 'You were her handmaiden—no more, no less. She's served her punishment to the Maiden Gods, and you need not suffer for her treachery.'

He fastened his grip on her shoulder, and the pair began to descend the hillside in the white-red light of the burning Temple.

It was only when they reached the first watchtower that it began to rain.

~ ~ ~

The mausoleum was smaller than Magmaya remembered, but it had served adequately against the fire. She had huddled in the corner as the world around her glowed, and all she'd known turned to ashes. There was a perfect symmetry about it that she hadn't noticed before, from the sculpted skulls to the demons covered from head to toe in antlers. The imagery was disturbing at best, but it was safer than the flames.

Magmaya forced herself to stare at the pitiful remains of Torth Fulton—a heap of flesh and bone. Soon, she might be like him, but not half as worshipped; she would just have been the high-born girl who threw away everything she had to travel south and die.

Clockwork artifices clawed at Torth as he lay, but somewhere under there the truth was buried. She felt for the ritual blade at her hip and hammered it down, and down again, hacking away at the glassy tomb. The first few attempts proved futile as the sword shimmered off pitifully. But when she persisted, the glass began to shudder, crack, and finally splinter until the chemicals spilt softly out. The corpse was even limper than it had been before, entangling itself on the remains of its own tomb.

There was a chiming of age-old brass, but it wasn't enough. Magmaya took a breath and forced her arm into the fleshy thing, but she felt nothing on her fingertips—nothing but the cold. That was until her nails found something hard and she clawed at it, wrenching it free from the corpse.

Magmaya held it aloft, and the clockwork heart burned like a flaming orb. Deih *had* been changed, and Torth too. Perhaps all the Belliousans had. Perhaps they would survive to walk again.

But not her. She had hoped to feel the light caress her fingertips, the warmth of mountains lash down upon her and stars sing up above; but it was a half-made death, and even if, somehow, she lived, there would be no sense in standing. Another girl would take her place and swagger off with Anclyn—it was a half-made death, but it was hers all the same.

Magmaya smiled and found herself thinking of the Summerlands before she fell into the pool of formaldehyde. It baptised her and embraced her, turning to roses in her palms. But all she saw was the floor take aflame and form riverbanks around her neck.

She tried to scream as the heat began to singe her hair. She had brushed it every day for as long as she remembered; she had dyed the blonde out of it; she had kept it tidy while Anclyn filled it with flowers. *No, my hair!* She wished she could've cried. *My hair.*

Magmaya stole a breath and closed her eyes. She drowned in an ocean of rose petals as they filled her lungs and kissed her neck.

Twenty-Seven

Anclyn broke her fast with Yalsus and the others before the sun had risen. No one spoke, save for Legatus Akanah, who sat and made lewd remarks at a skimpy servitor, while Krel threatened to cut the cook in two if he took any longer to prepare his food. The other Divinicus stood to attention, but Akanah's chosen few just sat and laughed and drank.

There were perhaps thirty feet before Anclyn and the Small Court were permitted to sit and eat, and they did so in the silence and smoke that rose from the shell of the First Temple. No longer did the rain beat down on the pavilion; Akanah had forced the captured Belliousans to set up the tent at the foot of the mountain and had taken great glee in watching them do so. Rumours were even circulating that Krel had raped half of them and beaten the rest. The thought made Anclyn sick.

Protests around the blockade had scarcely ceased all night; the jeers and shouts from those who'd lost their goddess echoed through the mountainside. The Divinicus had been dispatched throughout the morning darkness, and shortly after, the gutters ran thick with blood and rain. But it had only taken a few minutes for the protests to begin again.

'My mother was a whore.' Yalsus broke the silence with a grin. 'She was the greatest whore in all the land, they said, and I believed it. After all, she was infertile but shagged good enough to have me.' He smirked to himself, but his smile faded all the same. '*She* died in a fire; it was her and a man from the Silver City lying on sheepskin in front of an open fireplace. It doesn't take much imagination to guess what happened,' he chortled. 'You girls juggle your candlesticks all you like, but you'll drop them eventually.'

'Is this necessary?' Cheyne asked, biting into a slice of buttered bread. 'The fire has scarcely gone out.'

'Pah, what did that foreign girl ever do for us? She wasn't your friend, was she?' Yalsus asked Anclyn, who shook her head, sheepishly. 'Then may the Maiden Gods show her mercy.'

'Rumours say you were trying to escape with her, though,' one of the other handmaidens remarked.

'She was a means to an end. I just needed to get out of that hellhole,' Anclyn replied bitterly, but when she spoke, it was as if she was betraying herself.

Yalsus frowned and looked across the table to her. 'You've scarcely touched your food, dear.'

'It's dire.' Anclyn tore the bread into smaller and smaller chunks until her fingertips were sore and coated with crumbs. 'In the Summerlands, we had fresh fruit, and in the continent, we stole straight from the import ships. But here? There's mud, and there's bread.'

'At least it isn't burnt,' one of the others chimed in, and Anclyn dropped her food.

'I think I've lost my appetite, actually.' She stood, and the chair screeched behind her. She tossed the mutilated bread to an eager flock of crows, and forced herself into the rain outside, somewhere between the tent and the barricade of Divinicus.

But before she could clear the blockade, a shimmery hand clamped down on her shoulder.

'Where are you going handmaiden?' Akanah asked, his voice like cold milk.

'A walk, my lord. I would like some air.'

'There's air inside the tent.' He tugged at her arm, smirking. 'Come back inside. Aren't you enjoying the celebration feast?'

Celebrating what? Losing Belliousa? She wondered, and her heart sunk. But then, there was a flash of flowery robes, and the thin form of Cheyne forced himself between them.

'My lord,' he purred. 'She only wants a stroll. I'll watch her if you will.'

The Legatus waved her away and returned to his own kind. Anclyn breathed a sigh of relief.

'What are you doing?' Cheyne asked, but she'd already gone.

Anclyn felt his footsteps become her shadow as they left the curfew of the pavilion and disappeared into the upset of the crowds. They skirted their tormented shouts and escaped through the blockade with scarcely a splatter of mud about them.

They passed a beggar in the street, shrouded in discarded brown cloth, so Anclyn reached down and gave her some copper she had found about the tent.

'Perhaps if you'd stuck a needle in her toe, she would've at least danced for us,' Cheyne suggested. 'She'll go off and spend it on poison now.'

They found themselves at the foot of a small waterfall—no, it wasn't even that. The waterfalls in the Summerlands were vast and tremendous goliaths of rushing white and glistening emerald; this was a trickle of brown from a broken pipe in the mountainside. Around it, there were grey dogs lapping at the filthy water, bones jutting through their fur as if they hadn't been fed in an age. There were doves pecking at the dirt too, and occasionally, Anclyn noticed, they'd find a piece they both fancied and proceed to peck at one another's necks until they were bloodied and tired.

The handmaiden turned away and wandered through the streets until she found herself at the foot of those ivory stairs again, watching as they disappeared into the cloud and flame and smoke that shrouded the First Temple. The last time she'd climbed these steps, she'd done so with an army. Now, she would do it alone.

'Where exactly are we going?' Cheyne caught up. 'Have you quite forgotten how long it took us to climb up the last time? They'll be worried, girl.'

Anclyn laughed at that, taking the first dilapidated step. 'I intend to walk up this mountainside and throw myself from whatever is left of the tallest tower.' She paused. 'Or, maybe I'm going to go for a walk. Follow along and find out, if you want.'

There was an audible sigh from behind, but sure enough, a moment later, they had disappeared into the mist.

There was nothing to see, so she thought instead, but thinking hurt her head. When she had scaled the mountain before, she'd been furious with Magmaya for lying to her about Deih, but now she was furious with her for dying. Whatever her mistress did seemed to piss some part of her off, and so she decided it was better not to think about her at all—if that could be helped.

But Magmaya just kept rushing back through her mind wherever she moved, and no matter how much she tried to numb herself, the nothingness hurt too.

'It's bloody cold.' Cheyne's voice echoed down the cliff. 'It was never like this in Glassrock. There were only tropics and beaches and sun.'

'Sounds like the Water,' Anclyn said. 'With fewer pirates.'

'Oh, there were pirates.' Cheyne nodded to himself. 'But apart from that, it was a grand place, even when the mountains did start bleeding fire. Perhaps I'll go back there one day.' He looked to her. 'Perhaps you'll go back home too.'

Anclyn sighed. 'I fear there's no place in the world left for me now.'

'I wouldn't be so sure,' he said. 'The angels have far more trust in me than I do in them. I'm sure an eye could be turned while someone stole a small boat.'

'Oh yes, and then the trip would only take a few months,' she grumbled. 'Besides, I have no sense of how to row or sail. Maybe you could whisk me away from the angels as I was whisked away from my home, instead.'

'One day, if the price is right.' He laughed to himself.

'I don't have any money to offer you.' She shrugged. 'I have nothing to offer men like you anymore.'

'And what does that mean?'

'We don't know one another very well,' she mumbled, her cheeks red. 'Perhaps a girl was speaking out of place.'

'Carry on. I'm hardly offended,' he said. 'Besides, Legatus Akanah doesn't have to hear anything we don't want him to.'

'He doesn't?'

'Of course, he doesn't,' he said. 'I would consider myself an honest man, in truth, handmaiden.'

'How so?' she asked, intrigued by the prospect of his answer.

'I've been promised a sweet maiden of sixteen from Kythera,' he replied. 'She has auburn hair and is very beautiful, I hear. Little Yala, sister of Yala, daughter of Great Yala.' He laughed at that. 'And I haven't slept with another woman since our engagement.'

'How noble.' It was exactly what she had expected.

'You forget how deep the passion of men is,' he remarked. 'One moment we pledge ourselves for life, the next, we kill to stick ourselves inside someone new. But that's beside the point; this girl is from a high-born family on the Chain Islands, and I intend to make her my queen after this is all over. I just hope Akanah hurries up, in truth.'

'You're not alone in thinking that, my lord.'

'I am not a lord, sweet thing.'

'Oh,' Anclyn remarked. 'Why is that?'

'Glassrock doesn't have any lords, only the Holy *Malaquar*. The Bastard Mother's forces took me in after my father became shipwrecked off Vavaria, but she never cared to give me a title. Nor did I ask for one—I was but seven suns old at the time. I was more interested in the elephants.'

'So, what do I call you?' Anclyn asked.

He upturned his palms. 'I'm not your friend. You're still a handmaiden,' Cheyne spoke grimly. 'Try not to get too attached. I've had many names, but no titles. I never stay long enough for those.'

She was taken back but decided not to act like it. 'What should I call you, then?'

'Actually, I've decided I rather like being called *lord*. Especially when it's coming from *your* tongue.' He licked his lips, and she turned away.

The trip continued on past ruined watchtowers, long abandoned by the Temple Guard who had been cut down or captured on the way back down. Anclyn wasn't concerned with them, though; rather, she was growing sick at the thought of Cheyne following her from behind. She almost felt herself fall into some spiral of insanity as her head began to pound, and her footsteps faltered. But then, at last, the clouds trickled away into small brooks of rainwater, and the broken spires of the First Temple were in sight.

'What do you hope to find here?' Cheyne asked after a short while.

She ignored him and carried on across a mountain of ashen rocks, rain and ruin. All around her there was lamentation, and there was death. Perhaps two hundred Belliousans flocked over the blazing corpse of the Temple, draped in red and cowering over the blackened forms of their loved ones. Others cried Deih's many names to the heavens, while the rest scoured the embers for golden amulets or just about anything else of worth that may have survived the night.

The husk of the First Temple was grey and brooding, and those who scuttled at its feet were insects. And yet, it was a shadow of its former glory; proud banners and sigils had turned to dust, intricate murals were all but recognisable, and the towers and winding corridors stood like jagged thorns from the earth, still flickering orange. Morning sunlight struck down into places it had never before reached, like a spear intent on destroying whatever remained.

'Haggard old thing,' Cheyne remarked. 'Not a soul will pilgrim to Belliousa any longer. Better those cloaked in red find some new goddess to pray to.'

Anclyn sifted her feet through the muddy ground, watching pillars of smoke rise like young from a viper's nest. She was attracted still to the allure of the Temple—to its otherworldly ambience and deadly light. The closer she found herself, the louder the cries of the Belliousans grew, but the more beautiful the tortured remains appeared.

She stepped through a wall in such a way that would have been impossible several hours ago, ignoring the protests of Cheyne behind her. She skirted broken corridors and splintered heirlooms which she'd fled from in terror last night. She was calm now. The morning had brought the First Temple alive.

She chased the complex to the underground chamber. But in its place, there was only rubble and decay and some hint of an inferno raging still below. It was a good thing, though, she assured herself. The mausoleum was buried, and she wouldn't have to relive the night again.

The atrium was next, she decided. That's where Deih had been killed, bleeding as the angels leered atop the burning ground. She could even make out the remnants of it from the base of the Temple—how easy it was to walk through walls and carry out her every whim. Magmaya had cursed the ground she walked on the night before; now she was revelling in it.

She walked between the barricades and over the towers, following ruins which formed a trail of where she wanted to go. The First Temple had burned, and now they gathered in the ashes.

The atrium was how she remembered, save for Cheyne's presence. Parts of it were even preserved; from several busts and inscriptions which made up a surviving wall, to the mosaic floors and crusted remains of the fountain where Deih had died. But, of course, there was no sign of her now. The fire had seen to that.

In fact, Anclyn noticed, there was someone else there instead. She was facing away as she made her way through a burning arch, but it was clear she wasn't doting the ruby-red robes of the other Belliousans as they fluttered about in pursuit of gold.

She was wandering wistfully around the shell of the fountain, a mop of hair singed to her neckline and nude, save for a few bundles of cloth that just about stuck to her shoulders and thighs with rain. She held herself in a sort of delicate way that made Anclyn's heart leap into her mouth.

She was sobbing too, despite the murmurs of prayer and the downpour atop the mountain, there was a clear crying coming from her direction. And after a moment, it seemed she found the strength to turn around, her burnt hair swallowing her tears as she made a vain attempt to cover herself. She looked sad—that was the truest thing about her. But that sadness quickly enough turned to bewilderment.

The Belliousans murmured amongst themselves until one dropped gold at the girl's feet and the rest followed in tandem. They ran to caress her, drenched in rain and screaming 'Angelica, Angelica!' They flocked to cover her with their robes, but she just stood, quiet, and looking at Anclyn.

'Angelica, Angelica!' the Belliousans continued, scampering over to nurse her burns. Even Cheyne shied away, until it was only her and Anclyn, standing tall upon a shore of ash and smoke.

Magmaya Vorr smiled the same way a phoenix died.

And then, Anclyn's knees caved, and she dropped down before her. She closed her eyes and prayed; she prayed to every god, prayed to any god that would listen. She prayed until she felt a trickle of sunshine form fingers and brush through her scalp, and at last her prayers were answered.

A Note from the Author:

What started as a short story centred around the misdeeds of a man named Kharon Vorr has evolved into somewhat of an epic. *The Girl and the Goddess* has taken me four years to write and edit, from the first line, to the last full stop.

I dearly hope you enjoyed reading it.

There will be more to come.

I'd like to thank my parents and my sister for their continuous support, Edoardo Taloni for his incredible talent on designing the front cover, my friend, Alisha, for listening to me moan, and my rabbit, Yoghurt.